In memory of Albert Sydney Collard
Private, 7th Battalion The Buffs (East Kent Regiment)
Died aged eighteen on 1 July 1916

Glossary

<table>
<tr><td>arrack</td><td>native liquor/spirit</td></tr>
<tr><td>broadside</td><td>single-sheet advertisement</td></tr>
<tr><td>dak gharry</td><td>post cart/small carriage pulled by horses</td></tr>
<tr><td>diligence</td><td>long-distance coach</td></tr>
<tr><td>fandango</td><td>a party that includes singing and dancing</td></tr>
<tr><td>flash boy</td><td>young man known for villainy and gaudy attire</td></tr>
<tr><td>goober peas</td><td>peanuts</td></tr>
<tr><td>greybacks</td><td>Confederate States dollar</td></tr>
<tr><td>Gujar</td><td>semi-nomadic caste from northern India</td></tr>
<tr><td>jefe</td><td>boss/leader (Spanish)</td></tr>
<tr><td>johnnycake</td><td>cornmeal flatbread</td></tr>
<tr><td>lobsterback</td><td>slang for British redcoat</td></tr>
<tr><td>lollygag</td><td>to idle or waste time</td></tr>
<tr><td>loophole</td><td>hole or slit cut into a wall through which a weapon may be fired</td></tr>
<tr><td>lucifer</td><td>a match</td></tr>
<tr><td>mofussil</td><td>country station or district in India away from the chief stations of the region, 'up country'</td></tr>
</table>

Pinkerton	Allan Pinkerton, founder of Pinkerton National Detective Agency
rake	hellraiser and womaniser
rhino	money, cash
sawar	native cavalry trooper serving in the East India Company's army
secher	Northern slang for someone from the South who supported secession
sepoy	native soldier serving in the East India Company's army
specie	gold and silver coins
talwar	curved native sword
Tejano	Mexican born in Texas

THE UNITED STATES AND MEXICO 1863

- - - - Jack's route (including the El Camino Real de los Tejas trail
    from Natchitoches to San Antonio)

••••••• State border

We rely greatly on the sure operation of a complete blockade of the Atlantic and Gulf ports soon to commence. In connection with such a blockade we propose a powerful movement down the Mississippi to the ocean, with a cordon of posts at proper points, and the capture of Forts Jackson and Saint Philip; the object being to clear out and keep open this great line of communication in connection with the strict blockade of the seaboard, so as to envelop the insurgent States and bring them to terms with less bloodshed than by any other plan.

Letter from General-in-Chief Winfield Scott to
Major General George B. McClellan,
dated 3 May 1861

Chapter One

Near Matamoros, Tamaulipas, Mexico, February 1863

The Confederate officer covered his nose with his bandana as he rode through the slaughter. The bright red and white chequered cloth was usually employed to keep the dust from his mouth, yet this day it served a different purpose: it saved him from the stench of putrid flesh. Bodies rotted fast in the heat of the Mexican sun. These corpses had been left long enough for the stomachs to swell to the point of bursting, and for the open wounds to become rancid, suppurating messes, a feast for the thousands of tiny insects that swarmed over the ruined flesh.

'Capt'n?'

The officer turned his head as one of his troopers called out to him. 'What is it?'

'You seen that?' The trooper was one of the column's outriders, and had been the one who had discovered the butchered bodies. He had also been the first to find the foulest of all the depredations that had been visited on the men and women who had accompanied this particular wagon train. Now he pointed at a pair of corpses that had been dragged to one side of the trail. Both had been stripped naked, but it still took the officer a moment to identify the twisted and broken bodies as belonging to women. He had seen enough of the world to know the fate they had endured before their lives had been ended.

'I see 'em. Now search them other bodies.' The captain gave the order, then leaned far out of the saddle to spit into the dirt below. It did little to scour the foul taste from his mouth. 'When you're done, get all these folk buried. But don't take too long about it.'

'Capt'n?' Another trooper rode up. This man bore the twin yellow stripes of a cavalry corporal on his sleeve above the elbow.

'Corporal?'

'We found tracks. Heading south.'

The captain nodded. It was what he had expected. It was not the first ambushed wagon train he had seen, and he knew it would not be the last. The fate of the people now lying in the dirt would be just another footnote in this long and bitter war fought on the frontier, another atrocity to list alongside the hundreds that both sides had inflicted on the other.

He knew that the bandoleros who had attacked this particular wagon train would not linger. They would head due south with their loot. It did not guarantee their safety. Just as they would strike deep into American territory, he would not hold back from chasing them far into Mexico. Indeed, he had permission to do so, thanks to the accord signed between his commanding officer, General Hamilton P. Bee, and the governor of Tamaulipas, Albino López. Yet he could not afford to linger for long. The bandoleros had a head start, and his small command would have to ride hard if they were to catch the perpetrators of this latest massacre.

He kicked back his heels, walking his horse through the bodies that littered the trail. All were naked, the greying flesh the colour of putrid meat. The men who had driven and guarded this particular wagon train had been stripped of everything of value. It left their wounds on display, and he ran his eyes over the corpses, assessing the manner of their deaths with the practised eye of a man who had been fighting since he had been old enough to ride. He could see whom a revolver had shot, and who had died from a blade. Most had had their throats slit, the dark, gaping chasms telling him they had likely been left alive by the wounds taken in the firefight, death only arriving when their necks had been carved open. At least two were headless, the decapitated bodies crowned with great crescents of darkened soil where their life blood would have pumped out.

He reached the last of the bodies, then brought his horse to a stand. He waited there as his men went about the task he had set them, sitting silent, staring at the open trail that stretched out in front of him. To the north, he could see little more than a great swathe of ebony trees smothered with vines, which formed a living, twisted barrier forty to fifty feet high so that he had no sight of the great river that was no more than half a mile away. To the south, there was less for his eyes to look at. A lone mesquite tree and a thicket of thorn bushes was all he could find to break up the expanse of nothingness, the grey-green foliage doing little to colour the wide expanse of dusty drab yellows and muted browns.

Far off on the horizon, he could just about make out a line of distant mountains, their peaks half hidden in the haze so that they were little more than shadows. Scarred into the earth and running east to west were a pair of deep furrows, which thousands of heavily laden wagons had ground into the dirt and which led away for hundreds of yards before he lost sight of them in the shimmering heat haze. It was those wagons that had brought him to this desolate, isolated spot. It was his job to safeguard those who transported the cotton from the Southern states to the Mexican ports, where European buyers queued up to buy it. This time he had failed.

It left him with just one course of action. He would bury the dead and then he would ride south. He would find the bandoleros who had carried out this attack and he would bring them to justice.

His justice.

And his justice was death.

The Confederate outriders spotted the bandoleros just as the sun was setting.

The captain had led his men south, following the trail of the stolen wagons. It had been a hard ride, but he held them to the task, refusing to lessen the pace or even let them contemplate a rest. Only when he judged they were close had he taken his men away from the trail and led them in a wide, sweeping arc that he reckoned would place them far in front of the wagons.

He had found the place for the ambush an hour before. The ground fell away, the trail following it down into a deep gully that ran for a good five hundred yards before the terrain opened out once again. He had dispersed the men, lining them along either flank of the gully, their horses led away and guarded by half a dozen troopers chosen for the task. He had let those that remained choose their own spots. He trusted them. All had done this sort of thing before. He himself opted for a vantage point near the end of the gully. He would be the first to open fire, and he would do so only when the lead bandoleros were a matter of yards away.

He sat with his back resting against a boulder, checking over his weapons. The heat of the day had fallen away so that it was almost pleasant to be sitting there. It felt peaceful, serene and calm. With the sun low in the sky, the few mesquite trees and prickly pear cactus that managed to survive in this barren land cast long shadows across the ground, and the quality of the light changed from searing white to the palest orange, so that the world took on an unearthly feel.

He heard the wagon train long before he saw it. The screech of poorly greased running gear carried far, as did the braying of the oxen dragging the weighty wagons, and the crack of the whips that held them to their Sisyphean task. Only when the train was close did he ease himself forward. He took a moment to check that his revolver was loose in its holster, then aimed down the barrel of his carbine, lining up the shot that would bring fresh slaughter to a day that had already seen so much bloodshed.

Two mounted men led the wagon train. Both were dressed as he had expected, in skin-tight flared trousers open at the sides, paired with jackets made from dark leather. Both wore a sombrero on their heads. There were twenty wagons in all. Each would be heavily laden with ten or more five-hundred-pound bales of cotton, a cargo that was worth a fortune if it could be brought to the cotton-hungry traders waiting at Mexico's eastern ports. The rest of the bandoleros were spread alongside the train, with one group riding as a rearguard.

The captain made a rough tally as he waited. He counted two men at the front, twelve more scattered amongst the wagons and six at the rear. Along with the men driving the wagons, that made a total of forty. He had thirty-one men waiting along the top of the gully, but he felt not even a trace of anxiety at the uneven odds. He doubted he would take even a single casualty.

His justice would be delivered swiftly.

He sighed, then took a deep breath, settling himself into position. The lead pair were no more than twenty yards away. The gully was less than ten feet deep at the point where the captain waited. It was an easy shot, one he could make a hundred times out of a hundred.

He held his breath, then exhaled softly, releasing half of it. The barrel of his carbine tracked the nearer of the two riders. The distance closed slowly. Twenty yards became fifteen, then ten. When the pair were five yards away, he fired.

It was a good shot. The spinning bullet from the rifled carbine struck the first rider in the side of the head, shattering bone and spraying the second man with a gruesome shower of blood and brain.

The captain was on his feet the moment he had pulled the trigger, his left hand holding the carbine whilst his right drew his revolver. The handgun came up in one smooth motion. There was time to see a moment's fear on the second rider's face before he fired.

The bullet struck the bandolero in the chest. He jerked backwards, his arms thrown wide by the force of the impact. The captain fired again, the second bullet striking the bandolero's chest less than an inch to the right of the first. This time the man tumbled out of the saddle and into the dirt.

All along the gully, the Confederate cavalrymen were pouring on the fire. Some followed the captain's lead and used revolvers. Others switched to shotguns, and the air was full of the explosive blast of their firing. No matter their choice of weapon, every trooper hit his target, and the bandoleros were gunned down without mercy. The sounds of the shots blurred together so that they merged into one long-drawn-out roar. Underscoring it all were the cries of the dead and the soon-to-be dead.

'Hold your fire, goddammit!' The captain shouted the order, then scrambled over the lip of the gully and down the slope. The ambush had lasted less than half a minute. Not one of the bandoleros was left in the saddle or seated on a wagon.

He reached the bodies of the two men he had shot. One was clearly dead, his shattered skull unloading its contents into the sandy dirt that covered the ground. The second, the one shot by his revolver, was still alive. He lay spread-eagled on his back, gazing up at the sky whilst his mouth moved in a fast, desperate prayer for deliverance.

The captain stood over the man. He paused, making sure the bandolero was looking directly into his eyes. Only then did he move his right hand, aiming the revolver. The bandolero's prayer increased in tempo, the words pouring out of him in a sudden terrified flood. Then the captain fired and the prayer was ended.

There was nothing else to see, so he walked back along the gully. He fired twice more, killing two men too badly wounded to live for long. He found what he was looking for draped across the seat at the front of the second wagon in the now stationary line.

The bandolero who had been driving the wagon was still alive. He had been hit twice, once in the shoulder and once in the head. Neither wound would kill, even though the bullet that had grazed his scalp had released a great torrent of blood. It had left the man dazed and hurting, but alive.

'Get yourself the hell down.'

The bandolero blinked back at the captain, too dazed to understand.

'Goddammit.' The captain hissed the word under his breath, then holstered his revolver and approached the wounded bandolero. He took hold of the man's shirt, then half dragged, half threw him off the wagon and on to the ground.

'Don't you goddam move.' He gave the order, then stood back and waited.

All along the wagon train, his men were going about the same merciless task of searching the bodies for any bandolero left alive. Gunshots cracked out every few moments as the killing continued. Around him, the oxen brayed and fussed, but he ignored them, just as he ignored the riderless horses that pawed anxiously at the ground or roamed along the gully. His men would round them up when the bandoleros had been dealt with.

'Capt'n, we got ourselves one of the sons of bitches.' The corporal delivered the news to his officer as he approached. Two troopers followed, guarding a dishevelled, bloodied bandolero. The man looked pathetic. He had been shot in the arm, the wound now covered by his free hand. His face was bloodied, the flesh puffy and bruised from the blows it had taken from the fists of the men who now held him fast.

'Ramirez!' The captain summoned one of his men fluent in Spanish.

'*Jefe?*' Ramirez had already wandered over, expecting to be summoned.

'Ask these sons of bitches who they work for.'

Ramirez nodded. He posed the question in fast, fluent Spanish. Neither prisoner answered.

'Corporal.' The captain nodded.

The corporal needed no further instruction. He was a big man, easily over six feet tall, with broad shoulders and long, powerful arms. He knew what his captain wanted.

The bandolero with the bloodied arm looked up as the corporal came to stand in front of him. His mouth opened, but whatever words he wanted to utter were rammed back down his throat as the corporal smashed his large fist directly into his mouth. More punches followed, the corporal throwing his full weight behind each one. The men holding the bandolero gripped him hard, keeping him upright as the blows came without pause, hammering first into the Mexican's head, then into his chest and stomach.

'Enough.' The captain called a halt to the battering. 'Let him go.'

The bandolero fell to the ground as if his bones had been pulped into so much mush. The corporal stood back, chest heaving with exertion, knuckles speckled with blood.

'Ramirez.' The captain nodded to his Spanish speaker.

The question was asked again. This time it was addressed to just one bandolero. This time it was answered, in a gabbled, terrified flood.

'They're Ángeles,' Ramirez translated.

The captain grunted in acknowledgement. He knew the band Ramirez referred to well enough. There was more than one gang of bandoleros who thought nothing of attacking the wagon trains bringing the cotton from as far away as Louisiana and Arkansas, but the one known as Los Ángeles – the Angels – was the largest and most notorious. It was said that its leader,

Ángel Santiago, had as many as three hundred followers now, his men well fed on the wagon trains that he ordered them to attack. He was said to be a monster, a killer who had no notion of mercy and who would never take a prisoner. The locals referred to the gang as Los Ángeles de la Muerte. The Angels of Death.

'Bury them.' The captain had learned enough. He gave his last order, then turned away. The sight of the Ángeles sickened him to the stomach.

His men understood his order, and hurried to obey. It took them a while to dig the two pits to the side of the trail; long enough for the bandolero the corporal had beaten to come back to consciousness.

The two Ángeles were dragged towards the pits. Both knew the fate that awaited them, and both fought against their captors, their cries and pleas greeted with blows, slaps, jeers and laughter. Still they struggled. Both were weeping now, their tears cutting channels through the dirt and blood that smothered their faces. The Confederate cavalrymen gave no quarter. The two bandoleros were beaten into submission, fists and boots used without mercy until they were forced into the freshly dug holes in the ground.

The Confederates started to shovel the soil around their two victims. The captain stood by, listening to the sobs and muttered prayers of the two men he was committing to a horrific death. Both were weeping, and emitting a heart-rending series of moans and pleas as the soil was piled higher and higher. When it reached their necks, one of the troopers stepped forward, compacting the freshly turned dirt with his boots. Those watching laughed as he turned the task into a jig, their laughter doubling in volume as he deliberately kicked the nearly buried men in the head and face with his heavy boots.

Only when he had finished was the last of the soil shovelled into place. The Confederate cavalrymen took care not to pile it too high, stopping when it was firmly in place around the bandoleros' necks. Their heads were left free.

The captain called for his corporal and gave the order.

'Mount 'em up.'

'Capt'n.' The acknowledgement was brief. The troopers moved to obey, not one of them glancing back at the two men they had just incarcerated in the dusty soil.

The captain alone stayed where he was. He looked at the two men in turn. He was not moved by their tears or their whimpers. They faced a slow and painful death. The insects would come first, the tarantulas and the scorpions, the ticks, the fleas and the flies. None would kill, no matter how many times they stung or bit. That task would be left to the bigger animals that would follow: the coyotes and the rats that would begin to devour the flesh that had been left for them, and the rattlesnakes, copperheads and rat snakes that would sense the warm objects and come to investigate.

The two men would provide a welcome feast for the animals that called this forlorn, empty wilderness a home. That feast would continue until nothing but bone was left behind, the two men reduced to a pair of sun-bleached skulls. But the warning would endure, long after they were dead.

The captain turned his back on the two bandoleros and walked to his horse. His men were ready to move out, just as he had ordered. Some would drive the wagons that had been captured, whilst others would ride out ahead to scout the trail. They would proceed slowly, taking every precaution, wary of any more Ángeles who might dare to venture close. Not one would dwell on the fate of the men who had been left behind to die. Today it was their turn to administer the cruel, merciless justice of the frontier. Tomorrow they could be the ones on the receiving end of such a fate. Such was the bitterness of their war. Such was the destiny of the men who fought it.

The captain led his column north. Behind him he heard the first terrified shouts and cries as the men left buried up to their necks tried desperately to keep away the insects that had arrived to begin their long, tortuous deaths.

Chapter Two

Natchitoches, Louisiana, St Valentine's Day 1863

The man sitting in the dining room's corner seat eyed the room warily. He had not bothered to learn the name of the town he was in, for he would not linger there long. It was a place to rest for a few hours before he resumed his wandering, nothing more.

The settlement was prosperous, he knew that much, the main street lined with fine Creole town houses with iron balconies. He cared little for the aesthetics. He cared only for practicality. The town's location on El Camino Real de los Tejas, one of the main trade routes through Louisiana, meant there was enough passing custom for it to have a livery, and so his horse could be fed, watered and brushed. It was not out of compassion for the animal that he spent the last of his grey Confederate dollars on its care. It was out of necessity. He would need the beast if he were to continue to travel. Without it he would be reduced to nothing more than a tramp roaming the countryside. He might not have a destination in mind, but he was more than a homeless vagrant. Much more.

Or at least, he had been.

He had wandered for months now. The summer that had come after the bloodshed at Shiloh had passed easily enough. The warm weeks had been spent travelling across the Southern states, the days passing in a lazy torpor, the money in his pocket allowing him to rest and eat without interference. The autumn and winter that had followed had been harder. His supply of ready cash had dwindled, and he had been forced to find work, a succession of odd jobs in out-of-the-way places allowing him to continue to head south and west. He kept away from the war and, as much as he could manage, away from people too. He avoided both with assiduous care, wanting nothing to do with either. For he craved peace and solitude, or at least that was what he told himself as he spent night after night by his lonely campfire with no one but a stolen horse for company.

One of the logs burning in the fireplace spat out a fat ember with a crack loud enough to turn heads towards its fiery grave. The man in the corner seat did not so much as twitch. A man who had fought on a dozen battlefields was not startled by such an innocuous sound. Yet he still reached out to pull his repeating rifle towards him, keeping it within easy reach. Next to it was a Confederate infantry officer's sabre in its scabbard. On his right hip, the man wore a fine Colt revolver with ivory grips, the metal buffed and polished so that it shone like silver. He was never far from the three weapons; the tools of his trade always at hand and ready to be used.

The hum of conversation began again almost immediately. The simple dining saloon was almost empty, but there were enough men present to fill the space with grunted discussion and the scrape of metal on plate. Few would loiter there. It was a place for consuming the fuel needed to survive, not for enjoying a leisurely dinner.

The man in the corner seat used a wedge of dry day-old bread to mop up the last of the juices from the thick, fatty slices of bacon he had devoured. It felt good to have the food settle in his belly, even if it had cost him fifty cents, with another ten spent on the bitter coffee that tasted nothing like the thick, tarry soldier's tea that he preferred. Still, it was an improvement on the hardtack, desiccated vegetables and salted meat that was his usual diet. If he were being honest with himself, he had stopped at the backwater town for reasons other than just the care of his horse. There were times when a man needed warm food inside him.

There was little to see in the dining saloon. The simple pine tables were battered and scuffed from years, even decades, of long use. There was scant decoration on the walls, save for the large chalkboard above the fireplace that listed the fare on offer and its price. For a man who had once lived and eaten in a maharajah's palace, there was little to recommend it. But the food had been hearty, if not so fresh, and the truth of it was that the man in the corner seat had barely a dollar left in his pocket and had to live on the means at his disposal.

Food consumed, he stretched his legs out in front of him and belched softly. For once, he felt full, and he patted his belly to ease the arrival of the heavy meal. He burped for a second time, keeping the sound soft, unlike so many of the other men in the saloon, who shovelled their meal into their mouths at pace, then belched with the volume of a bullock being led to the slaughterman.

There was just a single woman in the room. The man in the corner seat had known she was a whore the moment he had entered the room. She was dressed to provoke interest, wearing nothing more than her lace-edged white underclothes

paired with a scarlet bodice that had been left with its upper-
most lacings undone to display enough flesh to arouse. But it
would take a needy man indeed to be attracted to the display.
The whore strolled listlessly around the room, her hands
caressing a shoulder here or sliding across a table there. All the
patrons, bar the man in the corner seat, had been approached.
Clearly none had voiced enough of an interest to keep the
woman from working the room, as she waited for men to
finish eating so that she could earn the first coins of that
evening's pay.

Eventually she approached the man at the corner table. He
had known she would, his arrival noted by the woman as
carefully as it had been by the old man who had delivered his
food and taken his money. He was just glad she had allowed
him to finish his meal before she bothered him.

'Are you lonesome, sir?'

The man in the corner seat said nothing. The girl came
closer in what he supposed she thought to be an alluring way,
but which to him looked like she was half cut. He studied her
eyes, noting the glazed look and the widely dilated pupils. He
had been raised in a gin palace in the East End of London,
his first friends the whores his mother had allowed to work the
crowd who bought her watered-down gin. Enough of them had
dulled the pain of their lives with opium, and although he was
thousands of miles from his childhood home, he recognised the
look of a woman, long past the early flush of youth, who had
turned to whatever local substance was available to get herself
through another night of being humped by any man with
enough coins in his pocket to pay for his pleasure.

As she came closer still, he could see the lines around
her eyes, her age revealed in the cracks and fissures gouged

across her forehead. She smelled as cheap as she looked, her overpowering perfume catching at the back of his throat. She opened her mouth to repeat her unsubtle question, but stopped abruptly. Her mouth remained open as she contemplated the hard grey eyes that looked back at her, then she turned on her heel and sashayed away.

The man in the corner seat was not sorry to see her go. But he did wonder what it was she had seen that had turned her away so swiftly. He knew he was no ogre, despite the thick scar on his left cheek that played peek-a-boo from behind his beard. There had been enough women in his life for him to realise that some found his battered charms attractive. But it had been a while since any had come to his bed, and he wondered if he were now repulsive; if there were something of what he had seen, of what he had done, reflected in his gaze.

He ran a hand briskly across his head, his fingers tingling as they touched the close-cropped bristles, and surveyed the room, checking for a threat. He was always alert, always looking for danger. He no longer knew why, but he could no more stop watching than he could stop breathing. It was who he was now.

It was time to go, but before he could rise, a young couple entered the room. Both were well dressed, the boy in trousers and shirt and a fine bright-red waistcoat that reminded the man in the corner seat of the flash boys of his youth. On his hip was the inevitable six-shooter, the revolver kept snug in a brown leather holster, and as he entered the room, he pulled a wide-brimmed black felt hat from his head. The girl was pretty enough to turn heads, with long dark hair worn in a neat braid that hung over one shoulder. Her dress was dark green and patterned like tartan, with white lace around the neck. To the man in the corner seat she looked a thousand more times attractive in her simple, respectable dress than the whore who paraded around with a large portion of her breasts on open display.

The pair whispered to one another, the conversation taking no more than a few seconds, before they separated, the boy walking into the room whilst the girl sat at one of the many empty tables near the door.

The man in the corner seat watched the boy – he could not think of him as anything else – as he approached a diner attacking half a cooked chicken with his pocketknife. He judged the lad to still be in his teens, and certainly well short of his twentieth birthday. It was rare to see a boy of his age. Most had left to join the Confederate forces that were fighting the armies of the Northern states.

He had heard tales of lads as young as eleven or twelve joining up, despite the age of enlistment being eighteen. He smiled as he remembered a pair of underage twins in the regiment in which he had served who had found a cunning way to enlist without lying. The boys, aged sixteen, had put a slip of paper into their boots on which they had written the number 18. When questioned about their age, they had been able to truthfully reply that they were 'over eighteen'. His smile faded. One of the twins had been killed crossing the city of Baltimore before the first battle in the War Between the States had even been fought. His death had meant nothing; had achieved nothing. He did not know what had become of the second twin, their parting coming on the battlefield as their battered regiment had begun a long and hazardous retreat back to Washington.

'Excuse me for interrupting your food, sir,' the lad said to the man tucking into his chicken dinner, 'but do you know the way to Shreveport?'

The man, a heavily bearded fellow in a red checked shirt with gravy stuck to his whiskers, scowled at the interruption to his meal and shoved a great chunk of chicken flesh into his mouth in lieu of a reply.

'I'm sorry to disturb you and all, but we're looking for our father. My sister and I, well, we heard he was there. We need to find him. You see, our mother, she passed and he doesn't know. We need to find him so we can tell him.'

The man looked the boy straight in the eye. 'It's north of here,' he mumbled, spitting out a morsel of chicken, which became caught in his beard where it enjoyed a reunion with a large dollop of gravy. 'Fair way aways, though.' He rammed another hunk of chicken into his mouth. 'If you head north, you'll find it easy enough. Plenty of folk know the way to Shreveport.'

'Thank you kindly, sir.' The boy held his hat across his belly, nodded his thanks, then turned and walked back to take a seat opposite his sister.

The man in the corner seat had seen enough. He would not stay to see how the game played out. For that was what he knew it was, a game, one in which only the young couple claiming to be brother and sister knew the rules. He pushed away his plate and gathered his weapons. He was about to rise when he saw the girl whisper again to her brother before she got to her feet and walked towards his table.

'Excuse me, sir. Do you mind if I ask you something before you leave?' She came to stand opposite him, her hands slipping on to the back of the empty chair on that side of the table.

The man in the corner seat paused. He was in no rush. He could wait to see what happened next.

'My brother and I, we were wondering . . .' She paused to fix him with a pair of wide eyes. 'Are you a serving man? Are you with the army?'

The man wondered why she felt the need to repeat the question. Did he look stupid to her young eyes? He did not answer immediately, though it was hard not to. The girl looked as if butter wouldn't melt in her mouth. She was older than her supposed brother, perhaps in her early twenties. She had darker skin than he had first noticed, as if she spent a lot of time outside. Her eyes were brown, the whites clear and bright.

'Are you a soldier, sir?' She repeated the question.

'Yes.' He spoke for the first time.

'I thought so. And if I'm not mistaken, that's the uniform of an officer. Am I right?'

The man let the words pass him by. They were a preamble, nothing more. He would have to wait a while for the real question, though he was certain even that question would disguise the reason for the pair's presence in the room. He kept a weather eye on the girl's brother, who was watching the exchange closely. He noticed the way the boy's hand hovered near the revolver he wore on his hip. It was a Navy Colt, he could see that much, similar to the one in his own holster. The lad was ready for trouble, maybe even expecting it. Maybe even hoping for it.

'Have you been fighting them Yankees, sir?' The girl pushed for his attention.

'I have.' He answered evenly. It was almost the truth.

'Why, sir, you are so brave.' She eased herself around the side of the chair, then pulled it out a little. Her eyes stayed locked on his the whole time. 'You being an officer and all, why I expect you killed a whole lot of them Yankees.'

The man paid the statement no heed, but he noted that the girl had identified his uniform easily enough. He was wearing the jacket of a major in the Confederate army, underneath the long, heavy overcoat that he had taken from a drunk a few months before. Like the overcoat, the uniform had been stolen. He had taken it when he had tired of being asked why he was not fighting in the war. It was for convenience, that was all, convenience and concealment.

Yet he had not been lying when he had said that he was a soldier. He had been one for more than a decade. He had led a company of British redcoats in the Crimea, and had defended the cantonment at Bhundapur against the forces of a rebellious maharajah. He had joined the campaign against the Shah of Persia, and had been in the first wave of men through the breach at Delhi. Then there had been the bloodshed at Solferino, carnage like nothing he had seen before or since. Even the First Battle of Bull Run, when he had fought in the blue uniform of the Union, had seemed benign in comparison, although the two days he had spent in grey at the battle at Shiloh had come close.

'Sir, may I sit with you a whiles? I think you might know a thing or two about the world that a young girl like me should learn.'

The brazen statement brought the man back to the present. 'Sure.' Once he would have risen to his feet, perhaps even moved around the table to pull the chair out, quite as a gentleman should. But he had never been a gentleman, at least not a real one. His career had been based on lies and deceit. He had been born poor, and his life and its opportunities had been limited the moment his mother had birthed him. That had only changed the day he took the scarlet uniform of a dead British officer for his own.

'I was wondering, sir, if you maybe might know our father, what with you serving with the army and all.' The question was posed as the girl slid on to the chair opposite. 'We're looking for him, you see. Our mother passed and he don't know. We need to find him so we can tell him. So we can be together again in our hour of need.'

To the mind of the man in the corner seat, it was a foolish question. Even a naive country girl would know that an army was made up of tens of thousands of men, and the chances that a man in a dining room in the back of beyond would know her father were impossibly small.

Now that the girl was seated, he studied her more closely. He wondered if she was a jilt girl. He had come across them before: girls who would promise the earth then be away on their toes with any payment they had demanded without delivering on a single one of their promises. She was faking, he was certain of that. There had been something in her voice when she had spoken the last time, something not quite right about her accent. The mistake was barely there, but every so often there was a different pronunciation to a word, or just a single syllable. The realisation was almost enough to make him smile. He had been an impostor for a long time, and he could spot one at a dozen paces. The pair were there for a reason, but one that had nothing to do with a missing father.

'So what's your name?' He asked a question of his own. He would put his head into the trap to see if it caught him.

The girl smiled, then leaned closer. 'I apologise, sir. What must you think of my manners?' She lowered her gaze to the table for no more than the span of a single heartbeat, then looked up at him again. 'My name is Jane Tucker. Over there, that's my brother Adam.'

The man in the corner seat had to admit that she was playing the game well, the change of gaze artfully done.

'What's your name, sir? I'd like to know it if we're going to be friends and all.' The girl kept up her side of the expected dialogue. Yet there was a subtle alteration in her tone, as though she had spotted something of the change that had come over him.

The man in the corner seat did not reply immediately. He stared at the girl, reluctant to reveal his name. Yet he felt no threat. Not here. Not in the middle of nowhere.

'My name is Jack, Jack Lark,' he said, and then he tried to smile. He failed, the smile dying as he felt a chill whisper across his skin. He shivered as the hairs on the back of his neck stood to attention.

He could feel the fingers of Fate tightening their grip on his soul the moment he uttered the words aloud.

Chapter Three

'Why, I do believe you're English. Do I have that right, sir?' The girl slid back in her chair, as if stunned by the realisation.

'You do.' Jack was impressed. Many people he came across noted his accent. Few could place it. It spoke of a rare intelligence, one that was quite out of place in a young country girl searching for an absent parent.

'So what are you doing in these parts, sir?'

Jack heard a different tone in the follow-up question. It was her first genuine one.

'I came to fight.' He would not admit to more. He had started the war fighting for the North, the hated Yankees. To confess to such, even in a backwater in Louisiana, was to ask for trouble. Not even his experience of the Indian Mutiny had prepared him for the deep-seated hatred that had grown between the two sides in this brutal civil war. They shared the same language and heritage. They even shared many of the same morals, beliefs and ideals. Yet the war had created such enmity that he could not foresee a time when the country could ever be as united as many of those in the North wanted.

'Why, sir, I ain't ever spoken to a proper fighting man before.' The girl's eyes widened, as if impressed. The game was back on.

Jack was spared an answer as a commotion erupted on the far side of the dining saloon. Jane's brother was on his feet, haranguing another diner. Jack had not seen the boy move, but now he was standing over the diner's chair, his narrow chest puffed out in anger so that he looked like a tiny starling fighting a pigeon for a crumb.

'Why the devil would you say such a thing?' Adam pointed his left index finger at the diner's chest whilst his right hand hovered over his holster. 'I asked you a civil question, that's all.'

'I didn't say nothing, boy.' The diner, a grey-bearded fellow dressed in a red and black flannel shirt and dirt-brown trousers, shook his head at the accusation.

'Lying won't help you!' Adam's voice rose in anger. 'I ain't going to let you say that kinda thing about my sister. No, sir, I won't stand for it.'

'Calm it down, friend.' The employee charged with serving the diners had come to intervene. Like most of the diners, he was old, his back bent with age, and his voice carried little authority. 'I'm sure your man there meant nothing by it.'

'I never said nothing.' The man in the flannel shirt repeated his defence. Thus far he was keeping his tone mild, refusing to be drawn into the one-sided confrontation.

'Why that's a lie and well you know it.' Adam raised his voice. 'You care to step outside and say it again?' His right hand slipped an inch lower so that it rested on the hilt of his revolver. The threat was clear.

'Now, boy, you want to button that lip of yours,' the accused replied with the first signs of anger.

'The hell I will.'

'Why don't you sit down, friend?' The ancient server placed a hand on Adam's shoulder in an attempt to steer him away. It was shrugged off angrily.

'Get your hands off me.' The boy's voice rose another level. 'Now you apologise, right this goddam minute.'

'I said nothing.'

'The hell you did.' Adam's revolver moved up an inch.

'What is going on here?' a new voice intervened. A tall man dressed in a well-tailored suit in a pale grey cloth with matching waistcoat strode towards the altercation.

Jack looked at the new arrival with interest. He had emerged from a side room, drawn by the ruckus. He carried an air of authority, and his single question was enough to lower the tension in the room.

'It's all right, Mr Sinclair, sir, nothing but a bit of fuss and nonsense about nothing.'

Jack noticed the way the old server wrung his hands at the sight of the man in the suit. There was fear there. He also noticed something else. The moment Sinclair had arrived, there had been an exchange of looks between Adam and Jane, and he had heard a barely audible sigh escape from the girl's lips.

'Now, sir.' Adam puffed himself up again as he addressed the newcomer. 'I don't mean to make no fuss,' he shot a glacial glare at the man he had accused, 'but this fella here, why, he insulted my sister and talked about her in the foulest terms. I ain't about to stand by and let stuff like that be said.'

'I didn't say nothing.' The man accused of the insult muttered his defence again. But any anger that had been building had subsided quickly. It was clear that the server was not the only man cowed by the new arrival.

'That's a lie.' Adam showed no fear, but his hand had moved from his revolver. 'Why, sir, I don't like to repeat what he said, but it was tantamount to accusing my sister of being a whore.'

'Where is your sister?' Sinclair sounded weary.

'She's just over there, sir.' Adam pointed to Jane, who immediately sat up straighter.

Jack watched for Sinclair's reaction carefully, looking for any change of expression. He saw what he expected, the man's lust coming as no surprise. As far as he could judge, Sinclair was handsome. He had thin dark hair that was slicked back so that it lay in a glistening layer over his scalp. Even his moustache and beard had been oiled. Jack judged him to be in his early thirties, and so of a similar age to himself. He wondered if the man had been the victim of as many taunts and comments as he himself had been before he had stolen the Confederate major's uniform. Men of their age who had stayed behind were subjected to a constant barrage of hostility from strangers whose husbands, brothers, fathers and sons had joined to fight for the right of the Southern states to govern themselves as they saw fit, rather than as the know-nothings in Washington dictated.

'Johnston.' Sinclair addressed the server. 'Get these two a meal, a drink too if they would like it. The same for my friend here.' He indicated the man who had been accused.

'Yes, Mr Sinclair, sir, I'll attend to it right away.' Johnston bobbed his head and scurried away with haste.

'Why, Mr Sinclair.' Jane rose elegantly to her feet. 'That is so very kind of you.' She moved gracefully across the room, her hands playing across the backs of the chairs that she passed.

As Jack noted the way Sinclair appraised her, he felt the

stirring of something deep in his gut. The first prickling of jealousy sat badly on top of the heavy meal.

'There is no need to thank me, ma'am.' Sinclair was all oily charm. 'It really is nothing.'

Jack ignored the urge to spit. He noticed the way Jane glanced at her brother, who immediately backed away. The accusation, which had supposedly been of such a heinous nature that it might have led to a gunfight, was forgotten with indecent haste.

'Would you care to sit and have a drink with me, Mr Sinclair?' Jane fixed the smartly dressed man with her gaze. 'My brother ain't got a good conversation in his head, and I reckon you might know a thing or two about the world. Stuff a young girl like me should hear about.'

Jack tried not to laugh as he heard the same line Jane had used on him. He saw the reaction in Sinclair's expression and he hoped he had hidden his own better. Yet Jane was no ordinary-looking girl, and any man, even one of obvious power like Sinclair, would be flattered by her attention.

'I would be delighted to sit with you for a moment, ma'am.' Sinclair gave another ingratiating smile, then indicated an empty table.

'Thank you kindly, sir.' Jane stepped forward so that she came within Sinclair's reach, then turned away to take a seat. 'It's mighty generous of you to feed us both. Why, my brother and I, we sure are grateful for a meal.'

Sinclair took his own seat. If he was surprised by the forwardness of his new companion, he did not show it.

Jack watched the pair for a moment longer. He had read Sinclair's intentions easily enough, and he would have had to be made of stone not to notice the obvious offer coming from

Jane. Yet he saw something else in the man's expression. Sinclair's desire for Jane was clear; Jack had spotted that immediately. Yet he was also no naive innocent, and was clearly wary. Jack could understand that well enough. Only a fool would not be cautious in the face of a beautiful girl who was throwing herself at him with all the subtlety of a tuppenny whore. Yet there was another emotion in Sinclair's expression, one that was much harder to read. It was as if he expected such attention. Perhaps it wasn't the first time a girl had thrown herself at him, or perhaps it was even a regular occurrence. Jack had seen enough of the world to know how some women would fawn at a rich man's feet, and it was clear that Sinclair was a rich man, at least rich enough to stand out here in Nowheresville, Louisiana.

Jack felt his interest begin to fade as the room settled back down. Adam took himself back to his original table. His righteous fury appeared to have evaporated, and any question of a missing parent also seemed to have been forgotten. Jack had an inkling that the siblings had achieved their first aim by bringing Sinclair into play. He doubted he would ever learn what the rest of the game entailed, but he was sure it involved Sinclair parting with something of value. He had been brought up on the hard streets of Whitechapel, a part of London few chose to visit unless they happened to be a rake looking for the type of vicious delight that only the seedier parts of the metropolis could offer. Adam and Jane were no different to the thieves he had known in his youth, and he was pretty sure they would get whatever it was they were looking for.

But he would not wait to see it. He got to his feet and gathered his weapons. Jane noted his departure with a fleeting glance that lasted no more than a heartbeat. He meant nothing to her. He had been a pawn, one discarded without a thought when the real move had been made.

With his weapons in hand, he paused. For a reason he did not understand, he felt that something had changed. He had been alone for months now. Yet he had always known that one day, Fate would intervene to put an end to his drifting. Now he felt her presence in the room. He did not yet know what plans she had for him, but he was sure they would be revealed to him soon. Then he would have to decide which path to take: one that brought him back into the lives of other people, or one that would see him turn his back on the world and continue his aimless, lonely wandering, perhaps for ever.

At that moment, he did not know which of those two paths he would choose.

Chapter Four

It was early evening by the time Jack was ready to leave town. He considered it to have been a day well spent. He had been fed, and his horse, a fine bay mare that he had stolen many months before from the Confederate army, had been given the best care he could afford and would be stronger for it. He had collected the animal, and now it was time to move on. He did not have the funds to pay for both him and the mare to be lodged overnight, and so he would spend another night sleeping outdoors with nothing but his horse and his weapons for company.

He heaved himself into the saddle, sighing as the weight of his full belly shifted uncomfortably. Once seated, he swept his long coat back, then settled his pork pie hat on his head before taking a moment to make sure everything was just so, his hand patting across his weapons in a familiar routine. He lived on the fringes of society, and there were plenty of folk who would not hesitate to make him fight to keep what he owned.

Experience told him never to take his safety for granted. That particular lesson had been learned many years before on the Grand Trunk Road on a journey from Bombay to Delhi.

The Gujar tribesmen who had attacked the dak gharry he had been travelling in had caught him unprepared, the ambush almost claiming his life and that of the young lady he had been escorting home. He had survived thanks to the timely arrival of the British cavalry, and from that moment on he had faced every day with his weapons loaded and primed.

He had been a soldier all his adult life. Most of those years had been spent at war. It had taken time to find a path to the life he had hungered for, and still more time to become the true soldier he had longed to be. Yet at the end, he had discovered that he had been deluding himself. He was no warrior, and most certainly no great hero. He was a man with a gun and a sword, a killer for sure, but only because he had been granted the one thing that a soldier needed more than anything else – luck. And one day, he knew that luck would run out.

It had taken him a long time to fully understand that. Once he had believed that it had been his talent for war that had kept him alive. Where some men shirked the fight, he had sought it out, sustaining his ambition in the bloody chaos of battle. Then he had learned the truth. He was alive due to blind fortune and the actions of others. Had circumstances been different, his body would have been left as food for the worms long ago. For a reason he could not hope to understand, he had survived when so many others had died.

He shivered. The same feeling that had come over him in the dining room made itself known to him again. Something had changed. The notion made him uncomfortable, perhaps even frightened him. He could handle his self-enforced solitude, even finding moments of genuine contentment in the simple life he now lived. He steered clear of conflict, drifting through the days with no aim other than to do what it took to survive.

He avoided uncomfortable thoughts, forcing his mind to live in the present without acknowledging his past. Memories were shackled and locked away so that they could no longer cause pain. People he had once cared for were forgotten, or at least ignored. He paid no heed to the part of his soul that wanted more. It was the coward's path, he knew that, but it suited him just fine.

The War Between the States had been going on for close to two years now. He had done his best to keep well away from it, his time spent with both armies now behind him. He had come across a few soldiers, even this far away from the main areas of conflict, and so he had heard something of the great battles that had taken place, but which appeared to have brought the war no closer to a conclusion.

There had been a second fight at the Bull Run River, the armies of North and South wrestling for control of the strategic railroad junction at Manassas. Once again the Union forces had been driven back, and there had been talk of a Confederate invasion of the North that would swiftly put an end to the war. That prospect had vanished a few weeks later, following a hard-fought battle at a place called Antietam, near Sharpsburg, in far-away Maryland. The Confederate army had withdrawn into Virginia, where they had beaten back a Union force at a place called Fredericksburg. In the west, the Union Army had pushed steadily southward, beating General Bragg's forces and gaining control of much of Tennessee.

As much as he tried to avoid the war, he was still drawn to the tales of the conflict in which he had fought, yet he did not choose sides. The fate of the country in which he existed no longer meant anything to him. He cared only for staying alive and staying alone. Now, with that aim firmly in mind, he eased his horse into motion and began to head out of town. As ever, it was something of a relief to leave the world of people behind. He was beginning to wonder if the strange sensation that had first come over him in the dining saloon was simply his imagination playing him false.

Then a girl screamed.

His revolver was in his hand in a second. The scream was not one of terror; he had heard enough of those to be certain of that. Yet it was still enough to capture his attention. He saw its source almost immediately, the flash of white undergarments bright in the fading light. The girl who had spoken to him in the dining saloon – Jane – was halfway out of a door that led on to a balcony on the upper storey of a handsome Creole town house, one in a line of identical buildings that pressed close to the turnpike. There was a brief struggle before she kicked her way free, then scrambled across the balcony. Without pause, she vaulted over the wrought-iron railings and on to the one next door, her dress held in her hand.

He saw her destination immediately. Another balcony door was open in a house further down the row. Waiting there was her brother, who was waving her over. The sight made Jack smile. He was witnessing the end of their game after all. His smile widened when he looked back to the door the girl had just exited to see the flushed face of Sinclair, the man who had worn the grey suit but who now stood naked in the doorway that led on to the balcony.

'You goddam bitch!' Sinclair took a single pace on to the balcony, where he stayed for long enough to shout the insult before disappearing back inside.

Jack waited where he was, watching Jane's progress. He wondered what it was she had taken from Sinclair; what it was that had inspired this game of bait and hook. He hoped it was worth the risk. Yet the girl was in no real danger, clambering easily across the balconies of the houses that separated her from her brother. Vaulting the last set of railings, she slipped inside his door, which was slammed shut the moment she was lost from sight.

Jack made no effort to move. If he were being honest with himself, he was rather enjoying the show. He did not have to wait long for the next act to begin, as the siblings' door opened for a second time and the pair came out one after the other. He saw that Jane had thrown on some clothes, and both now carried knapsacks. Neither showed any fear as they climbed over the railings of the balcony before lowering themselves down and dropping to the ground below. They landed no more than a dozen yards from where he sat in the saddle, an interested spectator to the evening's spectacle.

The girl bounded to her feet. She took a moment to brush the dirt from her hands, then she looked up at Jack and flashed him a momentary smile.

'Come on!' Her brother saw the pause.

She needed no further urging and turned to run after him, the two moving fast.

'Stop!' The shout came hard on their heels as a red-faced Sinclair burst out of the town house's front door no more than thirty seconds after the siblings had started to run. Two men came with him, both armed with revolvers. 'Stop them,' Sinclair snapped.

Both raised their weapons. The first shots rang out, the loud cracks echoing off the tall buildings that lined the street.

To Jack's ear, the sound was dreadfully familiar. It stirred memories of bloodshed, ones that he tried hard to contain. He distracted himself by watching the pair as they made their break for freedom. They were running fast, and he saw at once that they were already far out of range. None of the bullets were coming close.

'Hold your bloody fire!' He could not rein back the command. Angry faces turned his way.

'Shut your goddam mouth.' One of the men, a heavyset fellow with florid jowls, emphasised the message by firing off another shot.

Jack shook his head at the belligerence. 'Save your damn powder, you dolt. You won't hit them from there.' He offered the advice with a shake of his head.

'Do as he says.' It was Sinclair who echoed Jack's instruction. He stepped past the man, pushing down his raised arm, his eyes fixed on Jack. 'I saw you talking to that girl. Do you know her?'

'Never seen her before.' Jack gave the reply in a clipped voice. He looked Sinclair over more carefully now that he was closer. There was a dusting of grey in the man's moustache, and at his temples. Some of his hair stood to attention at the back of his head, the errant strands at odds with the glistening mass that still lay slicked against his skull.

'I don't think I believe you.' Sinclair ran a hand back over his scalp, smoothing his hair into place. From his tone, it was clear that the girl had ruffled more than just his locks.

'I don't give a fuck what you think, chum.' Jack's tone was unaltered.

Sinclair held his gaze a moment longer, but said nothing more before he turned on his heel and walked briskly back inside the house.

Jack sat where he was as Sinclair's men followed their

master inside. Aside from the whiff of powder in the air, it was as if nothing had happened. The young pair had taken whatever it was they had come for. The show was over.

He kicked back his heels, easing his mare into a walk. Whatever had happened was not his concern. Nothing was any more.

He rode out of town without so much as a backwards glance, heading back to the wilds, and back to being alone.

Chapter Five

Jack tore open a cartridge, then sprinkled the powder over the damp wood he had gathered, before striking a lucifer and setting the whole thing on fire. The powder went up with a flash, and he sat back, waiting to see if the flames would catch. It was an inefficient way to start a fire, but he had long accepted the fact that he was no woodsman.

He would need more cartridges before long. He had a full packet left for his revolver, and a single load of sixteen for his Henry repeater. The repeating rifle fired copper rimfire cartridges that were quite unlike the paper cartridges used by a revolver or a musket, and he had no idea where he would be able to find more, the weapon so rare and unusual that he had yet to see another man carrying one, in any of the states he had crossed. Until he located some of the unique ammunition, he would have to be careful, the last of his rounds saved for when they were really needed.

The flames caught, and he lay back, his task complete. He had stopped to make camp only when he could no longer clearly see the way ahead. He was not far from the turnpike, but the site he had chosen was well screened from the sight of any other travellers, the small clearing surrounded by tall oak trees and thick underbrush. There was a shallow stream a hundred yards away, and enough wood for his fire, even if it was all a little damp. He had no idea how far he had come from the town, and he did not care. Distance meant little to a man with no destination in mind.

He rested his head on the ground and stared up at the stars. They looked back at him, serene and unconcerned. The stars were his one true companion; a rare constant in a life that had seen too much change. He let the sight of them fill his mind, his eyes tracing patterns across the brightest of them. There was no thought of sleep. Closing his eyes would bring the nightmares that he knew would do nothing but torment. Sleep had long brought with it the faces of the dead. There were too many of those hidden in his memory. Men he had killed, and those he had watched die. People he had allowed to come close, only to lose them, alongside those he had spurned. They came in great legions, these faces that defined the years since he had first stolen an identity that was not his, and not one brought with it anything but pain.

A sound disturbed him. He listened carefully, locating the source then waiting for a repeat of the soft scuffle that had alerted him. It came almost immediately, followed quickly by another, and then another. He might be no woodsman, but he could tell the difference between an animal and the one creature that he tried to avoid at all costs.

He sat up and reached for his revolver, which had been kept loaded for just such an eventuality as this. There was no fear. Not yet. But he could feel it stirring deep in his belly. It was not far away.

He pulled the revolver carefully from its holster. The weight of the weapon was comforting, and as his fingers brushed across the ivory grips, the touch of the smooth surface was reassuring and familiar. The beautiful weapon had not always been his. He had taken it from one man before losing it to another. He had only reclaimed it when that man had been killed, and the touch of that memory shifted something in his mind. It was a memory of fear.

He scanned the gloom, searching for the source of the noise that had disturbed him. The flames of the fire cast an eerie, flickering light, so that shadows moved of their own accord. But still he saw the two figures easily enough.

'Stay right there.' He gave the command without hesitation. The pair halted immediately. If they had hoped to make a stealthy approach, then they had been disappointed.

He raised the revolver, aiming at the closer of the two shadows, and eased back the hammer with his thumb, the clicking sound it made loud, clear and purposeful in the quiet of the night.

There was silence then. He could almost hear them breathing.

'Are you going to shoot?' The question came at him from the first shadow. There was no fear in it.

'That depends.' Jack's voice caught in his throat, and he coughed gently. 'Should I?'

'We don't mean you no harm, mister.'

Jack held the revolver steady. He had his target now, the outline of the man just about visible. If he fired, he would not miss. Yet for a reason he did not fully understand, he felt no sense of danger. There was something familiar in the voice. It did not take him long to place it, for it was one he had heard only a short time before.

'I won't shoot you, Adam. You and your sister can go on your way in peace.' He glanced at the second shadow, which had yet to speak. The siblings from the dining room had disturbed his solitude for a second time. 'But I will shoot you if you stand there long enough.' He made a short, sharp movement with the revolver. 'So move along now, take it nice and easy and be on your way.'

The command was greeted with silence. Neither figure moved. Eventually Adam spoke again.

'You know us?'

'I saw you playing your game with Sinclair today.'

'Are you the major?' The second figure spoke for the first time. It was the girl. She sounded as calm as her brother.

Jack grunted softly as his identification was confirmed, but there was little satisfaction to be gained from it. The conversation was already too long for his liking. He contemplated shooting to drive them away, but the thought vanished quickly. He did not have ammunition to waste.

'Could we share your fire, sir?' Jane spoke again. Her shadow took a step closer. 'It gets cold at night, and we ain't got much of anything with us. We left in kind of a hurry and all.'

Jack lowered his revolver. 'You can come on out. I won't shoot.' The words emerged of their own accord even before the thought was fully formed. He wondered why that might be.

The pair came forward slowly.

'But if you try anything, I'll kill you, you hear me?' he warned.

As they approached, he looked them over. The boy was just as he remembered, but the girl had changed her clothing. She was dressed as a man, with a wide-brimmed hat, high black

boots, dark trousers that fitted snugly to her legs, and a grey
shirt worn underneath a heavy brown jacket with fringes across
the front.

'You too, girl. Don't think I won't.' He wondered if they
knew it was no empty threat. He had killed more people than
he could remember, some in the heat of battle, some in cold
blood. He would likely have to kill again before his own body
was left to rot in the earth.

'Yes, sir.'

Both gave the meek reply. Jack smiled. He could already
sense they were playing another game. He knew he should send
them on their way. Shoot at them too, if need be. But he had
not liked the man called Sinclair, and so he would let them
sleep by his fire. It was his prerogative after all. Even the lonely
could choose whom they allowed near.

'Well, if you're not going to jump me, you might as well sit
yourselves down.' Jack slipped his revolver back into its leather
holster, which he placed deliberately on the ground to his right.
He looked Adam dead in the eye as he moved his hand away
from the weapon, making sure the lad understood that it was
still in easy reach.

The pair looked at one another, then eased their small
knapsacks from their backs before sitting down. Both watched
Jack warily the whole time.

'Have you got any tea?' Jack fired the question at them.

'Tea?' Adam repeated. He laid his revolver on the ground as
he sat. Like Jack, he kept it close to his right hand.

'I haven't got any.' Ammunition for his repeating rifle was
not the only commodity Jack desperately needed. He was sick
of coffee.

'We don't have anything save what you see,' Jane answered.

'You saw us leave.' She laughed gently at the memory, as if feeling foolish, but Jack saw no trace of humour in her eyes. She was watching him closely and warily.

'So what you doing here, Jack Lark?' She spoke again. 'Will you tell us what a man all the way from England is doing here in Louisiana?'

Jack noted that she had remembered his name. He had been nothing but a minor distraction in the game she and her brother had been playing, yet still she had remembered. It was an indication of the sharpness of her mind, one that he would be wise to heed.

'Have you been in the fighting?' Adam probed for an answer.

Jack noticed the way the two of them worked in tandem. It spoke of a long partnership. Again he wondered why they were really there.

'It's none of your business.' He gave the answer gruffly.

'Are you a deserter?' It was the girl's turn now.

'No.' Jack kept moving his gaze between them. Watching them both. 'Why are *you* here?' he countered.

'We're looking for our father.' Adam started the tale. 'He—'

'Stow it,' Jack interrupted him. 'I heard that line of horseshit before, and I didn't believe a single word of it the first time.'

The pair exchanged a look, then fell silent.

Jack missed nothing. He saw the exchange of understanding. 'What are your names?'

'My name's Jane Tucker. This is my brother, Adam,' the girl replied immediately.

Jack shook his head slowly, then smiled. 'I know that's what you told that Sinclair fellow back in town. I figured since you're sharing my fire you might want to tell me your real names.' He watched her closely as he spoke, the flickering light of the flames playing across her face.

'My name is Adam Tucker and this is my sister, Jane,' the lad insisted. There was a touch of tension in his voice.

Jack laughed and shook his head. He had been an impostor for years now, and knew how to carry it off. You needed complete belief in who you were pretending to be. The boy wasn't good enough. The girl was better, but he had still noticed the way her accent dropped on occasion. They both needed more practice if they were ever going to be as good as him.

'So be it. I won't ask again. Just like I won't ask why you were setting up that oily prick back in town. Though I hope you got whatever it was you wanted, because I don't think he'll take kindly to you going back any time soon.' He noticed the way Jane's eyes narrowed at his wry comments. Was there something there in her gaze? Approval, perhaps? Or surprise?

'I don't rightly know what you mean,' Adam answered. There was sharpness to the words now.

'It doesn't matter.' Jack sighed. He had had enough of questions. They could keep their secrets, just as he would keep his.

'Jack, you look awful tired.' Jane leaned forward as she spoke. 'You can rest. We won't do nothing, I promise.'

Jack grunted at the comment. It was a fair observation. He was tired. But it was a tiredness that not even a month's worth of sleep could end. It was buried so deep in his bones now that he did not believe he would ever come fully back to life.

He looked at them both in turn. 'I'm going to close my eyes in a bit.' He spoke slowly and clearly, making sure his every word was understood. 'I'll be holding this revolver the whole time. You try anything, and I'll come up shooting, you hear me? And I warn you now, I'm a very light sleeper, and a very, very good shot.'

'We hear you, Jack,' Jane answered with a half-smile. 'We won't bother you none.'

Jack focused his attention on her. She might have been pretending to be someone else, and he had heard many lies come from her mouth that day. Yet this time, he believed she was telling the truth.

'Thank you for letting us share your fire.' She held his gaze.

Jack stared back. He knew he should look away, but for a moment, all he could think about was how attractive her youth was to him. There was such life in her eyes; a glimpse of a spirit that had yet to be worn down by the years. It was almost as appealing to him as the perfect symmetry of her flawless face and the shape of her slim figure. He wondered what it was like to feel that alive, to live without the grey murk of past suffering shrouding your vision of the world.

He looked away, then lay down and pulled a blanket over his body. He felt the coldness in his soul. It had been a mistake to allow the pair to stay. They had reminded him of a life he could never again possess. He would have done better to drive them away.

Life was easier when he was alone.

Chapter Six

Jack woke up with a start. He was surrounded by shadows. They fluttered past, tantalisingly out of view, flickering and fleeting, teasing him with their closeness, until they merged into the gloom of the last moments of the night. They were replaced by the empty quiet of the pre-dawn.

His fire had gone out. Morning was still far off, but there was enough light filtering through the murky greyness to allow him to see that the two people who had shared his fire had gone. He scanned around his meagre camp. Nothing was missing. The pair had left, but they had taken nothing of his with them, just as they had promised.

He eased himself to his feet, moving gingerly so as not to jar his back, which ached as badly that morning as it did every morning. The persistent ache in the pit of his spine was a reminder of a childhood humping barrels of gin, followed by a decade of soldiering. Like the scars on his face and skin, his body carried his memories for him.

He emptied his bladder against a tree then began to gather his things. It did not take long. It was only when he had everything ready that he understood the emotion that he was

experiencing. It had been a long time since he had felt disappointed. His life had been pared down to the bare bones, his
only desire to be left alone. Now he had allowed people into his
life, even if just for a few hours, and he felt their loss keenly. It
was a reminder, a warning even, that he was better off keeping
away from the world.

Jack rode along with his head comfortably empty. It was not
always like this. Often his own mind betrayed him, releasing
memories that would torment him. He would ride to the
accompaniment of echoes of gunfire, his ears ringing to the
screams of the dead. Some of the memories that haunted him
were so vivid he could even smell the acrid tang of powder
smoke in the air, alongside the reek of blood and mangled flesh.
He would travel without noticing his surroundings, the past
more alive, more real even, than the present. He would awake
from these long spells drained and shaking, his body sheeted in
sweat. He could do nothing to ease the discomfort, save to
carry on and keep moving until another day had been completed
and another night approached.

As he rode, his eyes were never still, as if he somehow
expected his bitter memories to come back to life, his world
once again returned to the horror of the battlefield. Yet there
was little danger that he could see that day. All was peaceful.
He had passed a great lake and now moved through a wide
swathe of woodland, his eyes drinking in the warm greens and
earthy browns that dominated the landscape. He saw little sign
of cultivation, aside from some evidence of logging. Thus far,
this part of Louisiana was almost devoid of people, and the
land was left to lie in peace to slumber through the seasons,
untouched and unsullied by the lives of man.

The crisp, cool morning air wrapped itself around him. For once, he was having a good day, and he felt almost at peace. He put it down to the belly's worth of food he had consumed the previous day, his body more content now that it had more than gristle and hardtack to sustain it.

A gunshot snapped out, shattering the peace, the sound angry and overly loud.

It was followed almost immediately by another, and then another, the flurry of shots urgent and demanding his attention.

He heard the first shouts then; men's voices rising in anger. Commands were barked, though the words didn't carry clearly to where he brought his mare to a stop. More shouts followed as the gunfire continued, the sounds half-drowned by the roar of many guns firing at once.

He gripped his reins in his left hand whilst his right drew his revolver. He held the pose, listening to the whip crack of bullets, mapping out where they were coming from. He was on a small rise that gave him a good view ahead. A wood stretched across his path, the trees – they looked to him to be oaks – widely spaced and the ground in between filled with thick clumps of tangled shrubs and bushes.

He could place three groups amongst the trees; as far as he could tell, there were no more than that. Two of them were firing revolvers, the distinctive sound easy enough to identify. The third group were holding their fire, but instead were moving fast, the blur of their bodies creating dark shadows amidst the trees.

Only when he was sure he knew where the shots were coming from did he ease his mare into motion and turn its head around. There was no question of his getting involved. The fight – or skirmish, or battle, or whatever it was – was no concern of his. There was no reason for him to carry on in the same direction. He could just as well turn back, then head towards a different point on the compass a few hours later.

It was as he began to turn that he saw more movement. He paused. Another of the three groups was on the move now. Two figures were running fast. He recognised them immediately. The pair of siblings who had shared his campfire clearly had a knack of finding trouble. Or creating it.

He was close enough to see them both twist and flinch as they ran. They skidded to a halt behind a fallen tree trunk. Both were on their knees instantly, their arms rising as they aimed their weapons back the way they had come. They fired in tandem, the crack of the shots reaching Jack's ears a few moments later. Both fired a second shot before the lad ducked down and began to reload whilst his sister slowed her rate of fire to cover them both and buy him time.

Jack had seen enough. He could only assume that Sinclair had caught up with them. He did not know why they were causing so much trouble, or why Sinclair felt the need to chase them down, and he did not want to. He kicked back his heels, starting the mare into motion again. He thought only of riding away.

He watched the third group as his horse took its first steps. They were still on the move. He saw that there were three of them, all men, and all held handguns of some sort. They moved slowly, manoeuvring carefully through the widely spaced trees. It did not take a military genius to know that they were planning to attack the pair from the rear.

Jack assessed the distance. The three gunmen would be in position to open fire in no more than a few minutes. There was little chance of either Jane or Adam spotting them, the pair fully engaged with the men to their front. Adam had now reloaded, and was on his knees, firing off aimed shots, whilst his sister reloaded her own revolver. Fire came against them almost constantly, the bullets cracking into the fallen tree trunk they sheltered behind or whipping past their heads. Yet the range for both sides was long, and it would be a lucky shot that found a mark in flesh.

That would surely change. When the three men in the third group were in position, they would have a clear shot. Then it would be as easy as knifing eels in a barrel. In a matter of minutes, the young pair who had shared his campfire would be dead.

It would be easy for him to intervene. He was no more than two hundred yards away from the fight. Thus far, none of the three groups had spotted his presence. He could ram back his heels and charge at the third group. Shooting from horseback was not so easy, but he had done it before. Even if he hit no one, his unexpected appearance would be enough to drive the three men to ground and warn the siblings of the danger. If he rode away, their young lives would come to a bloody and premature end.

The power of life and death was in his hands.

Jack did not move. The men in the third group advanced cautiously. They were dangerously close now, and on the edge of the effective range of their revolvers. If he were going to intervene, there was no time left to delay.

The temptation to fight was strong. He could feel a pressure building in his skull and in his chest, fear and desire mixing together to produce that peculiar, volatile cocktail that was more intoxicating than the strongest arrack or the most beautiful woman. The opportunity to reveal his talent was here, and it was ready to be seized.

Yet still he hesitated. He had promised himself that his days as a soldier were done. He had stared at the great mountains of dead that had filled the villages of Lombardy after the wholesale slaughter at Solferino, and gazed upon the piles of mutilated flesh scattered around the field hospitals at Shiloh. He knew that one day it would be his body left to rot amidst such a foul heap. So he had vowed that he would no longer allow himself to take his place on the fields of battle, where human butchery was committed in the name of some lofty strategic aim. He was a wolf now, not a sheep, and like a wolf he would fight when he wanted to, when he needed to, and not simply when he was told to. But still the lure of the battlefield was there, lingering in the darkness and never quite relaxing its grip on his heart. And he knew what he was, and what he could be.

He watched the pair fighting for their lives. Both were up and shooting before they ducked down to hide from the inevitable return shots. They fought well, both clearly capable, keeping up an almost constant fire that was holding their adversaries at bay. Yet as good as they were, their skills would not save them, not against another foe they had not yet seen.

Two of the men in the third group were creeping forward, whilst the third covered them. Jack could only approve of their action. It was the sensible option. In battle, the surest way to win a fight was to turn your enemy's flank. That tactic applied just as much to the skirmish he was watching, even though it was between just a handful of combatants.

He sat still, watching the two men as they took up their positions. He picked out the detail of their clothing. One wore a red shirt, the colour bright against the background of tangled greenery. The other was in grey, his flannel shirt open to the navel to reveal a dirty white undershirt. Both wore dark hats pulled low. He wondered if they were the same two men he had rebuked for wasting ammunition. The notion gave them an identity. It made them people, rather than a faceless foe.

He glanced across at Jane and Adam. Both were firing, their attention riveted on the men to their front. Neither showed any sign that they were aware of the danger behind them.

And so he made his choice.

He kicked back his heels, urging his mount into motion.

The mare increased its speed, hooves thumping into the ground as the animal stretched its neck and eased into a gallop. The rhythm of the impacts was mesmerising. It resonated through Jack's body, awakening parts that had lain dormant. Emotions stirred, excitement and fear swirling through him as he came truly alive for the first time in so long.

He raised his right arm, taking aim. The revolver jerked from side to side, his actions made clumsy by the motion of his horse. For a moment, he considered holstering the revolver and drawing the repeating rifle from its sheath next to the saddle. Yet he hesitated, unwilling to waste what little ammunition he had left. The distance closed quickly, the range reducing with every passing second. It was enough to settle his mind. The revolver would do the job well enough so long as he got close. He paused, settling himself, holding his hand steady so that his first target covered the end of the barrel.

There was a moment to reflect, a moment to doubt the sanity of his actions. Then he opened fire.

The first bullet missed, as did the second, the shots snapping through the air before burying themselves in the tangled foliage behind the pair of gunmen. The third took the foremost of the two in the side of the chest. The man crumpled with barely a cry.

Heads turned as a new player came into the game. The man in the grey shirt twisted on the spot as his companion died at his feet. There was time to see the sudden terror in his eyes before Jack shot him in the gut a heartbeat later. The man dropped his revolver to clutch both hands to the gaping hole in his stomach. He stood there, his mouth open in a silent scream, his eyes staring back at the rider who had shot him. Then he fell.

Jack paid him no heed. He turned his revolver towards the third gunman in the group. This man was no fool. He had seen the rider arrive to spoil their plan and had lingered long enough to see his two companions gunned down. Now he took to his toes, lumbering into motion as he tried to escape his fate.

It was too easy. Jack pulled hard on the reins, forcing his mare to the right, the action instinctive. He fired a moment later. The fifth bullet in his revolver stung the air beside the fleeing gunman's head. It came close enough to make the man stumble, and he dropped to his knees for a few seconds, then scrambled up and ran on.

The delay let Jack close the distance. He had a single round left. Yet he knew he would not miss again. He fired, then pulled back hard on the reins, forcing the bit deep into the mare's mouth and bringing her to a noisy halt. He did not bother to watch as the third gunman fell face down, a bullet buried deep in the pit of his spine.

Jack held his ground. His mare quivered and trembled beneath him, breathing noisily. For his part, he felt the thrill of the fight subside, the intoxicating emotions it had released now spent. They were replaced by an icy calm. He had likely killed three men, yet he was as composed as he had been when he had been riding alone. He felt the coldness in his veins, savouring its touch. But just for a moment he had been his true self. And it had felt glorious.

Chapter Seven

The fight had ended with Jack's sixth bullet. The group of gunmen that had been engaging Adam and Jane had run as soon as the odds had changed against them. It would have been as if the fight had never taken place were it not for the pitiful cries coming from one of the men Jack had shot down.

He rode towards the pair of siblings, who had stayed in position behind the fallen tree. Both were reloading. He watched them closely as he approached. It was clear that they knew what they were doing, both going through the routine with practised ease.

He said nothing as he reined his horse in.

'I reckon we need to thank you.' Adam spoke first. He did not seem pleased to have to acknowledge the stranger who had just saved their lives. He had finished reloading and now he spun his revolver around his finger before ramming it back into its holster, the action smooth and proficient.

'I reckon you do.' Jack's tone was ice cold. He did not relish the prospect of conversation.

'Thank you, Jack.' Jane spoke for them both.

Jack said nothing. He slid from the saddle. He would not linger; he had no need of their thanks. But he did have one last task that could not be left unfinished.

He turned his back on the pair, then fished out a fresh packet of six paper cartridges for his revolver. With it in hand, he turned and found a spot where he could sit and begin the slow process of refilling each of the weapon's six chambers.

'We're sure lucky you came by.' Jane approached Jack slowly, as if wary of the man who had killed to keep her alive.

'You are.' Jack half cocked the revolver, then spun the cylinder.

'You just happened to be passing?'

Jack grunted by way of reply. Her accent seemed thicker, somehow even more faked now than it had been before. He put it down to the stress of nearly dying.

He concentrated on reloading, filling each chamber with a fresh cartridge that he rammed home with the ramrod that hinged out from underneath the barrel, before glancing up at her once again. Her face was streaked with powder, and strands of hair were stuck in the sweat that glistened on her face. She might have looked dishevelled, but her eyes were bright, and there were points of colour on each cheek.

'You can drop the accent now, love,' he suggested, then offered a thin smile.

'What do you mean?'

He had not looked away. He noticed the frown that followed his instruction, and the way her eyes narrowed. It confirmed his suspicions. 'You know what I mean. But suit yourself. You can talk any way you damn please.' He returned his attention to his revolver. All six chambers had been filled, and so he reached into a pocket and fished out the small tub of grease that he would use to seal each one. Only when he was satisfied that the gun would not misfire did he carefully put a fresh percussion cap on to the nipple on each chamber and revolve the cylinder so that the gun's hammer rested in between two of the chambers. Then he got to his feet.

'Who are you, Jack?' Jane asked. The Southern accent was gone. It had been replaced with one similar to those he had heard on the East Coast.

'I have no idea.' He gave the honest answer, then pushed his revolver back into its holster before turning to walk away. There was something left to be done, something that he would not leave to anyone else.

The pair he had saved let him go. He heard their murmured conversation but paid it no heed. There would be time enough for talking if that was what he wanted.

He walked through the trees, taking his time. It was easy enough to find what he was looking for.

It took no more than a cursory glance at the man he had shot in the chest to know that he had died almost instantly. There was a moment's pride at the accuracy of the shot before the shame arrived. It had not been a fair fight. The man had died without ever really knowing who it was that had killed him. But that was not what shamed Jack. When the decision to kill had been made, the manner of its arrival had mattered not one jot. There was no fairness in death. Yet still he felt a prick of shame, one that concerned him. For he had killed a man and felt nothing.

He pushed on, drawing his revolver as he went. Cries and whimpers guided his footsteps. They came without pause now, the incoherent babble loud enough to hide the sound of his footfall.

The man in the grey shirt was lying on his back when Jack found him. He stared up at the sky whilst his hands scrabbled at the bullet hole in his stomach. His fingers were covered in gore, the blood already drying and blackening. Something pulsed deep inside the hole, as if a creature hid in the torn flesh and was about to emerge to bring terror to the world.

Jack gazed down at the wound his bullet had caused. He had seen many like it. It would kill as surely as a bullet to the head, just a lot more slowly.

The man looked up at Jack. His cries increased in urgency for a few moments before dying away as his eyes fell to the revolver held in Jack's right hand.

'Sorry, chum.' Jack whispered the last words the man would ever hear before he raised his revolver.

The gunshot that followed was loud, the sound echoing off the trees.

Jane and Adam were ready to leave by the time Jack returned to where he had left his horse. Both watched him warily.

He said nothing. He felt drained. With the gut-shot gunman dealt with, he had moved on to check on the third man he had shot down. That man had been dead when he had found him, yet the snail-like trail of blood smeared across the ground spoke of a drawn-out end, one that Jack regretted. He would kill without hesitation, yet he did not want to be the cause of suffering. He had witnessed too much to wish to inflict it on others.

He walked towards his mare, ignoring the silence and the stares. He carried one of the dead gunmen's revolvers and a pouch containing all the ammunition he had found on the three men. The little money they had had was in his pocket, as was a silver watch, a small knife and a cut-throat razor. Anything else they had owned had been left on their corpses.

'So are you just going to leave?' Jane asked. She stood next to her supposed brother. For his part, Adam said nothing, but his hand hovered close to the holster on his right hip.

'Yes.' Jack's reply was curt.

'Why did you do it? Why did you help us?'

Jack paused halfway through unbuckling one of his saddlebags. Then he sighed. Some things just could not be avoided. 'Tell me your real names first.' He finished unbuckling the strap, then busied himself stowing his new possessions and ammunition inside the saddlebag.

'My name is Katherine, but if you call me that, I'll shoot you.' The girl smiled as she made the threat. 'Everyone calls me Kat. It helps them forget I'm really a girl.' She nodded at her companion. 'His name really is Adam. He's too stupid to remember another one.'

'Are you truly brother and sister?'

'No.'

Jack tied off the strap then turned to face the pair. 'I thought not. You don't even look alike.'

'When did you know?' Kat was still smiling. Like Adam, her right hand was ready to draw her revolver.

'From the start.' Jack frowned. The pair were standing as if ready to fight.

'Then why did you help us?' Adam fired the question at him. Unlike Kat, he was not smiling.

'I have no idea,' Jack replied with total honesty. 'So who were those men?'

'You don't know?' Adam's right hand twitched.

'I've no fucking idea, chum.' Jack had spotted the slight

movement. 'Are you really going to draw on me after I just saved your necks?'

Adam's expression did not alter. 'We don't know who you are.'

'I told you my name once already. I didn't lie.'

'But you were back in Natchitoches, and now you're here. That's an odd coincidence, don't you think?'

'You think I'm following you?' Jack shook his head at the foolishness of the notion.

'I've learned to be cautious. That's why I'm still alive.'

Jack snorted. He didn't mean to, but Adam could not be much more than eighteen years old, which made his answer amusing, to Jack at least.

'You think I'm being funny?'

'Yes.' Jack shook his head as he sensed the anger building in the boy.

'That's enough.' Kat had watched the byplay and now chose to put an end to it. 'Adam, stop being so goddam dumb.' She moved her right hand away from her holster, then tucked her fingers into her belt, the action deliberate. 'Have you heard of the Sinclair gang, Jack?'

'No.' Jack kept his gaze on Adam, whose own hand had stayed near his gun.

'Well, you have now. And you just killed three of them. That puts you on our side, I guess.'

'And what side is that?'

'We work for a man called Brannigan. You heard of him?'

'No.'

'He's well known around these parts. You want a job done, you send for him.'

'Sounds like a stalwart fellow.'

Kat laughed at the turn of phrase. 'I've never heard him called that before.'

Jack liked her laugh. 'So why is your Brannigan fighting this Sinclair gang?'

'We're being paid to escort a wagon train down to Mexico. Sinclair thought he should have been given the contract. When he didn't get it, he figured he would take it anyway.' Kat spoke quickly, while Adam just scowled.

'Must be important, this wagon train of yours. What's on it? Gold?'

'Cotton.'

The answer surprised Jack. If men were fighting – indeed, dying – over this wagon train, then he figured it must be carrying something of high value.

'Just cotton?' he asked.

'It's worth almost as much as gold. Least it will be if we can get it down to the coast in Mexico.'

'So if this Sinclair fellow and his gang want to take your wagons, why were you paying him a visit?' Jack asked. Despite himself, he was intrigued.

'To find out where his men are waiting for us.'

'Did he tell you?'

'Eventually.' Kat gave a teasing smile.

'And now you'll take that information to this Brannigan fellow.'

'We will.'

'Seems a lot of trouble over some cotton.' Jack snorted as he made the remark. He had seen men fight and kill for a hundred reasons. But this was a new one. He did not understand why something so innocuous would cause such trouble. Gold he could understand, or weapons, or even food. But not cotton.

'So what about you, Jack?' Kat used the pause to change the direction of the conversation. 'You know why we're here. Will you tell us what you're doing?'

'Minding my own business.' There was a warning in his reply.

'Then why fight?' Kat seemed genuinely interested.

'Maybe I was just bored.' He spoke glibly. He had buried the truth deep, just as he hid away the joy he had felt when he had first spurred his horse into action.

He gathered his strength, then hauled himself into the saddle, his mare taking a single step to the side as it bore his full weight. He was ready to ride away and put this episode, this short chapter in his life, to bed. But something held him back. He sensed it was not over. Not yet.

'Bored men don't risk their lives for strangers.' Kat walked towards him until she stood close to his stirrup.

'I was never in danger.' Jack sat easily in the saddle. He was not bragging, just stating a fact.

'So where are you headed?' Kat looked up at him.

'Somewhere that's not here.'

'Do you ever give a straight answer?'

Jack laughed. It had been a while since he had last found something amusing. 'I guess I'm out of practice at holding a conversation.' He found her gaze, then offered a smile. 'I'm sorry.'

'Better,' Kat replied. 'You look less frightening when you smile. So . . .' she paused as if thinking something through, 'are you in need of employment?'

Jack did not answer immediately. He sensed that the moment he had been waiting for had arrived. It was time for him to choose his path.

'We need more men if we're going to get where we want to go. Brannigan will take you on when I tell him what you did. Anyone who kills Sinclair's men will be welcome. You've got your own gun and your own horse. He'll pay you well.' Kat offered the lure.

Jack rocked back in the saddle and looked up at the sky before closing his eyes. He had waited around for just such an offer as this. He might crave peace and solitude, but a man needed sustenance more physical than such lonely ambitions. Then there was something else, something more visceral. He knew what he was, what he wanted and what he needed. He had hibernated for nearly a year now. The short skirmish had given him a taste of what he had lost, and had stirred something buried deep in his soul into life, awakening the fear and the joy that he tried so hard to contain. It had reminded him what it was like to be truly alive.

He held his pose for several long moments before opening his eyes and looking down at Kat. There was a time when Fate demanded he be the man he was meant to be. And when life demanded he pay a price to keep living.

'Okay, let's do it.' The words came out flat. But they had been spoken.

It was time to rejoin the world.

Chapter Eight

---

*J*ack followed Adam and Kat into the small Creole cottage. It was a pretty one-and-a-half-storey building with walls made of roughened plaster that might once have been white but was now grey and mottled with age. There were separate entrance doors to both downstairs rooms and a neat porch across the front. It was set alone in a field next to the turnpike that the three had followed west in the hours since the fight with the men from Sinclair's gang. They had reached the out-of-the-way cottage shortly before noon.

The room they entered had little to recommend it. It was a mean affair that appeared to have been set up as some sort of saloon. There was no furniture save for a single wide plank of wood resting on trestles, and a battered dresser lined with bottles of cheap rotgut whiskey and dozens of tiny glasses. There was nowhere to sit, and the floorboards were covered with weeks of accumulated dust and debris.

Jack thought back to the ostentatious finery of his mother's gin palace, and wondered what she would make of such a place as this. His mother's place had been in the back streets of the East End. Its facade had been lit by bright gas burners that had acted as beacons in the gloom of the rookeries, and it had shone like a ruby in a pile of shit. He looked at the bottles of whiskey and saw the similarity to the gin palace in the raw spirit they contained. In their way, both places were a refuge, a sanctuary that offered its customers some respite from the endless grinding misery of their lives. That was no different despite the thousands of miles that separated them.

'Nice place.' He offered the judgement as the three of them stood in front of the dresser.

'No, it's not.' Kat answered over her shoulder as she walked to a corner of the room, where she dumped her knapsack. 'But the boys like it. They take over a place and fill it with whiskey as soon as we stay somewhere for more than a day. Makes them feel at home.'

'The boys?' Jack leaned his repeating rifle against the trestles at one end of the temporary table. He wore his sabre on his left hip and his revolver on his right. He had come ready to fight.

'Brannigan's men.' Kat removed her tasselled jacket before dumping it on top of her knapsack. 'He knows what they want.'

'What's that?'

'Money, whiskey and women, in that order. If he gives them those, they don't create.'

'Is that wise?' Jack remembered his days as a British redcoat, and wondered what his first company would have made of unfettered access to a few dozen bottles of whiskey. They'd have likely drunk the place dry in less than an hour.

'The boys know not to step out of line.' Kat reached behind her head and untied the bands holding her hair in place. She let it fall, then bent forward to shake it out.

'Is that what you want too? Money, whiskey and women?' Jack watched her, transfixed. He had been alone a long time.

'No.' Kat answered without looking at him, her attention focused on teasing some of the knots from her hair.

Jack wanted to keep watching, so he asked another question. 'So what *do* you want?'

'Nothing. I want to be *given* nothing.'

'Brannigan must like that.'

Kat laughed. 'Maybe. Might make me the worst kind of person to have around too.'

'Why?'

'That would be telling.'

Jack did not understand the intriguing answer, but he did feel himself beginning to stare at her, so he turned away. Adam was still standing in the doorway. He was watching Jack closely.

'I'll go find Brannigan.' He scowled as he spoke the words.

Jack met his glare directly. 'You all right, chum?' he asked.

Adam acknowledged the question with a slow shake of his head, then turned on his heel and walked away.

'Don't worry about Adam.' Kat had missed nothing. 'He doesn't like anyone. Except Brannigan.'

'Why's that?'

'You'll have to ask him.' Kat came back into his view. Her hair was once again bound tightly behind her head. 'Not that he'll tell you.'

'Then what's *your* story, Kat?' Jack did his best to keep his eyes on her face.

She laughed the question away. 'That's not something we ask round here.' If she was aware of the effect she was having on Jack, she let no hint of it show in her expression. 'And we won't ask it of you. We won't even ask you where you got that scar of yours.'

Jack's hand lifted to his face of its own accord, his fingers tracing the raised ridge of flesh that ran across his left cheek and under the beard that he had allowed to grow over the course of the last few months. The scar was the legacy of a mutinous sawar's sword, the blow that had caused it just one of the many moments when he had escaped death by no more than a fraction of an inch. He rarely thought of the bitter fight outside the walls of Delhi, the memory shackled and contained in the darkest recesses of his mind where he knew not to venture.

He was spared finding a reply by the sound of voices. He braced himself, sure that what was to follow would set down a marker for the weeks and perhaps months to come.

The men he had heard arrived on a wave of noise, one that got louder as they swaggered into the cottage, every man sure of his place and his right to be there. To Jack, it seemed that they were all talking at once, their voices brash and overly loud, as if they were well aware of the display they made and were proud of it.

One went straight to the wooden dresser and grabbed two bottles of whiskey, then swept up as many glasses as he could hold in a single hand. He dumped them carelessly on the simple table and began to fill each glass in turn, without bothering to lift the bottle, so that a river of spilled whiskey ran across the wood. Eager hands grabbed glasses, the contents tossed quickly down throats before the now empty vessels were slammed back on to the plank of wood for an immediate refill.

Jack watched the men carefully. All were older than him, with grey in both their beards and their hair – if they had any, that was. None looked friendly. They all noted his presence, but not one of them acknowledged him or changed their manner. A few greeted Kat with a curt nod or a smile, but there was nothing more, no leers or propositions or ribald comments. Their reaction made it clear that she was part of the gang, yet there was something more in the guarded expressions being sent her way, as if she were somehow a danger, too.

He noted the thought, then studied the members of the gang more closely. He saw two men in the grey uniform jackets of the Confederate army, and another in the dark blue of the Union. A tall, cadaverous fellow in a black morning suit hung on the periphery of the group, sipping at his whiskey with his little finger cocked at an odd angle. At his side was a man dressed completely in brown animal skins, his strange attire completed with a thick fur hat perched precariously on the back of his head. The rest wore dull, workmanlike clothes, many with simple waistcoats. They sported wide-brimmed hats, and most had bandanas around their necks. To a man they wore high boots with pointed toes and heavy spurs attached to the heel. All were armed with a six-shot revolver on their right side, and many wore a long bowie knife in a leather sheath attached to their belt. These were hard men, with faces to match.

'What we got here then?' One of their number spied the repeating rifle leaning against the trestle. The man, a broad-shouldered fellow with a thin smear of brown hair across his scalp and several days' worth of stubble on his face, took a moment to stare at Jack before lifting the weapon.

'Would you look at this beauty, fellas?' He held it in both hands as he inspected it 'Why, I ain't ever seen one of these fancy repeaters before.' He looked back at Jack. 'Where did you get a rifle like this from, friend?'

Jack noted the man's use of the word, but there was nothing

friendly in his tone. 'Give it back and I'll tell you.' He kept his voice even as he made the demand.

'I asked you a simple-ass question, nothing more.' The man cocked his head at an angle as he contemplated Jack. 'You're new around here, so I'll give you another chance to show a little more respect.' He spoke slowly, his voice full of challenge. 'Where did you get it?'

Jack forced a long breath into his lungs. There was only one way a conversation like this could end, and it wasn't with handshakes and cries for drinks all round. He took a moment to study the man holding his rifle. He was lean and well muscled despite his age. It would not be an easy fight if it came to it.

'Give it back.' He held the man's gaze as he repeated his demand. There could be no hint of weakness in front of men such as these, no matter what it cost.

The man ignored the request, instead making a play of admiring the rifle, turning it around in his hands so that he could look at the underside. 'Did you steal it?'

Again Jack held back a reply.

'Uh huh.' The man smiled, interpreting Jack's silence as a confession of guilt. 'I figured. A worthless varmint like you don't go getting a rifle like this all by hisself.' He made a play of looking Jack up and down as he spoke. The smile turned into a sneer. 'You'd have to be a man of means to get yourself this here weapon. And you? Why, you don't look like much to me, not like much at all. You look like you ain't got yourself much more than a pocket full of goddam goober peas.'

Jack brushed aside the judgement. 'I'll ask you one last time, *friend*.' He wrapped the man's choice of word in iron. 'Give it back.'

'And who might you be to tell me what to do?' The words were spoken softly.

'I'm the man who'll kill you if you don't give me back my rifle pretty damn fucking sharpish.'

The threat made the man smile once again. He turned his head to look at his companions, who were watching the confrontation. Most were smiling. Only Kat was not, but she said nothing as his eyes met hers.

'Isn't that the darnedest thing? This son of a bitch is threatening me.'

Jack stayed silent as the man played to the crowd. For a moment he contemplated drawing his sword, but the notion died a rapid death. Men armed with six-shooters surrounded him. He would be gunned down before he could aim even a single blow. Whatever was to come would have to be done the old-fashioned way.

He noticed Adam return, yet the lad whose life he had saved showed no sign of intervening. Instead he hung back, his expression guarded. There was no hope of any aid, so Jack kept his eyes fixed on the man holding his repeater. He knew how to deal with men like this. He knew what he had to do.

The man turned back to face him, a leering smile on his face. It was still fixed in place when Jack punched him full on the mouth. It was a fine blow, and it snapped the man's head back, crushing his lips against his teeth so that blood started to flow.

Jack stepped forward to snatch his repeater from the man's grip. Not for the first time, he wished he had ammunition to spare.

The room had erupted as the gang saw the first punch

thrown. It was a feral sound, the men whooping and cheering as the fight they had seen coming began.

'I'll break your goddam neck for that.' The man held the back of his hand against his bloodied lips and inspected what he saw. Then he attacked.

He punched hard, his right hand reaching for Jack's face. But Jack had seen it coming and swayed back, letting the fist flash past in front of his nose. The second punch came hard on the heels of the first, a low, rising blow that started down by the man's left hip. Again Jack saw it coming and stepped past it before ramming the brass-capped hilt of his rifle into the man's gut. It was well placed and it drove every scrap of air from the man's lungs. Before he could react, Jack snapped his head forward, smashing his forehead into the man's nose with enough force to rock him back on his heels.

The noise in the room intensified. Hands reached out to steady the bloodied man. There was no notion of anyone else joining the fight. In these hard lands, men fought alone.

Jack braced himself, ready to fight on. He had no choice. He had to stand his ground.

His opponent stood still for a second, his head hanging down as he drew in a few deep breaths. Then he lifted his head and came at Jack in a rush.

Jack ducked a shoulder and drove back at his adversary. The connection was brutal, but Jack was larger and heavier, and he knocked the man from his feet and sent him tumbling to the floor.

To his credit, the man did not stay down. He pushed himself up, but Jack had already recovered his balance, and he swung the rifle's butt, catching the man on the upper arm with enough force to knock him back down.

The anger was starting to flow. Yet Jack remained in control. He knew what he was doing. The example had to be set, and for a moment, he was almost glad that the man now struggling back to his feet had summoned the confrontation.

'I thought you wanted my rifle?' he mocked. 'Well, here it is. Come and fucking get it.'

The man regained his footing, then came at Jack for a third time. He bellowed as he charged, the bestial sound loud enough to encourage the men watching the fight to roar in encouragement.

Jack smiled. It was almost too easy. Despite being knocked down twice, the man was quick, yet still Jack managed to sidestep the rush. He swung the rifle again as he moved, bringing it around in a wickedly fast arc so that the butt slammed into the man's side. It hit him hard, spinning him around so that he faced Jack, who took a single step forward, then bludgeoned the barrel of the rifle directly into his assailant's balls.

The man crumpled. His mouth opened as he doubled over, but no sound came out. He stood there, his hands clutching at his groin for several long moments before the first wail came from his lips.

'Anyone else want to try me?' Jack turned to address the crowd. 'Any of you other pricks want to take this rifle of mine?' He fired the words at the faces that stared back at him, gesturing with the weapon. 'No one?'

Not one man answered. The room that had been filled with cheers and roars had fallen silent.

'What the hell is going on here?' The question came from a man standing in the doorway. It was asked in a mild, conversational tone.

Jack turned. 'I'm teaching that fuckwit some manners.' He

spoke with the same snap in his tone as he had used when challenging the other men to fight.

The new arrival did not reply. As he walked into the room, the men moved out of his way, their heads bowed like errant schoolboys suddenly taken to task by their master.

Jack stood his ground. From the men's reaction, there was no doubt that he now faced their leader. There was no hiding their fear of this man, yet to Jack's quick glance he looked nothing special. He was dressed shabbily, in well-worn brown trousers, a tired grey shirt and a brown jacket that was so old, large areas of the fabric had been worn to a faded black. On his head he wore a wide-brimmed tan hat pulled low.

'And who might you be, friend?'

Jack heard nothing dangerous in the man's tone. If he was concerned to see one of his men handled roughly then not a trace of it showed.

'His name is Jack Lark, and he saved me and Adam from some of Sinclair's goons.' It was Kat who answered the question that had been left to linger in the room like a bad smell. She alone showed no fear of the man. 'I'll vouch for him, Brannigan. Without him I'd be dead. Adam too.'

'So why the hell are we setting on him?'

'Because Wade is too damn dumb to do anything else.' Kat offered the damning verdict on the man who had attacked Jack. For his part, Wade hung back, head bowed and hands clasped to his balls while the blood from his crushed nose dripped on to the floor.

'Wade, why are you so damn stupid?' Brannigan removed his hat and tossed it casually on to the table, then came to stand in front of the man.

'That fellow disrespected me.' Wade made his defence in a voice laced with pain and fear.

'Oh he did, did he? Did he hurt your feelings?'

Wade said nothing. In the silence that followed the question, the only sound was the slow drip of his blood on to the floor.

'You really are one dumb son of a bitch.' Brannigan shook his head.

Jack did not see the blow coming. Brannigan's fist moved quicker than the eye could track, and he drove it hard and fast into Wade's gut. Wade grunted once, then doubled over again, puking out a thin stream of whiskey and blood that splattered noisily on to the floor. Brannigan did not let him recover. Moving quickly, he grabbed the man by the back of the neck and dragged him forcibly to the door. Once there, he threw him hard, so that he sprawled on to the porch.

Discipline delivered, he turned and strode back inside, the jangling sound made by his heavy spurs loud in the quiet that had followed Wade's ejection.

Jack stood tall, and got his first proper look at the man he now knew was Brannigan, the gang's leader. He was a good six inches taller than Jack, and older, his face weathered by the sun and the wind so that it was lined and tanned. On his right hip he wore the inevitable revolver in a battered and scuffed holster. He had close-cropped sandy hair and a thin beard of the same colour covering hollow cheeks. He looked as lean and as tough as if he had been fabricated from iron. But what really captured Jack's attention was his eyes. They were deep set, and the pale blue of winter's ice.

Chapter Nine

---

*B*rannigan's presence dominated the room. He poured himself a measure of whiskey from one of the bottles that had been left on the table. No one else was drinking any longer.

'Did you get the information?' He fired the question at Kat, but his attention was fully focused on the stranger who had beaten one of his men.

'Yes.' Kat's chin lifted as she answered.

'So where are they?'

'They've got a camp about ten miles south of here. But they're not going to attack us any time soon. They don't see the point of dragging the wagons all the way down to the border by themselves. They figure to trail us south then ambush us further down the trail.'

'Where?'

'South of the sands.'

Brannigan grunted as he absorbed the news. 'They figure they can take the wagons from us?'

'Sinclair thinks it'll be easy.'

'Well, he'll be disappointed. We're not all as dumb as

Wade.' Brannigan's expression was unaltered as he made the jibe. A few of his men muttered in agreement, and one even managed a half-strangled laugh. The sound died a slow death.

'So who is this fellow?' he continued. 'Did you find yourself a stray dog?'

'Like I said, he saved us from Sinclair's men. If he hadn't showed up, Adam and I'd both be dead, and you would know damn all about Sinclair's plans.' Kat took a few steps forward to stand at Jack's side. 'He's English.' She made the statement as if it offered proof of her tale.

'Is he now?' Brannigan was not impressed. He contemplated Jack for several long moments, then turned to pick up the whiskey bottle. 'Why is no one drinking?' he asked, then began to fill the glasses on the table. 'Come on, fellas, you know I hate drinking alone.'

The men were quick to obey, grabbing the glasses and throwing the liquor down their necks as quickly as they could before reaching out for more.

Brannigan emptied the bottle, then threw it behind the bar, the sound of it smashing loud enough to startle a good number of the men and make them flinch.

'So this fellow saved you all on his lonesome?' He took a full glass, then turned to face Jack.

'He killed three of Sinclair's goons. He's a good man, Brannigan. He knows how to fight, too.' Kat maintained her steadfast defence of Jack.

'Looks to me like he's lost his fair share of fights.' There was no hint of a smile as the remark was made.

Jack kept his expression even. The reference to his scar meant nothing.

'So why would you do that? Why would you help them?' This time Brannigan addressed Jack directly.

'It was an unfair fight. I figured I'd even the odds a little,' Jack answered warily.

'Are you some sort of hero?'

'No.'

'Then why do it?'

Jack shrugged. 'I do what I want.' He didn't like the tone of the questioning. Yet he wanted – no, he corrected himself, he *needed* employment. So he swallowed his pride and met the cold stare that searched his own.

'Do you now?' Brannigan clearly did not like the answer. 'I reckon that makes you dangerous, Mister Lark.' The verdict was given in the same flat tone.

'Maybe.' Jack matched his own tone to that of the man asking the question.

'So are you an outlaw? Got yourself a bounty on your head?'

'No.'

'You're not a talkative fellow, are you, Jack?' Brannigan's tone was scornful.

Jack said nothing. He was not sure where the conversation was going.

Brannigan nodded, as if the silence pleased him more than Jack's previous curt answers. 'You know who I am?'

'No.' Jack watched the other man's expression closely, but he was proving impossible to read. He tried to gauge Brannigan's age. His skin was tanned and weathered, but the lines there were not yet sunken and drawn deep. There was a thin scar under one eye and another high on the opposite temple, but neither was as large or as prominent as the one on Jack's own face. He guessed Brannigan to be in his mid to late forties, or perhaps a touch older. Both of them had seen enough of life to know what lived in their own souls.

'Good. That means you will make up your own mind about me, and I kind of like that.' Brannigan downed his whiskey, then carefully placed the empty glass on the bar. 'So why are you here, Jack? You expect some kind of reward for saving two of mine?'

'I want employment.' For once, Jack was not lying, or present under false pretences. He was who he was, nothing more and nothing less.

Brannigan contemplated the answer, then turned on his heel to face his men. 'Out you go, fellas. I need to talk to our new friend here.'

The men did not need to be told twice. They left quickly and quietly, the contrast with their noisy and boisterous arrival stark. Kat went with them, leaving Jack and Brannigan alone.

'So you fought in the war up north?' Brannigan asked when the last of his men had filed outside. He rested his weight easily on one hip, his right hand falling naturally to his revolver.

'Yes.'

'And you fought for the South?' Brannigan nodded towards Jack's attire. 'If I ain't mistaken, that's the jacket of one of their majors.'

'It is.' Jack kept a weather eye on Brannigan's right hand. He noted the way the man had used the word 'their' when talking of the Confederate army. He sensed something had changed. The conversation had become more serious. More dangerous.

'Why did you leave the army?'

'Because.' Jack let his own right hand rest easily on the hilt of his revolver. He would draw his gun and start shooting the moment Brannigan's fingers so much as twitched.

Brannigan contemplated the answer. His eyes never left Jack's. 'I don't need officers. I need men who do what they're damn well told.' His tone was mild. Yet there was still steel reinforcing the words.

'Fine by me.'

'You don't want to be in charge?'

'No.'

'You sure about that, Jack? I can smell it on you, just as easily as I can smell that there whiskey.'

'Then you're mistaken.'

Brannigan said nothing. But for the first time, his eyes shifted. They looked at Jack's right hand as it rested on his revolver, then moved over to the sword hanging on his left hip. 'I don't know another man that wears a sword these days.' The statement was made in a laconic tone.

'I find it useful.' Jack had relied on the sword for as long as he had fought. He had killed more men than he could remember with a blade. Once he had owned a beautiful talwar, a gift from a grateful maharajah. That weapon had been lost, but he had never been without a sword, carried in a leather scabbard that would not blunt its edge, that habit acquired in India. He could not imagine not wearing one in battle.

'You won't find it useful down here. You fight me and get close enough to use that thing, then I deserve to die.' Brannigan's gaze had returned to Jack's face. 'So are you travelling alone?'

'Yes.'

'Why?'

'None of your concern.'

'That's fair enough, unless, of course, you want me to give

you a place here. If you do, that makes it my concern. So I suggest you start answering my goddam questions.' The pithy instruction was delivered without emotion. 'Tell me why you want to work for me.'

Jack paused. He knew why he was there, but he could not reveal it, not to this man he did not know. He certainly needed the money, just as he needed ammunition, food and fodder for his horse. The notion of working as a hired gun did not concern him. He had sold himself before. He could do so again. But that was not all there was to it. The truth was, he wanted something more. He wanted to *be* something more. He reckoned taking a place in Brannigan's gang would allow that to happen.

'I need money.' He delivered what he thought would be the expected answer.

Brannigan's expression did not change. 'That's not enough.'

Jack drew in a slow breath. 'I need work.'

'Then buy a goddam shovel and start digging. There's plenty of work round these parts, what with everyone being off at the war, trying to make themselves heroes.'

Jack offered a thin smile. 'I'm a soldier. Least I was. I can do more than dig.'

'Then go back to the army. I don't want soldiers.' Brannigan shook his head, then looked away. The conversation, the interview, was done.

'Is that it?' Jack tried to hold the other man in place.

'I reckon so. Have a drink; take a whole goddam bottle if you want. Then you can be on your way.'

'You're going to let me go?' Jack could not help the surprise creeping into his tone.

'I don't need you.'

'Are you sure about that? Looks to me like you could do with my help.'

Brannigan turned to look at him. His stare was withering. 'We're done here,' he said, and walked away, leaving Jack to stare at his back.

Chapter Ten

---◆---

*J*ack stood where he was, quite unable to understand the surge of emotion that rushed through him as he was rejected. They were new, these raw feelings. Once, his skills had been sought out, men forced to convince him to serve them. He had not contemplated that a man like Brannigan could turn him away. That rejection revealed a truth that he could hardly bear to contemplate.

He was alone for one reason and one reason only.

He was alone because no one wanted him.

Brannigan stopped walking. He rested a shoulder against the door frame and leaned there, looking outside.

'Can you shoot?' He spoke without turning to face Jack.

'Yes.' Jack had to force himself to swallow, his mouth suddenly dry.

'Can you kill?'

He noticed Brannigan's hand move towards the revolver on his right hip. There it hovered, the fingers moving slowly as Brannigan stretched them out then closed his fist.

When he moved again, he did so with the speed of a striking snake.

In one movement, he turned on a sixpence, the revolver drawn and raised. As he twisted around, his body coiled as if he were about to leap into motion. The revolver was lifted so that it was held just about hip high, its muzzle pointed straight at Jack, whilst his left hand hovered over the top of it, ready to snatch back the hammer. He held the pose, not a muscle moving, so that he looked like he had been frozen in time.

'You're pretty quick.' Jack forced the firmness into his words as he broke the silence that had followed the dramatic display.

Brannigan said nothing. He did not so much as twitch, and for a second, Jack thought he might actually fire. He kept his own revolver stock still. He had snatched the weapon from its holster the moment he had seen Brannigan's hand move and was pointing it directly at the man he wanted to employ him.

Brannigan smiled and relaxed. He spun the revolver around his finger, then returned it to its holster in a single smooth, practised movement. 'And you're slow,' he remarked. He smiled. 'But it ain't speed that matters, not down here. Anyone who tells you that is a damn fool. Anyone who wants to can pull out a gun. It's being prepared to use it that matters. Killing a man, without pause, without hesitation, that's what keeps you alive. Can you do that, Jack? Can you look a man dead in the eye, then shoot him down?'

'Yes.' The single word left Jack's mouth shrouded in ice.

'You'll have to. You don't get a second chance. Well, not usually.' Brannigan gave a half-smile. 'Are you lying to me, Jack? Are you feeding me a line of horseshit?'

'I don't lie. Not any more.' Jack offered the qualifying statement with a wry smile. He was a thief who had stolen a life that was not his own. Much of the life that had followed had been held up by a foundation of lies. But that was not the case any longer. Now he had no lies left.

Brannigan walked towards the dresser. He said nothing as he opened a fresh bottle of whiskey and took two clean glasses from a shelf. He poured two measures, not spilling a drop in the process, then approached Jack.

'I've got work.' He held out one of the glasses.

'What sort of work?' Jack holstered his own revolver and took the whiskey. He did not drink it.

'I'm taking a wagon train of cotton down to Mexico, to a place called Matamoros on the far side of the Rio Grande. When we get it there, we'll sell it, then use the funds to buy guns that we bring back up here to sell to the Confederates.'

'Sounds simple.'

'It won't be. The cotton is worth a goddam fortune, the guns we buy even more so. That's why the owners pay me so much to keep it all safe.' Brannigan raised his glass of whiskey to his lips, then drank the measure down in one go.

'Cotton is that valuable?'

'It's worth a few cents a pound here, that's if you can find a buyer. It's worth twenty or maybe more once we get it down to Mexico.'

'Why?' Jack could not help the question. The desire to know more was genuine.

'The Union navy has shut all the Confederate ports. That Anaconda Plan of theirs.' Brannigan turned to refill his glass. 'That stops the plantation owners from selling their cotton. They're strangling the Confederacy good and tight. There're a few blockade runners out there, but they can't carry much, not if they don't want to get caught. The North is starving the South of the money it needs to fight this war.'

'Because the South has lost the tax it puts on sales of the cotton?'

'That's right. But of course there are some folk who think this is a great idea. They reckon if they stop selling cotton, then people like you English fellas will have no choice but to come in and fight for the Confederacy.'

'And are we?'

'I ain't seen any lobsterbacks around here, have you?' Brannigan drained his second whiskey, then poured himself another one. 'You English, you recognised the South all right. Said they have the right to fight and all. But that cotton of theirs, well, it ain't so important to you all that you want to fight the Yankees over it.'

Jack thought on the notion of forcing his homeland to side with the South by starving it of the cotton that its mills relied upon. He could easily imagine the possibility of British troops being sent to reinforce the Confederacy. The British government was not shy about dispatching its soldiers to some distant land to pursue a violent resolution to a situation where diplomacy had failed. He could only presume that the men in London who governed the gargantuan British Empire saw no need to involve themselves in this bitter struggle in its former colony. He considered it likely that they had found alternative sources of supply that meant they were no longer reliant on the cotton farmers of the Southern states.

He wondered how he would feel if Britain's policy changed and he saw men in red coats marching in the ranks of the Confederate army. Would he feel compelled to join his country-men? Would he want to do so? Would the lure of once again wearing a red coat be too strong? He shook his head, dismissing such thoughts. He had long ago learned not to waste effort on idle ifs and buts. The here and now was all that mattered. The future would take care of itself, with or without his intervention.

'So this idea of forcing you boys to fight, well, it ain't working so well.' Brannigan knocked back another measure of whiskey as he continued to talk. 'And last time I checked, ideas don't buy muskets and carbines. So now those fine fellows in Richmond don't have any choice but to tax anything they can think of. Now that they can't tax cotton, they charge duties on everything else they can find, including duty to buy a licence to take the cotton south. And the plantation owners, they're only allowed to take the cotton south if they agree to buy the stuff the sechers need to fight the Yankees.

'Of course if they do that, they'll only get paid in eight per cent bonds that ain't worth the paper they're printed on, but they don't have much of a choice. They can sell the cotton direct to the government, who'll stash it away in warehouses, but the price the government pays don't give them enough money to pay their taxes, or to buy the food and goods they need to survive. The biggest buyer, why that's you English. Down in Mexico, there's hundreds of ships waiting for the cotton. And there ain't enough of it to go round. That forces prices up, and makes it worthwhile to have fellas like me take it all the way down there.'

'So your job is to make sure the cotton arrives safely.' Jack took a first sip of his whiskey. The bitter liquid burned as he swallowed.

'That's right. The plantation fellas, they've got no choice but to send it south or sell it to the Yankees.'

'They sell it to the Union?'

'If they can. That's getting a hell of a sight easier now the

Yankees are pushing south. Things might get better when they win, but I doubt it.'

'You think the North will win?' Jack had never heard the sentiment once in all his time in the South.

'It's only a matter of time. The Confederacy is doomed. Always was.'

'Is that why you aren't fighting?'

'No.'

'But you're helping the South's cause?' Jack wanted to understand more.

'No.' Brannigan refilled his glass yet again. 'I work for myself.'

'What about the man who owns the cotton? Aren't you working for him?'

'You've sure got a hell of a lot of questions for someone looking for work.' The remark was delivered with a hint of irony.

'I want to know what I'm getting myself into.'

'What you're getting yourself into is some hard goddam work. You ready for that?'

'I'm not afraid to work.'

'You sure about that?' Brannigan's gaze bored into Jack.

'I am. I'll help you get your cotton wherever it needs to go.'

'That's mighty generous of you, Jack.' Brannigan acknowledged the statement by raising his glass. 'We take it along El Camino Real de los Tejas all the way to Brownsville, in Texas. We get it over the Rio Grande and into Mexico, then to a place called Matamoros. That's as far as we take it. From there it goes to a small village on the coast called Bagdad, from where they freighter it down the coast to Veracruz. That's where your countrymen are waiting to buy it up. We pay the people we have to pay along the way, then bring as many guns and as much ammunition as we can back up here. And we fight any son of a bitch who tries to stop us.'

'Sons of bitches like this Sinclair chap.'

'You learn fast, Jack.' There was not even a hint of a smile on Brannigan's face as he gave the praise. He turned to place his empty glass on the table. 'But it's not just men like Sinclair we have to worry about.'

'Who else is there?'

'Well, there's the army boys in Texas. They might want to have some of the cotton for themselves, or at least they'll impound it and conscript any of my boys they fancy if we don't pay 'em off. Then there are plenty of other men like Sinclair and his renegades who will do just about anything to stop us getting where we're going. And if it ain't white men like Sinclair, then it's the bandoleros like Cobos, or that vicious son of a gun Zapata. Then there's the worst of the bunch, Ángel Santiago.'

Brannigan paused, as if the name had left a foul taste in his mouth. 'I could tell you some tales about that fella. The locals say he's nearly seven foot tall and can kill a man with a single stare. Not that anyone has ever seen him, or at least, no one who has lived to tell the tale. That man is a demon all right, a killer if ever there was one. His boys even call themselves Los Ángeles de la Muerte.'

'Which means?'

'The Angels of Death. And they've sure earned the title. Santiago has about three hundred men now. They've been attacking the cotton trains for months, and there ain't much the Confederate cavalry boys stationed down there can do to stop 'em. And those bandoleros fellas, they don't stop at the border. They ain't shy about striking right up into Texas.'

'Bloody hell.' Jack was trying to remember all the names Brannigan was throwing at him. 'It's a wonder you get there at all.'

'I ain't finished yet. If none of *those* varmints get in our way, then there's still the French and the Mexicans to worry about.'

'The French?'

'You not heard about the war in Mexico?'

'No, nothing.' Jack could not help himself. He was lapping up the news like a thirsty dog.

'There was a civil war back in fifty-five. A fellow called Juarez won, only he bankrupted the country in the process. So he stopped paying all the countries that had lent him money. Well, you fellows, along with the French and the Spanish, you didn't much like that approach. So you sent over some men and captured Veracruz, Mexico's most important port. That should've been enough, but those Frenchies, they wanted more, and they've invaded proper. Now they're fighting the whole damn country, and you and the Spanish have left them to it.'

'Blow me tight.' Jack shook his head as he began to understand the enormous challenge Brannigan and his men faced.

'So I'm damn sure the Frenchies will be only too happy to take the cotton if they can. But then again, so will Juarez and his Juaristas. They're short of money as it is, and they need as much as they can get to buy weapons to fight the French.'

Jack noted all the information Brannigan was giving. He knew nothing of the struggle going on in Mexico. But he did know one thing. He had fought with the French army, serving with the Foreign Legion at Solferino. They were amongst the best troops he had ever encountered, and he was sure that if they had been brought to Mexico, then the Mexicans were in for a bad time of it.

'So it sounds like every man and his dog will want to stop you taking this cotton of yours to the ports,' he observed wryly.

'They'll want to try. It's our job to persuade them that it's not worth the effort. If they do try it, then we kill 'em.'

'It sounds like you do need my help then.' Jack held Brannigan's gaze as he repeated his earlier claim. He tried to sound convincing.

For the first time, there was just a hint of a smile on Brannigan's lips. 'I'll take you as far as San Antonio. There should be no trouble between here and there, if the tale Sinclair fed Kat is true. Keep out of my way, do as you're told and we'll see from there. If I let you stay, I'll pay you two hundred and fifty dollars when we get back to Natchitoches, same as my other boys. That's a year's money for a couple of months' work. That two fifty is all yours. When you work for me, I pay for everything: food, drink, women, whatever you want.'

Jack tallied the deal on offer. It was more than fair. He'd known men who would kill for little more than a bottle of gin. 'What about ammunition?'

'For that?' Brannigan nodded towards Jack's repeating rifle. He had not remarked on it, but he was savvy enough to guess Jack's predicament.

'I've got bugger all left. I've no idea where to get more.'

'I know a man in San Antonio. He might be able to help.'

'That would be kind.'

'Kind? No, I ain't ever kind.' Brannigan shook his head at Jack's choice of words. 'But if you accept my offer, then you're one of us. And we look after our own. We'll get you what you need.'

Jack heard the message behind the words. There were two types of people in Brannigan's world, those with him, and those against him.

'So do you accept?' Brannigan asked the inevitable question.

Jack didn't hesitate. He had known what he would say from the moment he had agreed to go with Kat and Adam. 'Yes. I accept.'

With those three words, his wandering was over. For better or worse, he would be in Brannigan's gang.

Chapter Eleven

———◆———

*J*ack let his mare come to a halt, then looked back at the wagon train that stretched out along the trail behind him. The sight still astonished him.

Thirty flatbed wagons followed each other nose to tail, each carrying twenty five-hundred-pound bales of cotton, stacked in two layers. Over the top of the cotton, the teamsters had stretched tarpaulins marked with the wagon's number. Each wagon was pulled by a team of ten mules, with at least half a dozen spare teams spread throughout the train, which were used when they had to haul the heavily loaded wagons uphill or across bad ground. Following the first thirty wagons were another ten that carried the fodder and supplies.

Brannigan's men numbered thirty in total, and he worked them hard. From riding alongside the wagons to being sent out as advance and rear guards, the men charged with guarding the precious wagons were in the saddle from dawn to dusk. Even when the wagons were circled at the end of the day, they were kept hard at it standing on picket duty in shifts through the long, chilly night. At dawn, riders were sent ahead to scout the trail, whilst others were dispatched back the way they had come to check for anyone on their tail. Brannigan was nothing if not cautious.

Yet if the nights were long, the days were endless. Jack had quickly learned that the long wagon train had two speeds: slow and stop. Yet somehow the unwieldy column was expected to travel hundreds of miles, following the main overland route from Natchitoches, Louisiana, first to San Antonio, Texas, then on to King's Ranch and Brownsville and over the Rio Grande into Mexico, where it would turn east and travel on to Matamoros. From there the cotton would be transferred to paddle steamers for the last leg of the journey through the shallows of the Rio Grande to Bagdad, then loaded on to freighters that would take it down to the deep-water port of Veracruz, where the European traders waited anxiously to buy every last scrap for the hungry mills thousands of miles across the Atlantic.

That the train moved at all was down solely to the expertise of the drivers. The men from Texas who drove the wagons were foul-mouthed and hard-drinking. Their days were spent fighting their animals, and the air around the column was filled with the curses and abuse they spat out constantly, and the crack of their whips. Yet for all their noise and bluster, Jack could only marvel at their skill. Driving the mules was as an art.

'Stop dawdling, goddammit.' Brannigan saw Jack stationary, and immediately bawled him out as he rode past on the far side of the nearest wagon.

Jack kicked back his heels and obeyed without question. Brannigan was a rigorous taskmaster, but he worked himself as hard as he worked his men, perhaps even harder. The man was tireless. The only time he allowed them to rest was at the stops along the trail. The names of the log houses, stone forts, missions, small towns and ranches where they had stopped meant little to Jack. Los Adaes, San Augustine, Nacogdoches, Alto, Crocket, Bastrop – they blurred together in his mind. That night they would stop at a place called San Marcos before pressing on to New Braunfels, and then San Antonio. There they would linger, the large Texan town one of the last places where they could make repairs and buy supplies for the last leg of the journey that would see them travel on to Brownsville and the Rio Grande.

Jack had learned that the last leg would be the hardest of all on their long journey. After a final stop at King's Ranch, the wagon train would have to cross a one-hundred-and-twenty-mile-long strip of land that Brannigan's men called 'the sands'. They had relished the chance to tell Jack about the hardships that lay ahead in the sun-scorched and wind-ravaged wasteland: venomous rattlesnakes, savage packs of coyotes that would not hesitate to hunt down a man walking alone, deadly Texan tarantulas and scorpions, along with a few million fleas and ticks that were sure to bury themselves deep in his flesh to make his every waking moment a misery.

If the threat to life from the animals and insects that dwelt on the trail was not bad enough, every man he had spoken to believed they would have to fight if they were to get the cotton to Matamoros. That notion sat badly in Jack's gut. He had not fought for months, save for the short skirmish with Sinclair's men that had secured his place in Brannigan's entourage. But that had been a one-sided affair. It had been a long time since he had been shot at, and he wondered how he would react now that he knew that it was just blind chance that decided whether he lived or died, his skill and experience of no consequence

once the bullets started to fly in earnest. Would he still be able
to fight? Or would he be paralysed with fear?

The question hung heavily in his mind, but he wanted to
know the answer. He had come looking for one thing that he
feared and loved in equal measure. Only time would tell if
finding it would satisfy his desire, or if it would reveal him to
be nothing more than a yellow-bellied coward.

Jack sat on the ground with his back against a wagon wheel,
gnawing on the strip of thick, fatty bacon that he had been
given for his dinner. It was so salty, he could already feel every
scrap of moisture being sucked from his mouth. He paused to
spit out a knuckle of fat, then began to chew again. The bacon
was as tough as hemp, but he preferred it to the thin strips of
sun-dried beef that was the alternative.

'Say, are you the Englishman?'

Jack kept chewing as he looked up to see who had come to
interrupt his dinner. The man who had asked the question
peered down at him from behind a pair of wire-framed
spectacles. 'That's me. Who's asking?'

'My name is Vaughan.'

Jack had heard the name from one of the other men guarding
the wagons. Vaughan was ostensibly in charge of the whole
wagon train. He was the man the plantation owners had trusted
to handle the sale of their precious cotton, and who would be
escorted back to Louisiana with the weapons he would buy
with the proceeds. Jack had seen him around the train, but this
was the first time they had spoken.

'Do you have a moment?' Vaughan asked, a friendly smile
on his face. 'I'd sure appreciate the chance to talk with you.'

Jack wiped a greasy hand on his trousers then used it to

lever himself to his feet. He was weary from another long day in the saddle, but he could not help but be intrigued. Vaughan was the one other man of consequence in the wagon train besides Brannigan. A conversation with him would likely be interesting, and the truth of it was that Jack was thoroughly bored of the talks he had with the other men in Brannigan's gang. The conversation tended to be limited to tall tales of their exploits with women, or an endless debate about the relative merits of oxen over mules for hauling wagons.

'I'd be happy to.' He gave his right hand another quick wipe on his trousers, then held it out. 'Jack Lark.'

'Benjamin Vaughan.' The introduction was given with a slightly damp but firm handshake.

Now that he was standing, Jack towered over Vaughan. The man had to be little more than five feet tall. With his spectacles and a receding hairline that had left what little hair he had clinging precariously to his temples and the back of his head, he looked better suited to spending his days in a comfortable office rather than on a wagon train. He was even poorly dressed for life on the trail, in a fine green tailcoat, with grey trousers and a matching waistcoat over a white shirt. He wore shoes rather than boots, and he even sported a cravat around his neck that was held in place with a pin topped with a single fat pearl. It would have been a fine-looking ensemble were it not for the layer of dust that had been ground deep into the fibres of the coat, and the stains and rents that were scattered across the trousers.

'I've been wanting to speak with you ever since Brannigan told me you had joined us,' Vaughan began.

'Well, here I am.' Jack lifted his strip of bacon to his lips to tear off another mouthful, then thought better of it. Vaughan reminded him of another life, one where gentlemen ate properly and did not attempt conversation with their mouths filled with fat. He pulled a handkerchief from the pocket of the plain waistcoat he now wore in place of his stolen Confederate major's jacket and wrapped the bacon before putting it away. The delay in its eating would not spoil its taste.

'Kat tells me you are from England.'

'I am.' Jack was oddly pleased that Kat had remembered that detail.

'And from your accent, I would say you are from London.'

'Yes.'

Vaughan grinned. 'I knew it. I was there once. Back in fifty-five, long before all this nonsense started.'

'You didn't want to stay?'

'Not for a damn second. The place terrified me! Half the time you couldn't see more than five damn feet in front of you. And somehow that was the best thing about it, the place was so goddam awful!' Vaughan chortled at his own jest. 'When that fog sets in, why, you can't even see your own hand in front of your face.'

Jack smiled. The Londoners called the fog that Vaughan described 'the particular'. It was as ghastly as Vaughan recalled, but it had its uses. Jack had lost count of the times he had been able to hide in it from someone.

'No, give me good old Texas any day of the week. Call me old-fashioned, but I want to be able to see what's about to kill me.' Again Vaughan laughed at his own words. 'So what brings an Englishman all the way over here?'

Jack did not answer. He was tired of the question. 'Is that why you wanted to find me? To ask me that?' There was pepper in his reply.

'I'm just making conversation.' Vaughan waved away Jack's churlish response.

'So why are *you* here?' Jack turned the tables. 'It doesn't appear to be your kind of place.'

'I don't want to be, I promise you that.' Vaughan shrugged at Jack's question. 'But when your master tells you to do something, you thank him for the opportunity and jump to it.'

'Who's your master?'

'Fellow named Trevathlon. Owns one of the biggest plantations in Louisiana. You might have heard of him.'

'No.'

'Well, there's no saying no to a man like that. Especially when he's married to your sister.'

'So this Trevathlon fellow trusts you?'

'He sure does.'

'He must do. Seeing as how he's expecting you to return with his rhino.'

'Rhino?'

'His money.'

'I forgot you London folk talk funny. Yes, he trusts me. Just like he trusts Brannigan.'

Jack frowned. He could understand Trevathlon trusting his wife's brother. But Brannigan was a different matter. Men like him were loyal to money, nothing more. 'Why does he trust Brannigan?'

'Don't you?' Vaughan grinned as he fired back a question of his own.

'I don't know him.'

'Yet you work for him.'

Jack could not help smiling at the fast retort. Vaughan might look like a mouse, but his mind was sharp.

'For now.'

'An enigmatic answer.' Vaughan appeared to be delighted by it. 'You don't know what to make of him, am I correct?'

'Yes.'

'Well, you are not alone.' Vaughan's smile faded. 'He terrifies me, that much I do know.' He reached out and held on to Jack's sleeve, pulling him closer. 'Don't let his appearance fool you. He might dress like a beggar, but Brannigan is a rich man. He is also the most dangerous man I have ever met. I urge you to treat him with the utmost caution.' Warning delivered, he let go of Jack's sleeve, then stood back. 'But my master trusts him, and so I find myself here.'

'What has Brannigan done to earn such trust?' Jack repeated his earlier question, which Vaughan had neatly avoided.

'They've worked together before. This isn't the first wagon train Trevathlon has sent this way. Brannigan has never let him down, and has always returned with the *rhino*.' Vaughan smiled as he took Jack's word for his own. 'And let me tell you, that weren't so easy. A wagon train like this,' he gestured around them, 'sure attracts a whole lot of attention. Brannigan always gets it through, no matter how many darn renegades try to take it.'

Jack absorbed the knowledge. He needed to know more about the man who had hired him. That Brannigan had a solid track record spoke well of his character. Perhaps he was a better man than Jack had first thought. Yet there was another nugget of information in Vaughan's words, one that he wanted to probe.

'So you think the wagon train is in danger?'

'Son, these wagons are worth a king's ransom.' Vaughan nodded at his words, clearly proud of the enterprise of which he was in charge. 'A man could live a dozen lifetimes on the amount of money we'll get for just selling the cotton. Then those guns we'll buy, well, they're worth twice as much again once we get them up here and sell them to whichever general wants them the most.'

Jack shook his head. It seemed odd that something that looked as innocuous as cotton could hold such value. He changed course and walked over to the nearest wagon, pulling back the corner of the tarpaulin so that he could see one of the great bales that were the cause of such peril. It did not look like much. He reached forward and ran his fingers over the coarse fibres. If Vaughan was correct, it seemed likely that men would fight and die for the stuff.

'How will we know if someone is coming for the cotton?' he asked.

'Well, son, seeing as how we're in the middle of nowhere, the only sons of bitches we're going to see are the dangerous ones. You spot something coming our way, you start goddam shooting.'

Jack smiled at the pithy warning. Vaughan made it sound simple. That notion appealed. He had allowed his life to become complicated in the past. He had let other people in, and they had caused him nothing but trouble and pain. Now that he had ventured back into the wider world, he would keep his existence pared down to the bare essentials. He would do as he was told, and if someone came to take the cotton, he would fight. Simple.

'So Brannigan tells me you know how to handle a gun,' Vaughan said.

'I do.'

'Have you killed a man before?'

'More than one.'

'Ah, yes, you were a soldier. You fought for Queen and country, isn't that what you English fellows say?'

Jack grunted. The soldiers he had known had fought more for their mates, and out of sheer bloody-mindedness, than for any such lofty ideals. Many had taken the red coat out of desperation, the life of a soldier, as brutal and unforgiving as it was, an improvement on the miserable existence they would have endured in the civilian world.

'The boys are already betting on you.' Vaughan raised both eyebrows as he made the statement.

'To do what?'

'To die.'

'Nice.' Jack smiled. The comment appealed to his liking for gallows humour. 'Why?'

'They say any fool who thinks they need to wear a goddam sword doesn't know shit.'

'You think they're right?'

'Partly.'

'Which part?' Jack saw that Vaughan too was smiling.

'About the sword. They're right about that.' Vaughan looked more serious. 'But I think they're wrong to discount you so quickly.'

'Thank you for the vote of confidence.'

Vaughan waved away Jack's words. 'Don't thank me. But you may have cause to if you stay with us.'

'What do you mean?' Jack sensed the conversation had changed. Vaughan was bringing it around to the real reason he had sought Jack out.

'You're new here. You've yet to learn our secrets.' Vaughan paused to glance around, as if someone might have crept up to eavesdrop on the conversation.

'And you're going to tell me them now?' Jack did not bother to hide his scepticism.

'No. That would rather spoil the fun.'

'Fun? Is that what it is?' Jack was tiring of the conversation. He did not want a part in whatever game Vaughan was playing.

'Of course. Life without intrigue would be dull. But I will say this, if you will allow me.' Vaughan leaned closer. 'Trust no one here,' he whispered. 'And I mean no one. Not even me.'

He pulled back, then offered Jack a tight-lipped smile. 'I enjoyed our conversation, Jack. I would urge you to consider all I have said, but I rather get the impression you are your own man and will do exactly as you please.' He turned on his heel and walked away.

For his part, Jack stood where he was. Vaughan had been quite correct. He would do as he pleased. Yet he still could not help wondering what the man had been attempting to achieve with the one-sided conversation. No matter what Vaughan had intended, and no matter how much Jack might wish that it were not so, the seed of intrigue had been firmly planted in his mind. It would take effort on his part to make sure that it did not root and take flower. But one thing was clear. He might have wanted his life to be pared back to the bare bones, but he was back in the world of people. And so nothing would ever be simple.

Chapter Twelve

Jack rode behind the wagon train in the rear guard. It was not a bad place to be, provided your horse had the sense to step around the copious amount of mule shit that littered the trail like slime from a snail.

Another day was drawing to a close. They would sleep in the open, just as they had every day, his bed a rug spread on the ground. He did not mind it. He was finding the life of a wagon guard pretty much to his liking. There was contentment to be found in the simple work, and he was always exhausted at the day's end, so that he fell into a deep sleep that was not disturbed by nightmares, at least not often. He would not admit it, but he was almost enjoying himself. Life was becoming routine. It had purpose. *He* had purpose.

Ahead, he saw Brannigan ride to one side and on to a knot of higher ground that would give a good view of the way ahead. Adam followed him. The young man spent a lot of time with Brannigan. From what Jack had seen, it was clear that he hero-worshipped the man, even going so far as to model himself on him. Brannigan's taciturn manner did not sit as well on Adam as it did on the older man.

Eager to break the tedium, Jack left his place with the rear guard to follow the two men on to the knoll. Brannigan ignored him, while Adam flashed him a glare that made it clear his presence was not welcome.

'Good afternoon, Adam.' He made a point of speaking to the younger man, knowing it would only deepen the lad's scowl. 'Problems?'

'You should stay with the wagons.' Adam's reply was typically abrupt.

'And you should learn some fucking manners.' Jack could only grin as he saw Adam's scowl intensify, just as he had predicted. He brought his mare to a stand, then reached down to pull his field glasses from their leather case. He cared for them with the same diligence he applied to looking after his weapons. Like most things he owned, they were not his. They had been stolen from an officer's bivouac at Fort Donelson in far-off Tennessee, shortly before it had fallen to the Union army. Jack had not been there to witness the surrender of thousands of Confederate soldiers that had ended the fighting, as he had made good his escape along with several hundred other men who had followed the hard-riding cavalry leader Bedford Forrest out of the fort the previous night.

Adam, scowl firmly in place, turned away as Jack concentrated his attention on what was ahead. He understood at once why Brannigan had stopped. The trail snaked downhill, following a meandering path down the side of a shallow valley. At the bottom, a wide river cut a gentle course through the landscape. The water looked to be shallow, no more than a few feet deep. It would barely reach the saddle skirt of a horse as it crossed, yet it was deep enough to make hauling wagons impossible, especially as both banks were smothered with thick undergrowth. Dozens of trees, both young and old, grew so closely together that in places they formed a natural wall, an obstacle no wagon could hope to push through.

Fortunately, a bridge spanned the river. It was narrow, but wide enough for a single wagon to pass over at a time, and from what Jack could see, it looked sturdy enough. It offered a way across, but it also represented danger, for the river crossing was the perfect place for an ambush.

He lowered his field glasses then looked across at Brannigan, who had just done the same.

'It's too quiet.' Brannigan made the remark to himself, then put his glasses back to his eyes to scan the crossing for a second time.

Jack had to agree. The trail they followed was a busy one, with wagon trains heading in both directions, those going south carrying cotton, the ones coming back in the other direction loaded with Mexican goods, guns, ammunition and a hundred other items that the wagons' owners believed they could sell on at a profit. Yet at this moment, there was no sign of another train for miles. The crossing was devoid of all life. It looked tranquil, picturesque even. It also looked dangerous.

Brannigan lowered his glasses, then looked at Jack for a long moment before he began to speak. 'That there is McGehee Crossing. It's the only bridge across the San Marcos River for miles. We have no choice but to take it.'

'You think someone is waiting down there to ambush us?' Jack understood immediately.

'Maybe.' Brannigan gave the single-word reply, then turned to Adam. 'It would be a good place for Sinclair to try to take us.'

'It's not what he said.' Adam's voice cracked a little as he spoke. 'We're still too far north. He told Kat that he would hit us later, and save himself the effort of hauling the wagons south.'

'Do you believe that?'

'I do.' Adam cleared his throat to remove the squeak of adolescence from his voice.

'You care to bet your life on it?'

'Yes, sir.' The boy's face had turned a good few shades paler during the conversation.

'Take Weston, Smith and Taylor. Ride down there and check it out.'

'Yes, sir.' Adam did not need to be told twice. He rode off quickly.

Jack heard him call out to the men Brannigan had named. Once rounded up, they galloped away, passing the wagons that rumbled along regardless of the sudden activity.

'Do you trust the boy?' he asked.

'Yep.' Brannigan sat easily in the saddle. He did not encourage conversation.

Jack took time to put his field glasses away before he spoke again. He approved of the decision to scout the way ahead. Brannigan was acting with caution, and sending away outriders showed sound judgement. It was what he would have done himself, were he in charge of safeguarding the wagon train.

'That lad worships you.'

Brannigan grunted at the remark. 'He's a good kid.'

'Has he been with you long?' Jack probed. It would be some time before Adam returned, and he wanted to know more.

'A while.'

'But he's young. If he's been with you a while, then he

must've been little more than a child when he started to work for you.'

'Uh huh.' Brannigan grunted the short reply.

'Is he yours?'

'Hell, no. His father worked for me. Got himself killed in a brawl in Brownsville. The boy had no one else.'

'His mother?'

'She was long dead.'

'So you looked after him.'

'Uh huh.'

'No wonder he idolises you.'

'He's a hard worker. He's good with a gun too.'

'But not as good as you.' Jack probed deeper.

'Maybe.' Brannigan gave a lopsided smile as he answered Jack's question. 'Man only gets one chance to find out.'

Jack laughed at the uncompromising answer. 'I'll make a note not to try.'

'You don't have to worry. You draw on me, and you'll be dead before that fancy Colt of yours is even out of its goddam holster.'

'Maybe.' Jack took Brannigan's earlier response for his own. It earned him another smile. Brannigan was a man of few words, but he faced the world with humour, based on the sure knowledge that he could kill any man who crossed him. It gave him an air of unshakeable confidence.

'No maybe about it.' Brannigan made a play of looking down at the sabre on Jack's left hip. 'Why are you still carrying that thing around with you?'

Jack patted the sword, which hung on longer slings now that he was mounted. 'You don't think I'll have to fight?'

'Hell, no. I ain't saying that. You'll have to fight all right.

But I don't think you'll need that. You killed men with it before?'

'Not so many with this one. But it's not the first sword I've owned.'

Brannigan considered the answer before he replied. 'That was in battle?'

'Yes.'

'Figures.' There was something disparaging in the remark.

'Have you fought in battle, Brannigan?' Jack held the man's gaze. There was something unsettling in it. It was as if Brannigan was always looking at something else, even when he was looking directly at you.

'Nope. Never wanted to. I've killed my fair share of men, though.'

'I don't doubt it.' Jack was trying to read the man opposite him, but failing. There was something inscrutable about him. To say he played his cards close to his chest was an under-statement.

'What's it like?'

For the first time, Jack heard genuine interest in one of Brannigan's questions. He was no longer just marking time.

'Most of the time it's as dull as hell. Nothing happens for hours.' Jack made sure he held Brannigan's gaze as he began to talk. 'Then it's like nothing else on this earth.'

'Go on.'

Jack turned away as he tried to find the right words. He wanted to choose them carefully. He did not want to boast, or try to show Brannigan that he was the better man for having experienced battle. Somehow he wanted to convey something more than that.

'At first it's nothing but confusion. It's the noise, you see. It comes from all over the fucking place, and it's like nothing you ever heard. Then you go into action. That's when you feel the fear for the first time, the real fear, not the thing you had before. This consumes you, and it's all you can do just to stand there. Then the enemy come at you. First it's the volleys, shooting as fast as you can, not thinking of anything save the next round. Men are screaming all around you as they're hit. That's a terrible sound, worse than anything. If you're lucky, you stand like that until the enemy break. If you're not, then you have to charge. That's when it gets really bad.'

He paused, and sucked down a deep breath before continuing. 'That's the worst fighting. Nothing prepares you for the violence. There's no sense to it; it's just chaos. When it's hand-to-hand, when you can see the man you're fighting – see him properly, I mean: look into his eyes and see his fear; even smell it – you fight like an animal then. Nothing else matters save for killing. You hack at the other poor bastard until you tear him apart. Then you find someone else to kill. You keep going like that until they run or you're dead. Or until you run yourself.'

He fell silent. He was breathing quicker now, so he concentrated on slowing it down. Brannigan was staring straight ahead, but Jack was sure he was listening.

'How many times have you done all that?' He asked the question without turning his head.

'I don't know. More times than I can remember.'

'Why do you go back?'

'Because I have to.'

'Why?'

Jack opened his mouth to answer. He had been about to say 'duty', but the word had stuck in his throat. He called himself a soldier, but it had been a long time since he had been ordered to fight. At first, he had fought for himself; to give his life purpose and then to become the man, and the leader, he had wanted to be. Then he had sought battle because he had believed he had nothing else save a talent for war. Yet that was all done now. Now he knew what he was. He knew what it was to fear for his life, just as he knew that there was something else that battle gave him, something he needed. And he wanted to go there again. He did not fully understand why that was. But the desire was there; the *need* was there.

'I can't explain it.' He gave the honest answer.

Brannigan glanced at him, then nodded in respect at hearing the truth. 'You kept going back knowing you could die.'

'You don't at first.' Jack watched Brannigan closely. He could feel his words having an effect. They might have led very different lives, yet they were both fighters. Both had killed and knew what it was to come close to death themselves. 'The first time you fight, it's so damn chaotic that you don't have a clue what's going on. You're too confused to be properly frightened. Then you believe that it simply cannot be you, that it will always be some other poor bugger that'll get hit. That thought doesn't last long. So then you think you'll live, but only if you fight harder than the other bastards. If you're quicker, faster, braver, if you're more vicious or a better bloody shot, then you'll live and others will die.'

He paused. There was a chill on the back of his neck. 'You become better at it too. Soon you start to believe that you're better than the other poor bastards out there. It almost becomes easy; too easy, perhaps. You begin to believe that you're alive because you're the fucking best.' Again he paused. 'Then you realise that one day it *is* going to be you, and there's bugger all you can do about it. You only stay alive if you're lucky. Or unlucky.' He spoke the last sentence so softly he was not sure if Brannigan had even heard him. Then he fell silent.

'Fighting looks different down here.' Brannigan eventually broke the silence. 'Now that repeating rifle of yours, that thing is a beauty. If we all had one of those, no one would dare come close to us, and we could mosey our way down to Mexico without anyone trying to stop us. But we haven't, and they will.' He turned to stare at Jack. 'Then you'll see it's not so different to what you're used to.'

Jack would be given no time to reply. Adam and the men he had taken with him were coming back. They arrived in a rush, the quiet broken by the sound of jangling harness and hard-breathing animals.

'There's no one there.' Adam shouted the news as he pulled his horse to a noisy halt. He spoke fast, excited by the ride, hauling hard on the reins as his horse tossed its head. 'What do you want to do?'

Brannigan looked at Jack. 'What do we do, Jack?'

Jack glanced once at Adam, then replied with a shrug. 'We have no choice. We need to cross.'

'Might be dangerous.' Brannigan's reply was sharp.

'Then turn around and go home.' Jack could see Adam glowering in his direction as Brannigan quizzed him. 'If it was me, I'd move the wagons down, but have at least two groups patrolling the surrounding area. There's so much dead ground down there, there's no telling what's waiting for you.'

'There's no one there,' Adam snapped. 'I went down there while you were sitting up here on your damn backside.'

'There's no way you can know that for sure. Just look at the ground.' Jack gestured towards the crossing. He had searched the areas up- and downstream with his field glasses. The heavy undergrowth and tightly packed groupings of trees created a hundred places where men could be waiting in ambush.

'There's no one there.' Adam repeated his assertion with all the confidence of youth.

'That's enough.' Brannigan put an end to the discussion. 'Jack's right. We need to cross, so we have no choice but to go down there.' He eased himself around in the saddle. 'Tell the boys to make sure they're loaded and ready to go. Adam, take four men; you're the advance guard. Tell Weston to take another four and follow you down, but to stay back.' He looked at Jack. 'Are you a betting man, Jack?'

'At times.'

'I bet you fifty dollars that Adam's right and there's no one down there.'

Jack kept his expression neutral. He didn't have much more than fifty cents to his name, let alone fifty dollars, but he recognised why the wager had been placed. It was to show Adam that Brannigan had confidence in him.

'Make it a hundred,' he answered, his words like iron. If he lost, he had just forfeited nearly half the amount he would be paid for risking his life to escort the cotton.

'Done.' Brannigan's reply was immediate. He spat on his hand and offered it to Jack.

The wager was made. And they would cross the river.

Chapter Thirteen

———◆———

Jack rode with his Henry repeater held in his right hand. He had loaded the gun, the first time he had done so for many months. With sixteen rounds in the magazine under the barrel, it would be a fearsome weapon in any fight. If there was one.

Brannigan might have backed Adam's opinion that no one was waiting to ambush the wagon train, but that did not mean he was not cautious. The two patrols he had ordered rode off, whilst more riders carrying drawn revolvers or percussion-cap muzzle-loading carbines flanked the wagons. Another group of four men protected the rear. Jack was impressed.

The wagon train came off the higher ground and moved cautiously down the slope, picking its way towards the crossing. Jack rode near the head of the long line of wagons. The position gave him a good line of sight all the way to the river crossing. If anything, the ground was worse than he had seen through his field glasses. The river twisted this way and that, its shallow banks thickly covered with undergrowth. It made a mockery of Adam's assertion that no one was waiting to ambush the wagon train. From what Jack could see, a whole battalion could be hidden there.

It started to rain, the first drops pattering softly on to the top of his pork pie hat. He pulled his long coat tighter around his chest, protecting his body from the worst of the rain, but made sure to sweep it back so that it did not cover either the holster on his right hip or the handle of the sabre on his left.

The gentle shower lasted no more than a minute. Then the heavens opened.

Jack had never known rain like it. It came down in great sheets, the water vomiting from the sky with a roar like a locomotive rushing up the line. The sky darkened, so that it went from daylight to dusk in a matter of minutes. The deluge cut visibility down to just a few yards. In the gloom, he immediately lost sight of the patrols Brannigan had sent out ahead.

The first flash of lightning crashed out with enough violence to make him flinch. Thunder followed hard on its heels, the sound so loud that it sounded like the very sky was being split apart.

The sudden storm was stunning in its violence. To his ears, it sounded uncomfortably like the start of a great battle; the thunder the roar of the artillery's opening barrage, whilst the cracks of lightning were the crash of rifles and muskets spitting out their massed volleys.

He rode on. The rain continued without pause. It drummed into the top of his hat, and soaked into his coat so that it hung cold and heavy around his body. The storm had barely lasted a matter of minutes, but already the ground was becoming treacherous, and the wagons were slowing. He could hear the shouts and curses of the drivers as they abused their teams of mules, whipping the beasts mercilessly as they made every effort to keep the heavily laden wagons moving.

Another great blast of lightning ripped across the sky. It seared through the blackened clouds to cast an eerie white light over the land for no more than a moment, before it disappeared, condemning the world to darkness once more. A great clap of thunder followed. The sound drew out, the deep, ominous rumble growing and reverberating until it lost its power and faded away. The rain pounded down.

Jack rode through the fury of the storm, his free hand working hard to keep his horse in check. He clutched his rifle to his chest, doing his best to cover it with his coat and keep the rain out of the long groove in the underside magazine. As he rode, he tried to peer through the sheets of rain, but he could see little more than what was directly ahead of him.

Again lightning scored through the grey, the dazzling explosion tearing away the darkness for a split second before his world was plunged back into shadow. Thunder followed, the rumble echoing across the valley. It was replaced by a different sound, one that Jack could barely hear over the drumming of the rain, but which was unmistakable to a man who had stood on a dozen battlefields.

He had just won his wager.

For he heard gunfire.

It was Weston's patrol that had sprung the ambush. All five men had drawn revolvers, yet not one had managed to fire a single shot before they were gunned down.

For a moment, Jack was unsure of what to do. This was not his kind of fight, and he did not know if he should stay and guard the wagons or ride ahead to return fire.

Lightning blasted across the sky once more, giving him a glimpse of the men who had lain in wait for the wagon train to arrive. They rode out of their hiding places on the far bank of the river, their shouts and whoops barely audible over the constant roar of the rain. Still he hesitated.

'Go! Go!' Brannigan called out as he rode past. Half a dozen of his men were at his side, with more rushing to join him.

'Get on!' Jack urged his mount to follow, angry at his own hesitation. He had fought for long enough to know that uncertainty was more dangerous even than making the wrong decision. The horse responded to his command. It scrabbled in the muddy soil, then found its footing and powered away. He felt the strength in its body as its hooves thumped into the glutinous ground, the sound dulled yet still mesmerising, the rhythm increasing in tempo as the animal stretched its muscles and began to gallop.

There was something intoxicating in this moment. He felt it thrill through his body, the sensation thrumming through his veins. Yet he fought against it, holding it at bay. He was no longer the man who had charged with the Bombay Lights at Khoosh-Ab. The madness that had once propelled him to the fight was an enemy as real as the men with guns who had come to steal away the cotton. It had to be corralled and contained, just as he contained the other emotion that surged through him. For alongside the excitement was fear; fear that twisted his stomach into knots and sent an icy rush deep into his bowels.

Gunshots seared through the gloom. Jack glimpsed muzzle flashes as men from both sides began to fire. He pulled his mount's reins, angling the animal to the north, acting on instinct, his first thought to flank the attackers. He kicked back his heels, then turned the willing mare off the trail, altering course so that he headed upriver. Gunshots came without pause now. With them came the first screams as men were hit.

He slowed his horse when he judged he had gone far enough, turning it towards the river and letting it pick its own path down the gentle slope and into a tight tangle of trees around a hundred yards away from the bridge. Flashes of lightning lit his path. He took his time, finding his way with care, holding his mare back when he could not see, and waiting for the next explosion of lightning to show him the way ahead. There had been times in the past when he had rushed into action, his desire to show what he could do overriding the need to remain in one piece. He had learned from those times, and so he let his mare walk, not willing to risk it shattering a limb or tumbling him from the saddle.

It took time to reach the riverbank. Once there, he paused to look across the gloomy battlefield. The rain hammered into the water, the sound of the thousands of impacts only adding to the noise. In the murk, it was hard to see more than a few yards. Yet he could make out enough to know that his plan had worked, and he was now well away to one side of the firefight.

The two sides were furiously engaged. Most of Brannigan's men had stayed on the near side of the river, taking up positions close to the entrance to the bridge. Only Adam and the survivors from the advance guard were on the far bank. They had dismounted, and now clustered together in a desperate huddle in the midst of a thick clump of undergrowth and spindly saplings about twenty yards from the end of the bridge. Their ambushers were spread out on the same bank, and moving to surround them.

A great sheet of lightning cut across the sky, casting an eerie white light. A man died at that moment, a bullet taking him in the face. Yet for all the gunfire, few men were being hit. The range was long for revolvers, and in the poor light there was more noise than accurate shooting. Both sides fired fast, but neither was securing an advantage. The rain came down constantly, and more than one man suffered a misfire as the water worked its way into the weapon's workings.

Jack brought his mare to a stand, keeping the animal away from the riverbank so that he was still screened by the trees that grew there. Only when the animal had become still did he raise the repeater and settle its brass-capped stock into his shoulder. He had just sixteen rounds. Each one would have to count.

He waited, slowing his breathing and steadying the rifle. He fired when the next bolt of lightning seared away the darkness, picking a target on the far side of the river in the split second of light. There was just enough time to see a man tumble from the saddle before the darkness returned.

He cranked the handle on the repeater, moving the bolt, ejecting the spent cartridge and bringing the next into the breech. He concentrated on his breathing, keeping it slow and rhythmical.

Another great flash of lightning lit the sky. He fired twice more, his rifle twitching from target to target in an instant. Both bullets hit.

He moved the moment darkness returned. He could just make out shouts and cries of alarm before a great peal of thunder rumbled across the sky. He paid the shouts no heed, concentrating his attention on the ground ahead. His horse moved slowly, so he kicked back his heels, forcing the animal to pick up a little speed. He would not risk staying in one spot for too long. He was being careful. He would not risk his life. Not yet.

The next lightning bolt let him pick his new position. In the few seconds that it lit the earth, he kicked hard, forcing his mare into a lurching canter. He reached a tree that was bent low, its branches almost touching the river, then came to another halt. The repeater was snug in his shoulder the moment the horse stopped.

He fired almost immediately, then cranked the handle on the rifle and fired again, aiming at shadowy figures on the far bank, hoping to spread confusion and fear as his bullets spat out from the darkness. More lightning came, so he fired again, this time sending a bullet spinning into a man's spine.

He had now knocked four men from the saddle. Already some of the ambushers were turning in confusion as they tried to locate him. Return shots came across the river, the men on the far bank firing hopelessly into the shadows yards from where he was. Bullets flayed the heavy undergrowth, whining as they ricocheted from the trees. None came close.

He steadied his mare as the animal pawed nervously at the ground. In the next moment, lightning cut across the sky and he fired again, missing his target as the horse fretted and jerked beneath him.

He was closer to the ambushers now that he had moved, the river bending and narrowing upstream from the crossing. The man he had just shot at must have felt the passage of the spinning bullet as it zipped past his head, and he turned, looking across the river directly at Jack.

Jack knew he had been spotted. Yet he did not move. As darkness returned, he reached down to lay his hand on his mare's neck, his voice soothing the animal. In the next flash of lightning, he saw that two men were picking their way down the far bank and into the shallow water at the river's edge. They rode towards him, their horses splashing noisily and kicking spray into the sky, then rammed back their heels, gouging their spurs into the horses' flanks and forcing the animals into the deeper water near the centre of the river. Both rode with right arms outstretched as they aimed revolvers his way.

'Steady now, girl, steady.' He spoke the words softly, patting the animal's neck one last time. He took a moment to wipe the rain from his face, then sat straight in the saddle and raised the repeater.

Lightning flashed. He saw the two men riding in his direction, their horses forcing a path through the water. Both men fired the instant the light came. Jack felt the air near him punched as both bullets snapped past. He held the repeater tight, then fired as the last of the light died.

He cranked the handle, holding his pose, every muscle tight. He waited, breathing slowly, feeling the fear in his gut. It twisted deep in his belly, worming its way upward through his body.

The next flash came. One man was left charging towards him, a riderless horse at his side. The man fired twice. Both bullets came close enough for Jack to feel the snap in the air as they seared by. He held his breath, then fired just as the darkness reclaimed the earth.

Again he held his pose. He did not know if his aim had been true, yet he knew with certainty that if he had not found his target, the man coming against him would surely be close enough not to miss him for a third time.

The fear was taking hold now. He could feel it picking and

gnawing at his courage. It urged him to move; to run, to do anything it took to get away. The feeling built until it was all he could do to hold himself still.

Another great surge of lightning ripped away the darkness, and he gasped.

His aim had been true. Two horses with empty saddles came towards him. Two corpses floated downstream.

Chapter Fourteen

---

*J*ack lowered the rifle and sucked a deep breath into his lungs. Around him, the firefight continued without pause. A man on his side of the river cried out as he was hit, whilst another on the far bank shouted unintelligible commands. In the gloom, it was almost impossible to pick out an enemy.

The rain was coming down in solid sheets now. It worked its way into weapons, causing misfires and blockages. Men cursed as revolvers jammed and carbines refused to fire. Those with spare weapons drew them. Those without tried to clear the blockages, their oaths and frustrated curses adding to the mayhem.

Jack knew he had to move. Yet he could not make himself do anything other than sit there, the rain running down his face. He could see shadowy forms rushing back and forth on the far bank, guns spitting short gouts of flame in the darkness. As the lightning flashed, he saw more, the shadows given life for a few tantalising seconds before the gloom returned. Men died as he watched, their despairing cries underscoring the claps of thunder and the almost constant roar of gunfire.

On the far bank, a single ambusher broke from the fight, his desire to capture the sodden cotton failing to hold him to the cause. Jack could hear the man's leader shouting, calling the deserter a coward and cursing him, yet nothing turned the man from his path. For his part, the leader stuck to the fight, rallying men to his side before turning to fire at the shadowy figures that huddled together on the opposite bank.

It was only then that Jack realised who was leading the ambushers. As a lightning bolt lit the gloom, he recognised the man wearing a pale grey suit that had been turned almost to black by the rain. Sinclair, the man Kat and Adam had played, had found a way to attack the wagon train after all.

The light died away. Even so, Jack lifted the repeater to his shoulder. He steadied it, holding Sinclair's shadowy form in its sights, ignoring the rain and the rumble of yet more thunder. A single bullet would surely end the fight. If he shot Sinclair down, his men would inevitably run.

Lightning ripped through the darkness with a crack loud enough to wake the dead, yet this time Jack did not so much as flinch. There was time to twitch the barrel a tiny fraction to the right, filling the sight with Sinclair's body, then he pulled the trigger.

Nothing happened.

'Shit.' He lowered the rifle and thrust it into the long holster attached to the saddle. He did not have to check to know that the weapon had jammed, the open groove under the barrel filled with rainwater or blocked by a scrap of dirt. The repeater was a fabulous weapon, one that could dominate a firefight. But only if it worked.

He hesitated. He knew what he should do to turn the firefight. But it would take courage – raw, passion-filled, courage. Courage he did not know if he possessed. And then the anger came. It was bitter and sharp, and he swallowed it only with difficulty. He did not like this man he had become. He had killed that day, gunning men down from his hiding places. They had died without knowing it was he who had taken their lives.

The thought shamed him. He had come searching for this moment. Now that it was here, he was skulking in the shadows. He was no longer acting like a soldier. He was acting like a cold-blooded murderer. A killer. A coward.

He was becoming a man he despised.

Jack sat and stared at the firefight in the rain. He saw what could be done to change the course of the skirmish. A brave man on a willing horse could scythe through the attackers' flank, cutting men down before they even realised what had charged out of the darkness to spread death and confusion amongst their ranks. Yet to launch such an attack took a certain kind of madness; that brave man on his fast horse propelled into the action by the wild, searing fury of battle. Jack knew he was no longer that man, yet he could see no other way of turning the tide of this gloomy fight. Someone would have to put an end to it. And that someone had to be him.

He kicked back his heels, urging his horse into motion. As the mare obeyed, he drew his sabre from the scabbard on his left hip. Despite the damp, the steel still rasped against the leather. The sword's weight felt good in his right hand, the balance of the blade familiar. Rain ran down its length, making the steel glisten in the white light cast by a bolt of lightning. The firefight was showing no sign of coming to a conclusion, the two sides seemingly content to blast away in the gloom. It was time for a proper soldier to show them how it was done.

He let his mare move slowly, giving her time to find her footing on the slippery mud of the riverbank. Another flash of lightning illuminated his path for a few seconds before it faded away, casting the world back into darkness. The rain still lashed down continuously, making it impossible to see more than a few yards.

He reached the bottom of the bank. Water surged around his horse's hooves, the sound it made loud enough to be heard even over the rain. He kicked back his heels, forcing the mare into the channel. The animal responded to his command, plunging forward without hesitation.

Jack gasped as the water splashed against his legs, the touch of its cold fingers sending a chill running through him. He urged the animal on, praying that the lightning would hold off for a few moments longer. Gamely the mare pushed through the deeper water at the river's heart, then picked up speed as the level fell. They were close to the far bank now, and Jack angled the horse's head so that the animal splashed obliquely through the shallower water, taking him further upstream and away from the fight. There was no lightning to show him the way, the storm starting to lose its power.

As he rode, he heard Sinclair shouting at his men, urging them to close with the scouts Brannigan had sent forward, and who still held on to a small patch of ground on the far side of the river. Many of the ambushers responded, gathering their reins before kicking their own horses into motion. Led by Sinclair, they charged forward, closing the distance on Adam and the handful of men with him.

Jack saw what Sinclair intended, yet he did not allow it to turn him from his course. He kicked on, forcing the tiring mare through the last of the shallows, then urging her up the far bank and into a gap between two stands of trees some two to three hundred yards upstream from the bridge, pushing on through the last of the undergrowth until he was on flat open ground. Only then did he change direction so that he was heading back towards the bridge.

He rode past the first man he came across, paying him no heed. Without the lightning casting its eerie glow, no one in Sinclair's gang would know that a stranger was now behind them.

Shots still snapped through the air. Adam and his party of scouts would be able to see the shadowy forms advancing towards them. To their credit, they held their ground. Those still with rounds in their weapons fired, yet it was no easy thing to hit a man on a fast-moving horse, and just a single attacker was knocked from the saddle as Sinclair led his men on their madcap charge.

Jack felt a stray bullet whistle past a few feet over his head. It fired the fear that he held contained in his belly, yet he pushed it down and rode on, keeping his eyes on Sinclair.

The attackers charged into the group of scouts. What had been a long-range firefight descended into chaos. More shots were fired. Men from both sides died as the range closed to just a few yards.

Brannigan had seen what Sinclair intended. As Adam and his scouts stood firm, he led more of his men across the bridge. They came on fast, hooves clattering on the wooden planks, guns blazing. Sinclair's ambushers saw them coming. Many turned, their revolvers returning fire so that two men close to Brannigan were shot down, their bodies tumbling from the saddle before finding a watery grave in the river.

The distance closed quickly. Brannigan and his men charged forward, revolvers and bowie knives in hand as the firefight descended into a chaotic, swirling melee.

As Jack surveyed the confusion, he saw Kat for the first time. She was riding not far from Brannigan's side, her Remington revolver firing fast. She was not shirking the fight, and he felt a moment's fear for her safety. The emotion disappeared as quickly as it had arrived. She was not his concern.

He pushed on, kicking his mare without mercy to find more speed. He kept his body low in the saddle, the sabre in his right hand held out so that he was ready to attack any man who came close. He followed Sinclair through the melee, dodging past a horse that went down with a scream of agony as a bullet buried itself in its neck, its rider thrown hard then trampled under the hooves of another horse being driven into the fight.

Sinclair was now in the heart of the skirmish. Even as Jack watched, he pulled a dry revolver from a holster on his right hip, the weapon saved for this moment. He was no more than two yards from one of Brannigan's men, and Jack saw him lift the revolver, then fire. The bullet struck Brannigan's man full in the face.

'Brannigan!'

Jack was close enough to hear Sinclair call to his adversary. The ambushers' leader had chosen his path well. Brannigan was no more than ten yards away. He called the name again, then fired, knocking another of Brannigan's men out of the saddle.

This time Brannigan heard the shout, and Jack saw his head whip around. It was clear that he had been caught unawares.

Sinclair raked back his heels. His horse responded, stretching its neck and powering forward. He held the dry revolver outstretched, the barrel stock still, the muzzle aimed squarely at Brannigan.

Jack knew what was to come. He stayed low and let his horse run, giving the animal its head. He was barely a dozen yards behind Sinclair.

One of Brannigan's men rode across Sinclair's path, forcing him to slow. A single gunshot followed, the bullet thumping into the man's chest with enough force to knock him from the saddle, his shocked cry cut off abruptly as he hit the ground.

Sinclair shouted in triumph as he aimed at Brannigan once again. The shot was so easy a child could take it. Brannigan was powerless to defend himself, his own revolver emptied of rounds.

Sinclair reined in his horse, bringing it to a noisy halt. There was a moment's pause. Gunshots echoed through the gloom. The rain came down in torrents, its roar constant and unceasing.

'And so it ends.' Sinclair could not resist the final jibe. Brannigan was at his mercy.

Then Jack struck.

Chapter Fifteen

I t was a poor strike. It was a long time since Jack had
fought from the saddle, and the suddenness of the impact
took him by surprise. Yet his rusty skills were good
enough for him to still hit Sinclair hard, the slashing blow
cutting deep into the arm holding the revolver.

Sinclair shrieked and whirled around in the saddle, his
revolver falling from his grasp.

Jack reined in, turning his mare hard and fast. He rode at
Sinclair as soon as the animal was ready. There was time for
him to see the surprise on Sinclair's rain-streaked face before he
was close enough to lash out with the sword for a second time.
This time his horse was moving more slowly and he was better
prepared. He half stood in the saddle, then cut hard as soon as
Sinclair was in striking distance. Every ounce of his strength
went behind the slashing blow that he aimed at the junction of
neck and shoulder. The blade hit, the shock of the impact
jarring back along his arm. The sword's leading edge cleaved
through flesh and gristle so that blood flew as he ripped the
blade from the wound.

Sinclair's mouth opened in a silent scream. Jack's hammer

blow had rocked him back in the saddle, yet he held on, keeping his seat even as the blood began to pump out of the gruesome crevice hacked into his flesh.

Jack stared at him, holding his gaze for the span of a single heartbeat before he drove his sword forward, ramming the point deep into Sinclair's chest. He felt the steel punch through ribs and into the softer innards beyond. He twisted the blade, fighting the suction of flesh, then tore it free and readied a third blow.

It would not be needed. Sinclair swayed in the saddle, his eyes locked on to Jack's own. Then blood gushed from his mouth and he fell to one side, tumbling to the ground without a sound.

Jack found himself staring directly at Brannigan. Neither man spoke.

'They're running!' A man away to Brannigan's left shouted the news.

Jack turned. Sinclair's ambushers had lost the will to fight now that their leader was down. Their shadowy forms were quickly lost in the rain as they rode hell for leather for safety. For their part, Brannigan's men were in no fit state to give chase. The bitter gunfight could not have lasted more than a dozen minutes, yet every man was spent.

Jack dismounted. His mare stood exhausted, with head lowered. He let the reins drop, knowing she would stay where she was, then walked towards Sinclair's body.

The man he had hacked out of the saddle lay where he had fallen, staring at the blackened sky. Rain ran across his face to dilute the blood that had vomited from his mouth. Somehow he was still alive, and he gazed at Jack, eyes wild with agony, his mouth moving slowly, as if he were whispering. Yet no sound came out.

Jack looked at the great cleft he had slashed into Sinclair's neck. It had been a while since he had seen a wound created by a sword, but he regarded the gaping, twisted mess of flesh, sinew and bone without horror. He had seen worse.

'What the hell did you do that for?'

It was Brannigan who shouted the question. He had ridden over and now loomed over Jack from the saddle, his face twisted with anger.

Jack looked up at the man he had saved. For a moment, he thought Brannigan would raise his empty revolver and use it to bludgeon him where he stood, such was the fury in his expression.

'He was going to kill you.' Jack was confused. 'Are you not grateful?'

'Grateful?' Brannigan spat out the word. 'Goddammit, why the hell would I be grateful?'

Jack felt the rain begin to slow, an insipid pale-grey light returning to the world as the storm finally cleared away. He did not understand Brannigan's reaction. 'You wanted me to let him shoot you?'

'I had him where I wanted him.' Brannigan's mouth twisted as if he was chewing on a fat turd.

Jack felt the touch of his own anger. He did not expect to be lauded as a hero for saving Brannigan's neck, but he did expect some common gratitude.

'I had him,' Brannigan sneered. 'Now I'm in your goddam debt.'

So this was the real reason behind his anger. 'Don't worry about it, chum.' Jack swiped a hand across his face, clearing away the rainwater and the sweat.

'That's not how it works.' Brannigan slid from the saddle,

his boots digging great holes in the rain-soaked ground. 'Not for me.'

He looked down at Sinclair, contemplating his fate. Sinclair stared back, his pain-crazed eyes flickering between the two men. His mouth moved continuously, emitting a strange mewing sound.

'Did you have to do it with that goddam sabre of yours?'

Jack heard a slight change of tone. Brannigan's anger was fading as quickly as the storm.

'I told you it would be useful.' He pulled his eyes from Sinclair to look at the man he had agreed to follow.

Brannigan shook his head ruefully. 'What the hell is a man like you doing in a place like this?' His expression changed as he made the remark. Any anger he had felt had been replaced with something else. Jack did not know quite what it was.

'Maybe it's just Fate.'

'Fate?' Brannigan grimaced as he repeated the single word. 'Do you believe in that horseshit?'

'I do,' Jack answered earnestly. 'We can't fight it. We can try, but nothing we do makes one scrap of bloody difference.'

'No. I will never accept that.' Brannigan denounced the notion forcefully. 'I make my own fate.'

Jack watched Brannigan carefully in the silence that followed the remark. He was beginning to think that the two of them were very much alike. They had both been fighting Fate all their lives. He knew he was losing that particular battle, but it appeared Brannigan had yet to feel the same.

'What do you think I should do with him?' Brannigan pointed a finger at Sinclair.

'If it were me, I'd put the poor bastard out of his misery.' Jack gave the honest answer. There was no surviving the wound he had inflicted on Sinclair.

'That's because you're soft.' Brannigan's voice hardened.

'That's not being soft. He's as good as dead. Why delay?'

Sinclair whimpered as the two men discussed his fate. A single hand reached out, but he did not have the strength to hold it in the air, so it ended up doing little more than claw at the dirt by Brannigan's feet.

Brannigan sighed, then gently moved Sinclair's hand back to his side with the toe of his boot. 'I have a reputation to protect. One that warns sons of bitches like this not to try to stop me going about my business.' He took one last look at Sinclair, then reached out to clap a hand on Jack's shoulder. 'I'll repay my debt to you, Jack. One day I'll save your lousy English neck, then we'll be even.'

He walked away, leaving Jack alone with Sinclair.

Jack did not move even as he heard Brannigan bawling orders at his men. He was still standing there when he returned with Adam and two others.

'Pick him up, fellas.' Brannigan stood back and pointed at Sinclair.

'Are you not going to kill him?' Jack felt an odd sense of ownership towards Sinclair, as if he were some sort of ghastly trophy.

'Not yet.' Brannigan did not so much as look at Jack as the three men lifted Sinclair up.

'What are you going to do with him?' Jack asked, taking a few steps back so that he was out of the men's way.

'You'll see.' Brannigan's voice was as hard as iron.

Jack stayed where he was as the men half carried, half

dragged Sinclair away. Already the first wagon was crossing the bridge.

He was not shocked at Brannigan's treatment of Sinclair. He had known plenty of men who were ruthless in the pursuit of their goals and would let nothing get in their way. It was worth remembering. Brannigan might talk of being in Jack's debt, but Jack had no doubt that that fact would quickly be forgotten if he ever got in the other man's way.

Chapter Sixteen

———✦———

Jack finished tending to his mare and walked towards the campfire, where Brannigan's cook would be doing his best to conjure something palatable from the bacon, dried beef, desiccated vegetables and hardtack that made up the bulk of their meagre rations on the trail south. He was not alone in doing so. The remains of Brannigan's gang, less those standing guard, were gathering around the fire. Four men had been killed outright that day, with another two lying on bedrolls with wounds that would likely finish them off before the night was out. Half a dozen men would have died to protect the great bales of cotton, and he wondered if there would be more deaths before the cargo reached its final destination.

He walked closer to the flames, the heat drawing him in. The cold had wormed its way deep into his bones. He had changed out of his sodden clothing, but even that had done little to warm him. It was as if a chill had settled in his soul.

'That was a close-run thing.'

Jack kept his face towards the flames. He recognised Vaughan's voice well enough and felt a moment's animosity. He had not seen Vaughan in the fighting. The plantation's agent had not shared that bitter experience, which in Jack's mind made him an outsider.

'The boys are talking about you.' If Vaughan sensed Jack's mood, he paid it no heed as he came to stand at his side. 'They say you fought as well as any of them.'

'No, I didn't.' Jack disagreed without hesitation. 'Otherwise I'd have stood there blasting away like a fool, just as they did.'

Vaughan laughed. 'I sense my words are angering you. I assure you that was not my intention. I merely wanted to offer my thanks. For keeping our cargo safe.'

'It's what you pay me for.'

'That is true. Yet from what I hear, you made the difference today. It proves you to be no ordinary man.'

'Oh, I'm no *ordinary* man.' Jack snorted as he revealed a trace of arrogance.

'I know, Jack, I know. You might be an outlaw, but you are one with a good heart.'

'No. I am me. Nothing more and nothing less.' He turned to look at Vaughan for the first time in the short conversation. The plantation's agent was warming his hands by the flames. 'You didn't fight.' He did not bother to hide his disdain.

'No.' Vaughan's expression was unchanged as he reacted to Jack's accusation.

'Why?'

'That is not my place here.'

'You are too valuable to risk? Is that it?'

'Perhaps.' Vaughan looked back at Jack, a smile creeping across his face. 'We have men much better suited to the fight than I.'

'Men like me.'

'Yes, Jack, men like you. You are a fighter, a warrior if you prefer. I believe this is what you were born to do. I was not. I have found I am better suited to other things.'

Jack did not reply at once. The words resonated. Vaughan barely knew him, but it seemed that he could see into the depths of his soul. 'And men like me are expendable.' His animosity was slipping away.

'Yes, Jack, you are.'

'At least you are honest.'

'I hope you will find me always to be so.' Vaughan smiled.

Jack held back a reply. He doubted he would ever trust the agent. He was too confident, too secure. A man who showed no trace of doubt was a man who was hiding something.

'Ah, here comes our esteemed leader.'

Jack followed Vaughan's gaze to see Brannigan arriving with a posse of men trailing behind him. Not one of them was speaking. They made their way to the fire, coming close to where Jack and Vaughan were warming themselves.

'You owe me a hundred dollars.' Jack addressed Brannigan. He noticed Vaughan sidling away, so as not to be part of the conversation yet to still be within comfortable earshot.

Brannigan faced the flames. He did not acknowledge Jack's presence.

'Did you hear me?' Jack lifted his hands to the flames, feeling the heat on his palms. His eyes closed as he relished the wash of warmth on his skin.

'I heard you all right.' Brannigan's answer was clipped. 'You'll get the money.'

'At least you can afford it now. How much did you save yourself today? A thousand dollars? Add another five hundred if those poor bastards over there don't make it.'

Brannigan did not so much as twitch.

'All in all, a good day's business.' Jack did not bother to hide the bitterness in his words. He wanted to nettle this man. Brannigan was warmed by fire and lit by flames, yet he himself felt as dark and cold as a midwinter's night.

'You talk too much,' Brannigan muttered.

'Maybe.' Jack looked deep into the dancing flames. 'So am I in?'

'In what?'

'Your gang. Did saving your life prove I'm up to this job of yours?'

'You want to stay?'

'You need me.'

Brannigan laughed then. 'You're an arrogant son of a bitch.'

'And you're a hard-nosed, miserable bastard who owes me a hundred dollars.'

'You'll get your money.' For the first time, Brannigan looked at Jack. 'And you're wrong, I don't need you. But I'll pay you back. For saving my hide.'

'No need. I was just doing my job.'

'No.' Brannigan's reply was as hard as granite. 'That's not how it works, least not round here. Like I said, I'll pay you back.'

Jack was saved finding a suitable reply by the arrival of Adam and Kat. Neither appeared to have been hurt in the ambush.

'You wanted us?' Kat spoke first. She stood half a pace in front of Adam, as if shielding him from the confrontation that was about to erupt.

Brannigan said nothing for a long time. He just stared into the flames, ignoring them both.

'Brannigan!' Kat showed no fear. She would not be left to

stand there, but demanded attention, her tone as hot as the flames that warmed them all.

'You screwed up.' At last Brannigan broke his silence.

'We told you what we learned.'

'Sinclair fed you a pack of lies, yet you believed him.' His tone was mild.

'We didn't know that. And maybe he just changed his plans. It happens.' Kat was defiant.

Brannigan grunted, then looked at Adam. 'You got a tongue in your head, boy?'

Adam visibly quailed as the full force of the gang leader's attention was directed at him. 'Yes, sir.' He took a step forward. In the light of the flames, he looked like the boy he still was.

'Tell me.'

Adam swallowed hard. 'We thought we'd got what we needed.'

'Then you clearly don't know shit.' Brannigan's tone did not change. 'I told you to find out where Sinclair would be waiting for us.'

'We thought we had.'

'It's not his fault.' Kat had stayed out of the conversation long enough. 'I was the one he told. I was the one who told you. If it's anyone's fault, it's mine.' She fired off the words, anger colouring her cheeks more than the heat from the flames.

Jack watched the altercation closely. It revealed much about the people he had allowed to enter his life. He saw that Kat had no fear of Brannigan, but she did fear for Adam, and was quick to come to his defence.

'I know whose fault it is.' Brannigan still spoke quietly. 'It's mine. I sent children to do my work for me.'

Kat and Adam both recoiled from the damning judgement.

Jack had known this confrontation was coming since the moment Sinclair's men had sprung their ambush. He had believed the pair had played Sinclair well, drawing the information from him that Brannigan had needed. He had been wrong, and he was not the only one. Four men at least had paid the price for such assumptions.

'I thought he told me the truth.' Kat looked around her. Brannigan's men were watching, but none would meet her gaze. Not one came to her defence.

'Why? Because you had that needle dick of his in your hand? Or did he tell you only when he clambered on top of you?'

'It wasn't like that.' Kat's eyes dropped.

'Then what was it like?' Brannigan loomed over her.

'I didn't . . .' Kat struggled to find the words. 'He didn't do that.'

'Then maybe he should have. Maybe then four of my men wouldn't have died.' For the first time, Brannigan's tone had changed. Anger coloured his voice, as bright and red as the flames of the campfire. 'I told you to find out what he had planned.'

'I tried.'

'And you failed.'

'It's not just Kat's fault.' Adam's voice wavered. 'I was there too.'

'Don't think I've forgotten you, boy.' Brannigan whirled to face him, but the anger had left his tone.

Adam lifted his chin as Brannigan focused on him. 'Don't just blame me.' He pointed an accusatory finger at Jack. 'He told you to take the bridge too.'

'Don't go trying to shift the blame now, boy.'

'Why not? Why do you listen to him? He ain't done nothing for you. Not like I have.'

'What have you done, boy?' Brannigan's tone was scathing.

'I've done everything you ever asked of me.' Adam's voice wavered, as if he was close to tears. 'You know me, Brannigan. I'm loyal. I'll do whatever you want; you just have to ask.'

'I told you to scout the river.'

'I did! And I fought. I didn't run. I killed two of them sons of bitches. I shot nice and slow and I didn't rush. I did it just like you showed me.' The words poured out of him now, the flood released.

Brannigan took a pace towards him. 'I told you to scout the river, boy,' he repeated. 'Did you do that with your goddam eyes closed?'

'I didn't see them.'

'Just like you didn't see that Sinclair played you both for fools. Did you ever think that maybe he would have been more vocal if it had been you who had gotten into bed with him? I'm told he's keen on boys like you. Boys that do as he wants.'

'Shut your filthy mouth.' Adam's eyes had widened as Brannigan's invective washed over him. Now they narrowed.

'Say that again.'

Adam was no coward. He met Brannigan's gaze. 'I said shut your filthy mouth,' he repeated slowly.

Brannigan absorbed the words, nodding calmly. He turned on his heel, as if about to walk away. Then he whirled back, his right fist rising fast.

The blow smashed into the centre of Adam's face. Blood flew as his nose was pulped. Brannigan's left followed hard on the heels of the first punch, slamming into the boy's gut with the force of a sledgehammer.

Adam bent double as the breath was driven from his body.

But Brannigan was not done. He reached out and grabbed the younger man by the hair, pulling him upright then hauling him forward.

'Leave him alone!' Kat came at him, her hands bunched into fists.

Brannigan saw her coming. He swung his free hand hard and fast, slamming the back of it into the side of Kat's face, bludgeoning her to the ground.

'Keep out of this,' he snarled. 'This is between me and him, you hear me?' He jerked his left hand, lifting and twisting Adam so that his bloodied face was almost touching his own. 'Now then, boy, what did you just say to me?'

Adam's face was covered with blood, and more pumped from both nostrils to run down into his mouth. 'I said shut your filthy mouth.' He stumbled over the words, blood flung from his lips like spittle as he formed them. Yet he spoke clearly enough for them to be understood.

'I thought that's what you said.' Brannigan's eyes roved over Adam's battered face. 'You want to challenge me, boy? You want to take over?'

'No.' Adam kept his hands at his sides. He made no attempt to fight back.

Brannigan's eyes bored into him. 'You sure about that?' His right hand dropped to his revolver. He drew the weapon, then held it up, pressing it hard into Adam's temple. 'I said, are you sure 'bout that!' He screamed the words into the younger man's face, grinding the revolver's barrel into Adam's skin so that more blood snaked down the side of his face.

'Yes!' Adam shouted. 'I'm sure.' There was real fear in his eyes now. They rolled around in their sockets as they tried to watch both Brannigan and the revolver.

'You think I should kill you?' Brannigan pushed his face closer. 'What say you to that, boy?'

Adam's resolve failed. Whatever reply he tried to form was lost as he whimpered in fear.

'Cat got your tongue?' Brannigan sneered. He pulled away suddenly, releasing his grip on Adam's hair as he did so. Adam's legs buckled as they took his full weight, and he fell at the gang leader's feet.

Brannigan did not so much as glance at him. Instead, he holstered his revolver, then turned to look at one of his men, who was lingering a few paces away.

'Is he ready?' His voice had returned to its usual dry, deadpan tone, as if nothing had happened. If he saw Kat get to her feet and walk over to Adam, he showed no sign of it.

'Yes, Brannigan.' The man could not hide his nervousness. 'I tied him up, just like you told me.'

'At least someone can do what I goddam tell them.' Brannigan glanced over his shoulder. 'Walk with me, Jack. I want to show you something.'

Jack felt a stirring in his gut. He did not know if it was fear, or something else, something akin to loathing. Brannigan's rage had shocked him. It had been feral and ferocious, two things that sat at odds with the quiet, taciturn manner that he had witnessed up to that point. He had learned much that day; not least that he had shackled himself to a man who possessed an uncontrollable temper.

Yet despite his newly acquired knowledge, he still did as he was told, and followed Brannigan as he walked away from the fire and through a gap in the line of wagons that had been parked in a circle around the temporary encampment.

Away from the fire, it was harder to see. Dusk was falling,

and the last of the sun's rays cast long shadows across the ground. But despite the failing light, Jack saw what Brannigan was leading him towards easily enough.

Sinclair sat against a spare wagon wheel that had been propped up against a lone oak tree. At first Jack thought he was looking at a dead man, but as they approached, he saw a single eye open to look in their direction.

It was only as they got closer that he saw the rope that had been hitched around Sinclair's chest, tying him to the wheel.

'What the hell is that?' he demanded.

'A warning.'

He shook his head as he absorbed Brannigan's answer. No effort had been made to ease Sinclair's last hours on earth. His wounds had been left unbound. His fine grey suit was stained with blackened blood, and the gruesome fissures and tears Jack's sword had rent in his flesh had been left open to the elements. That he was still alive was something of a miracle, but one that Jack had seen before. Some men went quickly, the wound that killed them barely visible. Others died hard, their body ruined and shredded so that it was impossible to believe they could linger for so long.

Sinclair's single open eye looked up at Jack from an ashen face cast into shadow by the sunset. The man was far beyond pleading for mercy, but Jack saw the appeal in the intense stare.

'A warning for what?' His mouth was dry.

'To tell others what happens if they come after me.' Brannigan spoke slowly, as if to a difficult child who had failed to grasp what they were being told.

'You don't need to do that.' Jack turned his head, moving his tongue around in his mouth as he tried to summon up enough moisture to spit away the foul taste there. 'They know.'

'It don't hurt to remind them.'

'You think he'd treat you like that?'

'No. He'd do far worse.'

'Worse?' Jack gave a short, bitter laugh. 'I don't think there's much worse than that.'

'You don't approve?'

'No.' He would not kowtow to this man.

'Have you never done something bad then, Jack? Never done something like this?'

'Oh, I've done bad things.' Jack did not turn to look at Brannigan. He kept his eyes on Sinclair, holding the man's agony-crazed stare. 'But I've never been as cruel as this.'

'Cruel? Is that what it is?' Brannigan asked, as if genuinely intrigued. 'Well, if it don't suit you, then you go right ahead and put the son of a bitch out of his misery.'

Jack heard the challenge in the words. He did not understand it, or know what the man hoped to achieve. Perhaps it was a warped test of character, and only Brannigan would know if Jack had passed or failed. Whatever the game was, he had no intention of playing along.

He held Sinclair's gaze for several long moments, then drew his revolver. He fired a single heartbeat later.

The sound of the gunshot echoed around the great expanse of open ground in which they stood. Jack looked once at Brannigan, then turned and walked away, heading back to the fire and its warmth. Not once did he glance back at the body that now lolled against the ropes that bound it to the wagon wheel.

Chapter Seventeen

To say the approach to San Antonio was busy was an understatement. Jack rode towards the long queue of wagons parked on the trail, and wondered how long it would be before they would make their way to the main plaza in the centre of the town. What had to be close to a hundred wagons were parked nose to tail in a semi-orderly queue that stretched back for over a mile. They might not have been moving, yet the noise of the stationary wagon trains was tremendous. From the shouts and oaths coming in a constant stream from the teamsters, to the brays and bellows of the animals they controlled, the cacophony was loud enough to be heard from several miles away.

Jack used the delay to study the other trains waiting to enter the town. Most were smaller than the one Brannigan escorted, the majority made up of just ten to fifteen wagons. He had learned much about the workings of these trains. Each one was under the control of a single wagon master, a cadre of hard-faced, dour men like Brannigan, who were charged with getting the precious cotton to its destination no matter what, or who, tried to stop them. Each was divided into two sections, commanded by men given the title of wagon captain, with another man, given the title of corporal, put in charge of the twenty to thirty spare draught animals that would be called into action when the wagons traversed the sands on their way to Brownsville, the last stop on the journey across Texan territory, a gruelling four-hundred-mile trek that would take four to six weeks.

Yet that part of the journey was still in the future, and instead of dwelling on the difficulties and dangers that lay ahead, Jack studied the town of San Antonio. From what he could see, it didn't look like much. Many of the nearby buildings appeared temporary, an array of wooden shacks and barns arranged in haphazard fashion along the main route into town. Alongside these ramshackle affairs were dozens upon dozens of great animal holding pens, each one filled to capacity with oxen, mules, horses and cattle. With so many animals came an earthy smell, the rich aroma of dung hanging like a low-lying cloud.

Yet not all was so temporary in nature. In the distance, he could see the bell tower of a cathedral, the cross at the top a beacon calling to the hundreds of cattle drivers and wagon trains. Not that he suspected many of the men who worked the trail would be thinking of finding salvation for their soul.

The men in Brannigan's gang had spent nearly every evening for the past week lauding the virtues of San Antonio. It was the last major staging post on that long journey to the Rio Grande, and the town had grown fat on the cotton trade. Every day, wagon trains piled high with cotton arrived heading south, whilst others travelled north loaded with cargo bound for the Confederacy. San Antonio provided for them all. There were depots for the wagons, the men who worked in them able to repair a great variety of faults. There were suppliers of food-stuffs and animal feed, the demand for the produce pushing prices to eye-watering levels. Others supplied the draught animals that the heavily loaded wagons would need on their long journey to and from the Rio Grande.

The debate over which animal was best at hauling the wagons had occupied a hundred hours on the journey to this point, and Jack had quickly tired of the endless back-and-forth. Some claimed oxen were best, the animals cheaper to purchase at two hundred dollars for eight, and strong enough to pull even the most heavily loaded wagon through anything but the thickest sand. Oxen also boasted one other advantage over mules, in that they could be eaten if the going got really tough. Yet Brannigan, and many other wagon masters, insisted on using mules. The animals were more expensive than oxen, at one hundred dollars each, and they required extra grain to be carried, as they needed a better diet. Yet nothing would dissuade their supporters from using them. As cantankerous and difficult as they could be, no other animal could endure like a mule, especially in the heat of southern Texas.

Jack had ridden slowly along the side of the wagon train and had now reached the head of the column. Vaughan, Brannigan, Kat and a few of the older guards had gone ahead, leaving just a few men with the train to wait out the long afternoon.

'Where do you think you're going?'

It was Adam who stopped him, his voice overly loud and full of challenge.

'Just taking a look-see.' Jack brought his mare to a stand, then turned to look at the younger man. Adam's face showed the aftereffects of his one-sided fight with Brannigan. Both eyes were surrounded by red and purple bruises, the whites of one shot through with bright streaks of red. His nose was close to double its normal size and both nostrils were ringed with crusty scabs.

Adam shifted in the saddle as he stared back. His revolver, a Colt, was in his hand. He was using the delay to practise drawing the weapon, completing the action by twirling the revolver around his finger before thrusting it back into its holster.

'You need to stay in your place.' He gave the order in a clipped voice.

'Are you in charge here?' Jack watched the boy toy with the revolver. It was an unnecessary conceit. It did not matter how fast a man could snatch his weapon out of its holster, or how fancy the tricks he could play with it. It was the ability to kill that counted. Adam could fiddle with this weapon as much as he liked. It would not make a difference when he came face to face with a man intent on killing him.

'Just do as you're told.' Adam tried to sound bored of having to repeat himself, yet there was an unmistakable tremor of tension in his voice.

Jack said nothing; merely sat and watched as Adam completed another round of his drill.

'That's not a toy.' He tried to keep his voice light as he addressed the younger man.

'You think I don't know that?' Adam scowled.

'Is it loaded?'

'Hell, yes.'

'Then stop bloody playing with it.'

'Playing with it! You think that's what I'm doing?'

'What do *you* call it?'

'It's none of your goddam business.'

'It will be if you blow your bloody leg off.' Jack heard the change in his own tone and drew in a sharp breath to stop himself saying anything more. He remembered what it was like to be Adam's age; how impetuous and headstrong he had been. Advice counted for nothing, not when you knew it all. 'What will Brannigan say if you shoot yourself?' He changed tack.

'I won't shoot myself.' The denial came back instantly. Yet Adam's hand stilled.

Jack noted the power of using Brannigan's name. 'You look up to him, don't you?'

'He's a fine man. A fine leader, too.' Adam sat straighter in the saddle.

'Have you been with him long?'

'All my life. All I remember, anyways.' Adam's hand rested on his revolver.

'Is that why you let him treat you like shit?' Jack wanted to know more, so he asked the deliberately barbed question.

'He does not.'

'He beat you pretty bad the other day.'

'That was my own fault.' Adam's neck began to turn crimson.

'That doesn't mean he has to wallop you.'

Adam shook his head. 'I screwed up. Just like you did.'

'Me?'

'Yes, you! You told him to make the crossing. Hell, you even suggested sending men forward. It was you who got Weston and the other boys killed.'

'Don't be stupid. Brannigan made the call.'

'Uh huh.' The flush that had started low on Adam's neck was rising so that it coloured his cheeks. 'I figured you'd say that.'

'What do you mean?' Jack felt the first touch of anger and made an effort to rein it in.

'Some fellas are like that.'

'Like what?' Jack knew he should shut up, but for some reason Adam always seemed able to get under his skin.

'They take the coward's way. "It's not my fault."' Adam put on a wheedling tone. '"I didn't do it."'

Jack barked a short laugh. There was nothing humorous in its tone. 'You really are a stupid little shit.'

'You care to say that again.' Adam's fingers curled around his revolver.

Jack saw the movement. He sensed the boy wanted the confrontation to go on, maybe even to the point where there was a fight. He could not let that happen. Adam was still young. He would likely learn life's lessons the hard way, just as Jack himself had done.

'You need to mind your tongue, boy.' He gave a last word of advice, then turned his mare's head around and began the long ride back to the rear of the wagon train.

As he rode away, he heard the telltale sound of a revolver being drawn.

Chapter Eighteen

───────◆◆◆───────

*J*ack stretched as he walked away from the main plaza. It was a relief to be on his feet, the six-hour wait to get into town leaving his back aching from the pit of his spine to the base of his neck. He sorely needed a chance to rest, and to sleep in a bed made from something more comfortable than his bedroll. Brannigan had hired rooms for them all in a boarding house that he used every time he came to town, yet it would still be some time before Jack could seek the respite he craved, as the gang leader had tasked him with ordering the ammunition they would need for the next leg of their journey. The firefight with Sinclair's gang of renegades had depleted much of their supply, and the list Jack had been given was long.

Despite the chore he had been tasked with, it was a relief to be somewhere other than on the trail, and San Antonio promised to make for a lively stop. The town did not just cater to the needs of the wagons and the animals that dragged them. It also looked after the teamsters and outriders who came with the cotton. There were brothels, bars, hotels, boarding houses, every manner of store, and dozens of gambling houses where the men could throw away their pay in a bewildering choice of games of chance. The citizens of San Antonio had become adept at emptying the pockets of the men who found themselves in the town, and the wagon teams were willing accomplices in the fleecing, the harsh reality of life on the trail fuelling their desire for a day or two of pleasure before they returned to the dangerous task of escorting the trains on their long, brutal journeys.

Despite the hardship of that work, every day men would fill the main plaza in the centre of town, trading themselves to the wagon masters and their captains. These men touted their skills and talents, holding out for the highest bidder for their services. It was a lucky wagon master indeed who arrived in San Antonio with a full complement of men, and so those looking for employment could demand a good wage. Many were Tejanos, Mexicans born in the new state of Texas. Others were deserters from one or other of the armies fighting the great War Between the States.

Jack had heard several of Brannigan's men talk of the temptation to jump wagon train in San Antonio and sign on for better money elsewhere. Yet as far as he could tell, not one of them was seriously contemplating doing so. Even here, on the frontier of the United States, men were fiercely loyal to their master. They reminded Jack of soldiers in that regard, their commitment to each other, and to Brannigan, worth as much as the wages they received.

There were also risks in leaving Brannigan's employ. Not every wagon train was paid for by private individuals like Vaughan's master, the plantation owner Trevathlon. Many were under the command of the Confederate quartermaster based in San Antonio, who was charged with taking the government's share of cotton down to the willing buyers in Mexico. With the power of conscription at his disposal, the quartermaster, a Major Simeon Hart, was not the sort of employer any of the men would choose, the wages he paid just a fraction of what they could earn working for a private merchant. Major Hart was also in charge of issuing the export permits the private wagon trains would need if they were to be allowed to take their cotton south. That made him one of the most powerful men in these parts, and not one to be crossed.

Then there was Brannigan himself. Few of his men would risk leaving his employ for any amount of money. Jack had heard many a gruesome tale around the nightly campfires of what had happened to those who had tried to walk away from the gang. He was not naive enough to believe every last detail, the men just like soldiers in their inclination to embellish, but the stories all had one thing in common: those who left Brannigan did not live long to enjoy the experience. The men had relished recounting the many and various ways, all cruel and many vile, in which Brannigan had killed those who abandoned him. It left Jack in no doubt whatsoever that signing on to the gang was a lifelong commitment. The only uncertainty was quite how long that life would be.

He walked away from the main plaza, then turned on to Commerce Street, following the simple directions Brannigan had given him. San Antonio was not a large town. It boasted a cathedral with a fine bell tower, and a large fort called the Mission de Valero, which Brannigan's men had referred to as the Alamo. As the wagon train had drawn closer to San Antonio, the men had regaled one another with tales of a great battle fought there between Texan rebels and the Mexican army commanded by Antonio Santa Anna. Jack did not believe all he was told, but the main thrust of the tale was that fewer than two hundred Texans had defended the Alamo against over two thousand Mexican soldiers for thirteen days before finally being defeated in a bloody battle that saw the Texans wiped out and hundreds of Mexicans killed.

'Hey, Jack! Wait up.'

Jack heard his name being called. He recognised the voice at once, and smiled as he turned to see Kat striding towards him.

As he waited for her to catch up, he did his best not to stare. As ever, her hair was bound tightly behind her head and hidden under a wide-brimmed hat. At first glance, it would be easy to take her for a young man. She wore the same clothes as the other men, from the pointed boots that were shaped to slip easily into a stirrup, whilst the thick leather sides protected the wearer from snake bites and scorpion stings, to the brightly coloured bandana that was worn loose around the neck so that it could be pulled up to cover the mouth, and so prevent at least some of the dust and sand of the trail from being inhaled. Her brown trousers were well worn at the thigh, and around her waist was a thick leather belt with a holster containing a six-shot Remington revolver. She sported the brown jacket with fringing that he had first seen her wearing when she and Adam had come to his campfire, and underneath it a plain grey collarless shirt.

'You got that list?' She fired the question as she came close.

'Right here.'

'Least you can do something right.'

'What do you mean by that?' Jack was immediately on the defensive.

'Shooting Sinclair was a damn-fool move.' Kat came to

stand in front of him. She was tall enough not to have to crane her neck to look him dead in the eye.

'Why?'

'Because it ain't what Brannigan wanted.'

'And he always gets what he wants?'

'Always.'

He grunted by way of response. He had not given the shooting of Sinclair much thought. Killing a man, even one who was dying, should have meant more, he knew that, but to him it was just another death, and a merciful one at that. It had not affected him in any way. The notion sat badly in his mind. He had given more thought to how to secure himself better rations than he had to the death of a man who had perished at his hand.

'Next time, just do as he says.' Kat lifted a hand to screen her eyes from the sun as she looked at Jack.

'Like you do?'

'Yes.'

'Bollocks. You'd not be sporting that shiner if you were such a good girl.'

Kat scowled. The skin around her right eye was puffy and bruised from where Brannigan had belted her. 'Call me "girl" again and I'll give *you* a goddam shiner.' She understood the strange word well enough to use it for herself.

Jack wanted to laugh at such a belligerent answer, but he held back, knowing it would likely do him no good at all.

'So like I said, you need to do as he says. Otherwise there'll be trouble.' Kat repeated her advice.

'No.' His reply was not defiance, or a way of attempting to impress the young woman standing in front of him. It was the simple, blunt truth. He was his own man now. Nothing and no one would change that.

'No?' Kat shook her head at such a recalcitrant answer. 'You think you know better?'

'At times I do.' He searched her eyes as he tried to assess her reaction. 'Do *you* do what Brannigan says? No matter what you think and no matter how many times he clouts you around the head?'

'Yes.' Kat's reply was stony.

'So you're just another damn lickspittle.' He shook his head in disappointment. He had thought there might be more to her than that.

'What the hell is that when it's at home?'

'You do whatever he says, as soon as he says it. No questions asked.' He made no attempt to hide his displeasure as he gave the definition. 'Am I right?'

'Something like that.' Kat's brow furrowed. She clearly did not like the tone Jack had taken.

'Does that include slipping into his bedroll whenever he wants you?' The question came from his lips before it had time to form in his mind.

Kat's right hand moved fast. The punch it delivered clipped Jack's jaw with enough force to rock him back on his heels.

'You got yourself a filthy goddam mind there, Jack.' She glowered at him.

Jack raised a hand and used it to nurse his jaw. He had been slapped a few times in his life, but Kat's punch hurt. He ran his tongue around his mouth. He was sure she had loosened a tooth.

'So you're not his woman?'

'You want me to hit you again?' She pulled back her arm.

'All right, enough.' He lifted both hands as if to ward her away. 'I apologise. It was a damn-fool question.' He borrowed her turn of phrase in an attempt to mollify her.

'You got that right.' Kat lowered her fist. 'I ain't no one's woman, Jack. Don't plan to be neither.'

'What about Adam? The lad is besotted with you.' Jack wanted to know the lie of the land, even if that meant getting another smack in the chops.

'Adam?' Kat looked astonished at the idea. 'He's no more than a boy.'

'You stood up for him. Took a punch for him too.'

'I'm just looking out for him. He's too stupid to do that for hisself.'

'Well, I reckon he's taken quite a shine to you.'

'If he has, which I doubt, then he's as big a fool as you. I don't plan to saddle myself with anyone – not Brannigan, not Adam, not anyone.' There was a warning in her tone.

'That must be hard. Out here.' Jack had seen enough of the world to know the dangers Kat faced.

'The boys know not to try anything now.'

'Did one of them have a go?' Jack heard what was left unsaid.

'Once.' A flicker of something that might have been a smile crossed Kat's face.

'And?'

'That man ain't here no more.'

'You killed him?'

'I gelded the son of a bitch.'

'Jesus.' Jack winced at the notion. 'Did he live?'

'For a bit. At least until Brannigan shot him.'

The answer went some way to explaining her loyalty to Brannigan. The gang leader allowed her to live the life she wanted without interference. That was a powerful thing. Jack was sure she would never admit to it, but he reckoned she knew that Brannigan protected her and gave her the opportunity to be something she could not be without his help.

'It must be lonely.'

'You would know.' Kat's retort was sharp. 'You reckon I need a man to be happy? You think I need a baby in my belly and a man running my life to be complete?'

Jack sighed. He had set off a firecracker. Now all he could do was wait for the display to be over.

'What about your family?'

'I don't have any family. Not any more.'

'What happened to them?'

'They were killed. Murdered by some goddam bushwhackers for little more than the clothes on their back. We didn't have much worth stealing. My brother and I only survived because we hid ourselves away.'

'Then what happened?'

'Brannigan looked after both of us. Took us with him wherever he went. When we were old enough, we started to work for him. My damn fool of a brother was good at it too. Everyone said he would be a wagon master hisself one day. Then he went off and the Yankees put paid to all that.'

Jack noted the way Kat spoke in a dry, clipped tone, as if keeping the memory at arm's length. He knew why she would do that; he had enough memories of his own. 'Where did your brother die?'

'Shiloh.'

The one-word answer resonated in Jack's mind. He had been at the fight around Pittsburg Landing in Tennessee, and had seen enough to know that it had been a brutal and bloody battle.

'I'm sorry.' He spoke with utmost honesty.

'I told him not to go.' Kat looked away. 'I told him what would happen.'

Jack could hear the emotion in her voice. For a moment, he saw behind the tough, capable exterior she maintained to keep the world away. It was like a hidden door opening to give a tantalising glimpse of what lay beyond.

'You were right,' he said.

'That don't matter none. Not now.' Kat's tone hardened. The door was slammed shut.

'Is that why you look out for Adam? Because you miss your brother?' Jack was connecting the dots.

'No.' The answer was immediate.

Jack smiled. He knew he was right, despite her denial. He was learning a lot. It appeared that Brannigan had a habit of collecting waifs and strays, and he wondered why that was. 'So now you're all alone. Save for your good chum Brannigan.'

'That's right.'

'And you have to do whatever he says.'

'I tell you this, Jack: I live my own damn life. I don't need some man telling me what to do, or where to go. Do you understand me?'

'I understand.'

'Good. I don't want to have to punch you again. Next time, I'll knock you on your goddam backside.'

Jack smiled. He knew she was more than capable of making good on her promise. 'I apologise, ma'am, for any offence I may have caused.' He put on an upper-class accent in parody of an English gentleman. He was relieved to see half a smile appear on Kat's face.

'I'm glad we understand each other,' she said. 'Now we'd

better get on with that list of Brannigan's. I don't think he'll take kindly to us standing around chattering away when there's work to be done.'

Jack nodded in agreement. He was glad to see her anger had subsided. It had been an interesting conversation, one that was almost worth getting clouted for. He had learned much; not least that Kat was not with Brannigan. The idea set off a chain of thought that he knew he should curtail. Yet it was there, lingering in his mind like a furtive shadow that he suspected would slip into his thoughts much more often than it should.

Chapter Nineteen

The gunsmith was located in a side street not far from the main plaza. Jack and Kat were not the only customers, and they were forced to idle away a good twenty minutes outside as they waited for the two men in front of them to conclude their business.

The smell of the place hit Jack the moment he stepped over the threshold. The twin aromas of gun oil and powder were as familiar to him as the stink of gin and sweat had been in his youth. The shop had a long wooden display case facing the door, its glazed top allowing the customers to gaze down at an array of pistols and their accoutrements – or at least Jack believed that was its original purpose. Instead, the view was of dozens of half-opened packets of ammunition, a number of parts that could, with patience, be reassembled into revolvers, and three unrecognisable stuffed animals with raggedy fur, patches of bare, overly pink skin, and glass eyes that made them look as though they were lost in an opiate-induced daze.

Behind the counter were two long musket racks that boasted a single ancient smoothbore flintlock musket between them, and on the side wall were a series of shelves that were nearly bare save for a dozen cardboard ammunition boxes, all of which had already been opened. Jack's hope of finding cartridges for his Henry repeater fell into his boots. Given what was on display, they would be lucky to be able to buy cartridges for their revolvers, let alone anything more.

'Hold yourselves there. I'll be out directly.' A voice came from behind a curtain that Jack surmised screened off a back room. The thick Southern drawl reminded him of Kat's mimicry when she had attempted to tease secrets from the unfortunate Sinclair.

They were left to kick their heels for five more minutes before the curtain was eased back and a man entered, taking up station behind the wooden display case and its sad array of items. He was short and stout, with a bald head and the fattest moustache that Jack had ever seen.

'Now then, fellas, what can I get for you all today?' The gunsmith smiled as he finally got around to dealing with his customers.

'We've got a list for you.' Jack spoke first, his tone making it abundantly clear that he thought he was wasting his time. 'But we'll just have whatever you've got.'

The gunsmith smiled as he took the list and perused it, his finger moving slowly from one item to the next.

'Have you got *anything* on that list?' Jack could not help trying to gee the man along.

'One moment there, sir.' The words were delivered slowly and deliberately.

For her part, Kat simply looked at Jack and smiled. Clearly she saw his impatience and it amused her.

'You want all of this today?' The gunsmith finally reached the end of the list and glanced up.

Jack made a play of looking around him, his eyes scanning the barren shelves. 'We'll just take whatever you have.' He could not help sighing.

'Oh, I have it all. I just need to know if you want it today or tomorrow.' The gunsmith shot Jack a withering stare, then turned his attention to his companion. 'It's Kat, isn't it?'

'I wondered if you would remember me,' Kat replied.

'We don't get many pretty girls down here. Least not ones that know their guns.' The gunsmith gave another smile, then turned slowly and moved towards the curtain. 'Come on now, come back here and let's see what we got.'

Pulling a wry face at Jack, Kat moved around the counter and followed the man into the back room. Jack hesitated for a moment, wondering how much of a fool he had just made of himself, then stepped through the curtain after her. The sight that greeted him was enough to make him gasp.

The room was at least ten times larger than the one that faced the street. Sunlight streamed in from two enormous skylights that made up a good half of the ceiling. All four walls were lined with musket racks, and there was not a single space on any of them. Much of the floor was filled with shelving, each unit packed to capacity with wooden ammunition crates, and great stacks of the card packages that contained revolver cartridges in packets of six. Another small series of racks stood in a long line at right angles to the shelving, each one holding a bewildering array of revolvers, many of which Jack did not recognise. Still more were laid out on a large dining table, which was where the gunsmith was now bent over, cross-referencing the list Jack had handed over against entries in a black leather-bound ledger.

Kat moved forward to stand at the gunsmith's side. It was

only then that she turned to raise both eyebrows at Jack in a silent rebuke for his doubts.

For his part, Jack walked reverentially to the nearest rack to run his hands over the first weapon he came to: a brand-new Springfield rifled musket that was identical to those carried by his former regiment at the first battle fought at the Bull Run River. He could feel the sheen of protective oil that had been put on by the factory, the touch of it, and its smell, bringing back the memories of the summer he had spent with the men from Boston.

'Who is this last item for?' The gunsmith had reached the final entry on the list.

Kat leaned forward. 'That's for him.'

The enigmatic answer was enough for the gunsmith to straighten up, then turn to face Jack. 'Sir, have you really got yourself a Henry repeater?'

Jack nodded.

'And you want six hundred rounds of rimfire cartridges?'

'I'll take more if you have them.'

The gunsmith barked a short laugh at the notion. 'I take it you know how rare that rifle of yours is?'

'I do.' Jack's Henry was a special weapon, one that he had yet to see anyone else carrying. He had taken it from a man sent to kill him, and he had no notion how that man had been able to get his hands on such an exceptional item.

'Would you be of a mind to sell it?'

'No.'

'Not even if I tell you I ain't got a single one of them fancy-ass rimfire cartridges?'

'No.'

'Not even if I tell you that there ain't a single one of them fancy-ass rimfire cartridges anywhere in the whole of Texas?'

'No.'

'It ain't no use to you with no ammunition.'

'I can still beat people to death with it.' Jack stared back at the gunsmith, expressionless.

'I bet you could.' The gunsmith's face creased into a wide smile. 'And looking at you, I reckon you've done that before too.' He gave another bark of a laugh. 'Have you got that rifle with you? I'd sure like to see it.'

'No.' Jack had left the repeater with the rest of his gear.

'Well, I'll have to console myself by taking a look at that gaudy Colt of yours.' The gunsmith indicated the revolver in the holster on Jack's right hip. 'If I may?'

Jack thought about refusing. But there was something about the man's manner that he liked, so he slipped the weapon out of its holster and handed it over.

'She's a beauty,' the gunsmith said admiringly. 'A '51 Navy Colt with custom ivory grips. Nicely polished, but no engraving on the barrel.' He ran practised hands over the weapon. 'Well cared for, too.' He glanced at Jack. 'But you've used it a lot. You don't often see a gun with this much wear and tear.' His eyes focused on the thick scar that was only partially covered by Jack's beard. He made no remark of it, but the comparison between weapon and owner was clear.

As he handed the revolver back, the gunsmith raised a finger, as if struck by a sudden thought. 'You know, I have something here that might interest you.'

He carefully tucked Brannigan's list under a corner of his ledger, then disappeared into the lines of shelves. He came back carrying a single handgun, cradled in his hands like a newborn babe.

'You'll sure appreciate this, if you've got yourself a Henry.' His voice was hushed and almost reverential.

Jack had never felt much for most of his weapons. They were the tools of his trade, nothing more. The only exception had been the Colt that now sat in his holster, and his talwar, a thing of beauty that had been given to him by an Indian ruler as a reward for the saving of a life, and which he had lost in the chaos of Delhi. He would never see the sword's like again, not in his lifetime. That thought, and the touch of its loss, made him feel a moment's anger, so that he almost snatched the proffered weapon from the gunsmith's hand.

The first thing that struck him about it was its similarity to his Henry repeater. It had the same shape and feel, even though it was only the size of a large revolver, albeit with a longer barrel. There was a ring-lever mechanism around the trigger similar to the one on his repeating rifle, and a comparable magazine, with follower and spring underneath the barrel. Its frame was made from brass, with a flared handle with wooden grips and an octagonal barrel that he guessed was about eight inches long.

'It's a Volcanic Navy pistol, made in '56 by the Volcanic Repeating Arms Company – that's the same folk who would go on to produce your Henry.' The gunsmith spoke in the hushed tones of a worshipper entering a cathedral. 'She holds ten rounds and I promise you won't find another gun with a faster rate of fire. She's quicker to load than any revolver too.'

Jack inspected the pistol, holding it in his left hand as he did in battle. It was a fine-looking weapon, but he could not imagine using it. It was heavy to the point of feeling clumsy, and he could not see how you could crank the ring lever without using both hands, something he could not afford to do in battle if he were holding his sabre in his right hand.

'Does it fire the same ammunition as the Henry?' he asked as he handed it back.

'Similar, but not the same. She fires a rocket ball.' The gunsmith paused, then reached into a pocket and produced a small conical bullet. 'This is it. It's been hollowed out, a bit like a Minié ball. There's a pellet of priming compound in the base with the main powder charge inside. The whole thing is sealed with cork, here at the bottom, making it waterproof, unlike the paper cartridges you carry for those revolvers of yours.' He twirled the bullet around in his fingers to show his small audience what he was talking about. 'In here,' he pointed a thick finger at the centre of the base, 'is a small anvil. The firing pin on the gun's hammer will hit it with enough force to fire the priming compound, which ignites the charge and shoots the whole thing out of the barrel.' He paused again, then tossed the bullet to Jack.

Jack snatched it out of the air and made a play of inspecting it. 'If it all goes out the barrel, then it can't be that powerful.' He was thinking about the rimfire cartridge on his Henry. When that was fired, the empty casing remained in the weapon and was ejected when the ring lever was moved. The Volcanic pistol was different, in that the whole cartridge was fired down the barrel. That made for a heavy, unwieldy bullet, and he could not see how the small amount of charge inside it could generate enough power for it to be a killer.

The gunsmith smiled and nodded. 'You have that right. This thing ain't going to gun a man down at a thousand yards. But you get this beauty up close and personal, and you've got yourself one hell of a weapon.'

'Maybe.' Jack sounded dubious. To his mind, it was still too clumsy for a weapon that was intended to replace his revolver.

'Can I see it?' Kat had stayed out of the conversation thus far. Now she reached for the Volcanic pistol.

Jack handed it over. The weapon was not for him. He trusted his Colt. But he could see something in Kat's eyes as she handled it. He recognised the spark of desire well enough.

'How much ammunition have you got for it?' He asked the question of the gunsmith, but kept his eyes on Kat, who was holding the weapon outstretched in her right hand so that she could sight down the barrel.

'Five hundred rounds.'

'There's lucky,' Jack said wryly.

'I've got four hundred for your Henry, too. Four boxes of a hundred each.'

'I thought you said you didn't have any?' Jack's reply was sharp.

'That's when I was trying to buy the weapon from you.' The honest answer was given without a trace of shame.

'And now you're selling.' Jack could only smile as he recognised the change of tack.

'You want to buy the Volcanic?'

'No.' Jack looked the gunsmith in the eye. 'But I reckon she might.'

'Who's she, the cat's goddam mother?' Kat interjected. But the Volcanic pistol was clearly distracting her. She was now cranking the ring lever around the trigger and watching carefully as the bolt slid backwards and the cradle for the bullet moved up and down.

'How much?' Jack asked the pertinent question.

'So you are buying.' The gunsmith lifted his right hand, his fingers reaching out to toy with his moustache.

'Maybe. Depends on your price.'

'One hundred dollars.' The answer was swift. 'That's for the pistol and its ammunition, plus the cartridges you need for your Henry.'

Jack snorted. A hundred dollars was a fortune. A second-hand Colt could be had for ten, whilst a brand-new Remington revolver like the one Kat carried cost around fifteen. Prices would be higher here, but it was still an exorbitant amount.

'It's a good price. No one else can sell you the rounds you need.'

'No one else will buy them. I don't reckon there's another Henry within five hundred miles of this place.'

'Then I'll hold on to them. Someone will want them. At my price.'

'I'd rather go without.'

'It's your choice.' The gunsmith smiled. The game was on. 'But then that fancy-ass rifle of yours ain't worth carrying, and you may as well sell it to me and get yourself something you can actually use. I'll do you a good price on a Maynard carbine.'

'I don't want a Maynard.' Jack looked the gunsmith in the eye. 'Seventy-five dollars, for everything, and you throw in a holster and gun belt for the Volcanic.'

'Done.' The gunsmith reached out a hand. 'You got yourself a deal.'

Jack shook the man's hand and even managed to smile. It was a small fortune, but it was also part of the money he had won from the wager with Brannigan. It was dirty money, tainted with blood, and he was happy to be rid of it. Besides, he was not spending it on himself. He had long ago learned the value of giving a gift.

He looked at Kat. 'So you like that thing?'

Kat made a face, as if she were unsure. 'I saw what your Henry did in the fight with Sinclair's fellows. That there Volcanic ain't the same, I know that much, but it's as close as I'm likely to be able to get down here. I could keep my Remington and put that on my other side.' She patted her left hip to demonstrate what she meant. 'Ten rounds out of that would sure give me options.'

She looked at Jack. She might be playing it cool, but he could see the desire in her eyes. She wanted the Volcanic.

'But I ain't paying that much for it.'

'You don't have to.'

'What do you mean?'

'It's yours. I'll keep the cartridges for my Henry. You get the Volcanic and its ammunition. I'm sure chummy over there will find you a gun belt that fits you.'

'What do you want in return?' Kat spoke bluntly, look-ing Jack dead in the eye. She did not glance away or play coy.

'Nothing.'

She arched her eyebrows. 'That the truth?'

'It is.'

'You swear it?'

'I swear.' Jack was lying, but he was good at that. He liked Kat, and he knew he would not be able to resist asking her for something more than friendship. It just waited to be seen if he would be gelded for his trouble, or if she would accept him for what he was.

'You sure about this, Jack?'

'It's Brannigan's money.' He found it easy to match Kat's smile. 'I didn't exactly earn it.'

'Then thank you. I'll find a way to repay you.'

'It's fine, honestly. It's my pleasure.' He held Kat's gaze. He did not mind spending the money. Money came and money went. It was not to be hoarded, or held fast for a rainy day that might never come. It was just another tool, like the weapons that he carried and the horse that he rode. It was a means to an end, nothing more.

Chapter Twenty

'Come on, I've got something I want to show you.' Kat made the offer as they walked away from the gunsmith's establishment. She was wearing the Volcanic on her left hip, its long holster close to the length of her thigh. It had taken a while to find a small enough gun belt. The one she now wore had only been unearthed after much rummaging around by the gunsmith, who had had to bore new holes in the leather so that it fitted her.

Neither spoke as they walked back through the town, then across the San Antonio River via a footbridge. It was only when their destination came into sight that Kat broke the silence.

'Have you heard the story of this place?'

'I've heard bugger all else all week from your bloody mates.'

'They don't have much in the way of conversation.' She smiled at Jack's exasperated tone. 'But they're good boys, every last one of 'em. If there's trouble, you'll be glad they're there.'

'I'm sure.' Jack believed her. Brannigan's men might not have much to say of interest, but they were a capable bunch who knew their trade.

They walked on. Jack could just make out the top of a

grand building over the walls that surrounded it. There was a gate in the south wall, and he could see a pair of bored sentries stationed outside, both wearing the pale grey of the Confederate army.

Kat led them straight towards the gate. To Jack's surprise, neither sentry bothered to challenge them, and he could only suppose that so many people came and went that the soldiers had long ago learned they were there for nothing more than decoration.

They walked through into a large plaza that was a good couple of acres in size. Thick walls surrounded it, and there were two single-storey stone buildings along the flanks. At the far end stood the mission. It was a two-storey building made from white stone, with a raised scalloped section in the centre of the upper storey that to Jack's eyes looked newer than the lower sections of the front facade. At its top flew the Stars and Bars flag of the Confederacy.

The plaza was buzzing with activity. From what Jack could see, the whole place had been turned into some sort of supply depot. A long line of wooden tables stretched along one wall, and dozens of offices and storage rooms had been erected around the stone buildings. At least a dozen wagons were parked in two neat lines to one side of the great plaza, and he could see what looked to be a blacksmith's forge tucked near one group of offices.

It was only as they approached the mission that Jack could see the scars of the battle Brannigan's men had talked of. There were pockmarks in the stone, and dozens of places where the walls had been patched with newer stone. He felt the fine hairs at the back of his neck tingle as he imagined the fighting that had taken place on the very spot on which he now stood.

He knew what it was like to be involved in such a fight. He had stormed enemy strongholds, first in Persia, and then again at Delhi. He remembered the fear of running towards the walls, and the way he had seemed to be moving so slowly no matter how hard he strained every muscle for speed. He remembered the feeling of helplessness as the first bullets spat into the earth around his boots, the moment of fear when there was nothing to be done save to run forward and pray not to be hit.

And he had been on the other side, mounting a desperate defence against the forces of a rebellious maharajah in the British cantonment at Bhundapur. He recalled the moment the maharajah's troops had launched their final assault, and just for a moment, he caught a whiff of something burning. It stirred the memories, bringing them to life with startling clarity. The smell coming from the blacksmith's forge turned into the taint of powder smoke, and he closed his eyes, seeing the defenders falling, men he had come to know and like dying as he stood with his small command, preparing to make their futile last stand.

'Are you all right, Jack?'

He opened his eyes to find Kat watching him closely. The memories swirled in his mind, refusing to disappear. He was back in the present, yet somehow still lost in the past. He felt the sun on his face, warming his skin, and he relished it, the heat forcing away the cold touch of death that had been released with the remembrance of his bitter history.

'I'm fine,' he replied, but his voice caught in his throat, betraying him.

'Do you want to talk?'

'No.' This time the single word came out firmly. He meant it. He did not want to talk.

'I wouldn't have brought you here if I'd known it would upset you so.' Kat reached out, her hand resting on Jack's upper arm.

Jack was aware that she was touching him, yet he could barely feel the placement of her fingers on his arm. He looked around, taking in the scene. There were many others nearby, bustling this way and that as they went about their business with purposeful steps. Yet somehow it felt as if they were the only ones present.

The melancholy air of the place wrapped around him once again, chilling and cold despite the sun's heat. He could almost see the ghosts then, the spirits that lived in this place of death, of suffering, making themselves known to him. They welcomed him into their world, recognising him as the killer he was. The faces of the dead started to flash past his eyes. They came in a great rush: people that he had loved and lost; those he had hated and killed. Others followed, some with names, then the legions he had slain in battle, their faces captured in perfect clarity at the moment of their death. They filled his mind so that he no longer saw the brightly sunlit plaza.

Something soft pressed against his lips. It lingered there, tender and calming. He felt warm breath whisper across his skin, the promise of life and more bringing him back to the present in a rush, the faces that haunted him whipped away and replaced by that of Kat as she kissed him.

He broke the kiss, pushing her from him. This was not the place. Not the time. He wanted her, he knew that, but not here, not when the dead surrounded him.

'Jack?' Her face revealed her confusion and concern.

'Let's go. Brannigan will wonder where we've got to.' His tone was made harsh by the sudden rush of desire. He shivered.

The memories left the cold buried deep inside him. Nothing, not even the touch of the woman in front of him, could warm him.

Kat searched his face, her eyes flickering back and forth, before she smiled and took a pace backwards, her hands falling to her sides. She said nothing as she turned her back and began to walk towards the gate.

Jack stood where he was, his eyes lingering on the woman he had pushed away. He sighed, wondering at his own sanity. Then he set off after her, knowing that the dead would come with him, just as they always did.

Chapter Twenty-one

———◆———

*J*ack walked across the rocky outcrop until he found a place where he could see the lie of the land ahead. The train had stopped for the day, and the wagons had been arranged into a defensive circle that Brannigan's men called a corral. The men themselves would not be allowed to rest. Some would be sent out immediately on picket duty, taking up sentry posts a few hundred yards away from the wagons to give warning should anyone approach. The rest would eat, then get what rest they could until it was their time for guard duty.

He pulled out his field glasses from their leather case and scanned the ground ahead, searching for something other than the dun, drab colours of the sandy wasteland through which they now trudged. He sighed. There was nothing to look at, nothing but mile upon mile of sod bloody all.

They had left San Antonio after two days of rest. The beginning of the journey had been spent travelling an undulating landscape dotted with fine oak trees and any number of creeks and streams. That pleasant rolling countryside had given way to a boundless prairie. There had been cattle feeding as far as the eye could see. It made for a dull ride, but the going for the wagons was good, and there was plenty of fodder for the animals.

They had stopped at a place called King's Ranch, the last major stop on the trail before they hit the infamous sands. There Brannigan had spent money like water to make sure his men would have all they would need. He had purchased dozens of hundred-pound boxes containing great hunks of bacon, which he had ordered to be filled with bran so that the fat on the meat would not melt away in the heat that was to come. They still had strips of beef from earlier in the journey, and more of it was bought to supplement the meat ration, along with salt, sugar, tobacco and butter. Then there was coarse flour in weighty sacks, along with crates of the inevitable hard-tack, and as many sacks of coffee beans as they could fit into the spare space in the wagons. Alongside these rations were great blocks of desiccated vegetables, the foul-tasting rock-hard substance that could be boiled into something that almost resembled a vegetable soup, and which was universally hated by every man in the wagon train.

Jack had been very interested to discover that Brannigan had also bought small sacks of antiscorbutic powder, which the cook would mix with water and essence of lemon to produce a drink that would prevent his men from developing scurvy. Few enjoyed it save for Vaughan, who claimed it to be more suited to his palate than the raw, rough whiskey that was purchased in large quantities and packed away with as much care as Brannigan's men could bestow.

At King's Ranch, Brannigan had also signed up four Tejanos. The men did not look like much, to Jack's eyes at least. All were a little ragged around the edges, their clothing weather-beaten, as though they had been on the trail for months on end without any respite. Jack had tried to speak to them just the once, but he had been rewarded with nothing more than a grunt and a look of disdain for his trouble. Since the moment they joined the gang, the Tejanos had kept themselves to themselves, even eating away from the rest of the group.

Not one of the Texans minded. Jack had overheard enough comments to know that the men of Brannigan's gang looked down on the Tejanos. It reminded him of the way the Hindus and Muslims had treated each other in India. The gulf between the two groups was simply too great for anyone to cross, their differences a chasm so deep and so wide that it would take more than a few well-meant comments to bridge. But for all their natural dislike and animosity, Brannigan's men were still happy to see the Tejanos at work, and they made up for some of the losses the wagon train had suffered at the hands of Sinclair's gang.

After King's Ranch, the wagon train had left the prairie behind. They now followed a trail through the wide, flat expanse known as the sands, a vast wasteland that was little more than one great sea of sand, broken only by a smattering of mesquite trees, prickly pear cactus, salt licks and rat ranches, the large molehills made from sticks and mud by the thousands of rats that called the place home. The sand covered Jack's clothing and worked its way into every nook, crease and crevice on his body. He could taste it in everything he ate, and he could sense it sticking in his throat after everything that he drank. When the wagon train stopped for the night, he was forced to spend hours cleaning his weapons to remove the grains that stuck to their every working part, knowing that they would be back there the next day, and the day after, and the day after that.

So far, the pernicious sand was the only enemy he had faced. None of the threats Brannigan had warned of had tried to interfere with their progress. Jack had talked with the other men. They all believed the wagon train would make it to Brownsville without any interference. They were certain that the tale of Sinclair's death would have spread far and wide. It would be a brave – or foolhardy – bandolero who would risk taking on Brannigan and his well-armed killers.

Jack lowered his field glasses then pulled out his canteen. He took no more than a mouthful of the warm, brackish water, then shook the canteen, listening to the sound of the liquid sloshing around inside. This far out, water was a precious resource, but he had learned in the violent heat of the Indian mofussil and the depths of the Persian desert to take care of his supplies. He would not run out before they were allowed a refill from the precious barrels that held the only water they would find as they traversed the sands.

The rocky outcrop he had chosen for his vantage point was crowned with a large mesquite tree that was at least fifty feet tall. The tough mesquites, with their vicious three-inch thorns, were one of the few living things that could survive in the sands, and they dotted the landscape, either standing alone or in forlorn huddles. Any near the trail were decorated with cotton snagged from the endless wagon trains that passed, the white fibres sticking out like spring blossom. The crooked trees also offered the men an emergency source of food: the seedpods they produced could be chewed raw or boiled until they were soft.

He lifted his field glasses again, then slowly panned around, taking in the great expanse of nothingness. He heard the soft scuff of footsteps as someone approached, but he did not let them interrupt his survey, and kept moving, scanning the landscape at his own speed.

'Brannigan wants you.'

Jack recognised the voice behind the summons easily enough. 'I'll be there directly.' He said nothing more as he finished his circle. Only then did he lower his glasses to look down at the man who had come to interrupt him.

'You need to go now.' Adam stood at the bottom of the outcrop. His face was flushed from the scorching heat.

'I'll be there directly.' Jack snapped the reply. Adam's enmity was wearing. The young man still hero-worshipped Brannigan, despite the beating he had received, aping his actions and manner in every way possible. Jack he despised.

'Don't you ever do what you're told?'

'It depends who's telling me.'

Jack put his field glasses back into their case, then started to clamber carefully down, checking the ground around his boots as he went. He had been warned about the rattlesnakes that infested the sands, but he had doubted the dreadful tales the men told of their dangerous nature right up until he had seen his first one. There was something in the rattle from the reptile's tail that had quite terrified him. Even seeing one of Brannigan's men grab the snake around the neck then sever its head with a bowie knife had done nothing to shift his new-found fear.

'Goddam Englishman.' Adam sneered, then turned away.

'What's your bloody problem, boy?' Jack gave his tongue free rein. He was hot and tired. The searing heat of the sands eroded everyone's temper, and at that moment, Adam's antagonism pushed his over the edge.

'You, you're my goddam problem.' Adam turned sharply on his heel. As ever, his hand fell to the revolver in its holster.

'You need to take that needle out of your balls, boy.' Jack scrambled down the last of the rocks and came to stand no more than six yards in front of Adam. 'And you need to learn to grow the fuck up.'

'And *you* need to stop telling everyone what to damn well do.' Adam took an angry pace forward. 'We're all sick of hearing your whiny English voice.'

'Is that so?' Jack turned his head to look away into the desert. He knew he should keep his temper in check. Nothing good could come of this confrontation. He held the pose, sucking his anger down. Only when he believed he had it under control did he turn back and start to walk towards the wagons.

'You don't like hearing the truth, huh?' Adam was doing his best to nettle Jack. Jack ignored him. 'That's it, keep on walking. Get back to your bedroll. You need some rest before you go back to licking Brannigan's ass.'

Jack stopped and held up a hand. 'That's enough, boy.'

'It's time it was said.'

Jack turned. He did not want the confrontation, but he would not avoid it. It had been coming for a while.

He took a few paces to one side, so that the sun was behind him and shining directly into Adam's face. 'So are you going to tell me what's bothering you, boy?'

'You.'

He pulled a face at such a poor answer. 'Come on, you can do better than that.'

Adam half sneered, half smiled as he got the quarrel he wanted. 'You like telling everyone what's what. It ain't so much fun hearing it.'

'And you're the big man who's going to tell me?'

'Mebbe.'

'Go on then.' Jack's temper was fraying. He stalked forward, closing the gap between him and the younger man.

Adam did not hesitate. His revolver was in his hand in a heartbeat, the muzzle aimed towards Jack.

'Are you going to shoot me?' Jack kept walking. He did not look at the revolver once. Instead he kept his gaze on Adam's eyes. 'You want to shoot me down, then here I am.' He spread his hands as he closed the distance between them. 'There ain't no one around to see it.' When he was just a yard away, he stopped. 'You want to kill me, then pull that fucking trigger.'

Adam's face contorted, his lips curling as if Jack was force-feeding him a turd.

'Killing a man up close and personal ain't easy, is it, boy?' Jack took a deliberate step forward so that the muzzle of Adam's revolver was against his breastbone. 'You want me dead? Then all you've got to do is pull that trigger.' He pressed forward, pushed the gun backwards. He held himself there for several long seconds; then, without warning, he snatched the revolver from Adam's hand.

'Seems you don't have the balls for killing.' His face was barely an inch from Adam's. 'I've seen you. You've got all the fancy tricks. Spinning that gun around your finger like it's a bloody toy. And I've seen you in a fight. You're good, I'll give you that. Brave, too. But it's easy when your enemy is far enough away that you can't see who it is you're shooting at. It's different when the man you want to kill is in your bloody face. When you can see his eyes. When you can see his soul.'

He had said enough. He reached out and pushed Adam in the chest with enough force to send the younger man staggering backwards. Then he turned on a sixpence and walked away, tossing the revolver into the dirt as he did so.

'You draw a gun on me again and I'll kill you.' He fired the warning without turning, confident that the lesson had been delivered. It had been needed. The lad was a fool who would get himself killed if he didn't wise up fast. Jack did not want to see that happen. Adam was still young. There was still time for him to learn.

Chapter Twenty-two

Brownsville, Texas

ack was heartily relieved when the wagon train rolled into Brownsville. It had been more than five weeks since they had left San Antonio, and after the best part of four hundred miles on the trail, the little Texan town looked a veritable Babylon. The simple houses lining the broad, straight streets were made of wood. The first ones they passed looked recently built, the wood still bright and yet to be weathered by the harsh, unforgiving climate. It spoke of a rapidly expanding settlement, the brisk and profitable trade across the Rio Grande enticing more and more people to live in this remote corner of the United States.

'I don't know about you, Jack, but I sure am glad to be back in civilisation.'

'You call this civilisation?' Jack tried to sound unimpressed. He had ridden into town with Vaughan at his side.

'Indeed I do. Give me a hot bath and the chance to read, and I promise you I shall be the happiest man alive.' Vaughan sighed at the expectation of such delights. 'Do you read, Jack?'

'Not much,' Jack answered honestly. He was literate. His mother had taught him his letters, and the colonel of his first regiment had been broad-minded enough to allow the brightest of his men a few hours a week in the barrack's library. 'I read the newspapers when I can.'

'That is good. A man should know what is going on in the world. But I really meant books, Jack. Books are what feed a man's soul. I look at you and I believe you are malnourished.' Vaughan paused, as if unsure whether to press on. 'I can lend you something, if you want?'

Jack considered the notion. 'I'd like that.'

'Excellent.' Vaughan seemed genuinely pleased to have secured his agreement. 'I have a copy of Thackeray's *Pendennis* that I think would suit you very nicely. I have but a few books with me. Back home, why, there is a whole library at my disposal.'

'Back home?'

'At Five Oaks.'

'And that's a plantation?' Jack did not try to hide his ignorance.

'Indeed it is. The finest in all Louisiana.' Vaughan's pride was obvious.

'So you have slaves there?' Jack could not help lacing the question with distaste. He had once hoped to make a new life with a runaway slave. That ambition, like so many over the years, had ended in grief and despair, and had left him with a deep-seated hatred of the institution of slavery.

'Of course.'

'And that doesn't bother you?'

'No.' Vaughan offered an easy smile. 'I know where you are going with this, Jack. Slavery is bad.' He said the words in a

stentorian tone of disapproval. 'Men who own slaves are evil.'
He continued in the same voice, then stopped to laugh at
himself. 'I take it you believe slavery is a wicked thing?'

'Isn't it?' For a moment, the image of Rose, the girl he had
loved, pushed its way into his mind. Even now, over a year
since he had lost her, it still had the power to hurt.

'Oh, it is, Jack. There is no arguing against that.'

'So then how do you live with it?' Jack forced the memory
of her face away by giving Vaughan his full attention. He had
expected a firm argument defending slavery. Yet the agent had
conceded the point immediately.

'I live with it and am content to do so.' Vaughan looked at
Jack and raised an eyebrow. 'I see your confusion. Let me
attempt to simplify matters for you. Have you been to a cotton
mill, Jack? I refer to one of the ones in your own country.'

'No.'

'A pity. I have. I enjoyed a memorable week touring the
north of England, where I visited a number of such establish-
ments.' Vaughan's tone had changed. All trace of mockery was
gone. 'The conditions there shocked me. Children barely able
to stand forced to work under these great thundering machines
for hours on end, despite the fact that dozens are maimed or
even killed each year. Men and women labouring tirelessly
with barely a rest, and in the foulest conditions our modern
inventions can create. I shall be honest with you, Jack. I looked
at the environment in which these countrymen of yours
worked, and I was ashamed. Ashamed that I supply the raw
material that leads to the creation of such hellish places.'

He paused and leaned across towards Jack. 'How do you
live with it?' He took Jack's question for his own and offered it
back to him in a much quieter tone of voice.

Jack did not answer, so Vaughan swayed back in the saddle and rode on. When he spoke again, his tone was flat. 'I shall not talk about the filth I saw in London. I would expect you know much better than I the conditions in which people there are expected to live their short, miserable lives. All I will say is that I saw the same squalor in every city I visited. And I will tell you this, Jack, and I say it without an ounce of shame. When I returned to Five Oaks, I felt nothing but pride. Pride for the lives our workers live and for the conditions we provide for them.

'Of course they are not free; I fully accept the iniquitous nature of their situation. But there are many types of slavery in this world, and I simply can't pretend that one is better than any other. I know there are places in this country of ours that are foul, and filled with evil men who perpetrate the worse kind of violations on the poor souls under their control. But not all are like that, and I know one thing with utter certainty. The conditions in which our workers live are a thousand times better than the miserable and wretched places that your own countrymen endure. Are they better for being *free*?' He laced the word with a fair dollop of sarcasm. 'I would say they are not. Not at all.'

Jack listened carefully to what Vaughan had said. There was some truth in the agent's words, yet he was not swayed. He had seen the legacy of an overseer's whip in the scars it had left on a young woman's face. There were many people who lived in misery. Yet no matter how wretched their lives, they still had something the slaves did not. They had freedom.

'You disagree with me, Jack?'

'Yes.' Jack spoke firmly. Sometimes one word said more than a dozen.

'I understand, indeed I do. But such things are rarely so

simple, so black and white, if you like. And sadly, it is the natural order of this world of ours. There have always been the haves and the have nots, and there will always be so, no matter how much we boast of improvements or believe we live in a civilised society. Rather than pretend such a situation does not exist, I simply acknowledge its existence. And of course, some people, some races perhaps, are more subservient in nature than others, just as some men are born to serve whilst others are born to lead. Just as you are.'

Jack held his tongue. There was much he could say, but he had long ago learned that you could not turn a man from a set opinion, no matter how forceful or telling your logic.

'I see I have not persuaded you, Jack.' Vaughan offered a wan smile as he watched Jack closely. 'I must say that pleases me. A man should have conviction in his opinions. We should agree to differ and leave the matter to those poor souls fighting for the right to decide which of us is correct.'

'Do you not feel the need to fight?' Jack held the conversation where it was. 'Men are dying so that plantations like yours can keep their slaves. Do you not want to help them?'

'There are many ways of serving a cause.' Vaughan gave the enigmatic answer without looking at Jack. 'And that includes providing an economic foundation for those who fight. Not every battle is won on the battlefield. Now then, let us turn our attention to this place. I take it you have not had the joy of visiting the delightful town of Brownsville before?'

Jack looked around him. The houses they now rode past were older, their wooden facades aged and weather-beaten. A few had broken windows or splintered door frames. 'It doesn't look very delightful.' He made the wry comment out of the side of his mouth.

'I would say that dear old Brownsville is the rowdiest town in all Texas, and if you took time to visit half the other towns in this state then you would understand what a bold claim that is.' Vaughan laughed heartily. He seemed pleased to have moved their conversation on to safer ground. 'But I tell you this, Jack, and it really is the darnedest thing. For all its raucous and unruly ways, I have never seen any injustice here.'

'Brannigan will have to watch himself then.' Jack spoke quietly. His attention was focused on the good folk of Brownsville, who were being drawn to the spectacle of the wagon train's arrival. He moved his hand so that it rested easily on the hilt of his holstered revolver. A few children ran alongside the train, earning themselves a curse, or even a flick of a whip from one of the more bad-tempered drivers when they ventured too close to the animals hauling the heavily laden wagons. Hard-eyed men stood in the shade of the nearest buildings, assessing the worth of the cotton and the calibre of the men who guarded it. There were few women about, and most of those he saw peered out from behind dust-streaked windows, as if too frightened to be outside.

'Do you trust him yet?'

'No.' Jack's answer was emphatic.

'He fought off an ambush. He protected the wagons. Does that not prove that he does what he is paid to do?'

'He won because I was there.' Jack grinned as he let his arrogance show. 'I saved his hide.'

'I heard.'

'Without me he'd be dead, and you'd be looking for someone else to guard your precious wagons.'

'Would that person be you?'

'No.'

'Are you not up to the job?'

'No.' Any good humour Jack felt evaporated as he gave the blunt and honest answer. Once he had considered himself a leader, an officer; a man who stood up and took charge when everyone else cowered or hid. Now he knew himself better. He knew the fear that hid deep inside his heart. He was not the man he had believed himself to be.

'I think you're wrong.' Vaughan watched him closely. 'I think you are born to lead men, even those as rough and ready as we have here.'

'Then it's you who are wrong.'

'Perhaps, though I am not often wrong.' It was Vaughan's turn to reveal a trace of arrogance. 'I think I am coming to know you, Jack. One day I may have to stake my very life on that opinion.'

'What do you mean?' Jack felt something close to anger, aware that Vaughan was trying to entangle him in some scheme. He had a sensation akin to fingers closing around his throat, the contact as light and delicate as a whore's touch, and just as fleeting.

'You'll see. If there's any justice in this world, then I shall not have cause to call on you. But something tells me that one day I will need your help.'

'There is no justice in this world.' Jack gave the cold answer in a frozen tone.

'You don't believe in justice?'

'No.'

'But you did.' Vaughan's eyes narrowed. 'Once at least, if not perhaps now. I can see it in you.'

'Then you need some damn spectacles,' Jack growled. He did not like the direction the conversation had taken.

Introspection was not one of his favourite pastimes, least of all when initiated by a comparative stranger.

Vaughan laughed. 'Perhaps I do, Jack. Perhaps I do. But we need justice in this world. I think you know that as well as I, perhaps better.'

'You should be talking to Brannigan, not me.' Jack sought to deflect the conversation.

'You think Brannigan does not understand justice?'

'Ask that Sinclair fellow.'

'You don't think he deserved to be left like that?'

Jack did not answer immediately. He thought back to the way Sinclair had been left. Brannigan's treatment of his adversary had been cruel, he knew that, and he felt a certain pride at having ended it. But Sinclair's corpse had still been left tied to the wagon's wheel, the gruesome sight a warning to any of his men who might return. Jack supposed it made no difference if the man had been left alive or dead, the warning, and the outcome, the same.

'No,' he said finally. 'He was as good as dead. He had lost. That's enough for anyone, I would say.'

'Perhaps.' Vaughan did not conduct a defence. 'But perhaps Brannigan knows what he is doing.'

'Perhaps. But he could have put Sinclair in a hole in the ground. I think his men would still have understood the message well enough.'

'Is that what you would have done, Jack? Do you always bury the men you have killed?'

'No.'

'Why?'

'Because that's war. I'm a soldier. It's different for us.' Jack heard the snap in his answer, so he forced himself to pause and take a breath. He had felt a moment's pride at his declaration; one that he did not deserve to feel. He had left his pride behind on the blood-soaked field at Shiloh.

Vaughan was watching him closely. 'I happen to agree with you. Soldiers are a different breed. They should not be held to the same account.'

'Why do you say that?'

'Because they do things we cannot comprehend. They are witness to the foulest depredations of man, and yet we expect them to hold on to their humanity, and to live amongst us as if they are normal men.'

'Have you fought?' Jack heard something underscoring Vaughan's words.

'I was at Manassas.'

'Where?' Jack fired the question back. He had fought for the Union at the same battle, which the Northern forces had called Bull Run.

'I was late to arrive. I came with Jackson from the Shenandoah Valley. We arrived in time to hold the hill on the eastern flank.'

Jack drew in a sharp breath as the memories of that day flooded through him. He had served in the 1st Boston Volunteer Militia. Along with dozens of other Union regiments, they had been ordered to flank the Confederate position that was lined up on the bank of the Bull Run River, not far from the strategic railroad junction at Manassas. They had fought hard, suffering badly against the brave Confederate soldiers, who stubbornly held their ground against superior Union numbers.

The flanking attack had pushed on through the long hours of that burning-hot day. Finally they had forced the Confederate defenders back. Jack had been in the blue-coated ranks when they had advanced for the last time. That advance had been on the point of success when thousands of Confederate reinforcements had arrived to snatch victory from the jaws of defeat. The 1st Boston had been broken and, like the rest of the Union army, forced to retreat. Now Jack rode alongside one of the men who had stood on the same ground, but on the opposite side; one of the men who had secured the Confederate army their first victory. One of the men who perhaps had killed those he had come to think of as friends.

'I was too late to see much fighting.' Vaughan spoke almost reverentially. 'I take it from your reaction that you were there too.'

Jack nodded.

'It was a hard day. We buried the dead the next day. I have never seen so many bodies.'

'I have.' Jack's voice was cold. 'After Solferino.' He said nothing more for a moment.

'I have not fought since.' Vaughan filled the silence. 'I came home a few months later.'

'Were you injured?'

'Not that you would be able to see.'

Jack frowned. It was an odd answer.

'And now here I am.' Vaughan kept talking. 'And so, it appears, are my former brothers in arms.'

Jack looked ahead. For the first time he saw the mounted soldiers waiting a hundred yards ahead of the column.

The Confederate army had arrived.

Chapter Twenty-three

The cavalrymen blocked the trail. There were perhaps as many as forty riders present. All were dressed in grey flannel shirts and trousers, and tall black boots with oversized spurs. Each man wore a large black felt hat decorated with the lone star of Texas on the front. It was a uniform of sorts, but the men were rough and dirty-looking, as if they had been wearing the same clothes for months.

One man at the front of the group carried a flag that Jack had not seen before. It was based on the familiar Confederate national flag, with the usual three bars of the same size, the top and bottom ones red and the middle one white. Instead of being decorated with small stars representing the states that formed the Confederacy, the blue canton in the top left corner was decorated with a five-pointed red star that was itself embellished with eleven smaller white stars, two on each point of the main star and one large one in the centre. On the white bar was a shield containing a single star and the word 'Texas'.

All the men were armed with carbines or shotguns. From what Jack could see, the weapons were clean and well cared for. The Confederate cavalrymen clearly knew what was important. Some carried six-shooters, mainly Colt Navy revolvers, whilst nearly all had a bowie knife attached to their belt. A few sported a lasso attached to the saddle, and he saw at least half a dozen armed with an Indian tomahawk. They might look a scruffy bunch, but they were as well armed as any cavalry squadron he had ever come across, and he was sure they would be more than a match for Brannigan's men in any kind of fight.

'Do you know them?' he asked Vaughan as they both tapped back their heels and forced their horses into a trot. Already the train was coming to a halt as the group of cavalrymen man-oeuvred into position to block its route a few hundred yards ahead of the lead wagon. Jack and Vaughan were not the only ones riding forward. Jack looked back to see Brannigan, Adam and Kat coming up the far side of the wagon train. They had been well to the rear, so he and Vaughan would be left alone to greet the newcomers.

'I do indeed.' Vaughan sounded slightly breathless as he answered Jack's question. 'They are stationed here to guard the crossing into Mexico.'

Jack did his best to run his eye over the men blocking their way.

'Dawson, you dog!' To Jack's surprise, it was Vaughan who shouted out in greeting.

A man at the head of the column looked back at him and waved. Jack supposed he had to be some kind of officer, but he looked as dishevelled as his men and bore no obvious markers of rank.

'You sure took your goddam time getting here.' Dawson made the wry remark in lieu of a greeting.

'We were delayed.' Vaughan gave the answer as they came

to the head of the stationary wagon train. 'Where were your men when we needed them, Captain? I thought your orders were to protect people like us.'

'We heard you had some trouble,' Dawson countered with an easy smile. 'We figured you and Brannigan would be fine without our help. Looks like we were right, too.'

'You might not have said that if it were not for my new friend here.' Vaughan gestured towards Jack.

'Well, I'm sure glad you had help.' The Confederate captain nodded at Jack. 'Who might you be, friend?'

'Jack Lark. Pleased to meet you.' Jack nodded curtly as he looked Dawson over. The man sat easily in the saddle, leaning forward with his left forearm resting on the pommel, his hat tipped back to reveal a sweaty mop of dark brown hair. Like nearly all the men who lived in these unforgiving borderlands, he was as lean as a whippet, with hard blue eyes and skin that had been tanned and weathered by the sun.

'You found an Englishman all the way out here, Vaughan?' Dawson guffawed as he identified Jack's accent.

'Where a leaf moves, underneath you will find an English-man. At least that is what the Farsi say, is it not, Jack?' Vaughan smiled at Jack as he showed off his knowledge.

'They have that right, whoever the hell they are.' Dawson looked over Vaughan's shoulder as the others arrived. 'Why there you are, Brannigan, I was wondering where you were hiding.'

'Dawson.' Brannigan did not bother with anything more polite. 'What has brought you here?'

'Just doing my job, nothing more.' Dawson's expression betrayed that there was no love lost between the two men. 'We need to make sure you have the right permits this time.'

Brannigan reined in his horse, then sat as still as a statue as he glared at the Confederate officer.

'That was a misunderstanding and well you know it.' It was Vaughan who added a dose of conviviality to the atmosphere, which had quickly turned hostile. 'This time I assure you that all is in order. Dare I suggest that we go somewhere a little more comfortable to look at the paperwork?'

'This'll do well enough.' Dawson did not move.

'Very well, if you insist.' Vaughan did not seem the least bit put out by Dawson's recalcitrance. He tapped back his heels, then walked his horse forward until he was within arm's reach of the officer. He reined in, then fished into a saddlebag and, after a moment's rummaging, produced a thin wad of papers. 'Everything is in order, I vouch for it.'

'You would say that.' Dawson sat upright as he took hold of the papers, which he did not so much as glance at before he turned and held them out to one of his men, who had ridden forward to take them. 'Is that all you've got for me?' He looked at Vaughan with disapproval.

'Ah.' Vaughan purred at Dawson's reaction, as if he had been waiting for it. 'Of course not.' He fished into the same saddlebag, this time producing a thick wedge of grey banknotes held together with twine. 'A little something for your trouble.' He tossed the bundle casually to Dawson.

'Greybacks?' Dawson caught the stack of Confederate dollars and considered it, his face betraying his disapproval. 'Is that all you think me and my boys are worth?' He turned the bundle of notes back and forth in his hand before shoving it deep in his own saddlebag.

'It is the currency of the Confederacy. You are a Confederate officer. I really don't see a problem.' Vaughan could not help a sly smile as he replied in an urbane tone.

'It's got about the same value as horseshit down here, as well you know.' There was the first sign of annoyance in Dawson's tone. 'And we sure have got ourselves one hell of a lot of goddam horses.'

'You expect something more?' It was Brannigan who answered. 'You already have the permits signed by Quartermaster Hart himself. We have paid you and your men for your trouble. I would say our business here is done.'

Dawson stared back at Brannigan. He did not reply immediately. The only sound that broke the silence was that of Dawson's men shifting in their saddles as they understood the change in the tone of the conversation, and prepared for any order their commander might give.

'Have you got yourself a problem there, Brannigan?' When Dawson spoke, his tone was openly belligerent.

'Not if you move aside, I don't.' Brannigan's words came out deadpan.

'We'll move aside when our job here is done.' Dawson's expression revealed nothing.

'It is done.'

'It's done when I say it's done and not before.' The officer sat up straight in his saddle. 'You challenging my authority here?'

'You have what was agreed. Now step aside.' Brannigan's words came out wrapped in iron.

'I'll step aside when I'm good and goddam well ready.' Dawson's hand slipped towards the revolver on his hip.

Jack watched the exchange with interest. The pair reminded him of two bull mastiffs before a dog fight. They were watching one another, wondering when they would be slipped free of the leash and given the order to tear the other's throat out.

'Now, gentlemen, please.' Vaughan spoke with surprising force. 'There really is no need for this.' He slipped a hand into the saddlebag that had already produced the papers and the Confederate dollars. 'I am sure we can sort this out in good humour.'

He pulled out a small oilcloth sack closed with a thick leather strap. He weighed the sack in his hand for a moment, listening as it chinked gently. Only when he was happy with its weight did he toss it casually towards Dawson, who snatched it from the air with aplomb.

'Thank you kindly.' The Confederate officer nodded his approval, then turned to pass the sack to one of his men. 'Specie is the only true currency in these parts. I'm glad one of you fellas knows what you're about.'

Dawson glanced at Brannigan and flashed a humourless smile. 'Now that that is out of the way, why don't you all come with us? Get yourselves out of the goddam sun for a while.'

'That is very kind of you, Dawson,' Vaughan replied with forced bonhomie. 'I rather think Brannigan and his men will need to stay with the wagons, but I am sure Jack here would enjoy the chance to share in some conversation.'

'Well then, it sounds like we got ourselves a plan.' Dawson nodded briefly at Jack before he turned his attention to Kat and Adam, who had sat silent behind Brannigan during the short confrontation. 'It's good to see you, Kat. Perhaps you'd care to accompany these good gentlemen here. Adam, you can come too, if you like.'

'That is kind.' Kat smiled her thanks.

'I need them to do some work.' Brannigan spoke before she could say anything further. 'I can spare those two, for a while anyways.' He nodded dismissively towards Jack and Vaughan.

'Why that sure is mighty generous of you, Brannigan.' Dawson beamed at the wagon master. 'I thank you for your consideration.'

'It is good of you, Brannigan.' It was Vaughan's turn to step into the conversation. 'If you can spare us for a little while, then it might be useful to hear what Captain Dawson can tell us of what lies ahead on the trail.'

'Call it what you will.' Brannigan was not in the least mollified by Vaughan's smooth answer. 'Just be back before nightfall.'

'We will indeed.' Vaughan nodded his thanks, then turned to smile at Jack. 'It seems we have been given some time off for good behaviour,' he murmured.

The Confederate cavalrymen turned their horses around, and Jack kicked back his heels to follow as they rode back the way they had come. For his part, he was pleased to accept the Confederate captain's invitation. It might present the opportunity of some better conversation than Brannigan and his men offered, and there was always the chance that Dawson might just have some tea.

Chapter Twenty-four

Jack rode into the Confederate encampment and immediately felt a sense of returning home. The cavalrymen had clearly been in Brownsville for an extended period. Most of their camp had been given over to wooden huts, the men stationed on the border building themselves some comfortable quarters. The huts were roughly made but snug, with bunk beds and trestle tables with benches. There was a sense of permanence to the place, but as he dismounted, he noticed that a good half of the huts, perhaps more, were empty.

'What do you think?' Dawson asked.

'It looks like you've done a good job of making yourselves at home.' Jack looked around. It had been a while since he had spent any time with soldiers. He felt a sense of profound longing. He had convinced himself that he was at his happiest living alone. Yet the feelings being stirred deep inside him made a mockery of that belief. The yearning to belong again was strong.

A soldier came to take the reins of his mare, whilst others did the same for Dawson and Vaughan.

'My boys will look after the horses for you.' Dawson gave

an easy smile, then gestured for Jack to walk on. 'For you fine gentlemen, I have some coffee.'

'Any tea?' Jack could not help the question.

'Tea?' Dawson repeated the word in what he clearly thought was a fine English accent. 'No, I'm afraid we are out of tea.' He laughed at his own humour, then clapped Jack on the shoulder. 'It's coffee or whiskey, my friend, that's all we simple folk drink down here.'

'Coffee will be just fine.' Vaughan answered for them both.

'Then step this way, gentlemen.' Dawson paused to retrieve his saddlebags from his horse, then led them towards the centre of the encampment. 'Most of my boys are out on the trail, so there should be something for us to drink. Something to eat too, if you're hungry.'

'That would be kind.' Jack was looking around him as he walked, taking in the details of the encampment. It was a well-tended affair, the huts arranged in neat rows. Other, larger structures had been built: stores, and a cookhouse with large trestle tables arranged outside it. It was to one of these that Dawson led them.

'You fellas take yourself a seat and let me go see what I can rustle up.'

He disappeared into the cookhouse and Jack and Vaughan did as they were told. It did not take long for him to reappear.

'Coffee will be out directly. Some johnnycakes too.' He took a seat opposite Jack and slung his saddlebags on to the table. He was keeping them close.

A few minutes later, one of Dawson's men delivered a pot of coffee, a thin trail of steam emerging from its spout, along with three tin mugs and a plate stacked with round golden-brown cakes. Dawson purred as the delivery was placed in front of him. He poured three mugs quickly without spilling a drop, then pushed one in front of each of his guests.

'We're lucky that so many of the boys are out and about.' He helped himself to a johnnycake and took a huge bite. 'There's no way in hell there'd be any of these left if they were all here.'

'What are they doing?' Jack asked as he too reached for a cake. He took a cautious bite, then paused as the taste flooded his mouth. The johnnycake was still warm, and it was simply delicious.

'Patrolling the trail. Taking note of who is coming and going, that sort of thing.' Dawson spoke with his mouth full, splattering crumbs from his lips without a care.

'Are there no Union forces down here?' Jack only asked the follow-up question when his own mouth was empty.

'Union? No, them Yankee sons of bitches are busy enough up north. Of course they took Galveston back in October. They didn't hold it for long, mind. And they tried to take Corpus Christi too, till we persuaded them otherwise. Now they leave us well alone; been concentrating on New Orleans and those folk over there in Louisiana. But don't you worry none about finding trouble, if that's what you're after. There's plenty of other folk looking to get in our way down here. It's our job to keep the trail open so good men like Brannigan can get where they're going.' Dawson rammed the remains of his johnnycake into his mouth and reached for another.

'And to charge them for the privilege,' Vaughan interjected.

'Well, now.' Dawson grinned at the rebuke hidden in Vaughan's words. 'You know that's just a little thank you between friends.'

Vaughan ignored the reply and looked directly at Jack. 'What Dawson here is not telling you is that he and his men are more than happy to charge a toll for their services, whether they actually provide them or not.'

'Aren't they just obeying orders?' Jack finished his cake and reached for his coffee. It was a poor substitute for tea, but it would do to wash the dust from his throat.

'Orders?' It was Dawson who replied. 'Oh, I got my orders all right. And I follow them to the goddam letter, let me assure you of that. But a man's got to eat.' He smiled wolfishly, then stuffed another chunk of johnnycake into his mouth. 'So we charge a little to smooth the way for people like my old friend here.' He showed no shame as he freely admitted what he was doing.

'What happens if they don't want to pay? If they expect you to just do the job you were ordered to do?' Jack's dislike of the Confederate cavalry officer was growing by the minute.

'Well, you know.' Dawson shook his head, as if saddened by what he was about to say. 'This here's a right dangerous place. There's all sorts of miscreants and goddam bush-whackers just waiting to take that fine cotton of yours for themselves. We try our best to protect you and all, but often times there just ain't nothing we can do. But if you pays us a little – and it is just a little when you think about how much that damn cotton of yours is worth – then we'll do all we can to make sure you get where you're wanting to go.'

Jack heard the words that were left unsaid. If Dawson and his men weren't paid, misfortune would likely befall anyone trying to cross into Mexico.

'Don't be fooled, Jack.' Vaughan eased himself to his feet. 'We know the arrangement here, and we're happy to pay. Now,

I need to walk my horse. Have you moved the latrines yet, Dawson?'

'Not yet. They're still in the same old place. You might want to wrap a neckerchief around your face. The smell can be kinda strong if you ain't used to it.'

Vaughan grimaced at the words but still walked away, leaving Jack and Dawson alone.

'So were you a serving man, friend?' Dawson had eaten his fill of cake and now started on his coffee.

'What makes you ask?' Jack was wary. He did not trust the man sitting opposite him one inch, just as he didn't yet trust Vaughan. The plantation agent was too smooth and too slick. And he played games. In Jack's experience, men like Vaughan used people for their own ends and nothing more, no matter how friendly or affable they appeared to be. He did not doubt that Dawson was cut from the same cloth.

'The way you carry yourself. The way you look about the place. That sword you wear.' Dawson paused to slurp down some coffee. 'I ain't prying none. A man's past ain't no one's business but his own. But you look like a soldier to me, that's all.'

'I was.'

'An officer too, if I ain't mistaken.'

Jack nodded.

'I knew it.' Dawson grinned at his own cleverness. 'I bet you've got a tale to tell.'

'Maybe.'

Jack's reserved answer only broadened Dawson's smile. 'You don't say much, do you now?' He shook his head, then reached out for the coffee pot to refill his mug.

'Depends who asking.' Jack couldn't help some snap peppering his reply.

'I ain't prying.'

'That's good.' He sucked down his aversion to the man, and asked a question of his own. 'So do you think we'll be attacked between here and the coast?'

'Maybe you will. We dealt with some of Santiago's boys not far from the trail to Matamoros just a little whiles ago. Could be there's more around here that might want to cause you some trouble.'

'I've heard of him.' Jack remembered the name from his discussion with Brannigan.

'Then you know he's a vicious son of a gun.' Dawson looked ready to spit.

'Have you met him?'

'No. No one has, or at least no one has lived long enough to tell the tale of what he looks like.' Dawson shook his head. 'Hell, if I did see him, well, I'd shoot the son of a bitch right between the goddam eyes as soon as I clapped eyes on him. That man is a monster. Got more men killed than any of them Yankee generals.'

Jack tried to keep his face neutral. He did not agree with Dawson's choice of comparison. This bandit leader might be a vicious outlaw, but nothing he could do could compare to the slaughter that was being committed on battlefields across the country. 'So what makes him so bad?'

'Santiago is a killer, pure and simple. That man ain't got a merciful bone in his body. If he captures you, he kills you.'

'And you've seen that?'

Dawson looked away and stared into the distance. 'I've seen it.' The words were spoken softly. 'Just a few weeks ago, his men captured a wagon train south of the Grande. Killed every man with it, and their women too, 'cept those poor girls got themselves a little special treatment first, if you know what I mean.'

Jack knew just what he meant, but he did not look away from the smug expression that had spread across Dawson's face as he described the fate of the wagon train. 'What did you do about it?' He asked the question that he knew Dawson wanted to be asked.

'What did we do? Why, we tracked those sons of bitches down, then killed every last one. Left two of 'em behind as a warning too.'

'You think that will deter this Santiago fellow?'

'Hell no! But Señor Santiago doesn't do the dirty work hisself. His Ángeles do that for him, and it might just stop some of them from following the son of a bitch. You know that folk round here call them Los Ángeles de la Muerte?'

'I know. Brannigan told me.'

'Did he tell you that Santiago killed two dozen of my men?' For the first time, real emotion entered Dawson's voice in place of his usual glib and boastful tone. 'Left the wounded with their bellies cut wide open so that any varmint that came along could feast on their flesh.'

'No.'

'Did he tell you that dear old Santiago is not above taking any women he captures and forcing them to whore for his men until they tire of them, whereupon he cuts their throats and dumps their bodies wherever he happens to be?'

'No.'

Dawson's gaze bored into Jack. 'I tell you this. If you ever see that son of a bitch, you either kill him right there and then, or else you run like the goddam wind before he kills you.'

'Thank you for the advice.' Jack held Dawson's penetrating

stare. There was no hiding the passion in the man as he talked about the bandit. It was rare to see such hatred on open display. 'So why don't you gather your men and track this Santiago fellow down? Deal with him once and for all.'

'You suppose I didn't think of that? We've tried, more than once. But Santiago knows what he's about. He's got those Union boys helping him now. Our old friends in the north are quite happy to supply him and his bandoleros, so long as they attack us. They claim to fight for the Union, but they're still just murdering sons of bitches. Raiding, thieving . . .' Dawson paused and held Jack's stare, 'killing.'

'How many of them are there in this gang?'

'Two hundred, maybe more. They don't hang around long enough for us to conduct a goddam survey.'

Jack raised his eyebrows. He could understand Dawson's problem. He had an enemy that fought on its own terms, and with its own methods, all of them vicious. His war was not a straightforward one where both sides lined up on a battlefield ready to kill and be killed. It was a war of ambushes and raids, where rape and murder were commonplace. Jack did not like the man, but he could sympathise. At least a little.

'Can I give you a piece of advice?' Dawson leaned forward, his gaze intense.

'Go on.'

'Don't go underestimating those bandoleros. They may look like crap, but they can sure fight. If they come for the wagons, you'll have to fight hard to stop them.'

'Won't you be there to defend us?' Jack made the wry comment without a hint of a smile.

'We can't be everywhere.'

'So why did Vaughan pay you?'

'Because if he didn't, I would've impounded his wagons and conscripted his men. Half of them are goddam outlaws or deserters anyways. Hell, I'd be doing my duty if I put them behind bars.'

'You can do that?'

'I can do just about anything I want down here.' Dawson smiled, but it didn't reach his eyes. 'But don't you worry none. If those bandoleros are still around, me and my boys'll find 'em. We'll deal with them too.'

'If you're there.'

Dawson laughed. 'That's right, Jack, if we're there. If we're not, well,' he shrugged, 'there's not a whole lot we can do about it!'

He was still laughing as Vaughan returned from the latrines.

'I see you two are getting on famously,' Vaughan commented.

'We are that.' Dawson answered for both of them.

For his part, Jack reached for another johnnycake. He had no faith in Dawson. The man was obviously there for the money alone. It was clear, to his mind at least, that if the wagon train was attacked, Brannigan's men would have to fend for themselves.

Chapter Twenty-five

———◆———

Jack lay back on the bed in the boarding house and savoured the sensation. After weeks of sleeping on nothing more than a bedroll, the moth-eaten and lumpy mattress on the iron bed frame felt wonderful. Not even the pervading odour of the room could spoil the moment, the potent mixture of piss and sweat the legacy of the thousand or more teamsters who had spent a night in the simply furnished room.

He had been lying there for no more than a minute when there was a knock at his door.

He laboured to his feet with a groan, the movement sending a spasm of pain shooting up and down the back of his legs. It was bad enough to make him pause, his hands moving to the pit of his spine.

A second knock followed the first.

'For fuck's sake, all right.' He did not bother to hold back the cantankerous response. He wanted peace, just for a moment or two, yet already he was being disturbed. 'What is it?' he snapped as he slipped back the bolt then opened the door.

'Well, that sure is a fine welcome.' Kat stood there, her arms folded across her chest.

'It's all you're going to get.' Jack felt his crabbiness shift as he saw just who it was that had come to disturb him, yet he tried not to reveal it. 'What do you want?' He delivered the line deadpan, and was pleased with his choice of tone.

'I wanted to speak with you for a moment.'

'Well, here I am.'

'I wanted to thank you for my pistol.' Kat's hand dropped to her left side, where she wore the long-barrelled Navy Volcanic. Her familiar Remington was on her right. The combination of weapons would allow her to fire off sixteen shots in a short space of time, firepower that was unheard of in a world of single-shot muskets and carbines and six-shot revolvers.

'You did that already.' Jack saw through the answer immediately. It was a poor attempt to divert the conversation away from her real reason for seeking him out. It also did precious little to distract him from the licentious thoughts that were beginning to rampage across his mind. He did not truly hold out hope that the thanks she wanted to deliver included pushing him back into the room so they could be alone, but just the notion was enough to shorten his breath and make his heart pump that little bit faster.

Kat stood there a moment without speaking. Then she took a step towards him before lowering her voice. 'I wanted to warn you.'

'About what?'

'Vaughan.'

'Go on.' Jack forced himself to concentrate on her words. Now that she was closer, he had caught the faintest whiff of her scent. Against the stink of urine that emanated from his room, it was intoxicating.

'You mustn't trust him.'

'I don't.' Jack searched Kat's eyes as she delivered her warning. He had been around enough women in his life to be reasonably good at reading emotions. But he had not the faintest clue what he saw reflected in her gaze. Was it fear, or cunning, or just nothing much at all? One thing he did not see was desire. 'Why are you telling me this now?'

'I saw you go off with him when we got here.'

'We were just talking.'

'Were you?' Kat frowned. 'That man's got himself the tongue of a goddam serpent. He's as slippery as an eel, too and he can talk the hind legs off a mule with all those fancy words of his.'

'I'll be careful.'

Kat shook her head, as if disappointed by his response. 'You need to be more than careful.'

'I can look after myself.' Jack wondered why Kat had felt compelled to give him the cryptic warning. 'What about Brannigan?' He asked a question of his own, to prolong the conversation as much as anything else. 'Should I trust him?'

'That's for you to decide.'

'But you do?'

'He's looked after me and kept me safe. Looked after my brother too until he got his head filled with nonsense and went off to fight for the damn rebels.'

'And that makes you trust him?'

Kat did not answer immediately. Instead she stared at Jack, as if trying to discern whether she could safely say more. 'I know him.' The words came out flat.

'And you stay with him, even though you could've left with your brother.'

'I've got no place else to be right now.' She took a half-step closer. 'Why are *you* here, Jack?'

'I've got no place else to be right now.' He mimicked her answer.

'Why's that?'

'That would be telling.'

Kat offered the slightest hint of a smile. 'You don't talk much, do you?'

'There's nothing much to tell.'

'Well, that's a lie. I reckon you got a whole lot to tell.' Her eyes flickered back and forth as she searched his gaze for something. Whatever she was looking for, she didn't find it. She stepped back. 'Just be on your guard around Vaughan.'

She opened her mouth as if about to say more, but then clearly thought better of it. Instead, she turned and walked away, leaving Jack standing in the doorway doing his best to understand the odd conversation. He did not know what she had intended, but she had sown the seeds of distrust. A mind like his was a fertile place for such a crop. He already trusted no one but himself, and he had needed no warning to continue to do so.

Jack turned in the saddle, looking back at the Rio Grande and the ferry that had brought them across its turbulent waters. He had not enjoyed the crossing, and he was heartily glad to be back on solid ground.

The area to the south of the river looked a little different to that around Brownsville. There were the usual thickets of mesquite trees, but nearer the river were dense swathes of huisache and juniper bushes, some up to seventy feet tall. Far off in the distance he could see a long chain of mountains that broke up the horizon and promised something other than more of the same desolate terrain that was all he had seen for days on end.

For once, there was something almost beautiful in the desolate landscape, something majestic. The sky was enormous, the great expanse of blue broken up only by a few wispy clouds. It was enough to make a man feel very small, yet at the same time part of something greater. Jack looked at the world around him and saw its beauty, then grunted as he acknowledged the strangeness of such a sentimental feeling. He put it down to their being close to their destination, the promise of some respite from the brutally hard trail weakening his resolve to remain detached from a world that usually delivered nothing but pain and discomfort.

They had a ride of around a mile to the Mexican town of Matamoros, their final destination. The route they would follow was clearly well used, and the wagons immediately began to kick up a huge cloud of dust. Once at Matamoros, they would deliver the cotton to the merchants who waited there, before purchasing the weapons and ammunition that they would then transport back to Confederate territory, to the grey-clad army that needed them so badly.

The first part of their long journey was almost complete.

The wagon train reached Matamoros late in the afternoon. It did not take long for Jack to decide that the town had little to recommend it. From what he could see, its nine thousand inhabitants had been through some tough times. Many of the buildings on the outskirts bore the scars of battle, their facades liberally scattered with bullet holes and broken stone. Vaughan had told him tales of the fighting that had broken out back in '61, when the cotton trade was only just beginning, the various factions that had tried to control the burgeoning trade scrapping it out until the great cotton barons had secured control of the town.

As they approached the centre, it became clear that the town was thriving. Fine red-brick buildings lined the streets, and as the wagon train pulled to a halt near a large plaza surrounded by iron railings, Jack could see that the place was teeming with life, whilst every building seemed to be engaged in some form of commerce.

Many belonged to the large commercial firms that had established themselves here to exploit the cotton trade. He had seen dozens of names on his way to the town's centre, and even two from back home, with Harding, Pullin and Company of London and Lloyd's of London both occupying large buildings that overlooked the plaza. The town also boasted its own cathedral, and he had noted the presence of a British consulate, a building that pointed towards the importance his cotton-hungry country gave to this place.

Alongside the offices and buildings connected to the cotton trade were the boarding houses, stores, saloons, dining rooms and brothels that catered to the needs of the men who transported the great bales of cotton. Those men were there in their hundreds. Vaughan had told Jack that ten stage-coaches made the journey each day from the village of Bagdad, twenty-five miles away on the coast, bringing a stream of seamen from every country in the world, along with as many smugglers and swindlers as could be found. All were drawn to the ready cash of the cotton trade, and the fortunes that were being made on the back of it.

Yet for all the finery of some of its buildings, and the prosperity that they alluded to, the town of Matamoros stank. The streets were filthy, with no pavements, and the roadway itself was deeply rutted. With so many people filling the town, water was scarce; every drop had to be carried in from the river by a constant stream of men and donkeys. Food and stores were horribly expensive, and Vaughan had warned Jack to keep a close eye on his possessions, the town lousy with pickpockets and thieves.

Jack was given the perfect example of the dangers of the place within five minutes of their arrival. Even before he had had a chance to dismount, a diligence made a noisy arrival nearby, a rowdy crowd of men surrounding it the moment it came to a halt, all of them pointing and laughing. The coach was covered in dust, but Jack could see no other reason for the noisy reception that had greeted its arrival. Yet it soon became clear that all was not well behind the coach's drawn curtains. As he watched, a hasty transaction was completed between whoever hid there and a fat Mexican who had arrived carrying a bundle of clothing.

'What's going on over there?' He fired the question at one of Brannigan's men who was nearby.

'Those sorry sons of bitches have gone and got themselves robbed.' Brannigan's man hooted with glee as he replied. 'Those bandoleros will have stripped 'em naked. Taken every last thing they own.'

'Does that happen a lot?'

'Often enough for that fat son of a gun over there to be waiting here ready to sell them a pair of pants for ten dollars! And that's only if he thinks they'll be good for the money.'

Jack looked back at the coach and saw clothing being thrown inside. He did not wait to see the unfortunate fellows who had been robbed. It was another example, if one were needed, that he was living in a world without rules, one where danger lurked around every corner.

Chapter Twenty-six

---

*B*rannigan did not let his men linger for long. The train stayed in the centre of town until he and Vaughan had presented their documents inside one of the red-brick buildings. As soon as the pair returned, the wagons headed down to the wharves, where the cotton was unloaded by what looked to Jack's eyes to be at least a thousand Mexican stevedores. It was then carried on to a pair of paddle steamers, which would transport it along the Rio Grande to Bagdad. From there, freighters would take it on to Veracruz, and the deep-draught merchantmen that waited for it at the port.

The first transaction completed, the wagons rolled back the way they had come, then turned away from the centre of Matamoros. A short while later, they lined up outside a huge wooden warehouse. Again the teamsters sat back and watched as more Mexicans worked tirelessly to reload the wagons with long wooden crates filled with rifles, and smaller ones packed with cartridges.

Jack could not resist taking a look. He slipped out of the saddle and made his made to one of the first wagons to be fully loaded. According to the stencilled letters on the wooden lids, these crates contained 1853 Pattern Enfield rifle muskets made by the Birmingham Small Arms Company. The percussion-cap weapons would be a welcome addition to the Confederate arsenal. Too often the Confederate soldiers were taking the field with smoothbore muskets, which were hopelessly outdated when compared to the more accurate and vastly more powerful rifled muskets like the Enfields.

The Enfields had an effective range of around six hundred yards, and a maximum of over twelve hundred, and they fired Minié bullets rather than the traditional musket ball. The conically shaped projectile had a soft metal base that would expand when the main charge was fired, meaning that it would grip the rifling in the musket's barrel, spinning the bullet so that it travelled further, faster and with much greater accuracy.

Jack had seen the effect of the powerful Minié balls at first hand. The heavy projectiles could shatter bone and rip limbs right off a man's body. They made for a dreadfully effective weapon. The Confederate soldiers fortunate enough to receive these Enfields would finally be able to match the power of the Union's Springfield rifle muskets. It would start to level the playing field and give the men in grey a much better chance of winning the war.

'You like what you see there, Jack?' Brannigan rode past. For once, he was smiling.

'I'm just glad to see you fellows have the sense to buy from us. These Enfields are a fine weapon.' Jack slapped a hand on the crate.

'You English boys want cotton. We want guns. That sure makes trade easier.'

'And now you take these guns back north and sell them on

for a fat profit.' Jack felt a moment's distaste at being part of such a transaction.

'We do. So long as we don't let anyone take them.'

'You think they will?'

'Well, we got ourselves two of the three most dangerous things in the world for a man to own. I reckon there's many folk who'd want to get their hands on either.'

'What are they?'

'Guns and money.' Brannigan's smile widened as Jack bit on his line.

'And the third?'

'Women.' This time Brannigan laughed. 'Guns, women and money. You ever think how many men died for those three things alone?'

'Oh, there are plenty more things to die for.'

'Like what?'

'Pride? Duty? Loyalty?'

'Shit, Jack. What century were you born in?' Brannigan scoffed.

Jack slowly shook his head, then looked away so that Brannigan would not see the loathing he was sure was reflected in his gaze.

'It's time you woke up and smelled the goddam coffee.' The gang leader's tone had changed. There was no longer any trace of good humour. 'Hell, you're lucky to still be here, if you believe in all that old-fashioned horseshit.'

'Well, here I am. I'm still standing.' He looked at Brannigan, his expression now neutral.

'For now. But you'll need to learn quick sharp if you're going to stay that way,' Brannigan warned. 'In my experience, men like you don't last long down here.'

'I think I might surprise you.'

'Mebbe.' Brannigan offered something that might have been a smile, but that could easily have been nothing more than a grimace.

'I saved your life, didn't I?'

'No need to remind me. I know there's a debt to be paid.' Any trace of that half-smile was gone. 'And it will be paid, I promise you that.'

'There's no need. Consider it my gift to the world.' Jack heard scorn lacing his words.

'No, that's not how we work down here. A Texan never lets a debt go unsettled.'

'Then forgive me if I don't look forward to giving you the opportunity to save my life.'

Brannigan shook his head. 'You really do think you're better than us.'

'No, I'm not better.' Jack answered with absolute honesty.

'You sure about that?' Brannigan leaned forward in the saddle to make a play of inspecting him. 'I can almost smell the pride on you.' He snuffled like a hound scenting a fox before pulling back and sitting up straight in the saddle once again.

Jack laughed. 'I'm not a damn dog.'

'No?' There was no hint of a smile on Brannigan's face now. 'You sure act like one.'

'What do you mean?' Jack's laughter died.

'You need a master. Someone telling you what to do.'

'So who's my master now? You?'

Brannigan shrugged. 'You're here. Doing what I tell you.'

'Because it suits me.'

'Tell yourself that if you want to.' The corner of Brannigan's mouth quirked in what might have been a wry smile. 'I know what I see.'

For a moment, Jack did not have the words to reply. There was truth in Brannigan's judgement, truth that he did not want to acknowledge. 'Is that why you do it?' He sought to divert the conversation away from himself.'

'Do what exactly?'

'Collect people like me. Or like Adam and Kat. The waifs and strays.'

This time Brannigan's smile was genuine. 'You're sharp.'

'You haven't answered my question.'

He acknowledged the remark with a short nod. 'Fair enough. You know much about loyalty, Jack?'

'A little.' Jack was evasive. This was not about him.

'It's an important quality in a man, or a woman, come to that. And it's not easy to find. Not the true kind. Oh, there's plenty of folk who'll swear they'll do whatever you tell them. They'll look you in the eye too; promise they'll be true no matter what. Then they turn tail and skedaddle as soon as you need 'em.'

'And people like Adam and Kat are loyal to you?'

'They sure are.' Brannigan's answer was immediate. 'You find people like that. Give them a home, give them a job and take care of them when they need you. You bind them to you and then they'll be yours for as long as you need 'em.'

'And when you don't? When you don't need them any more?'

Brannigan shrugged. 'Then you do what you gotta do.'

Jack shook his head. 'You're wrong. That's not loyalty. It's subservience. Loyalty's a two-way street. You to them. Them to you. It's a bond. One that ties you together, no matter what happens.'

'I ain't got no time for that malarkey.' Brannigan snorted. 'People? They're just tools, like a horse, or a gun. You appreciate 'em, hell you can even like 'em. But you use them. Adam's a good kid, and he's useful to me. Just like Kat's brother was until he went off like a fool and got hisself killed.'

'What about Kat?'

'Oh, she's useful too. Good in a fight. Got herself a sharp mind as well.' Brannigan gave his terse verdict.

'Do you trust her?'

'A little.' Brannigan acknowledged the fact with a grudging look on his face. 'But no more than that. Hell, at the end of the day, she's a woman. She ain't dangerous, not like a man. She just don't have it in her. None of her kind do.'

'And you'll still get shot of her when you want to?'

'Without hesitation.' Brannigan looked Jack in the eye as he gave the straight answer. 'These people, they have their uses. But when they're a burden, or they don't work right no more, why, then you just get rid. A man can't saddle himself with a lame horse, or a gun that won't fire. He does that and he dies.' He grunted to himself as he finished his explanation, as if surprised to have revealed so much. 'Now get back on your horse, Jack, and be ready to leave. We still got a long ride ahead of us. Who knows what could happen along the way.'

Without another word, he rode on, leaving Jack to stare at his back and wonder quite what was meant by the remark. Was it a warning? Or was it merely a reference to what they all knew would be a long, hard journey back to Louisiana? Whichever it was, he knew he would have to be on his guard all the way. He had never trusted Brannigan, but now he was sure that not all the dangers the wagon train faced came from without.

There were just as many within.

Chapter Twenty-seven

The wagon train left Matamoros at dawn. Many of the men were quiet, their heads heavy and sore after a night enjoying all the delights the town could offer. Jack, however, felt little but boredom. He had gone to bed early, forgoing the opportunity to drink and whore with the others. Now he rode out of town in his usual place with the rear guard, thinking only of the long, hard journey that lay ahead.

The wagon train kicked up a cloud of dust as they ground out the single mile that separated Matamoros from the ferry that would take them back over the Rio Grande and on to Texan soil once again. The trail was badly rutted, and the going was slow as the wagons bucked and scrabbled their way along. Yet for once, it was almost peaceful. The mules were fresh, and the wagon drivers did not have to work them hard. The only sound was the creaks and groans of any poorly greased running gear on the wagons. The constant noise, so familiar after many hundreds of miles, faded into the background, the melody of the wagon train lulling the men into a stupor.

Jack rode easy. Like the mules, his mare was fresh after time spent in a livery, and she walked steadily with the gait of an animal enjoying being back outside. Even the constant heat felt somehow less fierce than normal, the early-morning start giving the men some respite from the relentless power of the sun.

Brannigan was on the move. He had started the day at the front of the wagon train with the advance guard. Now he rode back along the column. He drew level with Vaughan, who was leading the rear guard, and nodded a greeting at Kat, who rode a few yards behind.

Kat came forward. She said nothing as she took a place to the right of Vaughan.

'Brannigan.' Vaughan greeted the arrival of the wagon master as he had a thousand times before. He did not notice Kat's movement, or if he did, he paid it no heed.

For his part, Brannigan turned his mare around so that he rode alongside Vaughan, ready to start a conversation.

Jack looked to the south and the long line of distant mountains. He thought back to the time he had spent in the mountains of Virginia. There he had passed the weeks frozen to the bone, the harsh, unforgiving winter the coldest time of his life. The memory of it was buried deep in his bones, and he twisted in the saddle so that the morning sun could warm his face. For once, he let his mind drift back, and he smiled as the image of Garrison and his daughter Martha came into his mind's eye. It had not been a happy time – he had been in too much pain for that – yet there were parts of the memory that were pleasant enough to recall: the silence of the snow-shrouded woods, and the satisfaction of honest hard work and a warm fire at the end of the day. There had been something that had filled a gap in his soul in the companionship of the two people who had saved his life. For a time, he had lived solely in the present, and in the simple task of surviving the harsh winter elements, his life pared back to essentials.

He tried to push the memory away before it soured. It was a morning for riding, and for daydreaming. A time for savouring the peace and for husbanding strength for the trials that most certainly lay ahead. Yet despite his efforts, the image of Garrison's grave slipped unwanted into his mind, the newly turned earth brown and warm against the cold snow that shrouded it.

He looked around, searching the horizon for something to distract him. He heard the murmur of quiet conversation between Brannigan and Vaughan, the words spoken too softly for him to be able to make them out. He saw Brannigan reach out, his right hand clapping Vaughan on the shoulder. Then it slipped to the holster on his right hip, the movement casual and ordinary.

Jack stared as the revolver was drawn. He was still staring when Brannigan raised it and aimed the barrel at Vaughan's temple.

The sudden gunshot shattered the peace.

The barrel of Brannigan's revolver was no more than six inches from Vaughan's head. At such close range, he could not miss, and the bullet shattered the agent's skull. For a single, grotesque moment, his body lingered in the saddle. Then it toppled silently to the right.

Murder had been committed.

Vaughan was dead.

And everything had changed.

* * *

Brannigan twisted his mare around in a tight circle, his right hand outstretched, the smoking revolver held ready to fire, shifting his aim from man to man as if expecting one of them to start shooting. The only pause came when his eyes reached Jack.

'Put it down, Brannigan.' Jack moved his own revolver a fraction of an inch. It would be an easy shot, one that he would not miss. He held Brannigan's life in his hands.

'Are you going to shoot me, Jack?' Brannigan stared at the revolver in Jack's hand. His own weapon was held stock still, but it was not aimed directly at Jack.

Jack hefted the gun, mind racing. He had drawn it without thought, his body reacting to the murder he had witnessed before any notion of a plan had time to form in his mind. He was the only man to have pulled out a weapon.

And he hesitated to do anything with it.

'You want to kill me, then pull that damned trigger.' Brannigan spat out the words. He seemed more annoyed than fearful.

Still Jack did not shoot. His finger took up the tension in the trigger. An ounce more pressure and the gun would fire.

'You not got the balls?' Brannigan did not move as he spoke. 'You not got what it takes to kill a man in cold blood?'

Jack was silent. He cared nothing for Brannigan's words. He had taken so many lives, some in the raging madness of battle, some in the cold light of day. He did not doubt that Brannigan deserved to die. It was the fate of murderers the world over. Yet still he did not pull the trigger. He did not fully understand why.

'Put the gun away, Jack.'

Jack recognised Kat's voice. He did not turn his head, but

he could sense that a gun was aimed at him. The situation had changed. Now, if he fired, he would join Brannigan on the long, slow, painful march into hell.

One half of Brannigan's mouth twisted upwards in what might have been an attempt at a smile. 'If you'd wanted me dead, you'd have fired already.' He gave a slow shake of his head, as if disappointed. Then he turned away, dismissing Jack's threat.

Men from further along the column were riding back, their passage noisy as horses blew and tackle jangled. Each man carried a drawn weapon.

Jack paid no attention to their arrival. Instead he twisted in the saddle and looked back at Kat, his eyes searching for hers. He ignored the pistol aimed at his spine.

Kat raised an eyebrow. 'Your gun's still drawn, Jack.'

He held her gaze. There was so much new information filling his head. He had no doubt that Kat had been in on the plan to kill Vaughan. He remembered Brannigan's nod towards her moments before he had drawn his revolver, and the way she had ridden forward. He had already known she was no ordinary member of the gang, but he did not know what else that made her.

'Put it away, Jack.' Some extra force entered Kat's tone.

Jack looked down at the revolver in his hand, then did as he was told. He said nothing as he turned his attention to the men who had arrived to find Vaughan a headless corpse lying in the dirt.

'Put your guns away, fellas. You don't need them.' Brannigan gave his men no time to dwell. 'Adam!' He called for the younger man, who had arrived with the others.

'Yes, Brannigan.' If the sight of Vaughan's corpse shocked Adam, he hid it well.

'Stop the wagons, then gather the boys.'

'Yes, sir.' Adam snapped the reply as he turned his horse's head around, eager to obey.

'You men hold here and dismount.' Brannigan gestured to the rear guard with his revolver.

Not one man replied as they did as they were told, Jack amongst them. As he found his feet, he looked across at Vaughan's body and wondered why he felt so little. A man had died; a man he had spoken to a dozen times. Yet that death meant nothing to him. It was why he had not fired at Brannigan. He wondered at the change inside him. He did not know when he had become so callous that a man's death did not move him.

He moved with the other men, leading his horse to one side as he waited for the wagons to circle. There would be time to think on what had happened. For the moment, he would go along with whatever he was ordered to do. Everything else would have to wait.

Chapter Twenty-eight

'There's been a change of plan.' Brannigan addressed the gathered men in a loud voice. 'I'm saving us all a whole load of bother.' He spoke slowly and clearly so there could be no misunderstanding.

Every man was there. The wagons had been circled, the horses tethered and the men gathered in the centre of the open ground between them. Every one of Brannigan's gunslingers was present, as were the teamsters. Only Kat and the four Tejanos were missing. The group had been stationed outside the circle to warn of any other trains approaching.

'We're not going back to Brownsville.' Brannigan paused, letting the words sink in. 'We're heading south.'

Jack noted that the men greeted the announcement without a sound. There was no sudden intake of breath or instant conversation. There was just silent obedience.

'We've got a journey of about a week ahead of us, but no more than that.' Brannigan paused again to assess the reaction to his words before carrying on. 'So no more sands. No more weeks in the saddle. Just a short ride south, and then we're done.' He looked around the gathering, studying faces. Few met his eye. Most looked at the ground or at the sky, anywhere but at the wagon master. No one spoke.

'Why did you kill Vaughan?' Jack broke the silence. He felt the gaze of every man shift on to him, yet he did not take his eyes off Brannigan.

'He had his own plans.' Brannigan did not shy away from the question.

Jack thought back to the warning Kat had given him. Now Brannigan was echoing the same sentiment. 'What were they?'

'He was going to double-cross us. Him and that son of a bitch Dawson. As soon as we got ourselves back to Brownsville, they were going to take the guns for themselves.'

'How do you know that?'

'Some of Dawson's men told me when we passed through Brownsville whilst you were off jawing with their leader.'

'Why would they do that?'

'Same as anyone. I pay them.'

'And you believe them?'

'I do.'

'Why? Seems to me there's so many lies down here that you lot wouldn't spot the truth if it jumped up and bit you on the arse.' Jack was scathing.

'Cos they'll want paying again the next time.' Brannigan's eyes narrowed. 'And a man only gets to cross me once. You might want to think on that, Jack.'

'What about the guns?' one of Brannigan's men called out.

'They're coming with us.'

'Where are they going?' The man fired off a second question.

Jack looked for the other brave soul prepared to stand out. It was one of the men dressed in Confederate grey. Jack did not know him beyond the fact that his name was Taylor. His uniform, what was left of it, bore the faded red stripes and red facings of an artillery sergeant. Jack had never said more than a single word to him, but he could only admire his courage in questioning the killer who stood in front of them.

'I've got us another buyer. One who'll pay more than any goddam soldier.'

'The Mexicans?' Taylor made the connection for anyone struggling to understand.

'Does it matter?' Brannigan did not move, but he turned the full force of his personality on the man questioning him.

'It matters to me.' Taylor took a half-step backwards as he replied, as if eager to get away from Brannigan. Then his chin lifted. 'These guns, they're for our boys fighting them Yankees.'

'Do you really care about that, Taylor? Are you forgetting that you ran?' Brannigan did not sneer or snarl. He spoke in the same soft tone as before, nothing about him altered by either the killing or the confrontation.

'I know what I am, Brannigan. But I ain't forgotten where I'm from. Seems to me like some folk have.'

Brannigan contemplated Taylor in silence. Then he walked forward.

'It's all right, Taylor. I understand what you're telling me. I know where you're coming from with this. I respect you for it, too.'

Taylor held himself tight as Brannigan approached. There was no hiding the fear on his face.

'This ain't for everyone, I know that.' Brannigan continued to speak as he walked. Every man was following his progress, every set of eyes riveted on the tall wagon master. 'Taking these guns, well, that makes us all outlaws, I guess. But there's money in it. I'll pay every man double for his trouble. That's five hundred dollars for just one more week's work.' He did the sum for anyone too slow to do it himself. 'But sometimes it ain't about specie. Ain't that the truth, Taylor?'

'Yes, sir.' Taylor gasped the words. Brannigan was close now. 'I don't mean no disrespect, Brannigan. You know me. We've been together a long whiles. Done this journey before together too. I ain't never let you down. Not once.'

Brannigan nodded. 'It's all right. I understand.' He took another step, then reached out with his left arm to clap Taylor on the shoulder. 'You don't have to come with us.'

Taylor relaxed, his relief palpable. 'That's good of you, Brannigan. You'll pay me my two fifty and let me be on my way?'

'It ain't no problem.' Brannigan gave a friendly smile and pulled the other man forward, as if about to embrace him. 'If you don't want to come, you don't have to.' His smile widened as he slipped his revolver out of its holster. He fired the moment the weapon's barrel touched Taylor's belly.

Every man flinched as the bullet ripped through Taylor's gut and exploded out of his back. Not one made a sound.

Taylor glanced down at the blood that gushed out of his stomach, then looked at Brannigan, his mouth opening in a silent scream.

'Like I said, it ain't no problem.' Brannigan held his victim upright. 'I said you don't have to come with us, and you don't.' He cocked his head, contemplating Taylor for one last moment, then pushed him hard.

Taylor staggered back. Both hands reached for his stomach, his fingers clasping at the ruined flesh.

Brannigan lifted his revolver. He took but a second to aim, then fired again. The bullet hit Taylor smack between the eyes and he dropped like a stone.

Silence followed.

'Anyone else feel like this journey ain't for them?' Brannigan asked the question in the same mild tone. He lowered the arm that held the revolver, holding the weapon at his side as he turned to look at the men gathered around him. 'You all know me. You've seen what I can do. I don't want none of you to be as stupid as Taylor here. I've said I'll pay you good money to get these guns where I want to take 'em, and I will. There'll be five hundred dollars waiting for each of you when we're done. Five hundred dollars.' He repeated the words slowly, making sure his men understood the choice they were making. It was a good amount. Not a fortune by any means, but it would allow a man to live in comfort for a while. And the alternative was death.

Jack looked around him, studying the men. There were more than enough of them present to take Brannigan down. If they joined together, the wagon master would be dead in a heartbeat. Yet not one man moved, or even spoke a single word. They made their choice with heads bowed and with fear and greed in their hearts.

Brannigan directed his gaze at Jack. 'You coming along for the ride, Jack?'

Jack felt no fear as the man who had proven himself to be a merciless and ruthless killer stared at him. He did not fully understand what he was thinking, let alone what he was feeling. Yet the answer sprang to his lips.

'Yes, I'm coming with you.'

Brannigan greeted the confirmation with a smile. Then he turned away. He did not look at Jack again.

For his part, Jack felt the decision settle. It had been an easy one to make. He needed the employment, he knew that for certain, and he sensed there was unfinished business with Kat that he wanted to resolve. Yet neither of those was enough to make him stay. There was one other reason, one truth that he could not escape. It reverberated inside his mind like the slow, pulsating drumbeat that accompanied a flogging. Without Brannigan, he would have nothing. Without the wagon train, he would have nowhere to go and would face a return to a life of aimless wandering. Being with Brannigan gave him purpose and allowed him to be the man he was meant to be. He might be serving a cold-blooded killer, but that killer gave him what he needed.

And so he would stay.

Chapter Twenty-nine

The wagon train ground its way forward. They had turned their backs on the Rio Grande and struck out into the flat, featureless country that stretched away to the south of the river. It was hard going, the mules worked to exhaustion as they hauled the heavily laden wagons along the rutted, broken trail they now followed. They had passed a couple of small Mexican villages, but had not stopped for anything other than to refill the water casks. They had all they needed, the supplies Brannigan had laid in more than enough for the shorter journey south.

After two hard days of travel, they reached a small town that one of Brannigan's men named as Valle Hermoso. The place was not much to look at. The trail led to a central plaza surrounded by a handful of stone buildings with white-limed walls and tiled roofs. The wagon train had arrived on a day of fandango, the townsfolk preparing to celebrate the birth or death of some saint or other; none of Brannigan's men knew the details. But they did know that the fandango would offer them the chance to drink, whore and gamble. To a man they looked to Brannigan and prayed he would slip the leash for that one night and let his wild dogs go free.

He did not disappoint. The wagons were circled outside the town, and the men made their plans for the evening ahead, the promise of a night's worth of depravity enough to lift their spirits so that the camp echoed to the sound of laughter. The wagons would be guarded by Brannigan himself and his four Tejanos, the five enough to keep the precious cargo safe.

Every man was given money. They were paid in silver coins, not Confederate dollars, and Brannigan was generous, handing out enough silver for them to live like kings for the night. For the first time since the wagon train had turned south, the men were loud and raucous, spirits that had been crushed by Taylor and Vaughan's brutal killings at least partially restored by the prospect of a night of debauchery.

'You want to stay here with me tonight, Jack?' Brannigan was working his way around the men, pouring coins into willing hands.

'Do you need my help?' Jack found it hard to know how to deal with the gang leader. He had not liked Vaughan and had not known Taylor, but their killings lingered in his mind. Yet he had made his decision, just like every man present. There had been a thousand opportunities for him to simply ride away. It would be a hard journey back to Texas and beyond, but not an impossible one. He had no ties to Brannigan, or to the men who served him. There was no sense of loyalty to any of them, or even a notion of duty. There was not even the feeling that he was doing something worthwhile.

And yet he stayed.

'Nope.' Brannigan held out the bag of silver, ready to pour coins into Jack's hand if it were offered. 'You can do whatever the hell you want.'

'How much are you going to give me?' Jack tried to read Brannigan's expression, but failed. There was nothing in the man's eyes, not even a flicker of emotion. 'Thirty pieces?'

'Enough for you to do whatever you want tonight.' Brannigan missed the reference.

'You're a generous man, Brannigan.'

'Just paying you what you're due.'

'Or buying our loyalty?'

'Have you got a problem, Jack?' Brannigan still held out the bag. 'If you want to go someplace else, then be my goddam guest.'

'And have you shoot me?'

'I wouldn't shoot you. I owe you, remember. You want to ride away, then I won't stop you. But have you got yourself someplace to go? Are there some folk out there that want you? Or have you got nothing? I seem to remember you coming to me begging for employment. Or am I mistaken?'

Jack heard the harsh truth in Brannigan's voice. He held out his hand. Silver was poured, the coins warm on his palm.

'You have yourself a good time now.' Brannigan gave him a leer that might have been meant as a smile. 'Find a whore and stop being an uptight English son of a bitch for the night. We could all use a break, especially you.'

Jack said nothing as he pocketed the silver. But Brannigan's words lingered.

Darkness had fallen by the time the men left the wagons and ventured into town. The place was lit by hundreds of paper lanterns of various colours and decorated with bright garlands of paper flowers that had been strung across the streets and which fluttered in the breeze to create a gentle melody. Not that Jack could hear much of it. The men he accompanied were loud. They were brash, these hard men of the trails, uncouth and vulgar, and they strode along like they owned the place. Not one of them glanced at the faces that turned their way, the people who called this out-of-the-way place home showing an obvious and distasteful reaction to the brazen Americans now in their midst.

Jack walked behind the group, distancing himself from their crude and offensive display. He deliberately slowed his pace still further, letting Brannigan's men press ahead. It was only as the distance between them widened that he heard the first sounds of music coming from the plaza. There were drums, the rhythm they played fast and pulsating like a racing heartbeat. Then there were guitars, and overlaying them all, voices singing and the high notes of flutes. The combination produced an effect the like of which he had not heard before, the music at once foreign and strange, yet somehow warm and inviting. It promised life, along with something more, something earthy and passionate.

He entered the plaza. Long benches had been arranged around its flanks, and already dozens of men, women and children were dancing in the centre, gyrating and jigging to the fast-paced music that filled the air with a riotous, joyous sound. A promenade was lined with drinking booths, gambling tables and stalls selling food, and people paraded past, many arm in arm as they perambulated, stopping for a moment's conversation, or to purchase something to eat or drink.

Jack worked his way into the stream of people. The men, nearly every one significantly shorter than he was, were smartly turned out in dark suits decorated with silver buttons, and most wore wide sombreros on their heads. But it was the

women that captured his attention. They exhibited a dark,
sultry beauty, their heads plastered with grease so that their
black hair lay slick against their skulls. All had heavily painted
faces, eyes rimmed with black lines that extended past the
socket, and cheeks and lips brightened with rouge. Most
wore full-skirted dresses with tight bodices in bright colours,
their outfits completed by flowers in their hair and the ubiquitous fan, which was moved back and forth in time to the
music.

Brannigan's men made a rowdy display as they stormed the
first drinking booth they came across. Leers and shouts rang
out, and the dignified procession of couples and families
immediately gave the raucous Americans a wide berth. Jack did
not have to be any closer to see the looks of disdain and disgust
on the faces of the locals as the foreigners arrived to cast a pall
over their celebration. He felt something close to it himself. He
had spent his life around soldiers and knew their coarse ways
well, but there was something about the behaviour of
Brannigan's men that repelled him.

He quickened his pace, walking past the throng around the
drinking booth. He paid no attention to the shouts sent his
way, or to the first roars of anger as the Mexican working the
booth failed to supply the drinks at the pace the Americans
demanded.

It was a relief to leave the other white men behind. He
slowed as he reached a set of gambling tables pushed into a
darkened corner. Four old women were presiding over them,
each assisted by one or two small boys, whose quick fingers
darted across the tables, withdrawing cards and coins with the
dexterity of youth. He saw that three-card Monte was the
game, and judging by the small piles of silver coins and

doubloons moving across the table, it was being played fast and hard.

Yet it was not the stakes that deterred him from playing. He had never been a gambler. There were plenty of ways in the world to make him part with money, so he had no need to look for another. He had known dozens of men who had lived for making wagers. He had never known one who came out on top.

Still he lingered at the table. He had no intention of joining the dancing, and he had little appetite for either the alcohol or the food being served to the crowd. His eyes turned to the women on the very edges of the plaza. They were from his world, those dim, shadowy places where life was hard. He thought back to Brannigan's advice to find a whore. There were plenty present, the women sashaying along on the fringes of the promenade wearing tight dresses with plunging necklines that left no doubt as to the trade they plied.

For a moment, he was tempted to approach one. He could feel the lure of the women, and he was sorely tempted to buy himself some comfort. Yet he had lived around whores for too long to be a willing customer. He knew the lives they clung to until their beauty failed them. He knew their fate when that happened.

He turned away, moving his gaze from the shadows and back to the card game, which was being played at a relentless pace. It was not a night for whoring or for gambling, at least not for him. He resolved to watch the game for a while, then find a quiet drinking booth, far from Brannigan's men, where he could turn the silver coins he had been given into whatever alcohol the men in the town favoured. Then he would drink enough to empty his mind of thought, before he went back to

the wagons. It felt like a good plan, a wise plan even. He just
hoped it would be enough to shift the loneliness that had
engulfed him from the moment he had set foot in the town.

Chapter Thirty

———◆———

'You fancy playing a hand, Jack?'

Jack started as he was addressed by someone he had not heard approach. Kat stood slightly behind him as she assessed the game in play. Her arrival brought with it a surge of emotions, ones that he would rather not have to deal with.

'No, I'm no good at cards.' He gave the honest answer.

'At last, something the great Jack Lark is not good at.'

Jack felt the wash of Kat's warm breath on the side of his face. 'Are you twisting my tail to see if I bite?' he asked.

'Why would I do that?' Kat leaned forward as she replied. She was close enough for her lips to land the faintest touch on the very bottom of his ear.

Jack relished the sensation, which sent a surge of fire through his veins, and fizzing through his chest before heading lower. 'I have no idea.' He heard his voice catch as he replied.

'Perhaps I just wanted your company.' Kat leaned into him, pressing herself against his side.

Those first tantalising and immoral emotions left him. He felt something else in their place, something akin to anger. Kat was playing one of her games, one where he did not understand all the rules; one that he did not want to play.

He stepped to one side, breaking contact. 'Why did you pull a gun on me, Kat?' His tone was harsh, coloured with the first strokes of anger.

'Why do you think?' Kat showed no fear.

'Because you're Brannigan's bloody lackey.'

She turned her head away. When she looked back at him, her cheeks were coloured. 'Is that what you think? That whatever I do, it's at Brannigan's request?'

'You pulled a gun on me to protect him.'

'You were never going to shoot.' Kat's reply came back laced with disdain.

'You know that for a fact?'

'I sure do.'

'Why? Did Brannigan tell you that I didn't have the balls for it?'

'I don't need Brannigan to tell me any such thing. Especially something that goddam obvious.'

'Is that so?' It was Jack's turn to be scornful. 'You were in on his plan, though, weren't you? You knew he was going to murder Vaughan.'

Kat did not answer. She simply glared.

'When did he tell you?'

'The day we arrived in Brownsville.'

The answer made sense. That was the day she had come to warn him. 'You didn't try to persuade him not to do it?'

'No.'

'Why?'

'Because it suited me.' Kat stared at him, her eyes locked on to his own.

He searched her face, looking for the truth. He found it. She was not lying, he was sure of it. 'Why?'

'Because Vaughan would never have allowed us to turn south.'

'And you wanted that?'

'It suited me to have him gone.'

'Because it suited Brannigan?' He did not fully understand.

'No.' Kat shook her head with exasperation. 'It suited *me*.'

'What the hell does that mean?'

'I do have my own mind. I'm not just here for decoration.'

'Bollocks.'

'That surprises you?' Kat hissed the words, lowering her voice, which had been getting steadily louder. 'I've been on my own since my brother ran off and left me. I take care of myself now. Do what I want to do. I ain't beholden to no one.'

'Maybe your brother was the clever one.'

'He was a fool.' The words were snapped back.

'Why?'

'Because he wanted to be a goddam soldier. Because he wanted to prove he was as brave as the next man, or even braver. Well, all that earned him was a bullet right in that stupid brain of his.'

Jack heard the pain in her words. He understood her brother's actions; after all, he had taken the Queen's shilling himself. The lure of a soldier's uniform was strong, no matter where or when you were born. 'And so that left you with no one but Brannigan.'

'It left me alone in this world.' Kat's chin lifted. Any sadness or grief was gone. There was just iron determination.

'To do Brannigan's bidding,' Jack added, watching her carefully.

'No, to do my own goddam bidding. You sure have got yourself one low opinion of women. Do you really believe that we're put on this earth just to please you menfolk and do as we're told?'

'And don't you? Don't you do whatever Brannigan tells you?'

'Not if it don't suit me.'

Jack gave a short, contemptuous laugh at the bold reply. 'Bullshit. You do whatever he says, even if that includes standing by when he commits murder.'

Kat did not flinch as he made the accusation. Instead she reached out to grab his arm, pulling him after her into the shadows behind the gambling table. Only when they were in a much less public space did she turn to address him again, still holding his arm. 'I told you before, it suited me fine what he did.'

'You wanted Vaughan dead? Taylor too?'

'Taylor was a goddam idiot.'

'And Vaughan? What had he done?'

'You didn't know him.'

'No, I didn't. So tell me, what had he done to deserve to die?'

'He had plans to take the guns for himself.'

'That's the same bollocks Brannigan spouted.' Jack fired back the words. 'I didn't believe them then and I don't believe them now. Why would Vaughan betray us all?'

'Money does strange things to people. Those guns are worth a small fortune, easily enough to live on for a lifetime, and in comfort too. That sure changes people's minds about things.'

'Do you really believe Vaughan planned to double-cross Brannigan?'

'Not just Brannigan. You think Vaughan would still have paid you and the rest of the boys if he'd got his thieving hands on the guns?'

'So Brannigan murdered Vaughan because one day soon Vaughan was about to murder him?'

'That would have to be part of his plan. Brannigan knew it.'

'What is he? Some sort of fucking clairvoyant?'

Kat glowered. 'I trust him. I trust him a damn sight more than I trusted Vaughan.'

'So Vaughan was some great criminal mastermind who was playing us all false. And Brannigan is some kind of hero who saved us?'

'Mebbe.'

'Bollocks.'

'Because you know better?'

'I know a murdering bastard when I see one.' Jack had no choice but to step forward as Kat tugged his arm with surprising force.

'You don't see what's right in front of your goddam face, Jack Lark.'

'And what's that?' he asked, his voice harsh.

Kat replied by pressing her lips to his.

Jack pulled her closer, his arm slipping around her waist so that his palm rested on the small of her back. He held her then, savouring the touch of her body under his hand. He had no idea what her game was, but he found he did not care, and he lost himself in the moment, closing his mind to everything save the touch, the smell, the feel and the taste of the woman in his arms.

Kat broke away from him. 'You still think I'm doing what Brannigan tells me?'

'I don't know what to think.' Jack could still taste her kiss on his lips. He wanted more – no, he corrected himself, he *needed* more. Kat filled his mind, every sense, every thought, every sensation riveted on the woman in front of him.

'I do what I want. Not what some man tells me to do.' She stepped towards him and kissed him again. This time it lasted longer, until she broke away for a second time. 'I don't know what Vaughan intended, not all of it. But to answer your question, yes, I was in on Brannigan's plan, and yes, I agreed that Vaughan had to die. Taylor, well he was a goddam fool, and his death is no one's fault but his own. And no, I am not Brannigan's lackey.'

Again she closed the gap between them. This time as she kissed him, she pushed her hips forward. He reached around and held her, hands dancing across her back, finger-tips tingling as he followed the contours of her spine. She stayed there for the span of a dozen heartbeats, pressing hard against him, before she took a step back and looked him dead in the eye.

'Whatever you do, don't discount me, Jack.' She reached forward to grasp his hand. 'Underestimate me at your peril.'

Jack dropped his gaze. He did not want her to see the naked lust that he knew would be reflected there. He savoured the feel of her hand on his, the warmth of her skin. When she dropped his hand, it was all he could do not to gasp out loud.

Kat did not say goodbye. She simply turned and walked away, leaving him alone in the shadows.

Jack watched her go. Only when he lost sight of her in the crowd did he start to move. He would stick to his earlier plan. He would find some alcohol, and he would get drunk in the hope that it would erase the feel of her from his mind. For he had a fearful notion that it would take root, and he did not know what to do if that happened.

It was only as he left the shadows behind that he saw Adam standing there. He could only presume the young man had been watching the whole time. He would have seen everything, and his hatred glimmered in the darkness like a lantern.

Chapter Thirty-one

———◆———

*J*ack rode along the side of the wagon train. They had left Valle Hermoso just after dawn. The men were quiet, the night's debauchery dampening spirits and hurting heads. Jack felt no better than the others, his own head reverberating to a pounding that threatened to split his skull in two. As ever, he was roasting hot, and he was contemplating taking a drink of water from his canteen when he noticed the wagon train's advance guard circled around something in the sand a few yards to one side of the trail.

'You should see this.' It was Brannigan who spoke. He too was riding up the side of the wagon train and called out to Jack as he passed.

'What is it?'

'Look for yourself,' Brannigan said without turning around.

Intrigued, Jack rode forward. There were two objects on the ground. Both were the same size, no bigger than a ripe melon. It was only as he rode closer that he realised what it was he was looking at.

'The poor bastards.' He breathed the words as he brought his horse to a stand next to Brannigan, who had halted just short of the gruesome sight.

Two heads stuck out of the sand. There was not a lot left of either, the faces and scalps ravaged by animals so that they were barely recognisable as having once been human. Nothing at all was left of the eyes or lips. Both mouths had been forced open by some creature or other, and Jack could see that all of the soft tissues inside had been ripped out.

'Is that another warning?'

'Maybe.' Brannigan answered Jack's question evenly. There was no trace of disgust in his tone.

'It's a foul way to bury a man.'

Brannigan turned to look at him. As ever, his eyes were cold. 'They weren't dead when they were left.'

'Someone buried them alive?' Jack did not bother to hide his revulsion.

'Of course.'

His stomach lurched at the notion. He was no stranger to death, and he had seen men die in a hundred different ways. Yet he could not recall having come across one as cruel as this. 'Have you ever done that to a man?' He asked the question, even though he pretty much knew the answer.

'A few times.' Brannigan offered a strange lopsided smile as he studied Jack's reaction. 'Does that turn your stomach?'

'Yes.' Jack answered bluntly.

'Why?'

'It's a horrible death.'

'Are there any good ones?'

'Yes.' Jack believed the answer he gave fully.

'Dead is dead.' Brannigan shook his head, as if surprised by Jack's folly.

'And cruel is cruel.'

'You don't approve.'

'You think I should?' Jack did not bother to remove the scathing tone from his voice. It might have been a better idea to hide his reaction, but he did not want to. He wanted his revulsion to register.

'You're soft, Jack. You think you're a killer, but in truth you're as soft as butter.'

'Soft?' Jack scoffed. 'I'm not soft, chum. But I'm not the sort of evil bastard who would do that to a man.'

'Does it frighten you?' Brannigan glanced at the animal-ravaged heads. 'You're a clever man, Jack. You must be thinking what it would be like to be that poor son of a bitch over there. What it must be like to be buried like that. What it must be like waiting for the first animals to come by. You'd last a fair whiles, I reckon: hours, maybe even days. You could shout at first, drive them away. But then one would come close. They'd take the first little bite, then another, and then another. Before you know, they're feasting on your flesh, ripping out your eyes and crawling into your goddam mouth.' He watched Jack's face as he painted the horrific picture. 'You think what that'd be like, and then tell me it don't make you want to shit in your pants.'

Jack forced himself to look at the remains of what once had been living, breathing human beings. Brannigan was right. He was able to conjure the scene in his mind's eye. He could imagine the terror the men would have felt as they were left like that, the sheer horror of that fate enough to turn his stomach.

'Who did this?' He swallowed the urge to vomit.

'Could've been anyone. Juaristas, bandoleros . . . hell, even another wagon master. My money's on Dawson and his men. I heard they killed some bandoleros. He'd do something like this.'

Jack fought the urge to spit. But Brannigan's words made sense. He recalled Dawson boasting of killing some of Ángel Santiago's men. 'You're all as cruel as each other then.'

'Oh no.' Brannigan gave Jack the widest smile. 'I'm far worse than any of them.'

Jack looked into Brannigan's eyes and saw that he was not boasting. He was simply stating a fact.

'And you're proud of that?' He did not bother to hold back the accusation.

Brannigan shrugged, unmoved. 'Pride's a funny old thing. Makes you act strange.' He paused, then offered a thin smile. 'You'd better be careful, Jack. Take care that pride of yours don't make you do something stupid.'

Advice offered, he kicked back his heels and left Jack to stare at the two ravaged skulls.

Chapter Thirty-two

───◆───

The trail they had been following stopped in a wide clearing surrounded on all sides by a high ridge. There was no way out, save for the way they had come. When they reached the middle of the enclosed space, the wagons rolled to a halt, just as Brannigan had ordered them to do.

Jack rode up the side of the now stationary train, his eyes scanning the ridgeline for the men he sensed would be hidden there. Brannigan had only told them that morning of the rendezvous with the Mexicans who would buy the guns. He had described the ground, and told his gang what was to happen when they arrived. So far, they were obeying his instructions, the wagons manoeuvring into neat rows off the trail whilst the men dismounted, tethered their horses to the wagons, then gathered in a group near a lone mesquite tree.

All was quiet. The slopes that surrounded the wagons were steep and covered with great boulders and loose fallen rocks. Jack lifted a hand to shield his eyes from the sun as he looked for another way out of the bowl-shaped clearing. He saw at once that there was no way in hell that the heavily laden wagons would be able to ascend the steep slopes. A man on horseback might manage it, but even that would be hard going, the loose rocks and sandy soil making for treacherous footing. He could not help feeling the tension as they waited in this place that God had made into the perfect location for an ambush.

The wagon train had followed the rough, rutted trail for three full days since they had turned south. They had been days of toil and hard graft, yet they had only covered the distance a man on a well-rested horse could travel in a single day. Other than the one night at the fandango, they had not stopped, one relentless, gruelling day following another.

Until they had arrived here.

Jack took his place amongst Brannigan's men. No one spoke, even the loudest and most raucous silenced by the forbidding atmosphere. They all knew the danger they were in, but Brannigan had ordered them to wait, and not one man considered following any other course of action.

Adam stood next to Jack, his hand resting on the revolver on his right hip. As the silence stretched thin, he drew the gun, keeping it low so that it would not be seen. Jack understood the need to hold a weapon. It felt unnatural to just sit there. They were like a fox who had wandered into a farmstead, and who now sat outside the hounds' kennel, waiting for them to be released.

Jack watched Brannigan arrive with the rear guard. The gang leader gestured for the men to join the others whilst he rode forward alone. If he felt any of the same tension as his men, he did not show it. He rode slow and easy, as if he hadn't a care in the world.

The wagon drivers walked over in a single group, taking a

place next to Brannigan's men, just as they had been ordered to do. At Jack's side, Adam was fiddling with his revolver, his right thumb cocking then un-cocking then re-cocking the weapon's hammer. Each action made the workings click, the sound repeating itself over and over.

Brannigan stood tall in the saddle and waved his arm from side to side. Then he sat down, both arms resting easily on the saddle's pommel.

Nothing happened for perhaps a full minute. Adam's revolver clicked repeatedly, the sound the only one coming from the men.

Then there was a new noise. It was barely audible at first, and Jack cocked an ear as he tried to pick it out. It sounded like a distant train moving down the line, the low rumbling of something a long way away on the move. It grew slowly louder, the sound echoing around the clearing.

Adam's revolver stopped clicking.

Suddenly, dozens of men swarmed over the ridgeline. They came in one great mass, flowing over the brow and down the slopes before spreading out to take up firing positions amongst the rocks and boulders that littered the ground.

Jack tried to tally their numbers, but there were too many to count. He reckoned there had to be at least two hundred, perhaps more. Every one was armed.

Brannigan dismounted. He took his time tethering his horse to the Mesquite tree before he turned to bark an order. 'Jack! I want you with me. Kat, you too.'

Jack glanced once at Adam. He took in the thunderous look on the younger man's face before he walked forward to do his master's bidding.

* * *

Jack, Kat and Brannigan walked in a line abreast. They left the mesquite tree behind and headed towards a group of four men who moved down the far slope on to the level ground at its base.

As they walked forward, Jack studied the men on the nearest slope. They were a strange-looking crew. Most wore skin-tight trousers that were open at the sides and widened at the ankle. Some were plain, but a few men sported pairs decorated with a row of metal buttons down the seam. On their top half, some of the men wore little more than a simple shirt, whilst others sported jackets made from dark material or some form of leather waistcoat. Nearly all wore the ubiquitous sombrero on their heads. Every man was armed, and Jack was not surprised to see a vast array of weaponry on display, from percussion carbines and shotguns to smoothbore flintlock muskets and even an ancient matchlock musket amidst a smattering of revolvers and single-shot pistols.

'You're late, Señor.'

Jack concentrated his attention on the man who had rebuked Brannigan. He was short, perhaps not quite five feet tall. And he was old, frail even, with a sparse thatch of thin grey hair and an even thinner grey beard. Yet he exuded an air of power, and he clearly did not fear the tall, rangy American who was standing in front of him.

'It's a hard ride.' Brannigan rested his weight on one hip, his hands slipping into his gun belt in front of his belly. He looked completely at ease. 'I told your men how long it'd take to get here, and look here I am, right bang on schedule. You should be more appreciative of my efforts, Santiago.'

Jack started as he realised who Brannigan was speaking to. This was Santiago, the man Brannigan himself had called a demon, and who had put the fear of God into Dawson. And he was nothing more than a weak old man.

'Do you have our guns?' Santiago demanded.

'Everything as we agreed.' Brannigan glanced briefly at Jack before he continued. 'Do you have our money?'

'Of course, Señor.'

'Gold doubloons?'

Jack heard a slight catch in Brannigan's voice. It was the first trace of unease. He understood it, for he felt it himself. But at least now he knew whom he faced. He wondered when the deal had been done, when Brannigan had met with the men who did Santiago's dirty work. Brannigan had not spoken of the buyer of the guns. The men had speculated, at least when they were certain the gang leader was out of earshot. Their favourite choice had been the Juaristas, the men fighting the French army that had invaded their land. It turned out that choice was wrong. Brannigan was selling the Enfields to Ángel Santiago. Jack thought back to the few sketchy details Dawson had given him about Los Ángeles de la Muerte. He had made it clear that the bandoleros lived up to their nickname. Now Jack would get the chance to see for himself if their fearsome reputation was well founded.

'You think I would try to double-cross you, Señor?' Santiago sounded as if he were genuinely affronted at the notion.

'I bet you thought about it.' Brannigan's reply was firm, any unease now well hidden.

Santiago smiled to reveal a few brown teeth. 'But then who will sell me more guns? I could kill you. I could take your guns and save my gold. But a man can only double-cross someone once. Is that not so, Señor?' He paused and made a play of looking around the small group. 'Where is Señor Vaughan?'

Brannigan laughed. 'He ain't here.' He spoke forcefully.

'So this is your last delivery to me?'

'Mebbe.'

Santiago's eyes narrowed as he contemplated the answer. 'Then perhaps I should kill you.'

'You can try.' Brannigan moved his hand so that it rested on the revolver at his right hip.

For the first time, the leader of the bandoleros offered a smile. 'I have given you my word that this transaction will be made. I must honour that, must I not, Señor? To do any less would be to condemn my soul to an eternity of suffering.'

Jack watched Santiago closely as he addressed Brannigan. The old man was speaking with utmost sincerity, he was sure of it. Everything he saw and heard sat at odds with the tales he had heard of this man and the terror he created in the minds of so many people.

'You can keep your God-fearing mumbo-jumbo to yourself, Santiago.' Brannigan was thoroughly unimpressed by the Mexican's words. 'Just pay me my money and I'll leave you the guns, and the wagons too, save for the one I'll need.'

Santiago nodded. 'Very well.' He looked past Brannigan, his gaze resting on Jack and Kat for a few moments before he turned. 'Do we still proceed with the rest of the plan as you requested?'

'We do.'

He shook his head slowly, his expression betraying nothing but sadness. 'So be it.' He turned to walk away. The men with him followed, one reaching out to take him by the arm and lend a steadying hand as they began to ascend the steep slope.

'What the hell is going on, Brannigan?' Jack had been listening carefully. 'What did he mean?'

Brannigan stood where he was for a moment, facing away from Jack. Then he turned, moving fast, snatching his revolver from its holster and pressing it into Jack's stomach. Only then did he smile. 'Give me your gun, Jack. That stupid sabre of yours too.'

'What the hell?' Jack looked down at the weapon pressed into his gut.

'Don't you say another word now, not unless you want a bullet in your goddam belly.' Brannigan reached forward with his free hand to deftly pluck Jack's revolver from his holster. He held it out to Kat, who took it and immediately raised it so that it was aimed back at Jack.

'What the fuck is going on?' Jack felt a sudden rush of fear. He had seen Brannigan kill in cold blood and knew he would not hesitate to do so again.

'I'm saving your life. I owe you, don't I? For what you did back in Texas.' Brannigan reached forward and carefully eased Jack's sabre out of its scabbard, moving the steel slowly. When he had it fully drawn, he tossed it contemptuously into the dirt.

'Saving my life?' Jack's mind was racing, but he was struggling to see any threat other than the one coming from the man in front of him.

'That's right.' Brannigan glanced at Kat. 'Cover this son of a bitch, Kat. Shoot him in the balls if he so much as twitches.'

He stood back, checking that Kat had her gun aimed at Jack, then turned and raised a single hand high.

At his signal, the bandits took aim at the small band of wagon drivers and gunslingers that had brought Brannigan and his precious consignment safely to this rendezvous.

Brannigan paused, his arm still aloft. Then he clenched his fist, and the Ángeles opened fire.

Chapter Thirty-three

Every one of the Ángeles fired at the same moment. The men on the slopes had been waiting for the command, and each one had been granted plenty of time to choose his first shot.

The great roar of the volley echoed around the enclosed ground. Hundreds of bullets and musket balls tore into Brannigan's men. At such close range, even the outdated muskets could kill. Some men cried out as they were hit, the vicious tempest ripping them apart. Others crumpled to the ground with barely a sound. A rare few stood long enough to draw a weapon and return fire. Wild shots cracked into boulders, or hit the slope to kick up plumes of dust. None hit a single Ángel. Those that fought back drew more fire, and were cut down in moments.

Those furthest from the Ángeles tried to flee. Adam led them, the youngest man in the band reacting faster than any other. Bullets chased them away, cutting down two of the men who followed him. Those still on their feet ran back along the trail, the ground around them hit repeatedly so that spurts of dust spat up from the dirt.

They would not get far. More Ángeles sprang up from

where they had waited by the trail and opened fire, their short-range volley knocking down men like skittles at the fair. Adam and just one other man were left standing. To their credit, they did not give up, but carried on, heads down, as if battling into the teeth of a gale. They ran into a melee, the Ángeles rushing forward to take them down. The two men never stood a chance as they were beaten into the dirt, musket butts used as clubs to batter them into submission.

Within the span of a few heartbeats, not one of Brannigan's men was left standing. Still the shots came against them, the Ángeles with revolvers firing on and on, their bullets thumping into any body that so much as twitched. Then suddenly, as abruptly as it had started, the firing stopped.

In the lull that followed, the moans and cries of those still alive could be heard. The pitiful sound filled the air. Here a man sobbed, whilst another cried for help. Most lay silent and still, their bodies twisted and broken, their blood pumping into the dirt on to which they had fallen.

Jack stayed stock still. He had been powerless as the vicious storm cut down the men who had ridden the trail with him. Now he stood there, his hands clawing at the seams of his trousers, the feeling of impotence like nothing he had felt before. He was like a lone bullock left in the butcher's yard after the day's meat ration had been culled, surrounded by the stink of blood and the threat of imminent death.

A man started to scream, the pitiful sound reverberating in the clearing. Jack heard footsteps. He twisted his head to see Brannigan walking towards the pile of bodies that had been created at his command, his pace slow and languid.

'Help me! Jesus, Brannigan, help me!' The scream turned to sobs as the man spotted the wagon master, who had come to stand over him. 'I beg you, Brannigan. Oh God, help me!' The words gushed forth, the babble almost incoherent.

Jack watched Brannigan. The heartfelt pleas did not move him, his face expressionless as he slowly drew his revolver and brought the gun up.

'No, Brannigan, don't do it. I beg you. Help me. Don't do it.' The man made a final plea for his life.

Brannigan held the gun still, taking his time to aim. Then he fired.

The single gunshot was loud. It cut off the man's pleas in an instant.

Jack held his head still, but his eyes followed Brannigan as he began to pick his way through the carnage, using the toe of his boot to push at the corpses that smothered the ground. As Jack watched, the gang leader paused. The revolver was raised and a shot was fired. The process was repeated a few moments later. Brannigan was checking every body and killing anyone left alive.

Jack held himself still. A part of him willed himself to make a break for it and risk a bullet in his spine. Yet he knew that to do so was to face certain death. Even if he evaded Kat's shots, he was still surrounded by a few hundred Ángeles. Escape was impossible, and so he stood there, resigned and docile, waiting for whatever fate Brannigan had in mind for him.

'Don't you even think about running.' It was Kat who spoke.

Jack wondered how she had been able to read his mind. She made the threat quietly. He was certain she was capable of making good on it.

'Were you in on this too, Kat?' He spoke without moving a muscle.

'Shut your mouth,' Kat snapped.

'Or you'll shoot me?' Jack could not contain the reply. He felt sick to the stomach. He was no stranger to death, but this was something far beyond even his bloody experience. 'When . . . when did you plan all this?' He struggled to get the words out, choked by loathing.

'A while ago.' Kat kept her eyes on him, ready should he try anything. 'Santiago's men have been with us since King's Ranch. And it was easy enough for one of his lieutenants to find us whilst you and the boys were drinking yourselves stupid the other night.'

Jack closed his eyes as he realised he had been played for a fool. The men he had believed to be Tejanos had actually been bandoleros. Then another thought hit him. He recalled the night of the fandango, and Kat's attention. He knew now why she had sought him out. It was not attraction. It was distraction.

'You murdering bitch.' He hissed the words, feeling another emotion start to boil inside him. It went beyond loathing. It was hatred so pure and elemental that it made him shake.

'I thought you said you were a soldier.' Kat's reply was biting. 'You're acting like you haven't seen a few dead men before.'

'That was different.'

'Why? Dead is dead.'

Jack had to swallow the urge to puke up his guts. He had heard Brannigan say the same.

'Way I heard it, there were so many dead at Shiloh that they were burying the poor sons of bitches for days, my brother with them.' Kat was scathing. 'But that's all right with you, is it, Jack? Because they were soldiers? Because they wore a uniform?'

'Yes.'

'If you ask him nice, maybe Brannigan will dress those boys up. If that'll make it all right with you.'

'How can you stand there and be a party to murder, Kat?' He spat the words, each one coated with disgust.

'It's not the first time. People have been killing each other around me for as long as I've been alive. Men killed my parents for their land, and then the Yankees killed my brother.'

'Doesn't excuse this.'

'You think I'd be better off if I'd been standing over there?' Kat's reply was immediate and cutting. 'You'd rather I was lying dead on the ground? You don't know a goddam thing. Why, you're nothing but a goddam babe.'

'And you know better? That's why you can stand by and watch that man kill?'

'Yes. I'll stand by and watch him kill. I'll stand here and watch him put a bullet right between your goddam eyes if it suits me.'

Jack shook his head, controlling his rage. It was all he could do not to throttle her with his bare hands.

'I'll tell you something else, Jack, I know exactly what I'm doing and why I'm doing it. So now I suggest you shut that big mouth of yours. Otherwise I reckon Brannigan will shoot you down right where you stand.'

Jack heard the jangle of spurs. He moved his head far enough to see Brannigan returning from his bloody task.

'You look shocked, Jack.' The wagon master spoke as he came close. 'You don't like what you see?'

'You're a murdering bastard, Brannigan.'

'I'll take that as a compliment coming from an Englishman, you fellas being the experts and all. Now you stand nice and easy. You ain't going to die. Least not if you're sensible. I told you. I owe you. Now I'm repaying my debt.'

The arrival of a group of Ángeles prevented Brannigan from saying more. They were half carrying, half dragging Adam and the man who had run with him. Of the pair, only Adam was conscious. His face was a mask of blood, whilst the other man – Jack thought his name was Brown, but he could not be sure – had been even more badly beaten. Blood flowed freely from his scalp and ran in a thick river down the side of his head, soaking into his shirt. There was enough blood for Jack not to be sure if he was even still alive.

'Good to see you, Adam.' Brannigan greeted the young man with a leer. He looked down at his revolver, then broke the weapon open to peer at the chambers. 'Looks like this gun of mine is empty, so that means you get to live a while longer.' He turned to the Ángeles. 'Take these two away. Him too.' He nodded in Jack's direction.

The Ángeles said nothing as they moved to obey. Jack was pulled forward to have his hands bound behind him with rough hemp rope that burned against his skin.

'You're safe for the moment. Just don't do anything stupid or it will be a whole lot worse for you. These boys won't stand for any of your nonsense.' Brannigan walked to Kat's side as he gave the advice.

Jack did not look at him once. He concentrated his gaze on the dirt between his boots. Nothing he could say would change what had just happened. Nothing he could do would alter his situation. He was a prisoner of Santiago and his bandoleros, and his life was in the hands of men who killed without a qualm.

Chapter Thirty-four

Jack rested his head against the wall behind him and closed his eyes. The pain in his back and shoulders was fierce, and his wrists burned from the hemp rope that still bound them tight behind him. He did his best to ignore the pain, just as he had ignored the shame of being stripped naked by his captors before being dumped into a small shed pressed hard into the flank of a large hacienda. The shed was filthy and half full of rotting straw. The brickwork was cracked, and in one corner a whole section of the upper wall had fallen in. The roof was made of beams and thatch. In two places there were gaping holes through which he could see the dark night sky. The single door was shut, and from the sounds coming from the far side, at least two men were stationed outside.

Jack had done his best to observe where he was being taken, his interest in his surroundings earning him a bloody nose from one of his captors as he had been dragged towards the hacienda. The building was sited on the side of a wide track. It was a two-storey affair, its walls made of stone that might once have been whitened with lime, but which now looked grey and forlorn, under a raggedy red-tile roof. There was a single doorway facing the track and no windows in the second storey save for four small square openings. To the rear was a yard of compacted earth, with an open-fronted barn to one side and three sheds down one flank. From what he had seen, the hacienda was in a poor state of repair. A sizeable section of the roof had caved in, and large patches of stone had fallen away from the walls. It had clearly been abandoned for a long time, and it looked as lonely and bereft as the three prisoners who had been dragged towards it.

'I'm going to kill him.'

Jack did not bother to open his eyes as Adam made the bold claim. It was not the first time the younger man had said something similar. The threats had come one after the other, some simple, others embellishing the ways in which Brannigan was to be put to death. Adam was sitting to Jack's left, his head hanging down so that it almost rested on his knees. The third prisoner, Brown, was still unconscious. He had been dumped without ceremony and lay where he had been left.

'I'm going to cut his belly wide open. He'll scream when I do it. He'll scream and scream, but I won't stop, not even when his guts are hanging out and he's begging me to kill him.' Adam broke off with a sob.

Jack tried to hold his tongue. He knew what the lad was doing. Conjuring images of Brannigan's death was a good way of passing the time. Yet the repetition was grating on nerves that were already stretched thin.

'I'm going to kill him real slow—'

'Shut the fuck up!' Jack snapped. 'I don't want to bloody hear it.'

Adam recoiled from the venom in his voice. 'How can you just sit there?' His face lifted and he looked at Jack, his bloodshot eyes filled with anguish.

'Because that's all there is to do.' Jack sucked down a breath, stilling his temper.

'I can't bear it.'

'You have to.'

'I can't.'

'You can and you will.' Jack's voice was hard. 'Sometimes there is nothing to do but suck it down. Crying and whimpering won't make it any better.'

'Nothing will.'

'No. So make a choice. Let it break you, or deal with it.'

'I can't.' Tears rolled down Adam's cheeks now. 'They're going to kill us.'

'Maybe. But we don't have any say in the matter.' Jack was not moved. 'All you can do is decide how you're going to face it.' He gave the fatalistic advice in a voice wrapped in iron. He had fought the battle with his own fear. After the first day's fighting at Shiloh, that fear had been like a beast living deep in his gut. It had lurked there, always present, always haunting him. At times it had reared up, swarming through his body like a plague of hornets. It had come close to winning the battle for his soul, but from somewhere – he did not know where – he had found the strength to take back control, and to master that fear. It had not disappeared, not completely, but like a bear whipped into obedience by a cruel master, it could be contained and corralled despite its power.

Adam drew in a deep breath. 'You're so goddam calm.'

'I pretend to be.' Jack sighed. He did not want this conversation. Yet he saw the need in the younger man, so he tried to

build a bridge, one that would lead Adam to some sort of peace
of mind.

'Really?'

'Yes.'

'No one would ever know. You're the surest man I ever met.
Save for Brannigan, goddam him.'

Jack grunted. 'It's an act. All of it.'

'I don't believe it.'

'I don't give a fig if you do or if you don't. But it's the truth.
Half the time I don't know what I'm doing, or why I'm doing
it.' Jack offered a short, bitter laugh. 'Look at me. Here I am,
as naked as a newborn babe, locked up God alone knows where
for a reason I can't even remember.'

'You did it for money. Same as all of us.'

'Not you.' Jack glanced across at Adam. The tears had
stopped. The distraction was working. 'You did it for
Brannigan.'

'And now I hate him.' Adam delivered the line with passion.
'And I'll kill him.'

'That's good. Hold on to that thought. Use it.'

'I hated you too. I wanted to kill you.'

'I don't blame you.' Jack snorted as the boy revealed
something he had already known. 'I'm a miserable bastard.
You can tell me why you hated me if you like.'

'I hated you because you were in the way. Every time I
turned around, there you were with Brannigan. Then you got
nice and cosy with Kat.'

'Not that cosy.' Jack shook his head as he considered that
particular folly. The first time he had seen Kat with Adam, she
had been playing a role. He had seen through it in an instant.
Yet despite that, he had not seen that she had been toying with

him the whole time since. He had been an impostor for years, yet he had taken her bait, hook, line and sinker.

'I was wrong about you.'

'Don't worry about it, chum. You're not the first. Looks like you might be the last, though.'

'I'm sorry.'

'Don't be.' Jack sighed. The conversation was awakening the fear in his own belly. Thankfully he was spared any more as a long-drawn-out groan announced that Brown was finally coming to.

The moaning stopped and Brown lifted his head as best he could. He was laying face down, his arms tied together behind his back just like Jack and Adam. 'Where am I?' His voice cracked as he spoke, the words grating and hoarse.

'In hell,' Adam answered.

Brown said nothing more. He tried to move, but failed to do anything more than writhe. He went still.

'Are we gonna die?' He finally spoke after a pause of several minutes.

'Maybe.' Jack took his turn to answer.

'Brannigan.' Brown spat out the word. Again he went quiet for several moments before he spoke again. 'Is there any water?'

'No.'

'Then they're going to kill us for sure. You don't give water to a dying man. Not out here.' Brown fell silent after he had made the dire prophecy.

None of the three men said anything more. Jack closed his eyes, trying to husband his strength. He made a final vow that he would not go quietly. At the end, he would fight, just as he always had done. However Brannigan intended to kill them, he would find a way to fight back. It might be futile, and it might earn him nothing but more pain on his way to hell, but he would not submit meekly to his fate.

A quiet mumbling interrupted his thoughts. It took him a while to realise that Brown was praying.

He listened to the barely audible words. For a moment, he wished he had faith. It would be a comfort to have something to turn to at the last. Yet his faith had always been in himself and the weapons he carried. He would rather trust a six-shot Navy Colt revolver to keep him safe than some faceless deity. Now, though, he felt that a part of him was missing. He did not know if some god could fill that space, but he did know that he had never felt more alone than he did at that moment.

Brown fell silent. There were no sounds other than the chirps and clicks of the thousand of insects that had come alive now that the sun was setting.

Jack screwed his eyes shut and did his best to empty his mind. There was no benefit in idle thought. Not now.

There was nothing left to do save endure.

And wait for the end of his days.

Chapter Thirty-five

J ack woke with a start. It was colder in the shed now, the cool air that had arrived with the dawn billowing through the gaps in the walls and roof. He had not meant to sleep. He had tried to stay awake, unwilling to miss a moment of his last night on earth. He had still been awake when the sky had begun to turn slowly from black to grey. Sleep had come only as the dawn breathed new life into another day.

He took a moment to look around him. Neither of his companions appeared to be awake, but there was no way of knowing for sure, and he had no intention of trying to find out. Outside, the chirrups of the insects were being replaced by the squawks and screeches of the thousands of green parrots that had come awake with the dawn.

A gunshot crashed out. It came from a fair distance away, but it still had the power to make him flinch. He could only presume that one of the bandoleros had taken a shot at the raucous birds. The cheer that had followed told him that the man's aim had likely been true.

He let his head rest back against the wall and closed his eyes, which were gritty and sore. His mouth and throat were parched, but he refused to dwell on his thirst. It was the least of his problems. He had just resolved to attempt to sleep once more, if only to avoid thinking, when there were footsteps outside his prison. A moment later, the bar that had locked the door tight was withdrawn, the sound of wood grating on wood echoing around the shed before the door was pulled back to send a wave of cold air surging into the confined space.

'Get yourselves on up, fellas.' Brannigan loomed large in the doorway. 'We're going for a little walk.'

The two men sharing the small space with Jack stirred at once. Neither had been asleep.

Jack looked at the man who had condemned them to this fate. Brannigan appeared well rested. Clearly the previous day's massacre had not prevented him from sleeping.

It was only then that Jack noticed that the wagon master had come to the shed carrying his sabre.

'I still don't get it, Jack.' Brannigan saw that the sword had caught Jack's attention. He made a play of looking at its hilt. 'I mean, it was made at the Nashville Plow Works, for Christ's sake. That's all this is. A farmer's weapon. It's not for men like us.'

Jack did not bother to reply.

Brannigan held the sword higher, sighting down the blade. He held the pose, then lowered the weapon. 'You sure this thing can kill a man?'

'Hand it over and I'll show you what I can do with it.' Jack's glib reply earned him a tight-lipped smile.

'I think you'd like that.' Brannigan laughed at the impossible idea. 'Try anything and my friends here have been told to shoot you down.' He paused, as if he expected an answer. He made a face when none of his three prisoners said anything. 'Come on, then. Stir yourselves, goddammit.' He snapped the words, good humour evaporating.

'You'll have to help me up,' Brown hissed. He was still lying face down. The words came out dry and hoarse.

Jack himself moved slowly. His head was pounding, and he had been sitting in the same position for so long that every muscle in his body protested as he carefully pushed himself to his feet.

'That's the way.' Brannigan greeted his obedience with a loud commendation. 'Boys, pick that there fella up.' He used Jack's sword to gesture towards Brown.

Jack had to lean back against the wall as two of Brannigan's Tejanos entered the small space. They spared no ceremony as they bent low and dragged Brown to his feet, one holding him tightly under each arm.

Brannigan stood easy in the doorway, a wide smile on his face. 'I hope you boys had a fine rest.'

'The devil will take you, Brannigan.' It was Adam who spoke first. 'We've done nothing save what you told us to do.' The passion burned in his words, but a barely controlled terror had sucked all the colour from the lad's face so that his skin was the colour of week-old milk.

'You have.' Brannigan stood foursquare in front of him. 'You've been loyal to me, and I sure appreciate it. But I have no choice. Not this time. Not if I don't want to spend the rest of my life with bounty hunters or Pinkerton's boys chasing my tail. You know what I've done and why I've done it. That makes you all dangerous to me.' He looked around the room at the three men, who stared back at him.

'You'll burn in hell.' The words spewed out of Adam and his face contorted, fear etched into every pore.

'Well, I ain't there yet. Maybe Jack will put in a good word for me when he moseys down there in a bit.' Brannigan looked away, as if bored by the conversation.

'You should let Adam go.' Jack was proud of the way his voice came out flat and level. His own fear was squirming in his bowels, but he had it whipped, for the moment at least.

'Now why would I do that?'

'You were his hero. He worshipped you. And he's right. He did every bloody thing you told him to. Why kill him now?'

'Because I have to.' Brannigan gave the answer in the same dry, lifeless tone.

'You don't,' Jack pressed on. 'You can let him live.'

'No.' The answer was given immediately. 'Like I told you, you don't keep a horse that's gone lame, no matter how good it's been to you. You shoot it right between the eyes. And you do that because it's no goddam use to you any more.'

'Adam's not a fucking horse. He's just a boy.'

Brannigan gave a wry smile. 'Now why are you defending Adam all of a sudden? He's hated your guts ever since the moment I took you on. Wanted you left by the roadside buried up to your goddam neck. Let me guess. Did you fellas become friends last night?'

'Just let him go. How can he hurt you?' Jack had to force the words out, his mouth as dry as the sands. Talking hurt.

'He can hurt me plenty. Hatred does funny things to a man. Last thing I need is to have to watch my back waiting for this boy to make his move. It's best this way.'

'Goddam you, Brannigan.' Adam had fallen silent, but now he spluttered the words, spit and tears flung from his lips. He was weeping openly, the tears carving channels in the grime that was crusted to his skin.

'First the devil, now God. Why, I sure got myself some pretty stern judges looking over me, haven't I just?'

'What about Kat?' Jack tried another tack. 'She knows what you did. Why aren't you killing her?'

'She knows plenty.' Brannigan's expression changed. 'But don't you worry yourself about her.'

'Why? Why trust her and not him?' Jack gestured towards Adam with his chin.

'She's a good girl. Knows her place and does what I says, when I say it. And a girl like that, she ain't no threat, not to me.' Brannigan pulled a wry face, as if that thought amused him.

'Because she does what you say? Because she flops on her back at your command?'

'Shut your filthy goddam mouth,' Brannigan warned.

'Why? Are you going to kill me?' The glib retort was immediate. 'You know she'll tire of you. You're an old man to her, Brannigan. When she's had enough of you pounding away at her with that dry old prick of yours, she'll find herself someone else. Someone younger.' He wanted to provoke the wagon master. He wanted anger. For angry men made mistakes more often than those who were calm and in control.

Brannigan took a pace towards him. 'Shut your filthy mouth.' He still held Jack's sabre. Now the tip of it rose, as if he was planning to drive it into Jack's breast.

'Why? Because you know I'm right? Because—'

Jack never finished the sentence. Brannigan punched fast and hard with his free hand. Jack's head exploded with pain as the fist smashed into his cheek with enough force to nearly knock him from his feet. He staggered, and only steadied when Brannigan reached out and grabbed him around the neck.

'It ain't like that between us.' Brannigan craned Jack's neck back so that he was rocked on to his heels. 'I found her and her brother just after some sons of bitches had killed their parents. I took them in and kept them safe. So you shut that foul mouth of yours, or I swear I'll kill you right here and now.'

Jack's throat was half crushed as Brannigan's fingers dug into his flesh. He could not have replied even if he'd wanted to.

'You ever say anything like that again and I'll kill you so slowly that you'll beg me to end it.' Brannigan's face was contorted with fury as he made the vow. His grip tightened, his fingers like claws, then he let go, throwing Jack away from him, his expressionless mask slipping back into place.

Jack slumped against the wall, his hands pressed into the cold stone, fingers scrabbling for purchase to keep him upright as he gasped down fast breaths. Brannigan had turned away the moment he had let go, and now he walked to the doorway. He stood there for several long moments. When he turned back to face his prisoners, a thin-lipped smile was firmly in place.

'Time for you to follow me, fellas. You can walk, or I'll have my boys drag you. I sure don't care which one of those it is.'

He looked down at the sabre in his hand, as if surprised to find himself still holding it. He contemplated the weapon one last time, then tossed it contemptuously aside before turning to amble out of the shed. The Tejanos supporting Brown followed. Two more waited outside, both armed with carbines.

Jack hesitated for a moment, then stepped outside into the chilly pre-dawn air. He would not allow himself to be dragged to his grave. Not when there was still strength left in his body. Not when he could still fight.

Chapter Thirty-six

There were few people present to witness the three prisoners' departure. Jack looked at the faces he did see, searching them for some shred of compassion, or some look or expression that would give him a glimmer of hope that someone would intercede on their behalf. He saw nothing but the cold, merciless features of men long used to cruel death. There was no hope to be found. Not there. Not that day.

He looked for Kat, too. Part of him wanted to believe she was not a party to everything that was about to happen. Yet he knew he was deluding himself. She had been the one person Brannigan had spared. To do that, he would surely have told her everything, just as he would most likely have told her his plans for the three men he had taken captive. It meant she knew Jack was going to die; yet she was not there to see it, let alone intervene. He would die believing she had played a part in his death.

But he found he did not blame her. She was nothing more than a pawn in Brannigan's game. And she was doing what she had to do to survive. He had done the same. He had taken his place in Brannigan's gang willingly, staying even after cold-blooded murder had been committed. Now he would pay the price for that folly.

The three prisoners and their guards walked away from the hacienda. Not one of the sad procession spoke. Brannigan led the way, followed by Brown and the two Tejanos holding him up. Adam and Jack came next, with the other two Tejanos and their carbines just behind. The captives were made to walk with their hands still bound tight behind their backs. One of the Tejanos had taken the necessary time to check the knots were still tight.

It was cold outside the shed. The cool air whispered over Jack's naked skin, raising goose bumps across every inch so that he shivered. Rocks and sharp stones cut into the soles of his feet, yet he paid them no heed, just as he did his best to ignore the numbness in his shoulders and the burn of the rope on the raw, bloody skin of his wrists. He thought only of when he would run, of when he would try to cheat the fate that Brannigan had planned.

They walked for a good mile without pause. Twice Jack thought about making a break for it, but a glance over his shoulder revealed that the barrel of a loaded carbine was no more than a couple of feet away from the pit of his spine. If he ran, he died. And it would not be a quick death. It would be slow, every one of his final minutes agony. On the battlefield, men relied on one another to administer a clean and merciful end. It was the creed of the soldier, the final act of comradeship between brothers in arms. Yet this day he was quite alone. He could expect no mercy.

They walked on. There was nothing to see save for mile upon mile of the same drab-coloured scrub. Jack's mind wandered. The colours reminded him of India, and the pale, dusty uniform he had worn during his ill-fated time as a lieutenant serving in Hodson's Horse, an irregular unit of cavalry raised and commanded by William Raikes Hodson, a man Jack had come to despise. The memory stirred something in his mind. It was a reminder of a time when he had fought through every adversity he had faced, a time when he had refused to give in to Fate.

'And here we are.' Brannigan spoke every word slowly as he turned to face the men who had trailed so dutifully in his wake.

Jack's mind snapped back to the present. They were in the middle of nowhere, the view of dusty scrub unchanged but for one thing. Behind Brannigan was a freshly dug ditch, the excavated dirt piled neatly to one side. The four bandoleros who had dug it waited patiently to one side, their shovels left on the mound of dirt, their hands now filled with brand-new Enfield rifle muskets.

He looked around him. The same bleak scene stretched away for miles in every direction. They were in a place where no one would ever find the bodies of the three men who now stood and stared at their own grave.

'So this is where it ends.' Brannigan looked at each of the three in turn. 'You are the last men alive who know what I did. Now it's time to put you in the ground so that no one comes after me.' He gestured to the two Tejanos supporting Brown to bring him to the edge of the pit. They did as he commanded, then let go, hesitating for a moment to make sure Brown could stand before they walked away.

'The authorities won't give up. They'll find out what happened here. They'll find out what happened to Vaughan and to all the others you butchered.' Jack found his tongue.

The words rasped as he spoke them, his throat burning from where Brannigan had half strangled him. There was not a drop of moisture left anywhere in his throat, and his tongue felt like it was glued to the roof of his mouth. Yet he forced the words out. He needed Brannigan distracted.

'The authorities!' Brannigan laughed. 'Hell, where do you think you are, Jack? Back in jolly old London? There ain't no *authorities* down here. I got myself all the goddam authority I need right here.' He patted his holstered revolver. 'There ain't no one going to care what happened to you all. As far as anyone knows, these Mexican boys ambushed the wagons and took the guns all by themselves.'

'You think they'll believe that?'

Brannigan shrugged. 'It happens. We'll just be listed as another missing wagon train. We won't be the first. Or the last.'

Jack tried to summon the will to continue, but his mouth and throat were on fire. Now they had stopped walking, his head was pounding, the pain filling his mind so that he was finding it impossible to think straight.

He looked around, trying to see where he could run. There were six guns covering the three men. Every one was held still. To move was to die.

He looked at Adam. The boy was the colour of whey. He had not made a sound since they had left the hacienda behind, but his face was twisted as he wept in silence and without tears.

Jack glanced at Brown. The man looked done in. He tottered at the edge of the freshly dug pit. Old blood caked his neck and shoulders, and there were thin streaks left across his bare skin from where it had run down his body. His prick had shrivelled with fear so that it was barely visible amidst his thick thatch of pubic hair.

Jack moved his gaze away from the pathetic sight. He saw that Brannigan was staring back at him. He searched the wagon master's eyes, looking for a spark of humanity; for something that would reveal that a man lived behind the expressionless facade. He failed. He stared into the abyss of Brannigan's baleful gaze and saw nothing but death.

'You done lollygagging now, Jack?' Brannigan turned on the spot, drawing his revolver as he did so. He fired a heartbeat later.

The bullet hit Brown in the side of the head. He crumpled without a sound, falling half in and half out of the pit, his ruined head coming down so that it lay on the dirt outside the hole, his body twisted at an impossible angle only the dead could make.

'Get him in there.' Brannigan gave the order to the Tejanos who had brought Brown to the grave.

The pair hurried to obey. They stepped forward, eager hands lifting Brown before tossing him forward so that his body fell fully into the pit. Task done, they moved away quickly, their hands bloody.

'Who wants to be next?' Brannigan addressed the question to his two remaining captives, the still smoking revolver held casually in his hand.

'Don't do it, Brannigan,' Adam whispered, the words barely audible.

'What's that you say?' Brannigan made a play of cocking his ear. 'I can't quite hear you.'

'Don't kill me.' Adam whimpered. 'Please don't.'

'Cat got your tongue, boy?' Brannigan shouted. 'Speak up now.'

'Don't kill me!' Adam lifted his head and shrieked the plea, his whole body shaking. 'I beg you.'

'Now I can hear you.' Brannigan smiled. 'But I'm sorry, Adam, this is just the way it has to be. Dawson knows you. Of all people, you might be able to convince him to trust what you say.' He turned to the Tejanos. 'Him next.'

'No!' Jack gave the word in the voice of command he had first learned all those years ago in the Crimea. 'Kill me, but let the boy live.'

'You giving me orders, Jack?' Brannigan had heard the snap in Jack's tone, and he made a face of mock surprise. 'You telling me what to do?'

'You owe me, remember? So now pay me back. He's just a boy. Let him live.' Jack stood straight, ignoring the pain and the shame of his bare flesh. 'Kill me and let him go.'

'No.' Brannigan's answer was immediate. 'Bring him up.'

The Tejanos did as they were told. The two without weapons each took one of Adam's elbows, then led him to the edge of the pit.

Adam tried to fight them. He kicked at the ground and leaned back, pushing against his captors, so that it was a struggle to get him into place, but he stood no chance against the strength of the two men, and they dragged him forward until his feet rested against the lip of the grave.

'Please, Brannigan,' Adam begged. He turned his head, terror contorting his features so that he was barely recognisable.

'I'm sorry.' Brannigan's tone was firm as he raised the revolver.

'No.' There was time for Adam to give a last wail before the gang leader pulled the trigger. The bullet hit him right in the centre of his forehead and he fell like a stone, his body toppling forward and into the pit, where it thumped into the dirt.

'And then there was one.' Brannigan did not look at the

body he had just committed to the ground. Instead, he turned on the spot and looked squarely at Jack.

Jack braced himself. The fear came then, an unstoppable shudder that swirled up from his guts, surging through his chest and into his heart before rushing on to fill his head with a silent scream. Nothing had prepared him for the intensity of this moment; this moment of his death.

He fought it then. He rallied his mind, forcing it to stand firm against the unstoppable forces that assailed it. Everything he had been had led to this moment. Every battle, every fight had preserved his life only so that he would die here.

There would be nothing redeeming in this lonely death. He was not laying down his life for his mates, or even for his country. He would die because he was an inconvenience.

That knowledge shamed him. He had not taken an officer's scarlet coat to die here. He had come so far, and he had changed so much from the naive, innocent young man who had embarked on the journey that had led him here. That his life should end in such a tawdry and insignificant manner seemed impossible. It was too sudden. Too simple. Too quick.

'You want to kneel?' Brannigan had raised his revolver. It twitched to one side, the barrel aimed squarely at Jack's face.

Jack found he could not speak. He looked at Brannigan. Everything felt unreal, like he was in a dream. This could not be happening. Not now.

'Take a step forward.' Brannigan gave the command. 'Save us the trouble of throwing you in.'

Jack did as he was told. He did not know why, and his meekness angered him. But he could see no other way. It did not matter if he tried to fight, or if he tried to run. There was no hope. There was no escape. There was just death.

'Good man,' Brannigan congratulated him. 'You boys get on now. I'll finish it. Jack ain't going no place.'

Jack almost choked on the indignity as he stood there, submissive and servile. Yet he could do nothing else. His mind was numb, the enormity of his own death engulfing every thought. He finally faced oblivion, and he faced it like a mouse. There was to be no last fight. No final attempt to save himself.

He heard the shuffle of men moving away. He could feel the breeze washing across his skin, and there was warmth on his back as the first rays of the sun spread over the scrubland. It was his last chance to run. Brannigan had gifted him this moment, his dismissal of the Tejanos and bandoleros reducing the number of guns aimed at him. Yet he stayed where he was, transfixed by fear.

They waited for many minutes like that, Jack standing stock still, Brannigan's revolver aimed squarely at his skull. The sounds of the men moving away faded. Then there was just silence.

'Goodbye, Jack,' Brannigan muttered.

Jack tensed. After so many minutes of quiet, the voice was too loud, too strident. It did not belong there. Not in the last seconds of Jack's universe. He felt a moment's anger then, a sudden urge to turn and confront the man who would kill him.

But he had left it too late. There was no time left.

Brannigan pulled the trigger. The last gunshot of Jack's life roared out, splitting the silence asunder.

Chapter Thirty-seven

'Get up, Jack. Come on now.'

Jack came back to the world. He had fallen when Brannigan's revolver had fired, his legs failing him at the last. He had hit the bottom of the ditch face first, the brutal contact with the ground knocking him out. Now pain surged through his head and face. He could feel blood pumping from his nose and lips where they had been crushed by the impact with the earth. But when he reached out through his body, searching for the impact of a bullet, he found nothing.

'Come on now. I ain't got long.' Brannigan snapped the command.

Jack slowly pushed himself up. It was not easy. He was lying face down with his hands bound tightly behind him. Somehow he managed to push his knees forward so that he could ease himself into an awkward crouch. With a lurch, he staggered to his feet and looked up.

Brannigan stood at the lip of the ditch, watching him. 'You surprised me, Jack. I swore you'd fight me.'

Jack had no capacity to speak. He could do nothing but stare.

'You getting out of there?' Brannigan gave a sickly smile, then turned to walk away, leaving Jack to look up at nothing but the sky.

For his part, Jack was struggling to keep up with what was going on. He stood there, every muscle shaking.

'Get out of there, Jack, or so help me God I'll shoot you after all.'

He heard the mockery in Brannigan's tone. He did not doubt the threat. He took a cautious step forward. Brannigan's bandoleros had worked hard, the pit a good three feet deep. He staggered to the edge, then bent his body forward on the ground above the lip. He pushed up and twisted, rolling himself on to the dusty soil above. He felt rocks catch his flesh, then he was out, and lying on the ground above. He took a deep breath, then wriggled on to his knees. It took everything he had to lever himself to his feet.

'Boy, do you look like shit.' Brannigan laughed as Jack finally stood in front of him.

Jack cared nothing for the abuse. He could feel the blood flowing across his lips and dribbling down his chin. His body was covered with dirt, and a hundred cuts and grazes. Yet he was alive.

'I expect you're wondering why I let you live.' Brannigan spoke carefully, as if concerned that Jack would fail to understand the words. He holstered his revolver, watching Jack as he did so to make sure the gesture was understood.

'You saved my life, and I told you I'd pay you back.' Brannigan hooked his thumbs into his gun belt. 'So here you go. I'm letting you live.' He paused, waiting for some sort of reaction.

He did not get one. Jack could do nothing but stand and

stare.

'Cat got your tongue?'

Jack moved his tongue around his mouth, trying to summon the moisture to speak.

'So be it.' Brannigan raised an arm and pointed into the distance. 'Off you go now.'

Jack turned his head with difficulty and looked where Brannigan was pointing. He saw nothing but more of the same drab scrubland.

'You still here?' Brannigan barked.

'Untie me,' Jack stammered.

'You'll be just fine as you are.'

Jack swallowed with difficulty. His mind was beginning to work once again. He was starting to understand that he was not going to die. At least not right at that moment.

'Go on now.' Brannigan snapped the command. 'If you don't want to go, I can still end it here and now.'

'No,' Jack spat. He could feel something shifting deep inside him. The fear was being beaten back and a sense of determination was starting to build, fuelled by shame. He had stood and waited for his death with passive acceptance. He did not know why.

'That's better.' Brannigan grinned. 'Now, I can't promise you that my Mexican friends won't come after you. I don't hold no sway with them. But I can give you a head start.'

'I'll come back.' The words rasped as they left Jack's mouth. It hurt to speak, but some things just had to be said. 'I'll come back. I'll find you. I'll kill you.'

'You're sure welcome to try.' Brannigan laughed off the threat. 'But if I were you, I'd concentrate my efforts on staying alive for the rest of the goddam day first.'

He shook his head as he contemplated Jack one last time.

Jack returned his stare. Then he summoned the strength he would need and began to walk.

Chapter Thirty-eight

---

*E*very inch of Jack's body hurt. The soles of his feet were the worst. After the first mile, he was leaving a trail of bloody footprints behind him, the rocks and thorns underfoot shredding the soft skin so that every step had become agony. Then there was the thirst. He could feel his lips splitting as the sun roasted the flesh dry, and his mouth was on fire. Water dominated his thoughts; at least those that penetrated the heavy pounding that reverberated around his skull as if a battalion of French drummers was beating out a *pas de charge* for him alone.

He kept moving. He could feel blisters starting to rise on the right side of his body as his skin was scorched. But at least the pain told him he was heading in the right direction. If he went north, he would be heading back towards Texas and American soil. He had no idea how long it would take him to get there, or if indeed he had the strength to cover that many miles, but it was all the plan he could summon.

As he put one bloody foot in front of the other, he thought of what he would do next. Revenge had sustained him before. Once he had crossed hundreds of miles to exact retribution from the man who had thrown his life into the balance. Yet this was different. He was not going to chase Brannigan down for some half-formed notion of avenging himself. He was doing it for someone else. He was doing it for Fate.

He would find Brannigan, and he would bring the man to justice. It was why Fate had led him south and to a place in Brannigan's gang. She wanted him there. She wanted him to deliver her justice.

He was to be her weapon and he would not let her down.

He saw the Ángeles the first time he fell.

There were dozens of them. All were mounted, and they were following the bloody trail he had left. He did not know why they were bothering. He could not see an outcome that did not finish with him falling into the dirt, where his struggle to survive would come to an end, his lonely death followed by his body being eaten by any animal that came along, until there was nothing left but sun-bleached bones. His pace had slowed in the last hours, so that he tottered along like an old man. He had stopped more times than he could count. Not once had he let himself sit, but on every occasion he had been forced to fight the urge to lie down and let the sun bake him to a lifeless husk.

He did not really understand what had kept him on his feet. The desire to kill Brannigan had sustained him for the first part of the day. The knowledge that he had been chosen as Fate's vengeance had lent strength to a body that was on its last legs. Yet such imaginings could only last so long. Now he was upright out of sheer bloody-mindedness. He would not give in again.

So he ground out the miles. Exhaustion and dehydration dogged every step, his life turned into a living hell. Somehow he kept going, fighting against his failing flesh, determination and pure grit keeping him on his feet for one more step, for one more minute, for one more hour.

Then he had fallen for the first time.

With his hands still tied behind him, there was no way to break his fall, and he hit the ground face first. His vision greyed, but this time he did not black out. He lay there, pain and fatigue swamping him.

That was when he saw the mounted Ángeles on his trail.

He almost cried out as he pushed himself first to his knees, then to his feet. It hurt to move, to breathe, to swallow, to carry on living, but he forced himself to move.

He ran then. It was not much, just an awkward lumbering gait that was all he could manage. He focused everything he had on putting one foot in front of the other. The futility of his actions bit at his heels, forcing him on. There was no outrunning a mounted pursuit, not even in the best boots or on the strongest legs. Yet he would run for as long as he could. Then this time he would fight.

As he ran, he looked for a place to hide, or at least to screen himself from view for long enough to change direction without being seen. Yet there was nothing and nowhere, just the same sparse, desolate landscape stretching for miles in every direction.

There was nothing to do save to keep going for as long as his battered, desiccated husk of a body could go on.

Jack was nearly delirious when he fell for a second time. This time he hit hard, his head bouncing up from the ground like it was on a spring. The darkness came for him almost immediately. It surged up, consuming and ravenous. The temptation to succumb was almost more than he could bear. But something had changed inside him. He felt strength stir deep down in his belly, a sensation that had not been there before, not even during the assault on the Great Redoubt on the slopes of the Alma River, or in the bloody confines of the breach at Delhi. It was as if there was a fire in his gut that sparked him back into life.

He rolled on to his side, and then on to his scuffed and grazed knees. The pain flared but barely registered. He was beyond such things now. With a great lurch, he got to his feet. Then he was moving again.

He laughed then. He did not know why, but something in that moment was inordinately funny. Perhaps it was a fleeting image of himself, this bloodied, filthy madman who ran naked across the bleak plain. Or perhaps it was the knowledge that he would surely soon be on his way to hell. Whichever it was, he ran on, cackling to himself like a Bedlam lunatic, even as he stumbled and almost fell for what would most likely have been the final time.

And then he saw them.

He stopped laughing. At first he believed he was deluding himself. He knew that he was falling apart, his mind breaking as the pain, thirst and fatigue consumed him. But somewhere deep inside, a small vestige of sanity remained alive. That part of him knew he was delirious, but it had not cared, not until that moment. Not until he saw the two men on picket duty.

He did not stop or cry out. Instead he kept moving forward, even as his addled brain tried to work out if his eyes were playing him false, or if he truly did see two men in grey jackets and wide-brimmed black hats with the lone star of Texas on their front.

'Hey!'

One of the figures shouted at him. It was enough to make him laugh out loud again.

'You there!'

Jack saw the men raise weapons, and he laughed all the louder. The idea that he had cheated death in the merciless scrubland only to be gunned down by an overeager sentry was somehow inordinately funny.

'Stop right there, or I swear I'll shoot.'

Jack slowed his pace and glanced over his shoulder. There was no sign of his pursuit. He could only suppose the bandoleros had seen the same cavalrymen he had and kept away.

He kept moving forward. Again he laughed, the idea that anyone could see him as a threat preposterous.

'I said stop right there!' The sentry repeated the command.

This time, Jack did as he was told. He staggered to a halt, and did his best to stand still.

'Raise your arms!'

Jack's laughter intensified. He threw back his head and whooped at the sky. Then the blackness came, and he fell.

'Hey, you waking up or what?'

Jack's eyes opened, but the light was too much and he could not see. Yet at that moment, something as trivial as blindness did not matter. For the first thing he felt was a pair of strong hands cradling the back of his head. Then he felt water on his lips.

Nothing had ever tasted so glorious. The warm, brackish liquid filled his mouth and he swallowed, dragging it over the raw flesh inside his mouth and throat. More came and he gulped it down. It was more intoxicating than the strongest arrack. He drank and drank, drowning himself in the beautiful sensation of water cascading down his throat. He could feel it running through his body and settling heavy in his stomach.

'Ease up there, Jack. You can have more in a minute.' A familiar voice ordered Jack to stop.

Jack still could not see. He blinked, trying to clear his vision. Only as the light became less intense did he recognise the man who was holding his head.

'Sweet Lord of mercy, I thought you were dead for a moment back then.' Captain Dawson was squatted down on his haunches as he peered at Jack.

'Are you sure I'm alive?' Jack coughed and spluttered as he spoke for the first time in what felt like forever.

'Ha! You don't look it.' Dawson shook his head.

Jack looked down. His eyes took in his own naked body. Every scrap of flesh was crusted with blood and grime.

'Can you sit?' Dawson asked.

Jack nodded, and did his best to struggle up. He made it with Dawson's assistance. It was only then that he realised his arms were no longer tied behind him.

'Jesus fucking Christ.' He could not hold back the oath. His arms had been numb for so many hours. Now they were on fire, and even moving them an inch set off a spasm of white-hot pain that was nearly enough to make him faint away.

'Take it easy,' Dawson advised, then handed over a canteen. 'Here.'

The pain was forgotten in an instant. Raising the canteen to his lips hurt like the devil, but his need for water overrode the need to protect himself from more pain, and he drank in long, desperate gulps.

Canteen emptied, he took in his surroundings. Dawson and

his men had bivouacked on a section of rocky ground several feet lower than the surrounding terrain. They were gathered around what looked to be a natural spring, the water bubbling up from a small pile of rocks. Several men were busy refilling dozens of canteens, whilst others had lit a fire and were brewing the inevitable pots of coffee. Jack had been around American soldiers for long enough to know they were fuelled by coffee just as the British redcoats were sustained by tea. Those not at work collecting or heating water were tending to the patrol's horses.

The ground around them was uneven and broken. The thorny bushes and patches of prickly pear cactus were higher here, in some places as tall as a man. Dawson had chosen the spot well, his men nearly completely screened from view. It was a good place to rest up for a while, and Jack felt a surge of relief as he realised he was safe.

'So what the hell happened to you?' Dawson was still squatting down next to him. His brow was furrowed as he contemplated the naked man who had run into his camp.

Jack held up the empty canteen. 'Can I have some more water?'

'No.' The refusal was given in a firm tone. 'Not until you tell me where to find either Brannigan or Vaughan.'

Jack saw the set of Dawson's jaw. The Confederate cavalry officer reminded him of Brannigan. Both had the same ruthless determination to get what they wanted.

'Then you'd better know the way to hell.'

'They're dead?'

'Vaughan is. Brannigan killed him.'

'The double-crossing son of a bitch.' Dawson scowled as he absorbed the news. 'When did that happen?'

'On the way back to Brownsville.'

'Then what?'

'We turned south.' Jack had to lick his lips. They were still raw and painful. He craved more water, but he knew Dawson would not be satisfied until he had the bare bones of his tale. 'We had to. To avoid you.'

'What the hell do you mean?'

'That plan of yours. You and Vaughan.' Jack searched through a mind as lumpy as yesterday's porridge, trying to remember Brannigan and Kat's claims about Vaughan's collusion with the Confederate officer now sitting in front of him. 'You were going to take the guns as soon as we got to Brownsville.'

'The hell I was. General Bee would string me up from the nearest tree if I tried something as goddam dumb as that.' Dawson's reaction was immediate. 'Who told you that nonsense?'

'They both did.'

'Shit.' Dawson turned his head and spat. 'It's a pack of lies. There was no plan. They fed you a huge pile of horseshit, my friend.'

Jack's addled wits were trying to keep up. 'So why are you here?'

'We knew the wagon train had gone missing. Those rifles make it one hell of a valuable cargo, one that Bee badly needs. So we've come to find it.' Dawson rocked back on his heels and shook his head. 'I knew Brannigan would be up to his neck in this.'

'And you're allowed to be all the way down here?' Jack asked a question of his own.

Dawson smiled wolfishly, revealing his fine white teeth. 'Bee agreed an accord with López, the governor here, that allows us to do whatever we like. Besides, I don't see anyone around to stop me. We're here to find the guns. When we've done that, we'll be on our way.'

'Brannigan's already sold them.'

Dawson's brow furrowed as he absorbed the bad news. 'Do you know who bought them?'

'Santiago.'

'Son of a gun.' Dawson winced at the news.

'That's not all.' Jack opened his mouth to say more, but at first no words came. Instead, his mind replayed the moment Brannigan's men were slaughtered. He heard their screams over the gunfire, and the heart-wrenching pleas for mercy that followed. 'He killed them. He killed them all.'

'What?' Dawson leaned forward.

Jack looked up. 'Brannigan had all his men killed save for three of us. Adam survived, as did one other man. Brannigan shot them both this morning.'

'But he let you go?'

'He owed me. I saved his life back in Texas.'

Dawson held Jack's gaze for a moment longer, then looked away. Neither of them spoke for some time.

'Where does a man like Santiago get enough money to buy a whole wagon train's worth of guns?' Jack broke the silence with the question.

'From the French. Santiago ain't picky. That son of a bitch will rob anyone. The French are pouring gold into Mexico as they fight the goddam Mexicans. Rumour has it that Santiago captured one of their convoys that had enough specie to pay their army for months. Hellfire and damnation.' Dawson cursed as he realised the enormity of the transaction Brannigan had undertaken. 'Now they're going to be armed with the best goddam rifles you English can make.'

'So take them back.' Jack sat up a little straighter. Either the pain was fading or he was becoming accustomed to it. Either way, he was feeling stronger.

'You know where they are?'

'I know where they were this morning.'

'Can you show me?'

Jack nodded. He reckoned he could find his way back to the hacienda where he had been held overnight.

'Then we'd better find you some clothes.'

Jack ignored the comment. 'I'll need a carbine, a revolver too.'

'You can have my spare. Hell, I'll give you the uniform off my own goddam back if you can show me where those guns are.'

'I can show you.' Jack looked Dawson dead in the eye. 'But there's a hell of a lot of Santiago's men with them.'

'How many?'

'Two hundred, maybe more.'

'Shit.' Dawson turned his head as he absorbed the news.

'How many men have you got with you?' Jack asked.

'Thirty-six.' Dawson looked back at him, a smile on his face. 'You like the odds?'

Jack shrugged. 'I've known better.'

'And I've known worse. But if we hit them hard and fast, it should be enough. Men like Santiago's don't hang around long.'

'And if they do?'

'Then we'll have ourselves one hell of a fight.' Dawson grinned at the thought.

'Sounds like we have a plan.'

The officer's smile broadened. 'We sure do.'

Jack saw the determination in Dawson's eyes. It was a good sign. For the first time, he felt his dislike of the man shift a little. The similarity to Brannigan was still there, but Dawson had something else, something totally lacking in the wagon master: a sense of duty and a willingness to do the right thing. For Jack, that was enough.

He held out his empty canteen. 'Now that that's sorted, be a good fellow and fetch me some more bloody water.'

Dawson laughed. 'Yes, sir.' He knuckled his head, then reached out to take the canteen and turned to toss it to one of his men with an order to refill it.

Jack sat where he was. He would not move until he had drunk his fill. Only then would he find the strength to get to his feet, and start the task of finding what he would need if he were going to ride with Dawson and his men when they attacked Brannigan and Santiago's camp.

Chapter Thirty-nine

---

*J*ack rode on his borrowed mare, one of the half-dozen remounts Dawson's column had brought with them, fighting the urge to fidget. Everything felt strange, from the animal beneath him to the clothes on his back and the weapons he carried. But he had to admit it was better than crossing the scrubland in nothing more than his bare skin. Dawson had been true to his word. Jack wore the Confederate captain's spare revolver in a holster on his right hip, a serviceable Remington like the one Kat carried. He was also armed with a double-barrelled shotgun borrowed from one of Dawson's sergeants.

The man who had lent him the shotgun had told him something of its characteristics. It was a short-range weapon, and Jack had been warned that it was ineffective beyond much more than thirty or forty yards. But up close and personal, he had been assured it was dreadfully effective. It fired buckshot cartridges, of which Dawson's men had plenty, and Jack had been given an ammunition pouch containing thirty cartridges along with a smaller pouch that held the percussion caps used to fire the main charge. The paper cartridges contained twelve individual pieces of shot, each one a smaller version of the musket ball fired by the smoothbore muskets Jack knew. Underneath the shot was a load of powder. A separate hammer and percussion cap fired each of the shotgun's two barrels. When the trigger was pulled, either or both of the cocked hammers would strike the percussion cap, which would explode and fire the main charge contained in the cartridge. Jack had not used a shotgun before, but he had no reason to doubt the cavalryman's word that it would be a brutal weapon in a close-contact battle.

Dawson's men had also found him clothes to wear: a grey flannel shirt and a pair of pale blue trousers that had a gaping hole at one knee. On his feet were a pair of the pointed boots that all the Texans wore, and they had even found him a spare wide-brimmed hat. Jack had to admit he looked every inch the Texan cavalryman. In addition, they had found him two spare canteens, a blanket and a small pocketknife. Their generosity had been humbling.

The Confederate patrol rode fast and hard. Dawson had sent outriders to scout the way ahead, and the main column rode with flankers and a two-man rear guard. They had all taken time to load their weapons before the column had set off. Jack had seen that they carried a bewildering array of carbines, revolvers and shotguns; every man also had either a bowie knife or a tomahawk, whilst many had a lasso. They might be outnumbered, but they were well armed and ready to fight.

'You good, Jack?' Dawson rode close to Jack in the centre of the main column.

Jack nodded. He was in pain, but he would not admit it. Everything hurt, not least his feet, and both shoulders were aching like the devil. But he rode with a weapon in his hand, and that was enough to stave off the agony.

'Are you sure we're heading the right way?' Dawson asked.

'Yes.' Jack was certain. After he had been released, he was reasonably sure that he had run north. All Dawson's men had to do was to ride due south and they should find the ruined hacienda. He glanced at the officer. He could see the worry on his face. It was no small thing to command men so far from safety, and he could well understand the feelings that Dawson would surely be enduring. But no words could lessen the burden of command that he carried, so he did not even try.

They rode on. It was not long before the outriders came rushing back towards the main column. Dawson raised a hand to halt the column, then rode forward to meet his scouts. Jack rode with him.

'It's right where he said it was.' The first man back, a sergeant, sang out the news as soon as he was close enough.

'How many?'

'Over a hundred. Maybe more.' The sergeant looked at Jack as he delivered the information, as if the Englishman were somehow responsible for it.

Dawson glanced at Jack.

'I told you.' Jack turned back to the sergeant. 'What about the wagons?'

'They're there.'

'How many?'

'Forty.'

Jack smiled. That was the whole wagon train. Dawson's patrol was horribly outnumbered, but at least their quarry had not already ridden away. There was still a chance to recover the weapons and to bring Brannigan and Kat to justice.

'Let's do this.' Dawson turned in the saddle and looked over his men.

'What's your plan?' Jack asked the only question he wanted answered.

'Plan?' Dawson laughed as if the idea was preposterous 'We don't need a plan.' He shook his head at Jack's foolish question, then stood up in the saddle. 'This is it, boys.' He said nothing more as he sat back down and drew a shotgun of his own.

'Ready?' He looked towards Jack.

'Yes.' Jack checked that his borrowed Remington was loose in its holster as he gave the reply firmly. It was time to start fighting back.

The column rode in fast. Dawson had pulled his flankers in, but he had left five men back as a rear guard, ready to cover any withdrawal. The rest of the men rode two abreast.

Jack was towards the middle of the column. The rhythm of the fast advance surged through him. His borrowed mare stretched her legs, and he could feel her power beneath him. Her hooves thumped into the sun-baked ground, the drumming increasing in intensity as she picked up speed.

No orders were given. The men knew their job.

As the column galloped along the trail, Jack caught his first glimpse of the hacienda. The wagons were parked to the rear. Some were ready to leave, the mule teams already harnessed up. Others were being prepared, with most of the mules and horses still corralled to the far side of the hacienda. A good number of Santiago's men were mounted as they prepared to escort the train away, but many walked around, some armed, others carrying water or other supplies. He saw no pickets. No sentries. No one to give warning.

The first man spied the cavalry. For a moment, he stood and gaped, then he dropped the sack he carried and shouted the first and only warning the Mexicans would get.

'Charge!' Dawson bellowed.

Every man gave his horse its head. The column surged forward, the pace increasing. Some men broke away, finding themselves a clear path ahead. Most stayed close together.

Jack could hear nothing save for the fast, staccato impact of hooves on hard ground and the roar of his own breath in his ears. He felt the thrill of the moment; fear mixing with exhilaration, fighting against the barriers he had constructed around it, desperate to escape its shackles. But he held all the emotions tight, emptying his mind so that he could fight without passion. He would no longer allow the madness of battle to control him. There was no room for rage, or some desperate desire for revenge. He thought only of what was to come. He was a weapon of war, honed for this moment, and he would fight with the cold, calculating mind of a killer.

Santiago's men saw the Confederate cavalry hurtling towards them. Those carrying weapons opened fire.

The first shots rang out.

Jack heard a bullet buzz past, then another. Neither came close enough to trouble him.

The men at the head of the column galloped into the yard behind the hacienda. Shotguns fired, a succession of blasts tearing through the air. The first Ángeles died as the buckshot tore them apart.

More shots came against the Confederate column. Not one of them hit.

The column broke up as it swarmed around the hacienda. Some followed the leading riders across the yard, the space echoing to the blasts of shotguns and the screams of men cut down by the vicious storm of buckshot. Others broke to the front of the hacienda, searching for targets of their own.

Jack followed Dawson into the yard. The air was filled with the stink of powder smoke and the raw, acrid tang of fresh blood and torn flesh. Revolver shots rang out constantly.

He rode past the first bodies. The devastating effect of a shotgun blast at close range was evident, with several bodies torn apart, great chasms ripped in their chests. A few corpses lay headless, the ground around them smothered with a grotesque display of brain, blood and bone.

But the Texans were not having it all their own way. Santiago's Ángeles were fighting back. Jack saw one of Dawson's men pulled bodily from the saddle. At least four Mexicans swarmed over him the moment he lay prostrate on the ground, coming for him with long knives that gouged and sliced as they hacked him to pieces.

Jack kicked hard, raking his spurs back. The mare responded, straining already finely stretched muscles. He picked a path, hauling on the reins to steer past a corpse with its stomach laid open by a shotgun blast, riding towards the swarm of Mexicans surrounding the fallen trooper.

He raised his shotgun only at the last moment, thumbing back both hammers then pulling the heavy trigger. Instantly the twin barrels erupted in an explosion of smoke and flame. The weapon's recoil was brutal, and far, far stronger than he had expected, and the shotgun was torn from his grasp. Still the twenty-four pieces of shot tore into one of the men hacking at Dawson's fallen trooper. At such close range, they split his flesh apart, blood and gore showering down like rain.

The three men left standing reacted immediately. As one

they raised knives bloodied to the hilt and rushed towards Jack, faces contorted with the intoxicating mix of fear and fury that sustained a man in a fight as brutal as this.

Jack watched them coming for him. It was easy enough to see what they intended. Together they could throw him from the saddle with ease. Then he would be at their mercy.

Yet he was not defenceless. With the shotgun torn from his grasp, he drew his Remington. He still held the reins in his left hand, and now he hauled them back, dragging his horse's head up so that it careered to a noisy halt. He fired a heartbeat later.

The first bullet hit one of the Ángeles in the chest. He crumpled, knife flying from his grip. The second hit the next man in the face flying at close to a thousand feet per second and dropping him in a heartbeat.

The third man stopped, his feet scrabbling as he tried to turn. Jack shot him down regardless, sending first one bullet then another into the Mexican's flesh. He fell forward into the dust, his blood pumping from his body with every beat of his racing heart.

Jack felt nothing as he killed, just like a slaughterman felt nothing as he swung the poleaxe to fell a bullock. He was just plying his bloody trade.

He turned his mare's head, swinging the animal around as he searched for a new target. The Ángeles had spread to the wind. Some had ridden away, and were already too far off for there to be any chance of catching them. Most were fleeing on foot, running in one great mass, spreading out into the scrubland that surrounded the hacienda.

They had left the wagons behind.

A dozen of Dawson's men gave chase, their horses thundering after those still running. The slowest-moving bandoleros were slaughtered, the air filled with the sound of revolvers firing and the screams of the runaways as they were caught. At least a dozen died, but there were not enough cavalrymen to ride them all down. The majority of Santiago's men would escape.

Yet not every Ángel had had the chance to run. Many of those on foot had made a break for the hacienda. Even as Jack looked for more men to kill, he saw at least four dash inside to join those already there.

'In the bloody house!' he shouted across to Dawson. He stretched out an arm to point at the ruined hacienda.

Dawson understood the danger. If he let men occupy the building, they could quickly turn it into a fortress.

'Boys! With me!' He shouted the order, summoning men out of the melee, then turned his horse towards the hacienda. Jack rode at his side, and together they made for the rear wall. This side of the building had no entrance; just four tiny square windows on its upper storey. The two men slewed their horses to a breathless halt.

'There's only one way to do this.' Dawson hissed the words as they both dismounted. Anything else he said was lost in the short, sharp roar of rifles firing from over their heads.

'Shit.' Jack could not help flinching as the volley snapped out. He saw its effect a moment later. Two of Dawson's men were down, one shot from the saddle, the other falling to the ground still atop his dying horse, which had taken a Minié ball in the neck.

'Move!' Dawson snapped the order, his jaw clenched tight. He grabbed Jack's arm, leading him towards the front of the building.

Men unscathed by the volley dismounted and joined them.

More were riding over when a second volley crashed out.
Another horse and rider went down.

There was no time to delay. Dawson's men might have
routed the bandoleros and captured the wagons, but the fight
was far from done.

Chapter Forty

———————◆———————

'Are you ready for this?' Dawson turned to hiss the words at Jack.

The two men were crouched down to one side of the entrance to the hacienda. Jack could see the strain on Dawson's face. Above their heads, more shots tore out from the building's upper storey. He had no idea how many Ángeles had rushed into the building, but they were already starting to exact a dreadful toll on Dawson's men. At least four bodies in grey shirts lay lifeless on the ground around the hacienda, with the same number of horses spewing their lifeblood into the dusty soil.

'Yes.' Jack gave the only reply he could. He reloaded his Remington quickly, pushing fresh cartridges into the empty chambers and ramming each one home with the loading lever attached to the barrel.

'You're good.' Dawson gave his verdict as he reloaded his own revolver: a Navy Colt, similar to the one Jack had lost when he had been captured by Brannigan.

'I should be, I've done this often enough.' Jack pulled away from the wall and looked up. Four rifle barrels stuck out from inside. As he watched, they fired again, another volley flung at

Dawson's men still chasing down running Ángeles.

'Well, now you get to do it again. We're going to rush them. Hit them before they settle.' Dawson snapped his Colt shut, all six chambers primed and loaded.

'Wait.' Jack was slower to load his unfamiliar weapon. He pushed in the last cartridge, then rammed it home before spinning the chamber to make sure all the cartridges were properly sited.

'Pope! Hunter!' Dawson looked around. 'Find loaded shotguns. You're in first.' He snapped his orders.

The two men turned to shout to the men behind them. Around a dozen of Dawson's men hugged the hacienda's flanks. Most carried revolvers, but a few had shotguns, and now these were passed forward.

'Here you go.' The man behind Jack handed him one of the weapons. Another followed, which Jack passed on to Dawson. There were four of the shotguns in total, all now at the front of the group.

'Ready?' Dawson looked down the line.

Pope and Hunter did not delay. Both men got to their feet and took up position opposite the hacienda's door.

'Go!' Dawson shouted the order just as another volley roared out overhead.

Pope stepped forward and smashed his boot into the door that barred the hacienda's only entrance. The wood juddered but held.

'Goddammit!' He stumbled back. Yet he was not a man to be deterred, and he stepped forward again and hammered his boot against the door for a second time.

Again the door juddered, but this time something splintered, the sound of breaking wood coming back clearly.

Once more Pope lashed out a boot. This time the door gave way, and it flew inwards, crashing into the wall behind it.

'Go!' Dawson shouted the order.

Pope was unbalanced, so Hunter took the bit between his teeth and stepped into the open doorway, lifting his shotgun as he moved. He fired into the hacienda, blasting both barrels into the dark interior. The explosion of sound was terrific.

Yet it was not enough. A volley of rifle fire came back almost instantly. More than one Minié bullet tore into Hunter's chest. At such close range, the heavy projectiles ripped him apart.

Bellowing a war cry, Pope stepped over Hunter's corpse and fired his own shotgun. Again the sound of the blast was deafening. This time there was no answering volley. Pope lurched forward, throwing himself into the hacienda.

Jack was on his feet. He tried to follow Pope inside, but his boot slipped in Hunter's blood and he fell back on to his backside. It let another one of Dawson's men get ahead of him, the trooper darting inside after Pope had cleared the doorway.

A second Ángeles volley roared out.

Neither of Dawson's troopers stood a chance. Both were cut down, their bodies shredded by the brutally powerful bullets. Jack clearly heard the splatter of blood on the hacienda's dirt floor as he got back to his feet. There was no time to dwell on the slip that had just saved his life, and he rushed inside, not once thinking to let others go first.

After the bright sunlight, the interior of the hacienda was filled with gloom and shadows. Yet there was no time to let his eyes adjust to the darkness, not if he wanted to live. He saw shadowy figures to his front, so he raised his shotgun and pulled the heavy trigger, arms braced for the recoil. The blast was terrific, yet this time he held on to the weapon. Screams followed, at least three men cut down by the explosion of buckshot.

'Out of the way!' Dawson had followed Jack inside and now bellowed the warning.

Jack barely had time to register it before another shotgun went off inches from his ear.

The sound deafened him. He reeled away, head and ears ringing.

More Texans followed their officer inside. Shots were fired, revolvers used at close range to kill. The hacienda was filled with the screams and shrieks of the wounded and dying, and those fighting for their lives.

Jack dropped the empty shotgun and drew his revolver. Yet he could not see a target in the vicious swirling melee erupting in front of him. It was like a chaotic brawl in a tavern, except here the men were using revolvers and bowie knives instead of fists and cudgels. The fighting was dreadful in both its violence and its immediacy. Men clawed and slashed at one another, killing and maiming. Fighting for the right to live; desperate not to die.

In front of his eyes, one of Dawson's men went down with a thin dagger driven through his eye and into his brain. At his side, a bandolero died as a trooper tore out his throat with his bare hands.

'Look out!'

Someone, Jack did not know who, bellowed a warning.

A bandolero came at him from the side. Jack only saw the blade at the last moment. He had just enough time to throw up his revolver in a desperate parry. The handgun caught the blade, throwing it to one side. Yet the impact tore the weapon from his grasp, the revolver falling to the floor.

His attacker shrieked in rage, then threw himself at Jack. Off balance and unarmed, Jack could do little to protect himself. He punched hard, but the blow bounced off the man's shoulder. It did nothing to stop his rush, and he grabbed Jack around the throat.

With his windpipe being crushed, Jack fell backwards, powerless against the force of the man attacking him. Yet even then, he felt nothing but calm. There was no wild rage. No visceral need to kill. Just a frozen, ice-cold mind, detached from the animalistic fight that surrounded him.

He hit the floor on his back, the impact brutal. The pain came in a great wave, but it was as nothing against the white-hot agony of the fingers clawing at this throat. Fingers that choked, suffocating, strong, remorseless.

He fought back, lifting his hands to his attacker's face. His fingers found the target they sought immediately. He dug them into the bandolero's eye sockets, nails like claws as they gouged deeper and deeper, ravaging the soft flesh. He heard the man scream as his eyeballs burst under the relentless pressure. Still he ground his fingers forward, ruthless and cruel, tearing through the mushy tissues then digging deeper still, blood hot and warm on his skin. He did not stop even as the man's hands released his throat and beat against his arms.

Keeping his fingers buried in the ruin of the man's eyes, he pushed hard, forcing his opponent up and away. He used the strength of his arms to manoeuvre the man to his feet then shove him backwards until it was the bandolero's turn to fall on to his back. Only then did Jack allow his fingers to tear free.

'Mother of God.' One of Dawson's men pushed past him as he staggered away from his victim. The trooper looked down at the man who lay writhing on the floor, hands clasped to his ruined eyes, blood escaping through his grasping fingers to run down his wrists. Then he glanced up at Jack, his expression somewhere between loathing and admiration.

Jack cared nothing for the man's opinion. He cared only for getting air into his tortured lungs, and he hauled down great gasps of it, his chest heaving with the effort. Around him the fight was dying out, the last of the Ángeles falling to Dawson's men.

The lower chamber of the hacienda stank. Powder smoke mixed with the stench of opened bowels, blood, piss and sweat. It was the smell of a bitter fight to the death.

'Heads up!' It was Dawson who shouted the warning.

Even as he sang out, rifles were pointed down the ladder that led to the upper level. They fired a moment later. Bullets whipped into the men near the foot of the ladder. Two of them crumpled, bodies like rag dolls.

'Return fire!' Dawson bellowed. Almost instantly, men raised revolvers and fired up through the opening at the top of the simple wooden ladder. Yet the angle made accurate shooting impossible, and the men sheltering upstairs were in little danger of being hit.

'Out! Out!' Jack saw the futility of the situation and pushed at the nearest men, forcing them towards the door. Another volley came from upstairs. Bullets ricocheted off the floor and walls. This time Dawson's men were spared, but the volley added impetus to the need to get outside.

Jack followed a trooper out into the light. Like the men around him, he flung himself back against the wall and out of sight of the bandoleros above. A moment later, Dawson slammed into a spot beside him.

'Sweet Jesus.' The words rasped breathlessly from the officer's lips.

Jack wiped the sweat from his face with hands bloodied to the wrist, leaving red streaks across his skin. 'Now what?'

'We burn the sons of bitches out.' Dawson's answer was immediate. He sucked down a single breath, then lifted his head to shout his instructions. 'Get me wood and straw. Anything that will burn.'

His men were battered and exhausted, but not one hesitated. Keeping away from the firing arcs of the upper storey, they did as they were ordered. Within minutes, a steady stream of broken wood and straw was carried towards the hacienda's open doorway.

'Get our wounded out, then shove it in there!' Dawson stood to one side of the door, pressing his back hard against the wall. His men obeyed, dashing inside with whatever combustible material they had been able to find, then coming out with any wounded troopers left inside. They carried on even as the Ángeles on the upper storey fired down, their bullets ricocheting in every direction. One of Dawson's men was hit in the leg, his curses adding urgency to the task their officer had set them.

'What about their wounded?' One of Dawson's men gabbled the question as he came out of the hacienda dragging the last of Dawson's own wounded men.

'Leave the sons of bitches to burn.' Dawson's reply was immediate.

Jack said nothing even as Dawson looked his way. If the Confederate officer wanted a response, he would be disappointed. He looked down at the blood and scraps of flesh caked on his hands and trapped under his nails. He had killed without a qualm. Not even when he had ripped out the man's eyes with his fingers had he felt anything. His emotions ran cold, just as they had to, just as he wanted them to. He had become something more than just a soldier. He was no master of war. No hero. No great warrior. But he was something else, something harder and colder. He had become a merciless killer of men; the instigator of Fate's judgement.

'Fire it up!' Dawson gave the order as soon as he judged there to be enough material inside to burn.

Two of his men came forward with lucifers at the ready. It took but a moment to light bundles of straw and toss them inside. The dry wood and straw caught immediately. Within seconds, a thick, choking smoke filled the interior of the hacienda. Flames followed, crackling and fierce.

Screams came within the first minute. Men too badly wounded to move cried out as the flames licked over their broken bodies, their shrieks of unimaginable agony lasting for a cruel length of time before they finally died out.

Shouts rang out from the upper level. The openings in the wall there were much too small for a man to slide through, and so the bandoleros who had fired at Dawson's men now faced a horrific choice. Stay and burn. Or dare to run through the flames only to be shot down by the men who waited for them.

Dawson's troopers knew the choice their enemy faced. As the flames caught, they moved away from the cloud of smoke that belched out of the entrance, forming a cordon to one side so that they would have a clear shot at anyone who tried to flee.

They had their first chance within a minute. A bandolero broke through the doorway. The man was screaming like a banshee, his clothing ablaze. Four men shot him down, their bullets knocking him over before he had taken more than two paces. He fell back into the doorway, the flames that engulfed him roaring and spitting as they cooked his flesh.

Another man followed. Like the first, his clothes were alight, and even his hair was on fire. He was felled with a single blast from a shotgun.

No one else came out.

The hacienda echoed to the screams of men burning alive.

Chapter Forty-one

The air around the hacienda was filled with the pungent reek of smoke, burned wood and charred human meat. There was little left of the building itself. The central section of the upper storey's floor had fallen in, as had a large portion of the roof. Flames still burned deep in the remains of the building, and a great column of thick black smoke rose into the sky, embers and scraps of burned clothing caught in the updraught.

Jack stood and stared at what was left of the hacienda. The bitter, acrid stink transported him to another time, to another catastrophic fire, one that had altered the course of his life. That had been in his home town of London, the building that had been destroyed the gin palace that his mother had clung to with all the fervour of a woman who knew she had nothing else. This day there was no one to mourn, and no thoughts of a lost future amidst the wreckage. So he stared at the twisted shapes that had once been men and felt nothing.

'We've found the guns. It looks like they took some, but I reckon we've got most of them, and most of the ammunition too.'

Jack turned to see that Dawson had come to stand beside him.

'Good.' There was nothing more for him to say.

'There are still too many for us to take with us. We can manage three wagons of rifles, no more than that.'

'What about the rest?'

'My boys are breaking the rifles up now. When they're done, we'll turn the animals we don't need loose, then set light to the wagons and anything else we can't take with us. That way we won't have to worry about Santiago's men being as well armed as us.'

'Seems a waste.'

'Have you got a better idea?'

'No.' Jack made the admission freely. Dawson's command had suffered badly in the fight: he had lost six men with another five badly wounded. That left him with just twenty-five to drive and protect the few wagons he could take with him. They would need that protection. Santiago's men had been mauled, but there were still a hell of a lot of them out there. And there was Brannigan.

'What about Brannigan's gold? Is there a strongbox here?' Jack asked.

Dawson smiled, white teeth bright against skin streaked with soot.

'You found it?' Jack felt no such urge to smile.

'It's all there.'

'And Brannigan himself?' Jack cared nothing for the specie.

'I didn't see him. Did you?'

'No.' Jack tasted something bitter as he made the admission. Brannigan would not have gone far from his money, but he had not been in evidence at the hacienda. There had been no sign of Kat either. 'He'll come for the gold.'

'He'll be welcome to try.'

'You might think differently if he brings a hundred of Santiago's men.'

'They won't be back.' Dawson gave the answer with confidence. 'They're not soldiers. We killed enough of them here. They won't have the guts for another fight.'

'Are you sure about that?' Jack was dubious.

'I know these people. Brannigan, well, he's different. But I don't see him wanting to take us on all by his lonesome. He's too clever for that.'

Jack heard the grudging respect in Dawson's answer. 'What if you're wrong? What if he persuades them to attack? What if *they* want what's in that strongbox?'

'Then we'll fight them off.' Dawson gave the answer immediately, but Jack saw the flicker of doubt in the officer's eyes. For all his confidence, Dawson knew the danger they were in. The threat of Santiago and his Ángeles was a real one. He did not need any reminder.

'So what's next?' Jack asked.

'We ride as soon as my boys are ready.'

'Have you sent out scouts?'

'Not yet.'

'You need to.'

'I know.' Dawson turned his head and glared at Jack. 'The boys are exhausted.'

'They'll have plenty of time to rest if you let them get killed.'

Dawson looked away. 'Fine. I'll send out a patrol.'

'And pickets, too. Three or even four pairs. One to each point of the compass.'

Dawson turned back to search Jack's face. 'Are you giving me goddam orders?'

'Just suggestions.' Jack met the stare calmly.

'Then tell me what I should do with them.' Dawson turned to point at a huddle of captured Ángeles. Each had been bound with ropes around his ankles and arms, with another, longer rope that went around every man's neck, linking them together.

Jack tallied their number. Six men had been taken prisoner. All were bloodied, either from bullets, shot or fists. They sat in a dejected circle, not one of them looking at their captors.

'I haven't got enough men to guard them if we bring them with us.' Dawson spoke quietly. 'And if that was my boys sat over there, that son of a bitch Santiago wouldn't hesitate to kill every last one of them. He'd take his goddam time over it too.'

Jack heard what was not being said as clearly as he heard Dawson's reasoning. 'You're going to kill them.'

'That's what we do. I've done it before.'

Jack looked Dawson dead in the eye. He saw something half hidden in the man's gaze; something that he read as shame, or at least close to it. 'That just makes us as bad as him.'

'As bad as Brannigan, or as bad as Santiago?'

'Both, I suppose.' Jack considered the man standing in front of him. To this point, he had not thought much of Dawson, his similarity to Brannigan and his readiness to work for his own account condemning him in Jack's mind. Now he saw something else; something better. 'So bring them with us. Find a way.'

'No. I don't see how I can do that.' Dawson spoke slowly, then sighed. 'We don't have any other choice. Killing them will warn the others what to expect if they come against us. It might put them off.'

Jack looked at the captured Ángeles. Empathy had never been his strongest suit. His mind went back to the massacre of Brannigan's men. These Ángeles had likely been there. They were the men who had pulled the triggers, killing without pity. They would know not to expect mercy. And yet to kill them in cold blood was more than he could stomach. The notion almost made him smile. It meant he was weak. But that was a good thing. He was not Brannigan, and neither was Dawson. So there was another way.

'Let them go.' He gave Dawson a different option. 'Turn them loose, like Brannigan did with me.'

Dawson looked at him sharply. 'You'd do that if you were me?'

'I'm not you. I'm not in charge here.'

'But if you were?'

Jack looked Dawson dead in the eye. 'I'd let them go.'

'And risk having them find their way back to Santiago?'

'Yes.'

Dawson looked at Jack for a long time as he wrestled with the idea. Jack said nothing. The decision had to be Dawson's alone.

'Shit.' Dawson looked at the ground, then over to the prisoners. 'Hooper!' he shouted at one of the men guarding them.

'Captain?'

'Strip those men naked.'

'Captain?'

'You heard me, Trooper.'

Hooper opened his mouth as if to protest further. But he clearly saw something in his officer's expression that made him close it quickly enough and go to do as he was told.

'I hope this isn't a mistake.' Dawson spoke softly, as much to himself as to Jack.

'Six more men isn't going to make a difference,' Jack replied.

'I hope you're right.' Dawson rubbed the toe of his boot in the dirt, a final moment's hesitation before he went to get rid of his prisoners.

Jack stood inside the shed where he had been kept captive. It felt like that had been days ago, not just hours. He could sense the presence of both Adam and Brown, their ghosts lingering like the smell that filled the cramped space. He remembered the long night before they had been led away into the desert, the night before Adam and Brown had been murdered.

He sighed. It was time to push their faces away and consign them to the dark recesses of his mind, where they could dwell with all the others. They would have company there, amongst the many faces of the dead and the lost.

Yet there was one more thing he had to do before he quit this place. It was the reason he had come back to the shed, and it did not take much digging around in the dirty straw that still littered the floor to find what he was looking for.

The sword lay where Brannigan had discarded it. Jack bent down to scoop it up and held it in his right hand, just as he did in battle. The weight felt right. He had always fought with a sword in his right hand and a revolver in his left. Brannigan had derided him for clinging to the past, his way of fighting an anachronism that had no place in a world where every man carried a six-shooter and a rifle.

He hefted the blade, then moved it in a slow arc, slicing it through the air. The movement was familiar, comforting. It was a reminder of the man he had been for such a long time.

Yet that had been when he was a soldier, an officer and a leader of men. He had moved on from all that, becoming his own man at last. One he knew well; the good and the bad, the strong and the weak. He knew what manner of man he was and he accepted it. He had even begun to like it.

He held the blade for one last moment, then he bent over and carefully returned it to the floor before kicking a covering of straw back over it. He no longer needed the sword to define him. It was time to move on.

He left the shed and did not look back.

The column rode away from the ruined hacienda an hour later. The men had barely had a moment to rest. They had stayed long enough to water the horses and heat some coffee, and then they were back in the saddle.

As before, Dawson sent out scouts and flankers. This time he had the three wagons to concern him, one carrying a full load of Enfields and their ammunition and another bearing the five most severely wounded troopers. The strongbox and its precious cargo were in the third wagon, with two of Dawson's men acting as guards. The dead had been buried and the rest of the wagons, rifles and ammunition had been set on fire, the enormous pyre filling the sky with a great column of dense black smoke.

Dawson's plan was simple. They would ride due north, heading for Matamoros. They would not stop save to replenish their water. It would be a hard ride, but none of the men minded the order. The sooner they were out of Mexico the better.

'Hey, you there.'

Jack turned to face the trooper who had addressed him. He

was riding with three of Dawson's men just ahead of the wagons. 'What do you want, soldier?'

The man was chewing on tobacco, and he spat out a stream of dark juice before he spoke again. 'You reckon Brannigan will be able to convince that son of a bitch Santiago to try to stop us reaching the border?'

'Yes.' Jack gave the honest answer.

They rode on for a while, the only sound the creaking of the axles on the three wagons and the slow, methodical sound of horses' hooves hitting the sun-baked ground.

'Hey, you there.'

Again Jack twisted in the saddle. It was the same man as before who had spoken. He had the stripes of a corporal on his sleeves and enough grey whiskers in his beard to be older than Jack. 'Corporal, my name is Jack. Feel free to use it.'

The corporal had the decency to offer a half-smile. 'Well then, Jack. Me and the boys here, we was wondering what the hell you did wrong to get yourself caught up in this fine old fandango.'

'It's a long story.'

'We got time. It looks like we'll be riding a whiles. The captain, when he says we ain't stopping, he sure as hell means we ain't stopping.'

Jack glanced at the three faces looking his way. 'Tell me your names first.'

'My name is Hennessey. That mean-looking son of a bitch over there is Moore. He's from Tennessee, so you can't trust a goddam thing he says. He's got a wife and five little ones waiting back home—'

'Six,' Moore interrupted.

'He's got six little ones waiting back home,' Hennessey

made the correction smoothly, 'so it's kinda important we see he gets there. And the baby-faced one yonder is Trooper Mills.' Hennessey waved an arm at a much younger man riding at the rear of the small group. 'He's a good Texas boy from Grayson County. He joined up with his big brother, but the Yankees killed him, God rest his soul.'

'He's with the Lord now,' Mills said earnestly. 'With my ma's little ones that died 'fore they was old enough to stand up all by themselves.' He spoke slowly, as if each word had to be prepared and checked before it was released to the world.

Jack looked at both men in turn, nodding as they were introduced. 'What about you, Hennessey? Where are you from?'

'I'm from a tiny little place 'bout twenty mile north of Brownsville.'

'Anyone waiting for you to get back there?'

'No, sir. There's no one out there with my name on 'em. Least, not that I know of!' Hennessey laughed at his own jest. 'What 'bout you, Jack? You got yourself anyone?'

'No.'

'Because of that scar of yours?'

'Maybe.' Jack was non-committal. He had never had cause to blame the scar on his face for his lack of a woman in his life. There had been enough of them along the way.

'You going to tell us where you got it?'

'I got it in India. Outside Delhi.'

'Now where the hell in the world is that?'

Jack grunted at Hennessey's lack of geographical knowledge. 'It's a bloody long way away from here.'

'So how did you get there, wherever there might be?'

'I was escorting a young lady home.'

Hennessey grinned. 'Now that's just the kinda tale we was hoping you might have.'

Jack laughed. It felt good to be with these men. They were his kind of people. They were soldiers. And he knew how to lead soldiers, if he chose to.

'Well . . .' he drew out the word, 'that is one of the interesting bits, I'll admit that. But if you want the whole thing, then I'd better start at the beginning.' He looked at the three men, smiling as he saw that he had their complete attention.

And then he began to tell his tale.

Chapter Forty-two

―――――――◆―――――――

By late morning, the temperature was ferocious. The sun pounded down, merciless and scorching. Jack rode along in something close to torpor, his mind wrapped in a heat-induced haze. The tinder-dry scrub stretched away to the horizon, the arid landscape desolate and empty save for the same tangled thorn bushes and smattering of prickly pear cactus that he had long tired of seeing. It made for a forlorn environment, as if this parched and lifeless expanse was an area that God had forgotten when creating the world.

The sun cooked the riders in their grey flannel shirts, and Jack could feel his exposed skin burning as the relentless rays scorched across it. His borrowed horse was suffering just as much as he was, if not more so. The poor animal was sheeted in sweat, with great globules of foam coated around its mouth. Yet like its rider, it would be given no respite. Jack pulled his borrowed wide-brimmed hat down on his head and wrapped his mouth as best he could in the bandana he wore around his neck. There was nothing for it but to ride on, every tortuous step taking the battered column closer to the Rio Grande and to safety.

The wounded suffered most of all. The air in their wagon was like that in an oven, and they were forced to lie there and endure as best they could, their wounds bound with dressings made from old blankets and torn shirts, their pain eased with water and whiskey. Their survival, just like that of the men riding the exhausted horses, depended on the column reaching Matamoros.

Jack rode near the heavily loaded wagon carrying the rifles. His tale had entertained the three men flanking him for a while. Hennessey and Moore had asked a few questions, laughing when they were meant to laugh and probing when they thought Jack had left something out. The young trooper called Mills had hung rapt on every word, the Englishman's story holding his attention for mile upon mile. But not even the tales of faraway lands and distant battles could hold sway for ever in such difficult and tortuous conditions, and not one of the group had spoken for over an hour.

Jack reached for one of his two canteens. This one was still half full, whilst the other had yet to be opened; even so, he hesitated, and let his hand fall back into his lap. He could endure a little longer. He had no idea when they would next be able to refill their canteens, and so he husbanded his supply of water carefully, as did the rest of Dawson's men.

He sat back in the saddle, stretching his spine. He could not imagine a time when he would be free of pain. His body ached from top to tail, his damaged feet burning in his borrowed boots and his back hurting like the devil himself was standing on his shoulders stabbing the pit of his spine with his fiery trident. Yet there was no respite in sight. The small column would ride on through the day and the night. Their sole objective was to reach the Rio Grande.

At that moment, it seemed impossibly far away.

Then the first gunshot snapped out, and any hopes of riding to safety were dashed.

The Ángeles burst out of a ravine no more than four hundred yards from the head of the column. They came in one great rush at least a hundred strong, every one of the armed bandoleros on foot. Those at the front opened fire. The range was long, too long, but the zip of Minié bullets stung the air around the two men Dawson had sent to scout ahead of the main column. Neither man needed more warning; both immediately turned their horses around and galloped back towards the wagons.

Dawson and his men had been fortunate. The dead ground that had hidden the ambushers from view was a good distance away from the trail. Had it been any closer, the column would have ridden straight into the ambush. As it was, they had been given a few, crucial, moments' warning.

'Turn the wagons around!' Dawson was riding at the head of the main column. He issued his order within seconds of the first bullets being fired. 'Sergeant Willis!' he bellowed at his senior non-commissioned officer. 'Go with them.'

Then he jabbed back his spurs and rode forward to meet the pair of scouts.

'You two, back to the main column.'

'We going to charge 'em, Captain?' one of the pair shouted as they slowed their headlong gallop.

Dawson gathered his reins, his head turning from side to side as he judged distances. 'Join the others. Tell them to form line.'

The two men rode off to do as their officer ordered. More

shots snapped out, but the range was still long and not one came close.

Jack rode forward. Like Dawson, his eyes roved around what had become a battlefield, looking for ground they could use, or which could be used against them, and assessing the distance between the two forces.

'We can't charge them,' he called over to Dawson. 'We're outnumbered, and those are Enfields they're shooting.' He had recognised the weapons being used against them by sound alone; it was distinctive, and quite different from that of a smoothbore musket. 'They'll cut us down before we get close enough.'

'I know, goddammit.' Dawson was already riding back towards his men.

'We can head over there.' Jack stood in his stirrups and pointed. He had spotted some broken ground to the east of the trail they had been following.

'Are you mad?' Dawson looked in the direction Jack indicated for no more than a few moments before he dismissed the idea. 'There's no way in hell we can get through that.'

'We've got to go somewhere.' Jack's mind was racing. 'They don't want to fight us here. They're on foot. They must know they cannot catch us if we ride away. They just want to turn us around and send us back the way we came.'

'Why?' Dawson was stressed, his voice rising as he snapped the single word.

'They must have men behind us too. None of those bastards over there are mounted. And I don't see Brannigan, do you?'

'No. Goddammit.' Dawson held his horse back as he looked around. Behind them, the three wagons had turned, and his men had formed line, just as he had ordered.

'They want to hit us from both sides. If we ride back that way,' Jack pointed back down the trail, 'then as sure as eggs is eggs they'll spring another ambush.'

'Speak clearly, goddammit.' Dawson spat out the words in frustration.

'There will be more of them behind us,' Jack fired back. 'Fight those bastards in front and you'll be caught between the two groups. You won't stand a chance.'

'So what are you thinking?' Dawson spoke fast. They did not have long. Already the Ángeles were closing fast. In a matter of minutes, the column would be in the effective range of their Enfields. There was no time for a debate.

'Head that way.' Jack pointed at the broken ground again. 'It'll be slow going, but we'll get through before those bastards can catch us. That'll fuck their plan right up, and maybe we can find a place where we can set up an ambush of our own.'

Dawson looked dubious. 'You had better be right.'

'We don't have much of a bloody choice. Go back the way we've come and we're royally fucked.' Jack twisted in the saddle. The Ángeles were close. 'Now make up your fucking mind, before those bastards make it up for you,' he snapped.

Dawson paused for no more than a heartbeat.

'Let's do it.'

They would gamble their lives on Jack's plan.

The column left the trail and rode towards the broken ground Jack had spotted. Away from the hard, compacted trail, their progress slowed instantly. The mule teams struggled to get the wagons going on the softer ground, and the troopers given the task of driving them cursed as they whipped the beasts cruelly in an attempt to make them move faster.

Half of Dawson's men rode ahead, whilst the rest formed a rear guard behind the wagons. Jack went with the scouts, whilst Dawson stayed with the men who might have to fight to keep the Ángeles at bay long enough for the wagons to get away.

The ground was worse than he had thought. It was broken by dozens of thin ravines and gullies. Between the ravines were boulders great and small, and acres of rubble and loose footing that would be almost impassable for the wagons.

'Shit.' Jack surveyed the scene.

'That way.' Corporal Hennessey rode at Jack's shoulder. He pointed out a narrow path that led around one of the large clumps of boulders.

'You think they can get through there?'

'Sure they can.' Hennessey's reply was certain.

'Fine. Go back and show them the way.'

'Yes, sir.' Hennessey obeyed without question.

Jack felt something pleasing in being addressed as 'sir'. It had been a long time.

'You men, follow me.' He shouted the order at the other men who were with him. He did not wait to see if they would obey as he rode forward, following the path Hennessey had spotted.

The corporal was correct. The path was wide enough, and the going was better than anywhere else. But the heavily laden wagons would still not be able to advance at anything other than a slow walk, with the mounted riders barely able to go much faster. Even on foot, the Ángeles would surely catch the column before they had gone much more than half a mile.

Something would need to be done to slow the chasing pack. Five hundred yards further on, Jack saw exactly what he had been looking for. One of the many gullies was wider and deeper than the others. It was not perfect, but it was low down and well to the left of the trail. It would suffice.

He raised a hand, halting his small command.

'Moore!' He summoned one of the two men he could name.

'Sir?' Moore replied without hesitation.

'Ride back. Tell Captain Dawson I've found a place to hide. Tell him to ride past us. We'll wait here, then give those Ángeles a bloody nose. Have you got that?'

'Yes, sir!' Moore snapped the reply, already turning his horse's head around before he raked back his heels to force it into motion.

Jack watched him go, then turned to lead his men off the path and down into the gully. It was time to plan an ambush.

Chapter Forty-three

The wagons and the rest of the column came past at little more than a crawl. Every man had plenty of time to look down at the dozen men waiting in the dead ground.

Jack sat at the head of the small group he had brought into the gully. It was hard not to feel some sense of jealousy as the rest of the Texan troopers rode past. The eleven men with him were about to ambush ten times their number. They had two advantages. They had surprise, and they were mounted. The success of the ambush, and indeed their survival, depended on hitting the Ángeles hard and fast. Even then, victory was not guaranteed. Yet something had to be attempted. If nothing was done, the wagons would be caught and the column shot down by the chasing Ángeles and their stolen Enfield rifles.

'Keep it quiet.' Jack hissed the command at two men who were carrying out a whispered conversation. He was pleased to see he was obeyed without question.

The last of Dawson's column went past. The trail behind them was empty.

Jack and his men sat in their saddles in silence. Waiting.

He could feel their tension as if it were a physical thing. The atmosphere was strained, like the air on a summer's day before a thunderstorm. It was the time for a man to feel fear. It was not an easy thing, to sit there and wait for an enemy to approach. If the Texans were spotted, they would make easy targets for the well-armed Ángeles. In the confined space of the gully, it would be as easy as knifing eels in a barrel. It would be another massacre.

'Quiet.' Jack was forced to hiss the command as one of the troopers cocked his shotgun, the sound of both hammers clicking into position impossibly loud.

In the silence that followed, he heard the sounds of men on the move. The Ángeles were noisy. They came on fast, shouting at one another, dozens of pairs of feet thumping into the rocky ground, the sounds combining so that it sounded like a single gigantic creature was advancing on the men waiting in the gully.

The first Ángeles rushed past. Not one of them looked down into the gully.

Jack held his breath and counted. He let at least twenty men pass. It would be enough.

'Charge!'

He bellowed the command he had been holding for this moment, the word releasing the tension that had been building inside him. Then he kicked back his heels, ramming the spurs into his horse's flanks, not caring that he was cruel. Nothing mattered now. Not now that it was time to kill.

Jack's men burst out of the gully. There was time for a few of the Ángeles to turn and stare as the ambush was released. Then the leading Texans opened fire.

Shotgun blasts cut bandoleros down in mid stride, whilst

those troopers armed with revolvers fired fast, picking their targets with care. At least a dozen Ángeles went down in the first salvo, their cries of surprise turned into shrieks of pain.

Jack rode hard, saving his shotgun's load. His mount scrabbled out of the gully and he turned its head to the right, riding it back down the trail.

The Ángeles scattered as the ambush was released. Yet there were too many of them to clear the trail completely. Jack charged forward, ignoring the men who dived out of his way, or who fell to the aimed shots coming from the troopers behind him.

Two Ángeles ran towards him. They shouted a war cry as they raised their rifles, both barrels aimed squarely at Jack.

He paid the threat no heed. He pulled hard on his reins, bringing the mare to a noisy halt, dust kicked high into the air as its hooves dragged across the ground. The shotgun was heavy, but he held it aimed at the two men. He fired the moment the barrel was up, arm braced for the strong recoil.

The two Ángeles were close enough for the spread of shot to tear through them both. At such close range, the effect was dreadful. The tightly packed buckshot ripped them to shreds, each man hit multiple times. Both crumpled to the ground, bodies jumbled together, arms and legs bent at impossible angles, blood smothering the thirsty soil.

Jack rammed the shotgun into a holster next to the saddle then drew the borrowed Remington. He paid the men he had slain no heed, searching only for his next target, for the next man he would kill.

He had plenty to choose from. Ángeles were running in every direction. Dozens already lay dead or dying.

He rushed the mare forward, forcing it back down the trail.

Even as its hooves scrabbled at the broken ground, he drew a bead on a running Ángeles. He fired, watching his bullet strike the fleeing man in the back. Then he twisted around in the saddle, firing at bandoleros running towards him. Two more fell, their despairing cries barely audible over the gunshots and screams that surrounded them.

He rode on, firing another pair of shots at Ángeles running as if the hounds of hell were on their tail. Both bullets missed, but they added impetus to the rout.

Not all the Ángeles were fleeing, though. A few of the braver ones were taking up positions to return fire. First one, then another bullet scorched past Jack, whilst a third spat up a fountain of dust as it struck the ground not more than a yard from his horse's hooves.

'That's enough!' He gave the order as he saw fewer and fewer bandoleros in range of his Remington. The ambush had killed nearly twenty of them and wounded as many more. The rest had scattered to the wind. It would take time for them to regroup. But the return fire was getting heavier, with more shots following the first few. If the Texans lingered, they would surely start to take casualties.

'Let's go!' He waved his arm high, then powered back along the trail. The ground was littered with the bodies of those bandoleros cut down by the ambush. Horses' hooves crushed those lying in the way, the Texans callous and cruel as they raced to get out of range of the Ángeles' rifles. They rode with the screams of the wounded ringing in their ears alongside the high-pitched whine of Minié balls zipping past.

Jack rode at the rear of his small command. For the first time, he allowed himself to feel a modicum of pride. The ambush had been timed to perfection, and the Ángeles foot soldiers had been hit hard. It had worked exactly as he had planned, and not a single one of the eleven troopers riding with him had been hit. They had bought the rest of the column enough time to get away.

'Good work,' he shouted. 'We hit those bastards hard.'

'Amen to that!' one man shouted in reply, whilst others whooped and cheered. With their fear spent, the feeling of elation would be strong.

They rode on, letting their horses pick their way, safe in the knowledge that their pursuers had been knocked on their collective arse.

Jack looked ahead. He could make out the rest of the column and the three wagons about half a mile ahead. Already they were on better ground, and as he watched, they seemed to pick up speed.

It was only then that he saw another mounted column, moving fast across the open ground.

The cheers and cries of triumph died out as the rest of the men riding with him saw the same threat.

They had beaten one group of Ángeles bloody. But they had forgotten about the rest of Santiago's bandoleros.

And those bandoleros were about to launch an attack of their own.

Chapter Forty-four

---

*J*ack and his men rode fast. Yet they were too far away to do anything but watch.

The mounted Ángeles came in firing. Armed with revolvers and carbines, they opened up with a deadly salvo of shots the moment they were in range.

From his distant viewpoint, Jack could not hear the cries of anguish and horrified surprise as the column came under attack. But he could see the troopers who were gunned out of the saddle, their bodies thrown into the dirt by the first close-range shots.

The mounted Ángeles swarmed forward. Shot followed shot as those with revolvers poured on the fire.

Dawson and his men fought back. Every Texan was a veteran of a dozen or more border skirmishes. They returned fire, shotguns and revolvers spraying bullets and buckshot into the mounted Ángeles. Well-aimed shots knocked down horses and men, the foremost Ángeles riders catching the full force of the return fire.

There was little time for anything more. With a defiant war cry, the Texan troopers counter-charged.

The two sides came together fast. Few men carried blades, so the fight descended into a chaotic melee, bullets coming from every direction. Men were shot from the saddle, their bodies trampled underfoot.

Jack rode towards the skirmish, spurring his horse on. He held the Remington ready to fire, knowing he had just the one bullet left in its chambers. The knowledge did not deter him. He would fight with what he had.

The ground passed slowly under the flying hooves of his horse. He could do nothing as more of the Texans fell, their despairing cries barely audible over the shouts and roars of men fighting for their lives and the constant snap of guns firing.

The distance closed. Yard by yard, each one crawling by.

He caught a glimpse of a familiar face in the melee. Brannigan was there, and he was using Jack's Henry rifle. In the close-quarters fight, the weapon was murderously effective, and he was making full use of the load of sixteen rounds. Even as Jack watched in horror, the wagon master fired a fast series of shots, the salvo striking a Texan trooper from the saddle, the bullets shattering his spine. Then he switched his point of aim, firing three more shots in rapid succession into the body of another trooper.

Jack could feel his horse slowing beneath him, so he kicked back his spurs, gouging the sharp steel into the animal's flanks, not caring that he drew blood. Speed was all.

He spotted Dawson. The Confederate captain was in the thick of the melee, hacking at countless Ángeles with a bowie knife, the blade striking down repeatedly. Corporal Hennessey had jumped on to one of the wagons and was grappling with a bandolero, the two men locked in a desperate hand-to-hand fight.

With fifty yards to go, Jack saw Kat. She was holding back, keeping away from the fighting. He could see the Volcanic pistol he had bought her clutched ready for use in her hands.

The last yards passed. Time sped up.

And he rode into chaos.

A Texan fell from the saddle just in front of him, a bone-handled knife sticking out of his throat. Another galloped through the melee, revolver firing fast, face twisted into an inhuman snarl.

A bandolero crossed Jack's path without seeing him, the man aiming an Indian tomahawk at a Texan riding the other way. He would never make the throw. Jack raised his Remington and fired. The bullet struck the Ángel in the back of his neck. The man arched his back, his body reacting to the strike of the bullet, before the tomahawk fell harmlessly into the dust as he tumbled from the saddle.

Jack thrust the Remington into its holster as he rode on. He flashed past a bandolero, the man's knife lunging at his side but missing by more than a foot. Close by, another bandolero's horse reared as it was struck by a bullet, the animal's bellow of agony loud even in the cacophony.

Jack pulled hard on his horse's reins, angling the beast in the direction he thought Brannigan would be. With his Remington out of ammunition, he was unarmed, so he dragged the unloaded shotgun out of its holster and spun it around in his grip so that he held it by the barrel.

There was no time to dwell on his choice of weaponry. A Texan rode past in the other direction, forcing him to swerve to one side. An Ángel followed hot on the man's heels. There was time for his eyes to widen in alarm as he saw Jack waiting in his path.

Jack saw his chance. He swung the shotgun hard. There was a moment when he felt his balance shift, then the butt slammed into the bandolero's face. It was a cruel blow, and it smashed the man from the saddle.

He rode on. He glimpsed Brannigan and altered his course. He did not care that he was heading towards a man firing a repeating rifle whilst he was armed with nothing more than an unwieldy empty shotgun. He would trust to Fate to keep him safe.

An Ángel charged by, revolver raised and firing. Jack was riding in the opposite direction, but he lashed out with the shotgun, acting on instinct. The clumsy swing missed the man, but it caught the revolver and sent it flying from his hands. The bandolero howled in anger and twisted in the saddle to see who had come to intervene. There was time for him to look into Jack's eyes before Jack backhanded the shotgun just as he would a sword, crashing the butt into the side of the man's head and knocking him half out of the saddle.

There was no time to land another blow. Jack rode on, narrowly missing a fallen Texan left writhing on the ground. He saw Brannigan again. The wagon master stood in his stirrups, face calm as he emptied the repeating rifle's magazine at targets Jack could not see.

'Brannigan!' A voice shouted for the wagon master's attention.

Dawson rode through the melee, his bowie knife held out like a sabre, blood and gore dripping from the blade.

Jack saw at once that the Confederate officer was riding directly at Brannigan, attempting the same feat as Jack was himself. It doubled the odds of at least one of them succeeding.

'Brannigan!' He shouted the name too, then laughed. There

was joy in this moment. It was foolish, idiotic even, yet it was joyous all the same.

Brannigan saw them both. His head whipped from side to side as he looked from Dawson to Jack, then back to Dawson.

Jack surged forward, breaking past a Texan and an Ángel locked in a ferocious wrestling match.

Brannigan stood his ground. The Henry emptied of rounds, he thrust the weapon into a holster next to his saddle and drew an Indian tomahawk. It was a vicious weapon, perfect for a hand-to-hand fight like the one they were about to embark upon. Yet Jack did not fear it. He knew Brannigan would not be able to hold his own for long against two men intent on his demise.

Dawson's horse surged ahead. He would reach Brannigan first.

Brannigan saw it. He jabbed back his spurs, and his horse lunged forward as it responded to the pain in its flanks. The two men came together at speed. Neither had a weapon with reach, so they reined in as they met, horses shoulder to shoulder, the animals snapping and biting at each other as the men lashed out for the first time.

Bowie knife met tomahawk. The two blades clashed, then came apart. Immediately both men dropped their reins and lashed out with their free hand. Dawson punched first, snapping Brannigan's head back. Before he could land a second blow, Brannigan's tomahawk came back in a wild, slicing blow that would have decapitated the Confederate captain had he not held back a strike of his own so that he could sway out of the way.

The two men traded blows, battering away at one another, trying to find a way through the other's defence, both looking for an opening. Yet neither could land a telling attack.

Jack galloped in. Brannigan was concentrating on Dawson, the two exchanging a fast series of blows without either securing an advantage. He did not see Jack coming.

Jack readied the shotgun, choosing his line with care. He would get only one chance, time for a single blow, nothing more.

He was still yards away when Kat rode into the fight.

She came in fast, her mount controlled with her left hand whilst her right held the Volcanic pistol. She skirted around Brannigan, then dragged the animal to a halt, its forelegs buckling under the strain.

Jack was too far away to intervene. He could do nothing but watch as Kat aimed the Volcanic at Dawson.

She needed both hands to hold the heavy pistol, so she dropped the reins, her left hand taking a firm grip of the Volcanic's barrel. It was skilfully done, the horse controlled with legs alone, her arms braced for the weapon's recoil.

The first bullet hit Dawson's right arm. The round lacked the power of a Minié ball, but at close range it was still capable of shattering bone, and the bowie knife was sent flying from a hand suddenly without the power to grip.

Dawson yelled out in pain. His head whipped around, his eyes wide as they searched for the source of the attack.

Kat fired a second shot. The bullet hit Dawson in the chest, rocking him back in the saddle.

His eyes found his assailant. There was time for a moment's surprise to register before her third bullet hit barely an inch away from the second.

Jack saw Dawson's clothing twitch as the rounds hit. Neither possessed enough force to knock the Confederate captain from the saddle, but with his knife gone and his arm fractured, Dawson was defenceless.

Brannigan saw it.

The tomahawk was a vicious weapon. Brannigan smashed it into Dawson's head with every scrap of power he possessed. The sharpened blade drove deep, splitting skin and cleaving bone.

Somehow Dawson remained upright, blood pouring from his head. For a moment he stared at Brannigan, his mouth opening as if about to scream.

Kat fired again. The bullet took Dawson in the mouth. Another bullet came a heartbeat later, and then another, Kat firing as fast as the Volcanic could manage.

Dawson stayed in the saddle a moment longer. Then he fell.

He was dead before he hit the ground.

Chapter Forty-five

*J*ack watched in horror from no more than five or six yards away as Dawson toppled from the saddle. Then he was hauling on his reins, turning his mare's head around, the decision made in an instant.

He rammed back his spurs, forcing the animal to find whatever strength it had left. With Kat now in the fight, he had no chance of taking on Brannigan, not alone and practically unarmed. So he took the only option open to him.

He fled.

'Pull back!' He shouted the command as he rode away from Brannigan. 'Pull back!'

He had no idea if any of Dawson's men would heed the command, but he repeated it over and over as he rode back through the melee.

The fight had been short and vicious. Dozens of men and horses had been struck down, the ground now littered with their bodies. Yet some men remained in the saddle, either still fighting or looking for a new target.

Jack rode past them all.

'Pull back!' he repeated. He saw Texans looking his way, so

he shouted again and again as he rode, sawing on his horse's reins to avoid the dead and the living alike. He saw Hennessey as he galloped by. The Texan corporal had won his fight for control of the wagon, and now sat in the driver's seat, gathering the reins.

The Texans had been in enough fights to know when the battle was lost. First one, then another turned their horses around. Cries of anger turned into the yips and yells of men encouraging their horses to run. Hennessey came with them, whipping the wagon's mules mercilessly, following Jack out of the chaos.

Jack heard the sound of men following so concentrated his attention on the path ahead. He gave little heed to direction. He thought only of getting the surviving Texans to safety.

His mare was near exhausted, but he pushed her on, kicking back his heels every time she flagged. The horse did its best, finding the strength for a final gallop. The ground flashed past, the sound of the bitter fight receding into the distance until he could hear nothing more than the rhythmic pounding of hooves hitting sun-hardened ground.

Only when he was sure that he had put a fair distance between himself and the melee did he allow the mare to slow. He twisted in the saddle, eager to know who, if anyone, was with him.

He looked back to see a handful of Texan troopers and a single wagon on his tail. It did not take long to count them. Just eleven men were left. All were filthy, and most were bloodied.

He brought the exhausted mare to a stand, the animal staggering for several steps before it found its footing. It gave him the chance to look back the way he had come. Off in the distance he could just about make out the place where Dawson had fallen. Two of the wagons were still there, and he could see Ángeles swarming over them.

'Oh my Lord.' The first man to reach Jack gasped the words as he brought his horse to a stand.

Jack said nothing. He sat in the saddle, sucking down deep breaths. Sweat sheeted his body and he could feel more running down his face. The heat of the day was pushing towards its height, so that it was like trying to breathe in an oven. But he could not complain. He was still alive. For the moment, at least.

Faces looked back at him, eyes bright against skin darkened by sweat, blood and powder smoke. He recognised some of the men. Hennessey was there, of course, driving the single wagon that had been saved from the ambush. Moore sat at the rear of the small group, the father of six drawing breath just behind the baby-faced Mills. Eight other Texan troopers reined in, each one with the wild-eyed stare of men who had just fought for their lives and come out the other side.

Yet they were to be given no respite.

'Jack!' It was Hennessey who shouted the warning. He was pointing back the way they had come.

'Shit.' Jack saw immediately what the corporal had spotted. It appeared that Brannigan and Santiago had no intention of letting the Texans escape. Dozens of figures on horseback were riding away from the two captured wagons. They galloped towards the small band of exhausted troopers. It did not take a genius to work out that they were riding to slaughter the last of Dawson's men.

Another notion filtered into Jack's tired mind. There was a further reason why the wagon master and the bandit leader would not let them go. He had seen the way the wagon Hennessey drove had covered the ground. It was the most lightly loaded of the three Dawson had brought with them. That meant it contained the strongbox filled with the gold doubloons Santiago had paid for the Enfields; a king's ransom in specie.

'Have you got a plan, Jack?' Hennessey looked at him. Ten other faces did the same.

For a moment, Jack hesitated. He was not these men's leader. He was no officer, not any longer. Yet they looked to him for direction.

The decision was an easy one. He would give the men the leadership they so badly needed. It was not out of duty, or because he was being paid to be there. It was not to earn glory, or to prove he was a better soldier, or a truer warrior. Instead he *chose* to lead these men. For he was who he was. And they needed him.

His first thought was to abandon the wagon and its precious cargo. It was a good option, one that might be enough to turn the bandoleros from their tail. But the idea died quickly. Brannigan would not let any of them go, not after the fight. He would want to kill every last one of them, and Jack most of all. Giving up the strongbox would almost certainly achieve nothing. He thought of heading for the border, but on their tired horses, the Texans had no hope of outrunning the bandoleros.

Then there was something else, something that he would admit only to himself. Brannigan had made his plans, and had acted upon them, killing the men who had served him with such loyalty and taking his master's specie for himself. Now only Jack stood between him and the successful completion of that plan.

It might have been bravery, or even some half-baked and fanciful notion of bringing justice to a world that would never know about it, and would likely not care even if it did. Or it might have been nothing more than sheer bloody-mindedness, his battered pride refusing to let a man like Brannigan have his way. Whichever it was, it was time to thwart Brannigan, and to put a barricade between him and the riches he had planned to steal. And so that left Jack with just one idea. One foolish, futile notion that would allow him and the Texans to hold on to the strongbox and, if they were lucky, their lives.

'The hacienda where we fought Santiago before – do any of you have any idea how far away that is?'

'A mile, maybe two to the south,' a stern-faced Texan replied.

'Right.' Jack searched the faces that were looking at him. These men needed a leader. They needed him. 'What's your name?'

'Brody Allen.' The Texan spoke evenly. He was tall, with a heavy moustache, and stubble that covered his cheeks and neck. He had been cut in the fighting, a gash running across his chin so that blood trickled down his neck.

'Right, Allen. You lead the way. Mills, you and Moore take the rear. Keep a close eye on those bastards. Sing out if they gain too much ground.' Jack gave his first orders quickly, his eyes darting from the men to the Ángeles on their tail. 'Let's go.' He gave them no time to think on what he had said. There was no time to spare.

It was only as he geed his horse back into motion, that he felt something shift deep inside him. It was not fear. It was something else. It had been a long time since he had given men orders in battle, yet the moment he had taken command, he had felt something awaken, something that had lain dormant for so long that he had forgotten it even existed. It was as if someone had just clamped a weight on to his shoulders. It sat there, heavy and unyielding, yet it was no burden, and he carried it willingly. He had taken responsibility for these men, and he would give them the leadership they needed. It might not be for long, and it looked more than possible that it would be the last thing he ever did, but he took on the mantle willingly.

They rode as fast as the exhausted horses and mules could manage. The going was good enough, the dusty scrubland rushing by as they pushed on. Allen led them, choosing their path.

Before long, Jack saw the hacienda in the distance. Smoke still rose from the charred remains of the building, the wispy column climbing high into the cloudless sky. It did not look like much, but it was the only building he had seen and so it would have to do. The Texans would have to turn it into a fortress – into their own personal Alamo.

The men arrived at the hacienda in a cloud of dust, horses snorting and breathless. There was no time to celebrate their arrival.

'Good work, Allen.' Jack slipped from the saddle, his legs buckling as they hit the ground. He wiped a hand across his face, smearing away some of the dust and grime, then looked at the burned-out husk of a building that he would try to defend.

The four walls still stood, yet at least half of the roof had collapsed, the charred supporting timbers unable to hold the weight. The building was just as he remembered, with a single entrance facing the track, no windows on the lower level, and just a few small square openings on what was left of the upper storey. The once white-limed walls were scorched and blackened, and the air was full of the acrid stink of woodsmoke. Yet there was something else that tainted the air, something far worse than the smell of burned wood. Underlying it all was the stench of burned human remains.

'Allen! Take two men and get the horses away. We won't need them now.' Jack gave the first order. The Ángeles would surely steal the horses, yet there was nothing else for it. The men were all that mattered.

'Hennessey!'

'Here.' The Texan corporal was the last to arrive.

'Dump that bloody wagon, release the animals, then start getting everything inside – every scrap of ammunition, every firearm, even the bloody saddles.'

'Yes, Jack. You want the strongbox too?'

'Yes.' Jack was already walking away. 'I want everything.'

He strode briskly to the hacienda. He reckoned they had five minutes, perhaps ten, before the Ángeles got there. They would have to use every precious second.

A span of timber from the upper storey half barred the hacienda's doorway. He kicked it out of the way, then walked inside, pulling up the bandana around his neck to cover his mouth and nose.

The interior of the hacienda was a mess. Broken tiles and charred wood littered the ground, crunching under his boots as he made a quick survey of the place he would try to defend. Amidst the wreckage were small mounds of what looked to be charcoal. He knew what they were, yet he paid them no heed, not even when his boot crushed what might have once been a man's arm into so much dust.

His eyes ran over the inside of the building. The walls were thick, which would make the cutting of loopholes either difficult or impossible. The centre of the upper floor had fallen in, but a good portion of the rest remained, and though the ladder was gone, he reckoned he could still get men up there. It would be a treacherous position – what was left of the floor was barely stable and sloped heavily towards the broken edge – but those men would be vital, as they could warn of the Ángeles' movements, and bring down fire if and when the bandoleros chose to attack.

He spotted something amidst the ash and bent down to retrieve it. It was an Enfield rifle, or at least the remains of one. It was a reminder of what had brought him to this place and to this hopeless battle. Brannigan had said it best. There were three dangerous things in this world: guns, money and women. Now Jack held one of the three in his possession, and he knew Brannigan would stop at nothing to take back the strongbox.

And so there would be another fight, another battle.

One that could well prove to be his last.

Chapter Forty-six

'Look lively.' Jack pulled down the bandana, which had done precious little to spare him from breathing the foul air inside the hacienda, and snapped the instruction at the Texans as he strode outside. They were tired. They were slow.

The first man bustled past carrying a set of saddlebags and half a dozen canteens. Others followed with saddles and every weapon they had.

'What do you want to do about the bodies?' One of the men asked the question as he came back for a second load.

'Leave them where they are.' Jack was busy with his own horse. Of all the men he had the least equipment.

'That ain't right,' the man mumbled.

Jack did not react. He concentrated on unbuckling the saddle's cinch and hauling it off. He nodded to Allen, who was waiting to gather the mare's reins. 'Take the horses away. Hide them if you can, but get them well out of range, then hurry the hell back here.'

He carried the saddle inside and dumped it without ceremony alongside the others that had been brought into the hacienda. All the men were inside now except Allen and the two other men who would get the horses out of harm's way.

'Right.' Jack pointed at two of the troopers. 'I want you two upstairs. Get your mates to give you a bunk-up. Make sure you have carbines, not shotguns.' He looked at the faces turned his way. All were becoming familiar, even if he did not know every name. They were becoming his men. 'And take that bloody strongbox up there with you.' He added the extra order as he saw two men holding the heavy wooden crate that contained Brannigan's specie.

'Hennessey!' He called for the corporal, the only non-commissioned officer left. 'Have the men start making loopholes in the walls. We need them on all sides.'

'Walls are plenty thick, Jack.' Hennessey pulled a face as he contemplated the order. 'Might not be able to make many.'

'Do whatever you can. Otherwise, all we have are the windows up there,' Jack pointed to the remains of the upper level, 'and that bloody doorway.'

'We need water, too.'

'How much have we got?'

'Less than one canteen each.' Hennessey gave the news calmly.

'Shit.' Jack knew how significant the lack of water would be. Every man would already be dry-mouthed, and the amount they would have sweated out in the fight and the madcap retreat would have left them in dire need of water. Yet it appeared they had precious little left.

'Where's the nearest water?'

'Out the back. There's a dam in a small creek at the back of the yard. We filled up when we were here before.'

'How many men do you need with you?'

'Two.'

'Go.' Jack did not hesitate. 'But be bloody quick about it.'

'You got it.' Hennessey had already turned away and was starting to grab the canteens that had been piled on the floor.

'You.' Jack pointed at a man he did not know. 'Get a mate and start dragging over some of these timbers so we can bar the door. We'll reinforce whatever you can find with the saddles.'

'Yes, sir.' The man did not need to be told twice.

Jack stood back as Hennessey and two other troopers dashed outside, their arms full of canteens. He had six men outside now. The rest were with him. Two were on the upper storey, and two were searching the rubble for enough strong wood to bar the door. That left just one man making loopholes, hacking away at the front wall with a bowie knife. Thus far he had made little impression.

'Jack!' One of the men on the upper floor called out.

'What?'

'I can see 'em. Brannigan and those Mexican sons of bitches. They're half a mile away. Mebbe less.'

'Shit.' Jack forced away the frustration. He had too few men and not enough time. 'Watch those bastards bloody closely. I want you to shoot at them when they are one hundred yards away. You understand me, soldier?'

'Yes, sir.'

Order given, Jack went back outside. The first seed of doubt was being sown in his mind. Brannigan, Santiago and more than a hundred bandoleros would be here in a matter of minutes. If Hennessey and his companions did not make it back, the handful of men left would be without water, and without three of their comrades.

'Hurry the fuck up!' He saw Allen and the two troopers

who had got the horses away jogging back to the hacienda. They were not moving quickly enough for his liking.

The men forced themselves into something close to a slow run. They were already exhausted.

'Get inside. Help make loopholes.' Jack would give them no time to rest.

He paced on, his eyes searching the ground in the direction from which he expected Brannigan and his entourage to emerge. He immediately saw the telltale dust cloud that revealed their presence. It was close.

'How long?' he shouted up to the windows above, where he could see one of the Texans peering out.

'Two minutes, I reckon. Mebbe less,' the man replied in a slow drawl.

There was no time left. Jack ran around the corner of the building. He saw Hennessey and his two men immediately. They were busy in the far corner of the yard.

'Hennessey! Get back here!' He cupped his hands around his mouth to help his shout carry.

'We ain't done,' Hennessey called back.

'Now!' Jack had no time to explain.

This time Hennessey did not reply, but he did obey. It took the three men a few moments to gather the canteens, then they started back.

A single gunshot cracked out, followed by a second.

'Shit! Hurry up!' Jack knew what the shots meant. Brannigan and Santiago had to be close now.

Hennessey and his men ran as fast as they could, the canteens draped over their bodies banging furiously together. One of the men dropped one. It was left where it lay.

'Come on!' Jack wheeled his arm as he ran back to the

hacienda's entrance. He half expected to see the enemy surging into view. To his relief, there was nothing but the cloud of dust. But that cloud was horribly close.

'Keep firing!' he shouted, then ran to the hacienda's open doorway. He was rewarded with two crisp shots from the upper level as the men there did as he ordered.

'Get ready to block this up!' he instructed. 'Get every gun loaded, and have the shotguns ready in case those bastards try to come straight in.'

Commands delivered, he turned and dashed back to the corner of the building to see where Hennessey had got to. He was relieved. He and his men were close.

'Get a fucking move on!' He took a moment to give the encouragement, then turned to run back to the entrance. It was then that he saw the first Ángeles ride into view.

The bandoleros were riding hard. And they were riding fast.

'Give me a shotgun.' As he reached the doorway, he called out to one of the men inside, his hand outstretched.

'Here.' The Texan thrust one of the freshly loaded weapons towards him.

Jack took the weapon. It was no repeating rifle, and he wished he had the firepower the modern weapon would give him. It had hurt to see Brannigan using the Henry, just as it hurt to know that the wagon master also had the Navy Colt that had served Jack so well for so long. Yet he would not dwell on their loss. He had lost finer weapons before, and he would find himself more. When they had won. When they were safe.

He glanced up the track that led to the hacienda. The Ángeles were close now. Almost in range.

Hennessey and the men with the canteens came rushing

around the corner of the building, their faces flushed crimson from the exertion of running in the heat.

'Inside! Now!' Jack bellowed his last instruction, then took two paces away from the doorway, clearing a path for the men and their precious load of water.

Two shots snapped out, the men in the upper storey keeping up their rate of fire. One of the closest Ángeles was struck, the bullet thudding into his shoulder and half throwing him out of the saddle. It caused his horse to swerve, and men around him were forced to slow as they avoided the sudden obstacle.

The rest still rode forward. They closed the distance quickly, revolvers and carbines outstretched.

Jack stood his ground. He heard Hennessey and his men scrambling towards the doorway. He did not glance round to watch their progress. Instead, he looked only at the leading rider, a hard-faced Mexican who rode straight towards him.

He raised the shotgun, settling the butt into his shoulder and easing his weight on to his front leg.

Behind him, Hennessey reached the open door, his two men just behind him.

The leading Ángel twitched his revolver to one side, changing his point of aim. Then he fired.

Jack felt the snap in the air as the bullet zipped past his head. He did not move a muscle.

Hennessey shouted instructions as he made it inside. They did not register in Jack's mind, the sounds ignored.

A second bullet snapped by close enough for him to hear the strange sound it made as it flew through the superheated air. He reached forward with his thumb, cocking first one of the shotgun's hammers, then the other.

Hennessey's two men rushed past just behind him. He could hear them panting.

More bullets flew, other Ángeles opening fire.

Jack braced himself for the shotgun's recoil. The sound of bullets cracking into the hacienda was loud, and he felt dust splatter against his leg from where one hit the ground by his right foot.

The leading Ángel was just twenty feet away. His revolver moved again as he adjusted his aim one last time.

The horse powered forward, goaded by the sound of the gunshots. The last yards passed quickly under its hooves. At such close range, the Ángel would not miss again.

Then Jack fired.

The shotgun's recoil thumped hard into his shoulder. The great blast of both barrels firing at once exploded out, shocking, deafening and powerful.

The buckshot tore into the Ángel riding at Jack, ripping through flesh and muscle. There was time for both horse and rider to scream, before the dreadful sound was cut off abruptly as they crashed into the dirt.

Jack did not wait to inspect his gruesome handiwork. The second he had pulled the trigger, he had bounded for the open doorway.

'Close it up!' He shouted the order as he dived inside.

The Texans hurried to obey. Some flung saddles into the opening, whilst others thrust forward scorched timbers and sections of broken roof. Within a few seconds, the doorway was almost completely blocked.

Jack handed the now empty shotgun to a trooper, then sucked down a deep breath, forcing air into his lungs.

It was darker now inside the hacienda, the only light filtering in through gaps in the jury-rigged barricade, with just a little more coming through the windows and the broken roof above. It gave the place an oppressive air, like a dungeon, the air heated to the point of being stifling.

He had got the men inside. They had weapons and they had water.

And they were trapped.

Chapter Forty-seven

It was the silence that worried Jack the most. None of the Texans spoke as they waited in the gloom. Every man breathed hard, the last-minute rush inside and the hasty barricading of the doorway leaving the already exhausted troopers panting and sweating.

The sound of men moving past outside was fading. With the Texans inside, the Ángeles had broken away, eager to get out of range of the Confederate cavalrymen's carbines. The men on the upper storey held their fire, the Mexicans allowed to pull back without interference.

Jack looked around at the faces of the men Fate had picked to stand with him. He knew only a few of their stories. He did not know where most came from, or what they had done before. He did not even know most of their names. Yet here they were. Ready to fight at his side. Ready to die there.

'Loopholes.' He said the single word loudly and clearly. 'Front, back and sides. We need as many as we can make, otherwise we won't know what Brannigan and those Ángeles bastards are up to. Work in pairs, and work quickly.' He did not raise his voice as he gave his instructions. He did not have to. In the quiet, every man could hear him well enough.

'Hennessey.' He picked out the corporal. 'What weapons have we got?'

'Carbines and shotguns.' Hennessey smeared a hand over his face, as if in an attempt to wipe away his exhaustion. 'About half a dozen of each. We've all got revolvers, plus a couple of spares.'

'Ammunition?'

'Plenty for everything except the shotguns. We've got maybe thirty or forty cartridges between us for those.'

'Right.' Jack took stock. 'I want all the carbines up there.' He pointed to the remains of the upper level. 'They've got the longest range so that's the best place for them. I want you up there too. Keep a bloody sharp eye on those bastards outside.'

'Got it.' Hennessey nodded. 'What's the plan, Jack?'

'The plan.' Jack gave a half-smile. 'We hold fast. If they attack, we drive them back. If we do that enough times, hopefully they'll fuck off and leave us alone.'

'That's not much of a plan.'

He shrugged. 'It's all I've got.'

'It's better than trying to outride 'em, at least.' Hennessey made the remark with a wry smile of his own.

'It is.'

'You think it'll work?'

'Maybe. Maybe not. There's fuck all we can do about it now, though.' Jack looked around him. The men were starting work on the loopholes as he had ordered, but all now paused to listen to the conversation. 'But you know what they say.' He spoke louder, making sure every man could hear him.

'What's that?' Hennessey played along.

'You shouldn't have signed up if you can't take a joke.' Jack delivered the old British army phrase with as wide a grin as he could summon.

He was rewarded with a few grunts of acknowledgement. Nothing more.

'You know what to do?' He spoke more quietly, addressing the question to Hennessey alone.

'Yep.'

'Good.'

Orders delivered, Jack turned his attention to the men working on the loopholes. The hacienda echoed to the sound of them scraping at the stone with their knives. It was hard going. The thick walls were resisting the men's efforts, but already the first slits were starting to emerge.

The sound of movement carried from outside. Keen to know what was going on, he walked to the doorway. The men had done a fine job of barricading it, but there were still enough gaps for him to see through.

The main body of Mexicans had arrived. The men on foot trudged in, taking up positions far from the hacienda. To Jack's eye, they did not look like much. They were a ragtag band, but every man was armed, many now with shiny new Enfield rifles. He remembered the volume of fire that had massacred the men of the wagon train. The bandoleros might look like a collection of scarecrows, but they could most definitely shoot.

As they came past, he searched their ranks for a glimpse of Santiago himself. He did not find the bandoleros' leader, but he did see two faces he recognised. Brannigan and Kat rode in towards the rear of the gaggle of foot soldiers. He did not know what that meant. Had Brannigan promised to give Santiago back a share of the gold held in the strongbox to make use of the bandoleros once again, or was their enigmatic leader happy to dispatch his men to rid himself of the last of Dawson's troopers? Whichever it was, one thing was certain. Jack and his men were horribly outnumbered. He tried to make a rough tally, but the Ángeles were spreading out as they encircled the hacienda, making the process close to impossible. Whatever deal had been struck, he reckoned Brannigan had well over a hundred of Santiago's bandoleros at his command.

Jack had just eleven men.

'Jack!' One of the men stationed on the remains of the upper storey hollered for his attention.

'What do you see?' Jack had been sitting on the ground as he finished reloading his Remington. Around him, the rest of the men were still working on the loopholes. They had been at it for a good thirty minutes now, but they had precious few to show for their efforts. The walls were just too thick.

'It's that woman of Brannigan's.' The man's tone was filled with contempt.

'What's she doing?'

'She's walking right this way. Got herself a white flag.'

Jack forced himself to his feet, pushing the Remington into his holster. He had no idea what Kat was hoping to achieve by coming forward to parley.

'You want me to shoot her?' the Texan asked. He did not seem overly concerned at the notion of killing a woman.

'No.' Jack gave the single-word reply, then turned to the closest pair of Texans. 'You two. Give me a bunk-up.'

The two men dropped their knives, then linked arms so they formed a cradle. Jack pushed his right boot into their grasp and reached for the edge of the upper floor as they boosted him.

With their help, he grasped the broken wood and hauled himself up.

'Bugger,' he hissed. Sharp splinters cut into his stomach as he scrambled over the lip.

'She's stopped.' The Texan who had called out to him gave him the update as he found his footing.

Jack walked carefully around the edge of the room, where the floor was still attached to the walls, until he came to one of the small windows. He saw Kat immediately. She was standing about twenty yards away from the front of the hacienda on the far side of the track, holding a square of white fabric that he reckoned was probably a handkerchief.

The sight of her brought him up short. As ever, she was dressed as a man, with her long hair pulled back and hidden under a wide-brimmed hat. She wore her Remington on one hip and the Volcanic on the other.

'What do you want?' He shouted across to her.

It took her a moment to work out where he was. 'Can I come closer? I can barely hear you,' she shouted up to him.

'All right.' Jack studied the scene carefully, looking for anyone else on the move in case Kat was merely there to provide a diversion. He saw nothing and no one.

As she approached, he felt the touch of the warm breeze washing across his face and recalled the attraction he had felt to this woman. 'That's close enough.' He stopped her when she was halfway across the rutted surface of the track. Any attraction had died, buried beneath a mountain of bodies.

'Are you going to shoot me down?' Kat looked up at his window as she spoke.

She was close enough now for Jack to see every detail of her face. He searched her expression, trying to read whatever emotion was displayed there. He failed, her half-smile, half-grimace as unintelligible as ever. But he knew one thing. It would be easy to kill her. To his left, Hennessey and another of the Texans were aiming their carbines towards her, tracking her movements. It would take a single word to order them to fire. Then there would be one fewer enemy to worry about.

'I might.' He shouted the honest answer. 'Depends on what you want.'

'I've got a message for you.'

'No shit.' He watched her carefully. Any desire he had once felt for her meant nothing. Not now. His duty was to the eleven men sharing his fate. He would do whatever it took to keep even one of them alive. 'Where's Brannigan?'

'He's here.'

'But he sent you to do his dirty work.' Jack was scathing.

'I volunteered.'

'Then you must be bottle-head stupid.'

'I must be. But I want to give you a chance to avoid more bloodshed.'

'What the fuck do you mean?' Jack sensed a trap.

'If you give yourself and the specie up, then those men in there can go free.' Kat raised her voice so that every man in the hacienda would hear her.

The offer took him by surprise. He had not known what to expect, but this was something he could not have foreseen.

'Did you hear me? Brannigan just wants you and the specie, Jack. If you come out, those boys in there get to go home.'

Jack's mind was racing. He assessed the offer. It made sense, to his mind at least. He was the only man there who had been a witness to all Brannigan had done. Without him to verify the tale, he doubted anyone would care what the Texans said.

Brannigan would be free to disappear with the strongbox.

'I heard you,' he shouted. He glanced at the Texans next to him. All three were looking at him, eyes bright white against dirty faces.

He understood now why Kat had been sent. Of all the people there, she had the best chance of getting Jack to listen. He *had* listened. And now he contemplated the idea of giving himself up.

He was no fool. He had no doubt that this time Brannigan would not spare him. He remembered the men they had seen by the side of the trail, the ones buried alive with just their heads left free. Such a fate would surely be his if he did as Kat demanded and gave himself up. The notion sent a wave of sickness deep into his gut, and he felt a twist of fear surge through his bowels as he contemplated being left to endure such a horrific death. It was not hard to conjure up the image of the insects and animals starting to feast on his flesh even whilst he still lived. He could not imagine the pure horror of that moment.

Yet he had known the answer he would give an instant after Kat had made the offer. He had no choice. Not with his men's lives at stake.

'So be it.' He closed his eyes as he whispered the words, a moment's terror threatening to steal his courage. He sucked it down, opening his eyes and staring at the woman who demanded his life. Then he shouted down his reply.

'I'll do it. I'll give myself up.'

Chapter Forty-eight

'No.' Hennessey snapped the word an instant after Jack had replied.

'It's not your bloody decision,' Jack fired back. 'They'll let you go.'

'Are you really stupid enough to believe that line of horseshit?' Hennessey's reaction was scathing.

Jack scowled. He did not take kindly to being insulted. 'They just want me. I saw what Brannigan did. I saw all of it.'

'You've got one mighty high opinion of yourself there, Jack.' Hennessey gave a lopsided grin. 'And you're a goddam fool.'

'I'm the only witness to all that bastard did.' Jack felt something close to anger starting to build. He had been willing to sacrifice himself for Hennessey and his men. He had not expected to be lauded as some great hero for doing so, but he had not expected to be insulted either.

'And yet you trust him now?' Hennessey poured a bucketful of scorn on his thinking. 'You think that if you walk out there, they'll let the rest of us mosey on down that track?'

'Yes.' He gave the only answer he could.

Hennessey shook his head. 'Like I said, you're a goddam fool.'

'What's going on up there?' Kat shouted. She would have heard Jack's reply. 'What the hell are you playing at, Jack?'

He looked Hennessey straight in the eye. 'You don't trust them?' He felt the fear shift. A part of him knew the corporal was right. This was just another one of Kat's games. She played so many, games where she did not share the rules, and where there could only be one winner.

'I don't trust a single one of them lying sons of bitches. We've been fighting them varmints for years now. We know them like they know us.' Hennessey paused to shake his head ruefully. 'It's a lie, Jack. The moment we walk out there, we're all dead men.'

Jack looked at the other two men crouched on the upper level with them. He could see their fear; he had been around soldiers long enough to recognise it with ease. But he saw something else. He saw their determination. He felt relief settle in his gut. Hennessey and his men were giving him the chance to at least go down fighting.

'Are you sure about this?' he asked.

'Goddammit, Jack, tell that lying bitch to go to hell.' Hennessey offered another of his half-smiles as the men around him growled their assent, one even going so far as to offer a shouted 'Amen'.

Jack held Hennessey's gaze for a moment longer, searching for a hint of doubt. He found not one shred of it there. Hennessey knew what he was saying, what he was committing the Texans to.

'What's going on up there?' Kat demanded.

Jack turned his gaze back to the outside. He had to blink,

the bright sunlight stinging eyes that had become accustomed to the gloom of the hacienda. Kat had not moved.

'I've got a message for Brannigan,' he called, his voice clear and strong.

'Are you not coming out, Jack?' Kat sensed something had changed. 'If you stay in there, he'll kill you. He'll kill you all.' She raised her voice to make sure every man in the hacienda could hear her. 'You go on and give yourself up now, give those boys a chance.'

'Horseshit!' It was Hennessey who replied. His men heard him and laughed, their scorn for the offer echoing off the walls of the building.

'You heard the man,' Jack barked. He was done talking. 'Tell Brannigan I thank him for his kind offer, but that I decline.'

'You're making a mistake there, Jack.' Kat would not let it go so easily. 'It don't matter what those folk up there say. It's your decision. You're going to get them all killed.'

'I'm going to count to ten. If you're still standing there when I'm done, we'll shoot you where you stand.' Jack kept his tone loud, clear and even. He wanted no misunderstanding.

Kat did not move. 'You're killing them, Jack. Same as if you slit their throats yourself.'

'One!'

She glanced down at the dirt around her boots, then up at the small window. Jack watched her. He could not read her expression. Was there regret there, some hint of sadness at the thought of his death? Or was there just stung pride at her failure? He did not know which it was. He did not want to know.

'Two.'

'You're a goddam fool, Jack Lark.' Kat held her position for a moment longer. Then she turned on her heel and walked away.

Jack did not bother to continue with the count. The decision was made. Brannigan was denied. And the twelve men in the hacienda knew the fate that awaited them.

Jack took his time loading the shotgun he had fired at the Ángeles. He kept the men hacking at the walls, their blunted knives gouging away at the stone in an attempt to add to the half-dozen loopholes they had managed to make so far. It was a brutally hard task, but at least it kept them busy.

As he rammed home a fresh set of cartridges, he wondered what else he could do to defend the hacienda. He had three men on the upper level, all armed with at least two carbines along with their own revolvers. The shotguns he would keep downstairs, where he would hold them back for any rush on the doorway. The eight men with him were still working in pairs, and he would keep them like that for the time being, two per wall, the loopholes they had created the only way they could see and shoot at any Ángeles working their way around the building. He would position himself at the doorway. There were gaps in the makeshift barricade that allowed him to see out towards the front of the hacienda. It was also the spot where Brannigan would most likely direct the first assault. When that came, he would summon one of each pair from the loopholes to join him at the barricade, the five of them all armed with shotguns. Any attackers attempting to break in would be greeted with a close-range salvo.

He ran through the simple plan in his head. There was nothing else he could do, he was sure of that. His only regret was that he had not had the time to return to the shed at the side of the hacienda where he had been held captive, and where he was sure his sword still lay, discarded and half hidden. It would be nice to end his fighting days with a blade in one hand and a revolver in the other.

'Jack!' Hennessey called down from his station on the upper level.

'What do you see?' Jack snapped the last shotgun closed, then got to his feet.

'Some old fella just turned up.'

'Took him long enough.' Jack had wondered if the bandoleros' leader would arrive to supervise the destruction of the Confederate patrol. He did not flatter himself that it had anything to do with the men themselves. Rather it would be for the strongbox that was safely stashed away on the remains of the upper level. He wondered what deal Brannigan had struck with Santiago for its return; what portion of its contents was being paid to ensure the death of one Englishman and eleven Texans.

'You know who that old fellow is, Hennessey?'

'Nope. But they sure do.' Hennessey sounded impressed. 'Every one of them is on their goddam feet.'

'That's Santiago.'

'Are you shitting me? That old son of a bitch is Santiago?' Hennessey could not hide the disbelief.

'As he lives and breathes,' Jack confirmed, just as the first cheers reached his ears, the bandoleros whooping and hollering to celebrate their leader's arrival. A few even fired shots, the sound echoing off the walls of the hacienda and ringing in the ears of the twelve men waiting inside. It spoke of what was to come.

Jack could just about make out a single voice hectoring the crowd. The words were barely audible inside the hacienda, yet they were clearly having an effect, and the cheering grew louder, the shots more frequent.

There was a final great roar, the sound building to a crescendo that battered against the walls.

'Here they come!' Hennessey shouted down the warning. Santiago had wasted no time in setting his men to the task.

The simple statement resonated in Jack's mind. The end was close now. 'How many?'

'All of them.'

'Where?'

'Everywhere.' Hennessey's tone was calm, as if he were reporting on the progression of clouds across the sky rather than on the movement of the men who would likely kill them all.

Jack glanced around the room. Every man looked back at him, the loopholes forgotten.

'That's enough.' He spoke softly. There was no need to shout. 'Take your positions.'

The men obeyed. Knives were dropped or put back in sheaths attached to belts. Revolvers and shotguns were readied.

'Hold your fire up there. Wait until the bastards are right outside.' He gave the last instructions to Hennessey. 'Make every shot count.'

He turned. The men were ready. It was the time when some leaders would offer up a speech assuring their men of victory, no matter the odds. Yet Jack did not have the words for that. He could speak of his gratitude, acknowledging the Texans' willingness to fight to the last. But anything he could say would just sound trite. They had made their decision to stay, for their own reasons. He could speak of his pride and his pleasure at fighting alongside such men as these. Yet he knew the Texans well enough by now to be certain they would not care for such mawkish sentiment. They were hard men from a hard land. There was nothing he could say that would make one jot of difference.

So he said nothing. He took up position at the barricaded doorway and readied himself for what was to come.

There was silence then, not one of the men in the hacienda making a sound.

Then the Ángeles opened fire.

Chapter Forty-nine

The opening volley roared out.

The sound was dreadful. The fire came against every side of the building, Santiago ringing the hacienda with men. Shards of stone were spat through the loopholes, the defenders stationed nearby showered with razor-sharp fragments. Bullets impacted against the walls like some sort of deadly hail, the sound echoing throughout the space.

There was a pause. It lasted for the span of two dozen heartbeats. Then they fired again.

The shots came constantly after that, the Ángeles firing at their own speed. The hacienda echoed to the cracks of bullet on stone and the curses of men hit by splinters.

There was nothing to be done. None of them had a weapon with the same range and power as the Enfield rifles. They would have to bide their time and wait for the right moment to strike back.

Jack hunkered down behind the barricade. Bullet after bullet slammed into the haphazard arrangement of saddles and wood that blocked the entrance. He was close enough to feel the power of the Minié balls, the barricade vibrating as each bullet thumped home. There was an odd pulsating rhythm to the firing now. The sound was constant, yet it undulated, as some men fired together whilst others fired alone. It was the overture to battle, one that he had heard more times than he could remember. Other sounds would follow, just as an overture would give way to the first act. But for the moment, the screams of the dead and dying and the yells of men fighting for their lives were still in the future.

Jack and his men held their fire. They were crouched down now, faces turned away from the loopholes to avoid the shards of stone flung through them. On the upper level, the men lay flat on the ground, bullets zipping through the windows to crack into the far wall.

The shooting continued, each of the Ángeles firing at least half a dozen rounds as they flayed the hacienda with fire. Jack listened to the sound of the countless impacts and felt nothing but scorn. Long-range rifle fire would not shift the Texans from the building. It was a futile effort, one that would do nothing but waste precious ammunition. He understood why Santiago had ordered the volleys. Few things inspired men on the battlefield more than standing in a cloud of their own powder smoke flinging shot after shot at an enemy. Yet on this day, they could fire for an hour and still have no effect. At some point the Ángeles would have to suck up the courage to rush the building and take on the Texans face to face.

The shooting stopped.

Jack tensed. This was the moment.

There was a pause. Silence wrapped around them.

Then came the first shouts. Orders and cheers; war cries and jeers.

'Hold your fire.' Jack spoke for the first time in a long time, taking charge of the moment, not willing to leave it to the men outside alone. 'Let the bastards get close.'

Outside, the cheers and yells came without pause now, the volume increasing. Underscoring it all was the start of a chant, a single word repeated over and over.

'Shoot the fuckers in the gut.' Jack spoke calmly, showing no sign of emotion. He did not know if the Texans needed the advice, or if they would heed it. They had been fighting this bitter war against the bandoleros since even before the struggle between the states had begun. They likely knew their job as well as he did, or better. Yet that did not mean they did not need to hear a calm voice reminding them of what to do, one that showed no fear in the face of the enemy, one that showed them that there was a man there to lead them.

The chanting increased in volume, and for the first time, Jack could finally pick out the single word that was being repeated over and over.

'Santiago! Santiago!'

'Wait until I give the command, then hit them with everything we've got.' He had to raise his voice to be heard over the visceral chanting. The sound echoed around the hacienda, the bandoleros stationed at the back and sides picking it up and repeating it over and over.

'Santiago! Santiago!'

There was nothing more for Jack to say. Around him the men held themselves ready. One of them murmured a psalm under his breath, the words barely audible over the voices of the bandoleros.

'Our God shall come, and shall not keep silence . . .'

'Santiago! Santiago!'

'A fire shall devour before him, and it shall be very tempestuous round about him . . .'

'Santiago! Santiago!'

'He shall call the heavens from above, and to the earth, that he may judge his people.'

The chanting stopped. There was one last cheer, the feral roar of the mob as it was released.

'Gather my saints together unto me; those that have made a covenant with me by sacrifice.'

The Ángeles charged.

Chapter Fifty

———◆———

The bandoleros came from every direction, Santiago committing every man to the attack. They shouted as they charged. It was no ordinary war cry, but something wilder. It rose in pitch as the Ángeles rushed forward, becoming unearthly as they shed their humanity and became the killers of men they would have to be.

'Ready!' Jack shouted the single word.

As one, the Texans stood up. Carbines and revolvers were aimed through windows and loopholes.

Jack peered through the gap in the barricade; the shotgun he would use when they rushed the doorway leaned against the wall, close at hand.

'Hold your fire!' he shouted. His men needed to hear him.

The Ángeles were moving fast now, feet pounding against the sun-baked ground, the noise building in volume as the charge came closer.

Jack watched as the distance closed with mesmerising speed. There was no order to the charge. They just came on anyhow, the men jumbled together. He could pick out faces as they rushed closer. He could see mouths moving as the Ángeles roared their unearthly war cry. He could see both fear and fury on faces twisted with emotion. He looked into the eyes of the men coming to kill him and felt nothing. No fear. No rage. No madness. He thought only of distance, his mind busy calculating feet and yards rather than dwelling on what was to come.

'Ready!' He judged the moment had arrived and held his breath, daring himself to hold on just a moment longer.

The Ángeles were close now, no more than forty feet from the hacienda.

Still he held back the command. Forty feet became thirty. The raucous noise of the war cry washed over the building, echoing off the stone walls and ringing in the ears of the twelve men who waited in silence.

Thirty feet became twenty.

'Fire!' Jack shouted the command.

The Texans fired as one.

The men on the upper level opened up with their carbines, aiming down into the mass of bodies. Every bullet hit.

Those at the loopholes fired the first round from their revolvers. Bullets scythed into the bandoleros' ranks, knocking men down. The bodies of the fallen tripped those close behind them, spreading chaos amongst the tightly packed mob.

More shots came as the men on the upper level fired their second carbines, the bullets ripping into the heads and shoulders of the men below.

The men at the loopholes poured on the fire, shots blurring together as they discharged their revolvers as fast as they could.

Round after round punched into the Ángeles' ranks. Men crumpled to the ground, flesh torn and blood pumping in the dry dirt beneath them. Screams came, louder even than the war cry.

Still the bandoleros came on. The dead and the dying were trampled as the rush continued, their comrades callous and uncaring as they carried the charge home. More men fell, the Texans at the loopholes emptying their revolvers into the mob. At such close range, it was impossible to miss.

Jack alone held his fire. He waited, watching the attackers as they charged, his mouth and nose filled with the familiar stink of powder smoke. Then he reached for the shotgun.

The Ángeles reached the walls of the hacienda. The first men shoved weapons through the loopholes and fired, sending bullets ricocheting around inside. Two Texans were wounded in the first instant, their cries of surprise and pain lost in the storm of sound that filled the building.

Jack felt the barricade shudder as the men outside started to batter against it. It was time.

He thrust the shotgun's barrel through the gap he had been looking through. He could hear the men outside. They were attacking the barricade with gusto, rifle butts hammering away, hands clawing at the rubble.

He fired.

The barrel of the shotgun was just inches from the men outside. At such close range the weapon was brutally effective. Two men were cut down, their stomachs ripped open as the swathe of shot eviscerated them both at the same moment.

It was not enough. The hammering continued apace even as the pair thrashed and died on the ground beyond the barricade.

'To me!' Jack summoned others to his side. The barricade was the weak spot and he had to defend it if he were to keep the Ángeles out.

Four men, one from each loophole, ran to his side. Each carried a loaded shotgun. The other men fought on, revolvers firing almost constantly as they tried to keep the bandoleros away from the openings.

'Shoot the bastards!' Jack stepped away from the barricade, letting one of the Texans reach the gap he had already fired through.

The man needed no more invitation. He stepped into the spot Jack had vacated, thrusting his own shotgun through the gap. He fired a moment later, discharging both barrels at once.

'Next!' Jack passed his own shotgun to the Texan backing away from the barricade. A second man stepped forward to take his place. A heartbeat later, another blast roared out.

'You two, get all the shotguns reloaded,' Jack ordered. They would need the firepower. Behind him the third man took his place at the barricade. He fired, then stepped away sharply.

'You're up.' Jack snapped the instruction at the last of the four men who had rushed over to join him.

As the Texan stepped to the gap, shotgun ready, a bullet seared through the opening. It took the man in the chest, hitting him with enough power to knock him back.

For one dreadful moment, his head turned to stare at Jack. Then he fell, his chest sheeted with blood gushing from the fist-sized chasm that had been torn in his flesh.

Jack did not hesitate. He stepped forward to grab the fallen man's shotgun, shoving the barrel into the gap and pulling the trigger. The weapon kicked in his hands as it spat out two more loads of buckshot. Screams followed as another man attacking the barricade was cut down.

Still the Ángeles would not give up. More ran forward, taking the place of the dead and the dying. They attacked the barricade with vigour spurred by fear.

With a cheer they managed to rip away one of the saddles,

opening a great gap in the upper quarter of the barricade.

Light flooded into the hacienda, illuminating the swirls of powder smoke so that the place took on an unearthly feel, as if the sun had somehow managed to penetrate the depths of hell.

Jack reacted first. He snatched his loaded Remington from its holster. This time he could see his targets clearly. He aimed his first shot, snapping off a bullet at a heavily moustachioed face that loomed into view as another great chunk of barricade fell away. The bullet took the man in the face, shattering bone. He fell forward, revealing a great sea of faces as dozens of Ángeles swarmed around the barricade.

'Shoot them down!' Jack gave the order even as he fired again. It was impossible to miss. The revolver's second bullet cut down an Ángel on the point of raising his rifle.

The Texans with him dropped their empty shotguns and stepped forward, revolvers in hand. The four men stood shoulder to shoulder, all firing fast. Their bullets tore into the tightly packed group of Ángeles.

Yet even as men screamed, the Mexicans fought back. Now with something to aim at, they drew weapons of their own that had been saved for this moment.

The man on Jack's left screamed as a bullet tore through his neck. The sound was cut off almost instantly as blood filled his throat. He fell forward, hitting the dirt in front of Jack's feet, legs thrashing and body writhing as he died.

Jack and the two men still with him kept firing, driving the Ángeles away from the barricade. Every bullet hit. Every bullet killed. The men stationed on the upper storey joined in, raining rounds down on to the heads of the men backing away from the building.

It was too much. The Ángeles had come so close to breaking

into the hacienda, yet now they fled, leaving the bodies of the dead behind them.

Jack fired the last round from his Remington, the bullet cutting down a man as he turned to run. Around him, those Texans still standing lowered their weapons. Not one had the breath in his lungs to say even a single word.

Jack thrust the Remington into its holster, then bent forward to put his hands on his knees. He closed his eyes, sucking down breath after breath, hauling the superheated air into his lungs. It had been close. Too close. Yet somehow they had held.

Chapter Fifty-one

———◆◆———

'Jack.'

Jack opened his eyes. The Texan called Moore was offering him a canteen. He took it gratefully and drank deeply, letting the water sluice away the dust and smoke from his mouth and throat. Only when he had drunk enough did he lower the canteen and hand it back. He made a mental note to thank Hennessey for having the forethought to get the canteens refilled before the Ángeles arrived. He could not begin to imagine how dreadful it would be at that moment if they had no water.

'How do we look?' He wiped the back of his hand across his mouth.

'We lost two men.' Moore took a mouthful of water from the canteen. 'Two more are hurt.'

'Badly?'

'Not enough to stop them fighting.'

'Good.' Jack looked around him. The two men who had died had been dragged to one side and laid neatly in a corner. He knew that his small command had been lucky, that the butcher's bill could have been so much worse. Yet it was hard to feel any sense of satisfaction as he looked at the two bodies.

He blew out his cheeks. The Texans had known what they were doing. Once he would have dwelt on the matter, his mind tormenting him with thoughts of what might have been, and of what he might have done differently. Now he let the matter fall away. What was done was done. The two men were dead and nothing would bring them back.

He turned his attention to the living. There were six men still with him on the lower level, with Hennessey and his two men above. They were ten men against God alone knew how many.

'You think they'll skedaddle now?' Moore asked.

'You never know.' Jack tried to sound hopeful. Brannigan might be paying Santiago, or the old man might be trying to wipe out the Texan patrol out of sheer spite. Whichever it was, the more bandoleros the Texans killed, the greater the chance the Mexicans would ride away. Hatred and money only went so far, and Santiago could surely not afford to lose too many men. If the Texans could hold out long enough, Jack was sure that Santiago would abandon the attack, no matter what Brannigan might want him to do.

It was not much of a hope, but it was all he could muster. He could feel the tiredness seeping into his bones. It would be a long time until any of them could rest.

'Well, we sure gave them boys a bloody nose.' Moore sounded satisfied. 'That son of a bitch Santiago will remember this day.'

'He will.' Jack cocked an ear. He could hear the groans of men outside. Not every Ángel they had shot down had been killed. Many lay wounded, and now they suffered. That suffering would continue until the Texans either surrendered or were wiped out.

'Make sure you and all the boys are reloaded. I don't think it'll be long before they try again.' He nodded as he gave Moore the order and was pleased to see the Texan turn to relay it without question. It was almost enough to make him smile. He had been wrong to spend so much time wandering. Only here, amidst the shit and the blood and the pain and the fear, was he the man he was meant to be. It did not make him a hero. He was no indestructible warrior who could cheat death no matter the odds. He was just one man, a man who had no more chance of surviving than any other on the field of battle. But he was a soldier and he was a leader. And he was back where he belonged.

The Texans were given little respite. It had taken the Ángeles less than a dozen minutes to regroup, and now they opened fire once again.

'Get down!' Jack shouted.

The men needed little urging. All bent low and crouched by the walls, tucking in their arms and legs to make themselves as small a target as possible. Bullets cracked off the hacienda's facade. Some zipped through the opening in the barricade before burying themselves in the far wall, or worse, ricocheting away in every direction.

This time the Ángeles fired slowly. Every shot was aimed, the bandoleros taking their time rather than just flaying the building with ineffective fire. More and more shots were flying inside, and the Texans flinched and cursed as deformed bullets and sharp splinters of stone flew this way and that.

'What can you see, Hennessey?' Jack called. He was

hunkered down by the remains of the barricade, keeping himself busy, first reloading his Remington then doing the same with the shotguns.

'Them sons of bitches are massing out front.'

'Can you see Brannigan or Santiago?'

'I see 'em both.' Hennessey's disdain was obvious.

'What are they doing?' Jack wanted to know more. He could not risk looking over the broken barricade. Its remains were being hit constantly now, the Ángeles making sure that none of the Texans could attempt to repair the weakened defence.

'Having a goddam powwow.'

Jack pictured the scene outside easily enough. The first assault had been poorly planned, the two men leading the bandoleros relying on numbers alone to shift the defenders from the hacienda. Now they were about to try again, and this time the assault would be premeditated and planned.

It was how he would do it were the roles reversed. Keep up a constant fire to pin the defenders down whilst advancing the assault party. The covering fire would be kept going until the last minute. Then the main group would rush forward, every man directed to the pathetic barricade that barred entry to the building. Once that had fallen, the Texans would not stand a chance.

'Is everyone reloaded?' he called. He could do nothing about the Ángeles, not with the hacienda under constant fire. But he could keep the men occupied.

Heads nodded. The Texans knew their trade.

'Take up positions on the front wall only.' Jack changed their placement. If Hennessey was right, the Ángeles were going to attack the front of the hacienda alone.

He paused, letting the men shuffle towards the front wall. Two crouched near a loophole that had been hacked from the stone. The rest gathered near the barricade.

'Hennessey!'

'Jack?'

'You boys hold your fire until the last moment. Then give those bastards everything you've got.'

'You got it.' Hennessey's answer was quick and sure.

Jack grinned. He liked these Texans. 'Are you boys ready to fight?' he asked the men crouching near him.

'Hell, yeah.' Moore was closest, and he growled the reply.

'Make every shot count.' Jack flinched as a bullet snapped through the opening in the barricade. He smiled as he saw the men nearby grinning at his reaction. 'Let's take as many of those fuckers with us as we can.'

The men nodded in agreement. All of them were ready.

'Here they come!' Hennessey sang out the warning.

Jack sucked down a deep breath. There was no fear. Not now.

He sensed devilment stirring in his gut. His end might be coming, but at least he was being given the chance to fight. He thought back to Adam and Brown, and then to Vaughan and the rest of the men in the wagon train. All had died a sad, ignoble death. At least Jack had the opportunity to end his days in the one place where he felt truly at home.

He would die in battle, with a gun in his hand and a snarl on his face.

Chapter Fifty-two

———◆◆———

The Ángeles charged for a second time. Once again they shouted as they pounded forward, unleashing their wild, eerie war cry. This time it was underscored by the crack of rifle fire.

Brannigan and Santiago had stationed men to either side of the assault. The angle let them continue to fire even as the main group rushed forward. Bullets thudded into the hacienda without pause. Rounds impacted into walls, cracking stone then hurtling on, fizzing and whining as they ricocheted.

'Ready!' Jack held himself still as he crouched behind the barricade, shotgun in hand.

The Ángeles rushed on. The covering fire died out as the charging mob finally blocked the gunmen's line of sight.

It was time.

'Fire!' Jack shouted the order as he rose, swinging the shotgun level. He pulled the trigger the moment the weapon was aimed outside.

This time he could see his enemy. The shotgun blast tore through two men leading the charge. At his side, the Texans stood and fired, the shotgun blasts merging into one. With the

Ángeles so close, every piece of buckshot hit home. Men tumbled over, screaming and shrieking as their bodies were shredded. More fell as Hennessey and his men on the hacienda's upper storey opened fire, their carbines dreadfully accurate at such close range.

'Pour it on!' Jack exhorted his men to keep firing.

Shotguns emptied, the men switched to revolvers. They fired round after round into the horde rushing towards them. The storm of bullets scythed through the Ángeles' ranks, killing and maiming indiscriminately. Men fell constantly, their dying bodies crumpling to the ground, where they were trampled by the callous feet of the living.

'Keep firing!' Jack picked another target. There was the shortest flash of triumph as his bullet took a man in the gut before he switched aim to fire again.

Still the bandoleros came on. As before, there was no order to their attack, no neatly aligned ranks. They charged in a mob, men running together, their faces contorted as they released their dreadful war cry.

Jack fired again and again. Every bullet hit. The men at his side were doing the same, yet there was no way to stop the men coming towards them.

The Ángeles reached the barricade, hitting it hard, hands and rifle butts hammering into the jumbled arrangement of saddles and broken wood. Weakened and already half broken, the defences collapsed inwards.

The Ángeles cheered as they poured inside.

The Texans could do nothing to stop them. But that did not mean they would not try.

Revolvers and shotguns emptied, the men defending the hacienda drew bowie knives and readied tomahawks. They counterattacked hard, ploughing into the first Ángeles to step inside, knives ripping into flesh. Men screamed as they were cut down, their bodies falling to writhe around the feet of the men fighting above them.

It was chaos. A moustachioed bandolero came at Jack, his Enfield rifle raised as a club. Jack saw the blow coming and arched his body, letting the rifle fly past his belly. Then he stepped forward, bowie knife rising in a fast strike. He punched the blade into the Ángel's throat, whipping the steel in and out so that it would not get caught in the flesh.

The moustachioed man's eyes widened, a moment's horrified surprise before blood poured from the wound in one great rush. His rifle clattered to the ground as he raised both hands to the gruesome tear in his flesh.

Jack gave him no time to dwell on his fate. He punched hard with his free left hand, smacking it into the side of the Ángel's head, bludgeoning him to the ground. The man fell without making a sound.

Without hesitation, Jack stepped forward into the gap he had created. He drove his knife into a bandolero's side, then grabbed another man's hair and threw him backwards towards the barricade.

Around him the Texans fought hard. They cut deep into the Ángeles' disordered ranks, striking men down one after the other and pushing them back. They did not have it all their own way. Two of the Texans went down, the bandoleros fighting back with rifle butts and knives. Yet the impetus of the Mexicans' rush had been broken by the stubborn defiance of Jack and his men.

'Keep going!' Jack bellowed the encouragement then stepped forward again. An Ángel came at him with a long knife with a fine bone handle. The blade was thrust forward, the tip aimed at Jack's gut.

He managed a desperate parry, throwing the strike wide so that the knife slipped past his hip. It gave him an opening and he thrust his left hand forward, grabbing the Ángel by the throat. As soon as his fingers took hold, he pulled hard, jerking his attacker towards him. Off balance, the man could do nothing to resist, and he stumbled forward just as Jack intended. He had taken no more than a half-step before Jack head-butted him right in the centre of his face. It was a vicious blow that came straight from the alleyways of east London, and it pulped the Ángel's nose and broke teeth.

The man's head recoiled from the strike. But Jack still held him around the throat, exposing the soft flesh of his neck. It was the work of seconds to recover his knife from its parry and drag it across his opponent's throat, cutting through sinew and gristle and opening the man's windpipe. Blood poured from the gruesome wound as Jack sawed the blade back and forth, driving the edge deep. The Ángel tried to scream, but there was too much blood in his throat, and he gagged on it, spluttering and choking as he died.

Jack threw the man backwards, then searched for a new target. Yet the bandoleros were backing away now, every one of them fearful of the white-faced men with their vicious knives. The attackers nearest the barricade stepped back again, creating space for those close to the Texans to retreat.

Jack stepped forward, blade dripping gore, blood slathered over his right hand and covering his jacket almost to the elbow. He saw the bandoleros were about to run. He could sense it. He could almost smell their fear. It would just take one more push.

He opened his mouth, readying the shout that would see the remaining defenders throw themselves at the bandoleros. The order never came.

A tall American stepped over the remains of the barricade. He held a strange-looking rifle in his hands, one with an odd-shaped lever around its trigger.

Jack saw Brannigan. He saw his Henry repeater.

And he knew that their stubborn defence was over.

Brannigan opened fire the moment he cleared the remains of the barricade. The Henry was never meant to be a long-range weapon, and the close confines of the fight in the hacienda were perfect for it to demonstrate its power. The first bullet hit a Texan in the gut, the second and third following so quickly that the sounds merged into one.

'Upstairs!' Jack shouted the only order he could think of. There was nowhere else to go.

The surviving defenders turned. Moore was in front of Jack. He ran to the place where the upper storey was lowest. One of the men already there squatted down, hands reaching for him, ready to haul him up.

Brannigan stepped further into the hacienda. He fired fast, cranking the Henry's handle and pumping bullets into the defenders even as they tried to escape. Three bullets hit Moore in the pit of the spine, knocking him face down on to the floor.

Jack could hear Brannigan laughing as he killed. Another Texan went down in a flurry of bullets, his body twisting and spinning as he fell. The bullets came without pause, the repeater firing as fast as Brannigan could make it.

'Jack!' Hennessey shouted. All three men on the upper storey were reaching down, their hands outstretched.

Jack needed no encouragement. He dropped his knife and ran towards them, his back twitching as his muscles tensed in expectation of being hit.

The last surviving trooper ran at his side. They jumped together, reaching up for the hands that could haul them to safety.

Brannigan fired.

The man next to Jack screamed as a bullet thumped into his spine. He fell away, pulling down the man who had attempted to lift him. Jack was scrambling up so he did not see either man fall, but he heard their screams as the mob below attacked them with knives.

There was a sharp stab of pain in his gut as he was dragged up and over the broken edge of the upper storey, then he was there, floundering on the floorboards like a freshly landed fish.

'Look out!' Hennessey shouted the warning before Jack could get to his feet.

Hands grabbed at his boots, which still stuck out into space. The Ángeles had swarmed inside as Brannigan gunned down the last defenders. Now they tried to drag Jack back down and into the clutches of the men below.

He lashed out, kicking away the hands then scrabbling forward on his stomach. Mills was there. The baby-faced trooper still had a loaded revolver, and now he fired down. The bullets took the nearest bandoleros in the head and face, driving them back and giving Jack the chance to scramble to his feet.

Yet he was far from safe. What remained of the upper level hugged the walls, the floor angled and twisted. The central section was missing completely, and as he found his footing, he looked down into a sea of faces as still more Ángeles poured inside. Already many were jumping for the upper storey, their comrades offering cradled hands to boost them up.

They came by the dozen. There were far too many to be stopped, but Jack refused to stop fighting. He stamped forward, crushing a set of grasping fingers under the heel of his boot. Then he kicked out, smashing his foot into the face of a man on the point of hauling himself up.

Everything was happening fast. Brannigan loomed into view below. Jack caught a glimpse of the raised Henry repeater, then the bullets came again.

Hennessey went down in the hail of lead, face smashed into offal by the impact of two bullets. His body tumbled over the edge of the floor and was immediately lost from sight as the Ángeles below swarmed over it, knives hacking.

The first bandoleros had reached the upper level. Mills battered one of them to the ground with his now empty revolver, but two others took his place. Both attacked the Texan with knives, their blades thrusting into his flesh at the same time. Mills staggered back, revolver tumbling from his grasp as his hands clutched at the two great crevices gouged in his flesh. The Ángeles went after him, blades moving fast, his despairing, terrified cries cut off as one of them stabbed him in the throat.

Jack fought like a man possessed. Two more men reached the upper storey. He punched the first one, the blow connecting with the man's face, bloodying his lips and nose. Then he twisted around, hands grabbing for the second. He managed to grip the man's jacket and swung hard, throwing the Mexican back over the edge and down on to the heads of the men still rushing inside.

The man he had punched recovered fast. He came at Jack

with a knife, the blade held low, ready to gut him. Jack twisted away, but with so little floor left, there was nowhere for him to go, and he thumped hard into the wall. Again the Ángel came at him. Jack swatted an arm across the front of his body, driving the blade wide. It saved him, but the Ángel's left hand was free, and he punched hard, hitting Jack in the side of his head.

The blow stung, but Jack butted his head forward regardless, striking the man hard, knocking him back. He went after him in an instant, his weight thrown forward, hands making contact with the centre of the man's chest. Off balance and hurting, the Mexican could do nothing to resist, and he went back over the edge of the floor, arms windmilling as he fell.

Yet there was to be no respite. Even as Jack fought, more Ángeles had made it to the upper level. And now there was no one else left to fight them. No one except one exhausted Englishman who did not know when he was beaten.

Chapter Fifty-three

———◆———

Jack charged across the blood-splattered floor. He hit one of the bandoleros with his shoulder, knocking the man over the edge. Another immediately came at him with a knife. Jack saw the blow coming. He blocked it with his left forearm, then punched, right hand cracking forward to catch the Ángel's chin with a rising uppercut that snapped his head back and sent him reeling away.

Still more Ángeles came for him. One rushed at him from behind. He twisted around, punching with his left hand then lashing out with his right, driving the man back.

Yet turning had left him open to an attack from the other side. Another Ángel came at him with the butt of an Enfield rifle. The blow connected with the back of his head, throwing him forward.

His knees buckled and his vision greyed. Somehow, he stayed on his feet. He turned around to grab at the man attacking him, but he was slow now, the blow to his head stealing his speed. He managed to get hold of the Enfield, but the man simply pushed forward, driving him backwards.

The back of his head hit the wall. Pain flared, bright and

hot. He could feel the blood starting to flow from the wound, soaking into his hair. Still he tried to fight. He lashed out, fists flailing at the men to his front. He hit one of them, his punch landing true, knocking the man backwards. Yet more of them came at him, fists and rifle butts hammering into his body. A blade scored across his forehead, opening the skin from temple to temple so that blood ran down his face and into his eyes.

More blows came. A knife slashed him across the chest, the pain sharp and clear. Then another rifle butt hit the side of his battered and blood-covered head.

He went down like a sack of horseshit.

As he hit the floor, his senses fled so that he could no longer fully see, or hear, or feel. But he knew that the blows had stopped.

Cheers penetrated the fog that engulfed him. The Ángeles had paid a heavy price to capture the hacienda. Now they whooped and hollered as they celebrated their victory.

Jack lay still, waiting for the killing strike. There was no fear at that moment. There was just mute acceptance that this was to be the day when everything ended.

Yet the blow did not arrive.

The moments crawled past. The cheers subsided. He heard Brannigan's voice, loud, clear and strident as he ordered the men outside. He heard the thump of boots hitting the stone floor below as the men around him jumped down.

Then he was alone.

A final, desperate idea came to him. He did not believe it would work, but still he rolled to one side, hands reaching out like a blind man. He had fallen next to Mills, the young Texan trooper who had listened so intently to Jack's long and sorry tale. Mills was dead, his body ripped to bloody ruin by the men who had cut him down. But he could still provide one last service to a comrade.

Jack slipped his hands across Mills's still warm body, then pushed his hands into the rents in the man's chest. He felt no revulsion as his fingers probed deep. They dug hard, nails tearing away scraps of flesh and bits of torn muscle. Only when his hands were full did he pull them away. It was easy then. He slathered the gore over his face and neck, adding it to the blood that had come from his own wounds, until his skin was covered. He went back for more, filling his hands with the grotesque mixture then layering it over himself until his face was nothing but a nauseating mess of blood and gristle.

Only then did he lie back, exhausted and hurting.

His breathing slowed, the pain taking over at last. The world faded away and he slipped into the darkness.

Chapter Fifty-four

ack awoke to a world shrouded in fog and confusion. At first, he was not sure if he was alive, or if he was awaking to his first moments in hell. Then he heard voices. They sounded far away, the sounds they made unintelligible, but it was a reminder that he still lived, that his arrival into hell was delayed, for a moment or two at least.

There was the sensation of movement, of being dragged, then a sharp moment of pain as his head hit the ground. He was barely conscious as he was moved again. He felt hands take hold of him, hard fingers digging into him, then he was dropped, the connection with the ground hard enough to send him back into the darkness.

He came to for a second time. He did not know how long he had been unconscious, but he was aware that this time he could hear more clearly. The voices no longer babbled, but instead spoke clear words, although in a language he did not understand.

He lay still, barely breathing. His thirst was terrible, yet still worse was the pain that rippled through him, his battered body making him aware of every hurt and every wound. For the moment, though, there was nothing he could do but endure.

He continued to fake his own death, lying as still as a corpse with his face and neck slathered with gore. And he would wait like that until either his death became a reality or the bandoleros left him.

He did not know how long he lay there. But then he heard familiar voices, the lighter tones of a woman and the quiet voice of a man he had come to despise.

'Where is he?' It was Kat who asked the question.

'Over there,' Brannigan replied.

'Is he dead?'

'Yes.' There was no doubt in the reply.

Jack felt the vibration in the ground as someone approached. He sensed someone standing over him, the touch of a familiar gaze wandering across his blood-smothered features.

'You poor son of a bitch.' Kat breathed the words. 'You came a long, long way to die here.'

'Serves the bastard right.' There was no remorse in Brannigan's tone.

'It cost you enough,' Kat said wryly. 'Santiago sure took a lot of our money.'

'My money,' Brannigan corrected her. 'And it was worth every last goddam cent.'

'Well, he's dead now. You don't have to worry about him coming after you.'

Jack heard something in Kat's tone. Was it sadness at his passing? Or remorse at the role she had played in bringing it about? Whichever it was, her remark resonated. Had Brannigan been afraid of him, or just fearful that someone had knowledge of his crimes? He had clearly spent a lot of his bloodstained specie to make sure Jack did not live to tell the tale of all that had happened.

'You going to bury them?' Kat asked.

'No.'

'That ain't right.'

'I don't care.' Brannigan's voice was cruel.

'No, you don't.' Kat sighed. 'So now it's just you and me.'

'Just like we planned.'

'Are you going to kill me next?' There was no trace of fear in Kat's voice as she posed the dangerous question.

Brannigan half laughed, half grunted. 'You ain't got no plans to double-cross me, have you, Kat?'

'No.'

'Then you ain't got a thing to worry about. I told you when I found you all those years ago that I'd see you right. I ain't never let you down, have I?'

'No.'

'No.' Brannigan repeated her one-word answer. 'Men like him,' he tapped Jack's body with the toe of his boot, the heavy spur attached to the heel jangling as he did so, 'hell, they're always going to end up like that. Don't matter if it's here or someplace else. You and me, we're different. And we got ourselves a future now. A good one.'

'Thanks to you.'

'Hell, yes, thanks to me.' Brannigan's voice rose as he replied. 'Now don't you fret none about old Jack there. His sort don't have a future and they know it. They live as hard as they can, for as long as they can. Then they die. It's as simple as that.'

'And you get to live on.'

'Damn right I do.' Brannigan paused. 'And thanks to me, so do you.' He spoke slowly and clearly, making sure Kat understood. 'I could've left you; you know that, don't you? I could've left you, and your goddam brother, all those years ago when I found you. You'd be long dead by now. Yet here you are, still breathing and living a fine old life. Now go get the wagon ready. We've wasted long enough here already.' He ended the conversation with his clipped instruction.

Jack heard them move away, the jangle of spurs and the heavy tread fading into the distance. It was quiet then, the only noise coming from the insects that buzzed and chirped their way through the day.

And so he lay there and endured.

He awoke to darkness. He opened his eyes, blinking hard until he could see the stars that filled the night sky. He lay there for some time, letting his mind adjust to the notion that he was still alive.

Fireflies flittered across his vision, their tiny bright bodies dancing to a rhythm only they could hear. He watched them, mesmerised, his eyes flickering back and forth as he tried to track one small body amidst the thousands.

As he lay there, he let his other senses reach out. The smell hit him first. It was rank, the familiar odour of blood, shit and torn flesh assaulting his nostrils. It was foul, but he had smelled it too many times for it to offend. He could hear nothing save for the buzzing of the million night-time insects. He could taste blood in his mouth, and the hard, metallic tang that only came with a thirst that had been denied for too long. And he could feel pain. It echoed through every part of his body. The worst was in his head. Something pounded away deep in his skull, the dull ache fighting for control of his mind. The rest of him hurt, but he could feel nothing that would kill him.

With a groan, he started to stir. Something heavy lay across his chest, and so he pushed at that first, only belatedly realising that it was an arm. He took it easy, moving slowly and gingerly, allowing his body to become accustomed to one position before he attempted the next. Still, any movement doubled the intensity of the pounding in his head, and more than once he felt faint. Yet by taking it slowly, he eventually managed to get to his feet.

As he stood there, swaying like a sapling in the breeze, he recognised where he was. He had been left in the yard to the rear of the hacienda. And he was quite alone.

For the first time, he saw the pile of which he had been a part, the bodies of the Texans treated without ceremony or respect. Their ruined corpses lay in a heap, arms and legs contorted into grotesque, twisted shapes. Familiar faces stared back at him with sightless eyes.

He coughed, wincing as pain forked through his skull. He needed water, so he turned away from the mound of the dead and walked at a slow, careful pace towards the rear of the yard, where he knew the dammed creek was. It took him a long time, the simple act of taking one step after another draining him of what little strength he had left. When he finally reached the creek, he fell to his knees like a pilgrim arriving at his much-longed-for destination and scooped up the water with cupped hands, relishing the feel of the cool liquid as it ran across his skin. Desperate and needy, he threw the water into his mouth, repeating the action over and over. It took him a long time to drink his fill.

Stomach aching, he sat down. He could feel the water soaking into his clothing and he shivered, the cool night air chilling him to the bone. Yet he felt stronger now, the water revitalising.

As he sat there, he pondered what to do next. He could scarcely credit that he was alive, and that his gruesome deception had worked. But he knew what it was like after a hard fight. The exhaustion once it was over was like nothing else. Along with the fatigue came the joy of having survived. The twin emotions made men careless, too tired and buoyed by exhilaration to take time to thoroughly check the bodies of the clearly dead. It made him wonder if he had ever been deceived by the same simple ruse. Images of past fights replayed in his mind's eye, his tiring mind wandering through his memories.

Time passed. He did not know how long he sat there. Twice more he forced himself to his knees to repeat the task of scooping up water. Twice more he slumped back to sit on the soil that he had soaked.

It was only after his third refill that he had the presence of mind to force his thoughts back to the matter at hand. It seemed to him that he had two choices. He could walk back to Texas, and find a new life far removed from this moment. There he could try to forget all about cotton, and the men – and woman – whose lives had crossed his for a while. He had done it before. Moving on was one of the few skills he had mastered. He knew it would work. He knew the memories, no matter how bitter and painful they were now, would fade away with time. This moment would be just another nightmare stored away in the darkness alongside all the others. The pain, the remorse and the guilt would recede until they no longer had the power to hurt him.

Or he could take a different path.

He could stay. He could find Brannigan. And he could bring justice to the world.

Alone in the darkness, he laughed aloud. There was no

choice to be made, not really. It had already been made for him all those months before when Fate had brought him to an out-of-the-way dining room where a young man and a woman would play the first of many games.

He was to be Fate's vengeance. He would find Brannigan and Kat, and he would bring them to account for their sins.

And if he could take the money too, then he would. He was a boy from Whitechapel, after all.

He pushed against the dampened soil on which he sat, forcing himself to his feet, and began to walk, feeling the strength returning to his limbs as he made his way to where he had been held captive.

It was pitch black inside the shed, so he got down on his hands and knees and began to search. It took time, but at last he found what he was looking for.

As he emerged outside, the light of the fireflies and the moon was reflected in the blade. He held it still, moving the sword this way and that as he let the light shimmer across the steel. The power of the weapon resonated deep within him. He might no longer have the power of his repeating rifle, or be able to rely upon a six-shot revolver. But he had killed more men than he could count with a blade, and he reckoned he could find a way to add a couple more to the tally.

Chapter Fifty-five

Jack lay on his belly and looked down over the bandoleros' encampment. It was a good place to spend the night: a natural bowl in the ground surrounded by a dense chaparral of thorn bushes. There was just the one track leading in, making it easy to guard.

It had not taken him long to find the place, the trail that Santiago and his men had left clear enough for even a blind man to follow. He had spotted a rise in the ground a few hundred yards away from the camp, and there he had settled down to watch and wait.

He had chosen his ground well. The knoll was no more than a few yards from the trail that led to the encampment, and it was covered with prickly pear cactus. He had burrowed under one of the largest, taking care to avoid its viciously sharp spines, and made sure he had a clear line of sight over the encampment so that he would not miss anyone leaving.

As he lay there, he listened to what was going on inside the encampment. At first, all he could hear was the pitiful cries of the wounded. From the volume, it seemed there were plenty of men who had been hurt in the fight at the hacienda. Many would die that night.

As time passed, however, another sound took over, that of men celebrating their victory and their survival. There was music and singing, and even the occasional gunshot, as the bandoleros who had lived through the vicious fight drank and danced and sang.

Jack lay there listening to the twin sounds that so often followed battle. Misery and joy. Agony and relief. Death and life.

And he waited.

He did not try to sleep. He let the night pass slowly, savouring the minutes, watching the stars and listening to the sounds coming from the encampment. He found peace there, alone in the dark, and he was content. For once, there was no doubt in his mind. For he knew he had made the right decision.

It did not concern him that this night might be his last on earth. The thought of his death no longer terrified him as once it had. He would live or die at the whim of Fate, and there was nothing he could do about which of those it would be. All he could do was follow his instinct and act as he thought best. There was no room for doubt, recrimination or fear. He was to be Fate's servant. He would let her choose whether he lived or died.

A group of men emerged as the first rays of the sun pushed back the shadows of the night. They brought with them half a dozen corpses. They did not linger. They scraped a single shallow grave into the dusty soil and dumped the bodies without ceremony before retreating back into the encampment.

An hour after the sun had risen, Santiago and his Ángeles

left, taking the same trail they had ridden in on the previous night. The wounded, those who lived, had been loaded on to one of the wagons they had recaptured from Dawson and his men. Jack saw no sign of either Kat or Brannigan, but he spotted Santiago easily enough. The man who commanded Los Ángeles de la Muerte rode on another wagon, surrounded by a mounted escort.

The old man had paid a high price to rid himself of Dawson and his cavalrymen, but Jack understood why it had been done. The war between the men of Texas and the bandoleros was a ferocious one, with no quarter given on either side. He thought back to the two skulls he had seen on the trail, all that remained of men who had been unlucky enough to be captured in this most vicious of frontier wars. Both sides inflicted the worst of atrocities on each other, and there was the kind of hatred between them that Jack had only seen once before, when the sepoys of the East India Company had risen up to mutiny against their white masters. Hatred such as that left no room for anything other than bloodshed.

He understood the emotion well, for he had once felt it himself. Then he had crossed hundreds of miles to find a man he loathed with all the passion he had in him. He had killed that man, and had earned himself the bitter peace he had sought. He felt no such hatred for Brannigan or for Kat. But he would still kill them both. For they deserved to die for all that had been done.

There had been another reason for Santiago and Brannigan to capture the ruined hacienda, one that likely surpassed even the deep need for revenge. The prize it had contained was worth more than even the dozens of lives that had been sacrificed to secure it. Now, Brannigan had taken back the strongbox and the king's ransom it contained. Jack knew from what he had overheard between Brannigan and Kat that some of that fortune had been returned to Santiago. But he also knew that Brannigan would still be a wealthy man, whatever remained in the strongbox enough to secure his future.

He turned his attention to the one wagon that remained behind. He knew that it belonged to Brannigan, and he was sure that it contained the remaining gold he had been paid for delivering the rifles to Santiago, just as he knew that Brannigan would have a plan for where it would be taken next. It was a plan that would not come to pass. For the wagon master had forgotten about Jack Lark.

That mistake would kill him.

The single wagon left the encampment no more than half an hour after the Ángeles had departed. Jack watched from his hiding place under the cactus as it moved at a leisurely pace along the trail. He bided his time. Waiting for the moment to strike.

Brannigan drove the wagon. Like the men he had once employed, he was forced to use his whip regularly to keep the mules in motion. He had the easy skill of an experienced driver, and the wagon rolled along steadily. There was no sign of Kat, and Jack guessed she had chosen to ride inside the wagon, her eyes, and likely her revolver, aimed back down the trail, watching for anyone coming up behind them. It was a wise precaution, one that on another day might have saved the pair from being ambushed. But not that day.

The wagon would pass no more than five or six yards from the knoll on which Jack hid. If he timed it right, Brannigan would die without ever knowing who had attacked him.

The wagon ground its way closer. The running gear screeched and whined, the sound louder even than the braying of the mules and the crack of Brannigan's whip. Jack stayed stock still, holding himself tight. His sword was in his right hand, the blade angled so that it would not catch the sun and so warn of his presence.

The wagon bucked over some rough ground. For the first time, Brannigan yelled at the mules, his curses loud.

The moment came.

Jack sprang his one-man ambush.

Chapter Fifty-six

He burst from cover, running hard, his boots pounding into the rocky ground, eating up the yards in great loping strides.

Brannigan looked up, a mixture of shock and anger in his expression.

Jack charged, the sandy soil flashing past under his feet. He focused everything he had on the man driving the wagon.

Brannigan reacted fast. Dropping the reins, he reached for the revolver holstered on his right hip. He drew the weapon, half rising to his feet as he did so, preparing to shoot. The gun was just out of its holster when Jack struck.

He came in fast, bounding up on to the wagon's seat at full speed. He hit Brannigan hard, leading with his shoulder and pumping his legs. Grabbing the wagon master with his free hand, he dragged him backwards so that they tumbled from the far side of the seat together. He held tight as they fell, bracing for the impact with the ground.

When it came, it was brutal. They hit with bone-jarring force, teeth clashing together, legs and arms jumbled this way and that, Brannigan's revolver flying from his grasp.

Jack was on his feet first. He sucked down a single breath, then swung the sword. It was a rushed blow, but Brannigan was still crouched and not ready. The blade thumped into his left arm, cleaving the flesh to the bone and throwing him to one side.

A rush of violent exhilaration surged through Jack, powerful and intoxicating. It lent him power, and he stepped forward, readying the next strike.

But Brannigan was fast, and he was tough. Even with blood pouring down his left arm, he fought back. As Jack came for him, he drew a bowie knife with his right hand, holding the blade low, aiming the tip at Jack's belly. He struck the moment Jack stepped towards him.

Jack spotted the blade's movement. Attack turned to defence. He slashed his sword across his body, sparks flying from the clash of steel on steel as he parried the knife's strike. Brannigan advanced regardless, smashing his head into Jack's face and knocking him backwards.

Jack fought to stay on his feet. Blood cascaded from his nose and filled his mouth. Brannigan gave him no respite and came for him again, bowie knife stabbing forward.

Again Jack parried the blow, deflecting the blade wide. It came back at him a heartbeat later, moving faster than the eye could trace. This time Jack's flailing parry missed, the knife slipping past then cutting deep into the flesh of his sword arm, just below the elbow.

Brannigan snarled as he twisted the blade, ripping it free. A moment later, he darted it forward again, the tip aimed at Jack's eyes.

Despite the pain tearing up Jack's sword arm, he parried the blow before it could reach his face. He stepped back then, spitting the blood from his lips and gathering his strength.

But Brannigan had other plans. The moment Jack broke from the combat, he turned and ran. For a big man, he moved fast.

Jack saw what he planned and set off after him. But he was hurting. And he was slow.

Brannigan skidded to a halt near his fallen revolver. He snatched the weapon from the ground and twisted around, gun already levelled.

Jack came to a stumbling halt five yards away from the barrel of the revolver. He stayed there, blowing hard, his sword held low in his right hand, blood running down his arm and on to the hand that gripped the blade.

Brannigan's chest heaved with exertion, yet he held his pose, the barrel aimed squarely at Jack's chest. He had the power of his revolver. He held Jack's life in his hands.

'You really don't know when to die, do you, Jack?' The words were delivered breathlessly.

Jack said nothing. He stared at the barrel of the gun. He was just a couple of yards away. He could still strike.

'You know I'll shoot you down.' Brannigan was bringing his breathing under control. A laconic smile spread slowly across his face. 'You so much as twitch and I'll put a bullet in you.'

Still Jack refused to speak. He had seen Brannigan shoot enough times to know the man would not miss. He would kill without hesitation.

'Put that goddam sword down.' Brannigan spoke calmly now.

Jack hefted the blade in his right hand, checking his grip. The blood ran across his hand, but he could still wield the blade one last time.

'I told you what would happen if you came at me with that thing. So put it down.' Brannigan paused, waiting for a reaction. When none came, he shook his head slowly. 'You not going to do what you're damn well told?' He raised an eyebrow. He was in complete control now. 'Well then, I guess that's the end of it.' The revolver lifted a fraction of an inch as his thumb pulled back the hammer.

Jack saw the movement. He knew Brannigan was about to shoot, just as he knew he was a moment away from death. So he did the only thing he could think of.

He charged.

Chapter Fifty-seven

Brannigan saw Jack coming and laughed. At such close range, he could not miss.

The first gunshot was loud. A second followed close behind it, then a third and a fourth, coming so fast they blurred together.

Jack cried out, the sound torn from his lips. Every muscle quivered in expectation of a bullet's impact.

An impact that never came.

More shots roared out, one after the other, the explosions of sound shocking and loud.

Jack stumbled forward, confusion filling his mind.

Brannigan still stood with his revolver raised. Then his mouth opened wide to release a cascade of blood. He stood there a moment longer, staring at Jack as the blood ran over his chin, before he fell forward, hitting the ground face first.

Jack staggered to a halt. He had expected to die. Yet somehow he still lived. He did not know how or why.

He lifted his gaze to see Kat standing no more than two or three yards from where Brannigan's body lay, the Volcanic pistol cradled in both hands, a cloud of black smoke pouring from the barrel.

He searched her face, looking for a sign that she was going to draw the Remington that was holstered on her hip to shoot him too, but he could read nothing in her expression. All understanding of her was far beyond him.

Brannigan groaned. He was still alive. Blood poured from the wounds to his back. It ran into the dust, staining the thirsty earth black.

Jack walked forward. It was time to end it.

Brannigan looked up as he approached. Somehow he found the strength to hold his head up. His eyes bored into Jack.

Jack lifted his sword so that it pointed towards the wagon master, letting the man it would kill see it coming for him.

He paused when he was within an arm's length. At the last, Brannigan's head lolled forward, his strength failing him. Jack was grateful for it. There was little pleasure in this moment. No sense of righteousness, or of satisfaction. He took a last step forward, then plunged the sword down, pushing hard so that the blade cut deep through muscle and sinew. He worked it between bones, tearing and ripping the organs deep inside until he was sure he had done enough. Only then did he twist the blade and tear it from the flesh.

It was done. Brannigan was dead. The irony of the moment was not lost on Jack as he stood there hauling down deep breaths. In this world of revolvers and repeating rifles, it was a sword that had ended Brannigan's life. Jack's sword. One that Brannigan had mocked as an anachronism, and a reminder of a dying age.

Gruesome task complete, Jack looked at Kat. She had not moved.

'It's over.' He felt the need to speak and so break the silence.

Kat's expression did not change. She stared back at him coldly.

'You shot him down.' He took a step towards her. 'After everything that happened, you shot him now?' He was struggling to understand. He had believed that Kat and Brannigan had been working together, that they had been in collusion since before Vaughan's death, and had stayed together through the massacre of first Brannigan's men and then Dawson's. Yet now she had killed Brannigan. And she had saved Jack's life.

'You don't get it?' Kat shook her head as she replied. 'I thought you were cleverer than that, Jack.' She looked down as she holstered the still smoking Volcanic, taking care to make sure it was secure in the long holster on her left hip.

He took another step towards her. His mind was racing now. She was right. He didn't get it.

'Why did you do it?'

'You tell me.' Kat's reply was sharp.

'I don't know,' he replied honestly.

'You think I did it for you?'

He took another step, then stopped. She had saved him. He thought back to the times they had kissed, the times he had held her in his arms. Was that enough? Was that the reason he had been spared?

'Did you?' He took another step, moving quickly now, his instinct pushing him towards her.

Finally her expression changed, a wan, sad-looking smile creeping across her face. Then she drew the Remington.

'No.'

'Then why?' He came closer.

'Take another step and I'll kill you.'

'What?'

'You heard me.' The Remington was held still.

He was confused, yet he obeyed, stumbling to a halt.

'I've planned this for a long, long time, Jack. Did you think it all happened by chance?' There was a mocking tone to her voice now. 'Did you really think I was just here for decoration?'

'No.' He watched her carefully as emotions played across her face. 'I never thought that.'

'No?' Her expression twisted, as if he had forced something sour between her lips. 'Are you sure about that?'

'Yes.' He watched the Remington. It did not so much as twitch.

'Horseshit.' Her smile widened. 'I saw the way you looked at me. I saw it back in the dining room when I first came to sit at your table, and I can see it even here and now.'

For the first time, she moved forward, coming towards him with slow, even steps. 'I know you want me, Jack.' She spoke quietly. 'And I like you, I really do.' She kept walking. 'But you men, you're all the same. You think with your dicks.' She laughed then, the sound coming easily. 'I'm grateful for it. It makes it so much simpler for me.'

She was closing the distance between them, her eyes locked on to Jack's. 'You see, all this,' she waved her free hand, 'it all happened the way I planned it. Well, except for one thing. I'd have kept Brannigan alive if it hadn't been for you, I'll tell you that much. I'd have kept the evil son of a bitch alive at least until we'd reached Veracruz. I needed him until then, to keep me safe and to get this specie where it needs to go. Now I suppose I'll have to make my way there all on my lonesome.'

'You planned all this?'

'I sure did.' She smiled and shook her head, as if amused by something she heard in his tone. 'The day they told me my brother was dead, I knew I had to do something. So I waited. It sure took a long time to come to this, but here we are.' She paused, her head tipped to one side as she contemplated the man standing in front of her. 'Does that surprise you, Jack?'

'Yes.' He watched her as she came closer. He focused everything on this one person, this one woman.

'Good. I like that.' She was close now, standing within arm's reach. She looked at him, her eyes searching his face one last time. Then she stepped forward and kissed him. When she pulled away, she was smiling. 'You're a goddam fool, Jack Lark. But you're a good fool, and I meant what I said. I really do like you.'

He stared back at her. He never saw the Remington that she raised then smashed violently into the side of his head.

Kat, the world and everything in it disappeared, and he fell.

When Jack awoke, he was lying on his back, staring up at the sky. The pain swamped him at first. It was so bad that he was sure his skull had been split open. He did not try to move, and slowly it faded away until it was no more than a dull pounding. It still hurt, but it no longer felt as if his brains were spilling out of his head.

He moved slowly and carefully until he was sitting up. He took in his surroundings. He was alone.

Brannigan's corpse lay next to him on earth darkened by the blood that had been spilled across it. There was no sign of Kat, or the wagon with its precious cargo.

He moved gingerly, keeping his head as still as he could, getting slowly to his feet. It was only when he was standing that he noticed the items that had been left for him. They lay in a neat row in the centre of the trail. His repeating rifle, with two packets of one hundred rounds at its side. Next to that, his Navy Colt, the metal polished and the ivory grips clean and bright. Then there was his sword, the blade wiped clear of blood and gore. Beside that lay a haversack and two canteens. The final item in the line was a small cloth sack of the same type and size that he had seen Vaughan give to Dawson back in Brownsville. It sat on a single scrap of paper.

Still moving carefully, he walked to the sack. It chinked as he picked it up, and it was heavy. Yet he did not bother to open it to inspect its contents. Instead, he picked up the note that had lain beneath it.

It was short and to the point: *I said I'd pay you back*. It was signed with a simple letter K.

With a sigh, he crumpled the paper and tossed it to the ground. He took his time gathering what had been left for him. He discovered that the haversack was filled with rations and both canteens were full. Kat had left him all he needed to survive.

And that was what he would do. He would survive. He had believed himself to be Fate's vengeance, yet it turned out that she had not needed him at all. Her vengeance had been a young woman called Kat.

Jack started to walk south. He did not know where his path would take him, and at that moment he did not care. He had what he needed to survive.

And once again, he was alone.

Epilogue

Veracruz, Mexico

Jack stood outside the ticket office, studying the broadsides and sailing schedules that had been pinned to a noticeboard there. They promised fast transit times to a hundred different destinations, and he ran his eyes over the list, trying to decide where he should go. He had enough money to buy a ticket to any one of them, thanks to Kat's generous payment, but for now, he put the decision to one side. It could wait.

He turned and walked away. He had no plans for that day, or for those that would follow. There was a big world out there.

The Lost Outlaw is the third Jack Lark novel set against the backdrop of the American Civil War. I was keen to take Jack somewhere other than the battlefield, and I thought long and hard about the novel's location. My original plan was to use a cotton train simply as a vehicle to take Jack down into Mexico, where he could then find his way into the war being fought between the invading French and the Mexicans. However, the more I read of the effort to get the Confederacy's cotton to Mexico, the greater the temptation to base the whole novel around the trade.

There is no doubt that the cotton trade was of vital importance to both the Confederate government and the plantation owners who grew the valuable crop. It was this that made the Union's Anaconda Plan such a powerful weapon, one that starved the Confederacy of the income it derived from taxing the exported cotton. With their seaports blockaded, the plantation owners had few options left, one of which was to take the cotton south to the Mexican ports that were still open to the European trade.

One of the trails that the wagon trains took, El Camino

Real de los Tejas, still exists in part, and there is a fantastic guide available on the website of the National Park Service, a valuable resource for armchair-bound (well, train-seat-bound) authors like myself. However, some parts of the trail, such as the village of Bagdad, no longer exist. Bagdad has been swept away under the changing course of the Rio Grande and today is just a beach.

The task of getting the valuable cotton all the way to Mexico was a difficult and dangerous one. There are many gruesome tales of the vicious fighting between the men charged with guarding the cotton and the many bushwhackers and bandoleros who tried to steal it away.

Despite the violence and the risk, or perhaps because of it, the trade attracted men of every country, creed and colour. Many made their fortunes, by fair means or foul. I like to think that men like Brannigan and Vaughan were there, although neither is based on a real person. There were certainly many renegades and bandoleros waiting to prey on the wagon trains, the most famous being José María Cobos and Octaviano Zapata. Ángel Santiago and his Ángeles de la Muerte are inventions, as are Dawson's cavalry. As ever, I try to tread as lightly as possible over the history of the real men and units that fought in the years I am covering, whilst still trying to bring their stories and adventures to life as best I can.

As you might expect by now, the fights in this novel are based on nothing more than my own imagination. The battle at the hacienda was inspired by the Battle of Camarón, the most famous action ever fought by the French Foreign Legion. I gave a great deal of thought to trying to include Camarón in the novel, but it just didn't fit. However, I was still fascinated by the idea of a small group of defenders holding out against far superior numbers (blame my love of the film *Zulu* for this), and so the idea for the fight at the hacienda was born.

There are not a great number of resources for those wishing to learn more of the cotton times. *The Matamoros Trade* by James W. Daddyman is the best book I have found. A long-term favourite of mine, the website of the National Park Service, www.nps.gov, is invaluable for those like me who cannot travel to the places they are writing about, and I recommend it wholeheartedly once again.

As to what is next for Jack, well, this time I am not sure. He has come a long way from that gin palace in Whitechapel, and so much time has passed since he took Captain Sloames's officer's scarlet for his own. Now he finds himself in a deep-sea port with money in his pocket and no one to tell him where he should go next. He really can go anywhere.

Let's see where he turns up, shall we?

Acknowledgements

The Jack Lark novels are a delight to write. I still find the whole process of constructing a novel deeply satisfying and I will be forever grateful to those who have put me in this position. My biggest thanks, as ever, goes to my agent David Headley. He has a huge influence on my career as a writer and I am fortunate indeed to have such support. My editor at Headline, Frankie Edwards, is simply brilliant. Frankie is a superb editor and these books would not be what they are without her insight, suggestions and guidance. I must also thank Jane Selley, my copyeditor, for her input and for her patience.

I also want to take a moment to thank everyone who has ever taken the time to write a review of my books online or to contact me. Each and every one means a great deal. At times, it can feel like you are writing in a vacuum, and I will always be very grateful to those who reach into the void and offer a kind word or suggestion.

Finally, I must thank my family for putting up with me. They are simply the best.

After five years away, Jack Lark – soldier, leader,
imposter – is once more called to fight . . .

FUGITIVE

London, 1868. Jack has traded the battlefield for business,
running a thriving club in the backstreets of Whitechapel.
But this underworld has rules and when Jack refuses to
comply, he finds himself up against the East End's most
formidable criminal – with devastating consequences.

A wanted man, Jack turns to his friend Macgregor, an
ex-officer, treasure hunter and his ticket out of England.
Together they join the British army on campaign across
the tablelands of Abyssinia to the fortress of Magdala,
a high-stakes mission to free British prisoners captured
by the notorious Emperor Tewodros.

But life on the run can turn dangerous, especially in a
land ravaged by war . . .

Coming August 2020

HEADLINE